CLARE KELLY

To Cathy,
who may enjoy
a small town
Ontario tale.

Margaret

CLARE KELLY

Margaret Reilly

If you try to change it, you will ruin it.
Try to hold it, and you will lose it.
Lao Tzu

Contents

Dorothy

The month of May in Lawrenceville was heaven. The grass in the fields was long and blew in the wind like a green sea. The ice was gone from the river, and the blue and silver waters sparkled like a million diamonds in the sun. Tulips, daffodils and lilacs bloomed in front yards. There was a faint scent of cows and plowed earth from a farm on the edge of town. Red-winged blackbirds called to each other from the swampy edges of ponds. I knew I should be outside enjoying nature; instead, I was indoors, standing as close as I dared, watching my mother Dorothy as she drew on her black eyebrows. She frowned into the small round mirror.

"Why don't you go out and play. It's a nice day."

She said this so often I almost didn't hear her. I tried to be invisible, barely breathing. I was fascinated by her concentration. I had a curious obsession with seeing her face come to life as she added lipstick, eyeliner, mascara and rouge.

"Okay, Mummy."

I wasn't trying to be annoying. I just wanted to be close to her, even though she hated having me at her elbow.

"Clare, I'm Dorothy. How many times do I have to tell you? Now scoot."

I was used to her pushing me away. I'm not even sure I minded. I often thought she wasn't my real mother. I tried to imagine various scenarios in which my real mother left me with Dorothy, but couldn't come up with anything that made sense.

Dorothy's casual indifference and coldness didn't get me down. My life held many joys; chief amongst them was my friendship with Isabel Bergeron, who lived up the street. We had been best friends since Grade One and had made it to Grade Five together without so much as a quarrel. We seemed to be a perfect match.

I spent a lot of my time at Isabel's house. She had three sisters; Madeleine, May and Arlene, and two brothers; Timothy and Peter. They lived in a three-bedroom house, which was small for such a big family but they never seemed to mind.

Isabel's mother was always home and always busy, yet she welcomed me at their house and often allowed Isabel and me to help her in the kitchen. She also taught us to sew clothes for our dolls; giving us bits of fabric, and threading needles for us with great patience. Isabel's sisters treated me exactly as they treated Isabel, which is to say, like a little sister.

Isabel's father was a mystery. He worked at a factory that made tin cans, and came home each day exhausted. Even for a man, he was exceptionally silent. Isabel's brothers were mysterious too. They lived in their own world of toy soldiers and firecrackers. Our worlds didn't intersect, except on summer nights, when boys and girls would join together for thrilling games of Hide and Seek or Red Rover.

In response to another suggestion from Dorothy that I 'scram', I called Isabel, and said "Want to play?"

"Okay," she said.

Within a few minutes we met on the sidewalk.

"What should we do?" I asked.

Isabel was always full of ideas, and I was happy to go along with them.

"Let's have a donut and Coke at Woolworth's," she suggested.

The lady at the counter warmed the donut, so chocolate icing melted onto the white china plate. We shared it, as we shared everything, although I always paid. I was the only one with a regular allowance.

After we finished our donut, Isabel licked the last of the chocolate off her fingers and said, "Want to go to the park? I can use Madeleine's bike today."

I quickly agreed. I had my own bike, a red CCM. Isabel had to share with her sister Madeleine, who almost always claimed their old brown Raleigh for herself.

It took us only a few minutes to bicycle to the park. We threw down the bikes and headed to the playground equipment. We believed ourselves to be extraordinarily talented in that we could stand, one at each end of the teeter-totter, and go up and down without holding on to anything. After a few minutes of this, with perfectly synchronized timing we jumped off and ran to the swings. These had wooden seats, perfect for standing on. We pumped hard until we felt we were flying, masters of the playground. We played until we heard the twelve o'clock whistle.

Isabel jumped off. "I have to go home for lunch."

Isabel's family kept regular meal times, even on the weekend. I knew no one would be looking for me. I returned home to our third story apartment, creeping in quietly in the hope of discovering something; ever on the lookout for an answer as to why Dorothy was so unlike other mothers.

Dorothy was at the kitchen table with her cards. Our neighbour was sitting across from her, focussed on the cards being laid in front of her. I had seen this so often it no longer interested me. Women came to her again and again to hear the same lines: *you are facing troubles with someone close to you*; *you will be coming to a turning point with something you have long wished for*; *I see change for the better.* By the age of ten I could see through the game. Dorothy's readings were vague. Her clients filled in all the details.

"Dorothy, that's amazing. That must mean my husband's brother is going to find a job and get his own place."

"That's what the cards say," Dorothy would reply.

At school we were taught that fortune telling was the work of the devil. When I explained this to Dorothy, she told me to keep my opinion to myself. I didn't see religious teachings as mere opinion, but as rock-solid truth. She wasn't interested in hearing this point of view either.

I wished my father was home. When he was around on Saturday, he would cook us a nice lunch of beans and wieners, and turn on the radio to a cheery station. Unfortunately, he was a salesman and on the road most of the time. He was always back by Saturday night, even if it was late, so we could go to Sunday Mass together, then have our wonderful Sunday rituals; the newspaper, percolated coffee, fried potatoes with eggs, and the crossword, which we worked out together.

I made my usual lunch, a peanut butter sandwich with a glass of chocolate milk, and took it to the porch. It ran along the back of the building, looking out over the river. It was one of the best features of our apartment and was my refuge. I brought the morning paper with me and scanned it while I ate.

I heard Dorothy say, "You were a famous artist in an earlier life."

Yes, I thought, in a previous life when you weren't a lazy slob.

Darn, I caught myself being mean once again. Why couldn't I be kind and loving in my thoughts? I'd have to add this to my list for confession. Father Belfast came to our school once a month to hear confessions and I liked to be prepared with something colourful to tell him. I didn't feel it was good enough to say I was unkind or I was disobedient. I hoped details would make his job more interesting.

I continued to peruse the paper, reading every word, even the sports scores. I learned that the mayor had hosted a party for our Member of Parliament, our junior hockey team was having a banquet to celebrate the 1961/62 hockey season, and the editor of the paper was musing on whether it was time to plant tomatoes. Then I came to something of vital interest to me: Children's Fun Day, coming up next Saturday; the annual event in which the children of Lawrenceville dressed up, paraded down the main street, and had our costumes judged. I looked forward to this, although I knew my costume was never going to take a prize. I paraded every year in a long sweater and black tights, what I called my beatnik look. I had a vain hope Dorothy would take an interest in helping me with a costume, but she never responded to my pleas.

Newspaper finished, I sat daydreaming. I thought about what Isabel told me about gypsies trying to steal their family car in the night. Awakened by sounds in the yard, her father and her oldest brother, Peter, got up to investigate. They discovered intruders attempting to break into their garage. The whole family woke up when her father started shouting. Madeleine had daringly gone out to the front porch and saw several men running away. Her father stormed back in the house and shouted, "Gypsies! Trying to steal the car!"

I envied Isabel having had this exciting disturbance. We had all had been warned about gypsies; how they would steal babies and whatever wasn't locked up, even pets. I didn't understand why they wanted babies, but I could definitely understand stealing pets. I didn't have a pet because we lived in an apartment, but I longed for a dog. I was acquainted with a cocker spaniel belonging to an old woman up the street. I stopped every day to scratch his ears and give him some small treat; usually bacon or toast from breakfast.

I went back to thinking about the gypsies, wondering where they lived and why I'd never seen any in town. It was another of life's mysteries.

I went inside and saw Dorothy smoking and looking intently at the cards.

"The parade is coming up, and I wondered if..." I didn't get any further.

"Not now. I'm busy!"

On Sunday after our leisurely breakfast, Dad suggested we go see if it was warm enough to swim in the quarry. At mid-May the river was still cold, but it was possible the past week of sunshine had warmed the quarry enough to get in. My father loved to swim. He always kept his

4

swim trunks in the car in case we found a good spot for a dip. This was one of the rare things we shared with Dorothy. I suspected she enjoyed it for the chance to display her beautiful figure.

Dad was delighted to have Dorothy along with us. He was extra attentive to her and set out a plaid blanket for them to share, while I sat alone on my towel, dripping and cold.

Dorothy was at her best that day. She was kind to Dad and attentive to me, the model of a smiling, happy mom.

When we got home we had a wonderful Sunday dinner. Dorothy made fried chicken, a rare treat, and we watched Walt Disney together.

When I went to bed I could hear my parents talking. Dorothy was suggesting they take a vacation.

"Call in sick this week. We need to get away, have an adventure together."

I couldn't hear Dad's response, but knew he would never agree to an impromptu holiday. Our life might have been different, if only he had agreed to Dorothy's request.

Life with Father

I was up in the morning and off to school as usual, without seeing either of my parents. Dad was always gone by seven and Dorothy was seldom up before I left.

It wasn't until after school that I realized she was gone. Our neighbour was at the door waiting for me, wanting to know why Dorothy wasn't around for their regular afternoon chat. She came into the apartment with me. That's when I noticed a difference in the air; there was no smell of perfume or cigarettes. The cards that were always on the side table wrapped in a silk scarf, were gone. I went into my parent's bedroom to find the dresser drawers open and empty. The closet had been ransacked. I found an envelope on the bed addressed to my father.

I needed to be alone so I could think.

"I just remembered, my mother went to the city for the day. She must have forgotten to let you know."

I got her out of the apartment and sat down to figure out what I should do. Should I read the letter? I was torn. It was possible I'd discover things I'd rather not know. On the other hand, I didn't want to be left in the dark.

I couldn't resist. Inside the envelope I found her wedding ring and a slip of paper with these few words, "By the time you get this note I will be gone. Please don't try to find me. Forgive me, I cannot go on."

I put the ring and paper back inside and resealed the envelope. I realized I had to keep this quiet, otherwise I wouldn't be allowed to stay alone until my father returned. When he read the letter, I'd have to convince him I was okay on my own. I couldn't bear to have someone come to look after me, or worse, to be sent to live somewhere without my father.

I never believed Dorothy was my real mother and this confirmed it. She was leaving us, and she didn't even mention me in the note. I told myself I wasn't sad Dorothy was gone, but suddenly found myself in a flood of tears, feeling shocked and abandoned. In the past, whenever I felt sorry for myself, I would have visions of the woman I imagined to be my real mother, a woman with blonde hair, in a sensible skirt and sweater set, wearing an apron in the kitchen, peeling potatoes. Right then I longed for her to appear.

I soon as I calmed down I began to make a plan. I wasn't afraid to be alone and I knew how to take care of myself. The first thing was to make sure no one came snooping around. I knocked on the neighbour's door and told her Dorothy had returned with a migraine. This had happened before and meant two or even three days of total silence. That would give me time to prepare my case for when Dad came home, to show him I could be the woman of the house.

I longed to tell Isabel but I couldn't trust her to keep this secret. It was too big. After school each day I did what I'd normally do; come home, do my homework, make Kraft Dinner with hot dogs, go over to Isabel's for an hour or so, and then return to watch TV until bedtime. I wasn't nervous about being alone at night, and the week passed.

Dad was home early on Friday. He didn't seem as jokey as usual. I wondered if he had a suspicion about Dorothy's flight. I was not prepared for him looking so serious and worried. I had thought I would make light of it – say something like, "I don't know where Dorothy is. I've been fine on my own," to set the tone, let him know it was no big deal.

Before I had a change to say anything, he sat down in the kitchen and said, "I have bad news. Where's your mother?"

"She's gone. She left a letter on your bed."

All hell broke loose. He went in the bedroom, found the letter, read it and began to sob.

"Clare, it couldn't be worse. Dorothy's gone and I've lost my job. What am I to do?" He sat down with his head in his hands.

Whenever God closes a door, he opens a window. I thought of saying this, but saw the wisdom of keeping quiet. I was aware that this new situation was perfect. Dad would be home while he looked for a new job, and maybe he'd find a better one that didn't keep him on the road all week. My troubles were over.

I was right about this. Gradually life settled down. It became known that Dorothy had run off but no one said much about it. Isabel told me I could share her mother. Dad found a better job, selling home remedies, spices, flavourings, and cleaning supplies. His territory was all within an hour of town, which allowed him to return home each day. It was working out better than I could have imagined.

I had supper ready each day when Dad got home, and kept our apartment tidy. It may not have been up to the highest standard, but Dad never complained. I may have had too much responsibility for a child, but it was a wonderful life. I was freer than my friends. I couldn't imagine how they could live with no privacy or autonomy. With our apartment close to school, I could invite girlfriends over at lunchtime to watch TV while we ate our sandwiches. They must have envied my independence.

I was proud of my kitchen skills. I developed a regular menu for each day of the week, beyond the Kraft Dinner and hot dogs of the past, and enjoyed the shopping and planning that accompanied this task. Because it was just Dad and me, it was easy to handle. On Sunday, Dad cooked a roast with potatoes, gravy and canned peas, along with his specialty, Apple Betty, for dessert. On Monday we ate leftover roast and potatoes, fried with onions to create a delicious hash; Tuesday there was still roast, which would make a lovely hot sandwich with gravy; Wednesday we had sausage in tomato ketchup sauce with mashed potatoes; Thursday was hamburger patties with mashed potatoes and canned peas; Friday we had fish sticks with fried potatoes. Everyone I knew ate fish sticks on Friday. Saturday was less predictable, as it was our one day to eat in front of the television, watching baseball, hockey or a cowboy show. Sometimes we had TV Dinners, which I considered a treat, with a Coke for me and a beer for my father.

My father wasn't terribly strict but he did everything he could to stop my television habit. He tried to keep our evenings devoted to homework and reading. I appreciated it later, but at the time I felt I was missing out if I couldn't watch The Beverly Hillbillies and The Lucy Show. I would sometimes go to Isabel's to watch television. Her family would all sit around or lounge on the floor close to the screen, laughing at Jethro and Mr. Drysdale. Mr. Bergeron loved this stuff, but Mrs. Bergeron would either be sewing or working on something in the kitchen. When she did sit down, she would immediately fall sound asleep. Mr. Bergeron would say, "Mommy, you should go to bed."

Every Saturday Dad gave me enough money to pay for Isabel and me to see the Saturday afternoon double feature at the Princess Theatre, and to buy a McIntosh Toffee Bar which lasted through the entire afternoon. He insisted I deserved this weekly treat and seemed to enjoy giving it as much as I did receiving it. Isabel was thrilled, as her family didn't have money for this sort of extravagance. We sat through hundreds of hours of movies and enjoyed them all – although we preferred comedy. We were in heaven if it was Jerry Lewis and Dean Martin. In winter we would head home in the early twilight, heads spinning from hours in the flickering light of the theatre. Dad would ask what we'd watched. I'd try to tell him the highlights and see if I could convey how side-splittingly funny we had found it. In summer we would emerge from the theatre dazzled by sunlight and hit by the wall of heat after four hours in dark, air-conditioned comfort.

The first Christmas on our own, Dad thought I would be sad without Dorothy. He made sure I had plenty of presents. He apologized because it was just the two of us sitting down to a stuffed chicken and the trimmings. I was at pains to assure him I couldn't be happier, although I didn't want to admit how happy. Dad was smart, but had obviously been unaware of lots of things regarding life with Dorothy. He didn't seem to have any clue what a terrible mother she had been. He seemed to have moved on from missing her, though. After the first few months he barely mentioned her and I noticed one day that he had removed their wedding photo from his dresser. If he knew where she'd gone, he never let on.

That winter, since Dad was home every evening, we did a lot of skating at the rink in the school yard. As soon as dishes were done we walked to the rink with our skates and put them on in the shack. There was usually a pick-up hockey game at one end and skaters at the other. It kept me alert, trying to avoid an errant puck. My father was a fast skater. I wished he had the whole rink to himself so he could let loose. One night I asked him if he used to skate with Dorothy.

"No, she used to come to watch me play hockey though."

"Didn't she skate?"

"I don't think she ever learned."

"What did she like to do? Did she have friends like I have?"

"Oh, she was like any girl. She had friends."

Dad answered my questions but I never learned anything that helped me figure her out. I was lucky to have Isabel and her sisters in my life. They kept me informed of everything I needed to know as I grew up. They were open in discussing sex, boyfriends, the cruelty of high school girls, and most important, which Beatle was the best. I never felt at a loss for guidance. Mrs. Bergeron told me explicitly to come to her if I needed a confidante. I took comfort in knowing she was there if I needed her.

With Dorothy gone, my father spent more and more time in the kitchen, sitting at the table listening to the radio. Sometimes I would wake in the night to the faint sound of voices and laughter. The radio signals came from far away in the late night. Dad's favourite show was Long John Nebel, broadcast from New York. He also loved to hear baseball on the radio, preferring this to television. He said he could see it more clearly when he was listening to the radio.

On hot summer nights we would open all the windows and the door to the back porch, hoping for a breeze. There were no sounds, save for the occasional yowling cat, and never any traffic. We would sit in the dark; my father in the kitchen with his radio, me on the porch with my book and a flashlight, enjoying the silent, sleeping town.

When I got up, Dad would be gone, and it would be bright, the heat beginning already. I read while I had my coffee and toast. Then I would pull on my shorts and pop top, and walk over to Isabel's.

When I turned eleven an outdoor pool was built in the park by the river. That was one of our best summers. Isabel and I spent every afternoon swimming in the clear turquoise water, playing a game of throwing down a coloured stone, then seeing who could retrieve it fastest from the bottom of the pool. We stayed in the water until our fingers puckered and our eyes were red. When we got chilled, we would lie in a row with the other kids on the grass, a charming sight in our brightly coloured suits on top of equally colourful beach towels. There we basked in the sun, talking of all sorts of foolish things. We liked to create stories about the lifeguards, who were college boys and wonderfully unattainable, perfect as the subject of our hopes.

Isabel and I had other girl friends in our circle, but when we were in grade eight, some of them changed drastically, and left us behind. They moved on to smoking, stealing, and a hardness revealed in their expressions. They wore identical blue pea jackets and developed a slanting, slutty walk. While they were going to the Tiki Club to dance, Isabel and I were still dressing dolls and reading novels about girls who love horses.

Isabel and I had been sitting side by side in every grade through Elementary School, so it was a big change when we went to high school. Suddenly there were many new kids, and we weren't in the same home room. We managed to get together for lunch break, which was a welcome respite from all the strange new experiences.

Home Economics class was a welcome part of my first two years of high school. Miss Smart was very kind. She must have known I didn't have a mother because she seemed to seek me out for extra attention. When I came in after school hours to work on a sewing project, she told me I could call her Anna, as long as it wasn't in class. She gave me hints on fashion and hairstyles. I wore my hair straight, parted in the middle and cut to shoulder length. One day she said, "You know, big hair won't happen by itself," and she suggested I should use curlers and hairspray, and showed me how to tease my hair. She always had her red hair coiffed in a perfect beehive. I expressed my thanks for the tips, but I never felt the need to change my hair style. Possibly as a reaction to my mother's over-the-top sexiness, I preferred to be as plain as possible.

Isabel's oldest sister, Arlene, got married when we were in grade ten. She was twenty and had been working as a cashier at the grocery store. She had always talked about becoming a teacher, and had been saving her money for teacher's college. She met Bill at the grocery store where he was the produce manager. He was a few years older than her and it seemed like a perfect match. When I asked her if she minded not becoming a teacher, she acted surprised.

"Oh, heavens, I never think of that now. I have everything I want with Bill," she told me.

Isabel's next sister, May, had a lot of boyfriends. Every time I went to see Isabel, the front porch was full of teenage boys waiting for May to come out. Isabel and I promised each other we would never act so ridiculous about boys. We saw how it could change someone into a complete fool. May used to be a lot of fun, but now all she ever thought of was make up and getting her jeans to fit as tightly as possible, even going to far as to wear them in the bathtub to get them to shrink tight to her legs. In the kitchen, sitting around chatting with Mrs. Bergeron, we mentioned that we missed the old May. She agreed with us, but said life was full of change and we'd have to get used to it. I didn't agree. I planned to have as little change in my life as possible.

In Grade Twelve I had the second biggest shock of my life, after my mother's disappearance; Isabel fell in love. Suddenly she wasn't available for our walk to school, lunch break, or watching soap operas after we got home from school. I had other friends, but it wasn't the same. No one else understood so much with barely a word spoken. No one else had her sense of humour. Madeleine, who was spending the year at home recovering from mononucleosis, started spending a lot more time with me, which took up some of the emptiness left from Isabel's loss. She helped me keep my connection to the Bergeron family, and she was familiar, but she could never replace Isabel.

Joe, Isabel's boyfriend, was a great guy; handsome, kind, and smart. He was even gracious to me, suggesting I accompany them on the walk to school, at lunch, and even to dances, but I couldn't do it. There is nothing worse than being around a couple in love. The fact that he was a worthy partner to Isabel was some consolation. I also knew that if it wasn't Joe, it would be someone else. Isabel had become so beautiful, this was inevitable. I was philosophical about it. They initially tried to match me up with Joe's friends, but I had no desire for a boyfriend. I wasn't ready for the cataclysm of falling in love.

After I graduated from high school I enrolled in secretarial training at the college in Williamsville. Mrs. Bergeron tried to convince me to go to Grade Thirteen.

"Stay in high school for one more year," she urged, "with Isabel."

"I don't need Grade Thirteen for the work I plan to do," I said.

"But wouldn't you like to have more options," she asked?

I was mystified. Secretary, nurse, or teacher; these were the only options I could imagine. None of them required university.

I got a ride to college every day with two girls from my class. In October they decided to get an apartment in Williamsville and asked me to join them. The idea was unthinkable. I couldn't possibly leave my father, and I certainly didn't want to leave Lawrenceville.

I managed to find another friend to ride to school with, which was slightly better for me as she was on my schedule. We could both leave school at three every day, and I could be home in time to make dinner.

Business College was easy. I loved sitting at the big black Underwoods, pushing my typing speeds higher and higher. Shorthand was fun, like a secret language. Best of all was double entry bookkeeping which felt like a game. I decided my ideal job would be as a bookkeeper. I loved the elegance and orderliness of it.

One winter day, I had come home from school and was in the midst of getting dinner ready, when I received a call from my father, telling me he was at the hospital emergency room.

"I had some minor chest pains. The doctor says it's a touch of angina. I'll be late for dinner."

"Should I ask Mr. Bergeron to come and get you?" I was at a loss. My father had never been sick.

"I'll be fine."

"Wait there. I'll come in a taxi."

My father seemed remarkably nonchalant. "No need for that. I'll see you later."

I sat by the phone wondering what I should do. He was at the hospital so they must be taking care of him, I told myself, trying to be calm. I called the hospital to see if I could speak to him again. I was sure he shouldn't be driving himself home. The receptionist assured me the doctor would make sure he was fine before they let him go.

I never got a chance to say good bye. He had a massive heart attack while he was at the hospital, and they weren't able to save him. My father, the centre of my life, was gone. This was a situation I had never imagined. My life had been planned around him.

The funeral Mass was held at Sacred Heart Church. The Bergeron family sat in the front pew with me as I had no family to share my grief.

As soon as the funeral was past, I turned to the practical matters of his bank account and will. I discovered Dad had no savings and no life insurance. Within a month, I was broke and soon to be homeless. I was a year away from a college certificate, but couldn't afford to continue. I quit school and began my search for work.

The Ashram

I responded to an ad in the Lawrenceville paper that said, "Housekeeper/Nanny wanted. Live in." A live in job would immediately solve my money dilemma. I was invited to an interview at an address a few miles from town. There I discovered the Haari Shiva Devenanda Retreat Centre, known to those who stayed there as The Ashram.

Although it was close to Lawrenceville, I'd never known it was there as it was behind large gates, the buildings not visible from the road.

I arrived on my bicycle at a gate where I was directed by a man in a security booth.

"Take the first turn off the main driveway to the left for about a quarter mile until you get to a house."

I knocked at the door and was met by Haari, the leader of the ashram. He had on what I took to be white pyjamas but discovered were his everyday clothes. His hair was jet black, greased and combed back and he had a long beard streaked with grey. He appeared to be well fed. To my surprise he spoke English with no accent.

I was expecting a lot of questions about my credentials but Haari didn't seem at all interested in my background.

"The most important part will be to take care of my children. There's a bit of housekeeping as well," said Haari.

I started to tell him about my cooking credentials.

"Meals for you and the children will be delivered. You won't need to cook."

He explained the hours and the pay, asked if they were acceptable to me, and when I said yes, asked how soon I could start.

I was surprised at how easy it was. He offered me the job without knowing anything about me, and I suspected he chose me entirely for my appearance.

I had no experience with young children, but I was confident I could handle the work. There were two children to look after, Gita, a five-year old girl, and Jiddu, a three-year old boy. Both were exceptionally beautiful, with blonde hair and rosy cheeks. I started work immediately, moving into Haari's house with my few possessions.

The saddest part of my life at this time, apart from missing my father, was the loss of our home and all the things I had grown up with. I was forced to send all we had to auction, and kept only my clothes, books, and Toasty, my stuffed dog.

Night after night, I found myself dreaming I was back in our apartment, wandering from kitchen to living room to bedroom and out to the porch that looked over the river. I saw the couch with its crocheted granny square afghan, the portable radio on the kitchen table, the sparkling white ceramic sink, and my bed with the reading lamp beside it. My heart longed to return to these things. I would often wake up disoriented and heart-broken.

Despite my grief-stricken state, I was cheerful around the children. I felt I owed it to them to be happy and enthusiastic, and being with them made me feel happier.

I soon discovered Haari was almost a god to his flock of devotees. I didn't see much of him at first as he spent almost all his waking hours at the ashram. When we did meet, however, he rarely spoke of anything personal, never mentioned the children's mother and gave no hints about where she had gone. He repeatedly told me he wanted the children to have a normal, Canadian childhood, which was where I came in.

One of the devotees who brought us meals gave me some insight into what went on at the ashram. She wasn't supposed to stay and talk but she couldn't help herself; she was naturally gregarious. Her spiritual name, given to her at the ashram, was Madeeha, which she told me meant praiseworthy, but her real name was Brenda. She was friendly with the kids and we all looked forward to the days when she brought the food. Brenda said Haari was an enlightened being who could have stopped being reborn, but chose to come back in order to serve.

"This is definitely his last lifetime," she told me.

Brenda's confidence was amusing.

"I'm getting married next month to Saadar. We met here and plan to make this our life's work. I wasn't sure if he was the one for me, but I talked to Haari and he assured me that Saadar and I belong together. I actually went to Haari to tell him that I was thinking about leaving the ashram and going back to my old boyfriend in Toronto, but he helped me to see how wrong that would be. It's bliss to know we're following our Divine path."

"Are you sure about that? Isn't marriage an awfully big decision to leave to Haari?" I asked.

"Haari takes care of us all. He speaks for the Divine."

"Maybe you should go and see your old boyfriend before you do something you can't reverse," I suggested.

"I've already got my wedding clothes," Brenda said, as if that put an end to it.

Most of the time I was left on my own with the children. They had a large playroom with all sorts of wonderful toys, and a swing set in the yard. I read to them from my books, and when these were exhausted I borrowed books from the Lawrenceville library.

Gita and Jiddu were remarkably easy to entertain. We soon had an enjoyable routine; watching Romper Room in the morning while I made beds and did some tidying, followed by a walk on the grounds on a trail that wound through fields and woods. It wasn't a long walk but with their short legs and many things to stop and look at, we used up a good portion of the morning. We looked for trilliums and stopped at every lilac to revel in the flowers' fragrance.

The children were enthralled by stories of my childhood, especially memories of my mother. Despite their youth and short attention spans, they hung onto every word of my early recollections. Gita immediately started calling my mother Mummy Dorothy, something I had never thought to do.

Gita would sweetly ask, "Clare, what did Mummy Dorothy sing to you? What colour were her scarves? Did she smell of flowers?"

What a lot of questions from such a small girl! Despite the fact that memories of Mummy Dorothy hadn't been all that pleasant, I managed to find things to tell them that satisfied their curiosity. The truth was, when Dorothy left, her place in my life disappeared and I barely ever thought of her. I dredged up what I could for their startling questions and in doing so I began to wonder about the mother I'd lost.

"Her scarves were bright flashes of colour on a black background, smelling of coffee, cigarettes, and Chanel, her perfume."

Gita closed her eyes. "I can smell this," she said solemnly.

What could Gita know about cigarettes, coffee and Chanel? She was truly a character, maybe even a budding mystic.

Jiddu wanted to know more practical matters. "Did she cook? How many bracelets did she wear? Did she wake me up in the morning with a cup of sweet tea?"

I was bemused, but happy to find a topic that could so easily hold their attention.

"Was she beautiful?" Gita asked.

"Beautiful? I think so."

But how could I know? I was only ten when she left. She was a charmer; sexy and glamorous. She was occasionally warm, but mostly she didn't even notice me. It made me wonder, if I had been as golden and winning as Gita and Jiddu, might she have loved me more? I began to invent stories about Dorothy, and in the telling she became the mother I longed for.

"Yes, Mummy Dorothy sang me to sleep and told me lots of stories. She loved to make cookies. We decorated them with coloured candies and served them at a tea party for my teddy bears."

All lies, but the children loved it. What harm could it be?

Sometimes I missed adult company, but I saw my friends on my day off, and Haari kept us company now and then.

As the children's trust in me developed, they began to talk about their mother. They called her Mummy Maureen. No one else mentioned her and I still had no idea where she was. I assumed she must be blonde and lovely, like the children.

One warm day, late in June, as we were taking our morning walk, a young man appeared out of the bushes. He grabbed my arm and whispered, "Can we talk somewhere?"

"Who are you? How did you get in?"

This part of the ashram was off limits to anyone but Haari and his family.

"I can't tell you now. Please meet me in town tomorrow. It's about Maureen."

Despite the strangeness of this request and the intrusion into our private space, I didn't feel any fear of him. It may have been because he was extremely attractive. I hoped I was more discerning, yet it was his looks that had me agreeing to meet him at Woolworth's lunch counter; that and my curiosity about Maureen. What did he know? I had to find out!

He had come and gone so swiftly that Gita and Jiddu, running ahead of me up the path, hadn't seen him. I didn't understand why, but somehow it seemed right to keep this encounter to myself.

The next day I waited at the lunch counter wearing my best outfit, a pale green linen sheath dress, with my white flats and white purse. Who was I trying to impress? I still didn't even know his name, let alone what he needed to talk to me about. I felt excited, as if embarking on an adventure.

I ordered a Coke and sat facing the mirror so I could see anyone who approached. I had only been there a few minutes when he slid onto the seat beside me.

"I'm Patrick." He extended his hand and I offered him mine in a rather awkward shake, as we were sitting side-by-side on the red leatherette rotating stools.

"I'm Clare. Clare Kelly." I turned so I could look directly at him. "What do you want to talk to me about?"

"My sister Maureen, Gita and Jiddu's mother. I need your help to find out where she is."

"I've never met her. The only things I know are what the children tell me."

"You're the only person who can help me."

"I don't see how. The children don't know where she's gone. No one else ever mentions her. I asked Haari where she is and he said it's a painful subject that he doesn't want to discuss. He asked me not to encourage the children to speak of her, but I let them talk about her all they want. They seem to be really missing her. Don't you know where she is?"

"She hasn't been in contact lately, which may be my fault. I made it no secret I find all this ashram business creepy. About six months ago we stopped hearing from her. I finally got in touch with Haari. He told me she was in India, but I can't believe she would leave the children."

"How can I help?" I asked.

"I'd like you to let me know if you hear or see anything at all that could help me to find her." Patrick turned away, trying to hide his sadness. "The thing is, Haari will fire you if he sees us together. We'll have to be careful."

"I'll do what I can."

I didn't think I would be able to find out anything, with only the children to talk to. My contact with people at the ashram was entirely superficial; dropping off food and barely acknowledging my presence, except for Brenda. I'd already asked her about Maureen and she said she didn't know her. I told myself not to start building up a case – after all, I knew mothers were capable of disappearing.

We agreed that I would call him in a week when I was back in town – or sooner if I had anything to report.

A few days later, Haari came in for a visit with the kids. Before he headed back for the evening meditation, he told me there was a speaker coming in a few days.

"Her name is Stargaze. She's from Lost Coast Community and will be telling us about the experience of being on a magical farm. You'd enjoy it. Take the night off and come hear her presentation."

He handed me a flyer with a little more information about the upcoming lecture.

"Thank you," I said. "It sounds fascinating."

"Great. I'll arrange for someone to stay with Gita and Jiddu that evening."

Stargaze

When I arrived at the meeting hall I saw posters on the door advertising the talk. There were pictures of giant cabbages, carrots and absurdly large onions, with a kneeling figure beside them to give perspective. There were round stone cottages that looked as if they would be inhabited by elves, and groups of men, women and children holding hands, dancing in circles. The people were dressed in a wild rainbow of colours, the grass was dazzling green, and the sky as blue as any sky could be. The speaker's photo showed a black haired woman in a gold spangled sari, sitting behind the flames of a campfire.

I entered and took a seat on the floor amidst the eager crowd of disciples. Haari appeared and gave the introductions. All eyes turned to the figure on a cushion on the floor. Dim light cast shadows across her face. She was dressed in sparkling robes and adorned with jewellery. She sat ramrod straight, her head held high, as if she were a goddess.

"My beloved spiritual seekers, it is a magnificent blessing to see you again. I am certain we have known each other across many lifetimes."

As soon as she started to speak my heart began to pound. I knew that voice.

"The very fact that you are here means that you have arrived. The Holy Ones have led you." Stargaze went on and on.

I got up, made my way to the back of the room, and tried to decide what to do. I wasn't sure I could bear to stay, but neither was I able to leave. There was a cloakroom at the back. I went inside and paced up and down. I heard her describing the powerful spiritual forces that had been unleashed at Lost Coast where she lived. It was agony listening but I couldn't tear myself away. Stargaze presented herself as a priestess of a new pagan spirituality and as a leader of psychological transformation. She told them that the Lost Coast Institute had found the secrets of longevity; that there were members of her community who were approaching two hundred years old, and still were in fine health and unwrinkled. She was promising every kind of spiritual delight, as well as material riches. It was thrilling and nauseating at the same time.

Stargaze spoke for at least an hour, proselytising to bring seekers to her community, and to solicit donations. Then she opened the floor to questions. I could hear wholehearted belief and acceptance of her promises from the audience. This was an admittedly gullible group, but she definitely had charm.

Then, as if possessed I returned to the hall and called out a question from the back.

"What do you think of a woman who would abandon her husband and daughter to set out on a selfish quest for spiritual fulfillment?"

As there were many in the group who fit this description, it was sure to be an uncomfortable question for more than just Stargaze. I could hear people shifting in discomfort and murmuring to each other.

Stargaze didn't blink.

"You are asking the wrong question. The real question is what in the karma of the spouse and child led them to choose a life where they would be left behind."

I didn't respond and the discussion immediately moved on to other topics. Now I was furious. I waited until the talk was over. As she was preparing to leave I stood in her path and said, "Dorothy..." and then to my shame, I started to cry.

She took my arm and led me down a flagstone path to the cottage where she was staying. Once inside she turned and looked at me.

"You are very much changed. I might have walked by you on the street without knowing – but your voice still has the same demands in it."

This was our re-introduction. No love, no affection, merely a cold-hearted analysis of my shortcomings.

"Don't you owe me an explanation?"

"Oh Clare! If only you could share the spiritual heights I have ascended, you would feel nothing but happiness for all that has transpired."

"I don't want to hear from Stargaze. I want Dorothy, my mother, you owe me that. I'm an adult now. You can't push me aside the way you always did." I despised the pleading in my voice. "I've been left on my own, with nothing. Dad died a few months ago. Don't you even have any interest in what you missed of my life?"

I was talking fast. Fearful this might be my one brief chance to find out the where and why of Dorothy's hidden life.

For a moment Dorothy softened. "I know about your life. Ned kept me informed. He knew where I was."

I was shocked. "He knew you were at Lost Coast?"

"Ned knew, but wasn't the type to come running after me, and by then he had Anna Smart. He didn't really want me back."

"Miss Smart? What are you talking about?"

"You have been in the dark. Ned was too respectable to let it be public. He carried on with Anna, but somehow kept it secret from you. Everyone else knew."

Dorothy was breaking my heart. Unfortunately, it seemed plausible. Now I understood why Miss Smart had been so attentive. If only they had let me know, I wouldn't have protested. I liked her. On the other hand, maybe I wouldn't have accepted it. This was too painful to think about.

"Dad loved you. He was good to you. Why weren't you happy with us?"

This was the heart of what I needed to know.

"I wasn't cut out to be a mother. I was doing a terrible job of it. I'm sure I saved you from a lot of suffering by leaving you behind. I'm not trying to say I did it for you. I'm not a selfless person. I had to get out of that town. These years of travel and becoming Stargaze have been great. I won't apologize!"

It was entirely believable that she could move on, leave me behind without regret. It was what I had always known. Why did I want more? But my longing for justice or – what? – a loving mother – could not be so easily dismissed.

I could barely look at her and yet I could not let her go. "Could we at least stay in touch now?"

"Clare, what could we possibly have to say to each other? Do you think you could be a friend to Stargaze? I would make you furious every time I spoke. You would be calling me a phony and criticizing the Lost Coast spirituality. I won't allow negative energy into my life."

I tried to play her game. "But we have been led together tonight, despite the odds against it. Maybe we're meant to continue our relationship?"

I was desperately seeking the right words to elicit her sympathy.

"You are the only relative I have in the world."

"I can help with that. I come from a big family. I was only too glad to get away from them, but if it's relatives you want, I'll get you connected."

Another bombshell. What else didn't I know?

"Why didn't anyone tell me?"

"They aren't far away. They live on the Fourth Concession Road back of town. Do you remember the tar paper house, with the front door five feet up and no stairs?"

"That's your family?"

"You asked for it. All you have to do is drop in. I'm sure they'll welcome you with open arms, but don't be surprised if they want to borrow money. Don't worry. They won't reject you if you don't have any."

Stargaze, reached out and held me in the phony embrace that was practiced by the disciples.

"Don't worry Clare. Now that you know where I am you can write to me at the Lost Coast Institute. I must say goodnight now. I'm flying to New York in the morning."

I went back to my room and realized I no longer felt sad. My philosophical acceptance of life was back in place. I was thankful that I knew where Dorothy was. I was even optimistic about having relatives. It's possible I have a grandmother, I thought. I went to sleep, full of hope.

Looking for Maureen

Stargaze was gone by the time I was up. I decided I would not speak to anyone about our meeting. My mother was right; there was no way she could fit into my life. I was Catholic. I was dutiful. Maybe I was prim. I couldn't be around Stargaze without criticising and judging her.

I turned my attention to finding out what happened to the children's mother, Maureen. For this I needed access to more of the ashram and the disciples. I could pretend to have an interest in their spirituality; ask to join in some of the activities, but Haari hired me precisely because I wasn't on that track. I would have to come up with something else.

The ashram had a large vegetable garden tended by disciples. If I could work in the garden, that would allow me to get to know some of the volunteers. I approached Haari and he was agreeable. As I really had no free time, I had to fit it in on my day off.

My life was becoming very full; phone calls to Patrick, work in the garden while trying to get information, my weekly visit with Isabel, and a library visit. When, I wondered, will I get to meet my relatives? Given that my only means of transportation was my bicycle, I was going to be busy indeed.

One concession from Haari was permission to attend early Mass on Sundays, returning straight after to have breakfast with the children. I suppose all this activity was a blessing. It kept me from brooding on my losses.

Ignited by our meeting, I started having dreams of myself as a child, and of Dorothy. They weren't nightmares, but they left me feeling shaken. Dorothy often appeared to be rounding a corner, with me running behind her shouting, "Wait." Or Dorothy would be dancing and I would look in the window and see her. I would be locked out and couldn't get her to open the door.

***

The children and I came in from our daily walk with our hands full of Black-eyed Susans, daisies and dandelions, picked from the meadow we named The Friendly Field. The kids loved making up names for all of their surroundings. They saw differences of landscape that would have been missed by a grown-up's eye.

I found water glasses for the flowers, then opened a can of tomato soup, which we enjoyed with saltines and a glass of milk. I was now making our lunch every day, as the children preferred the food I cooked over lentils and brown rice from the ashram. As we ate I launched into a tale of my mother in an attempt to inspire the children to talk about Maureen.

"One day Mummy Dorothy went away and I didn't know where. Her suitcase was gone. She took her cigarettes, her silver lighter, and her purse. Even her perfume was gone. I was terribly lonely. I kept looking out the window, hoping to see her coming up the walk. Then, out of the blue, she came home again. I was so happy I hugged her and said, 'where did you go?' and she laughed and was surprised I didn't know she was visiting her sister. Oh, we were so happy then, but the sad thing is she came home with the most dreadful cold. Coughing."

"We aren't to talk about coughing," Gita said, "but Mummy Maureen had a terrible cough. It went on for ages and ages."

"Is Mummy Maureen visiting her family?" Jiddu asked sadly. He was close to tears, but I had to learn more.

"Do you mean she was sick when you last saw her?"

Before anyone could answer, Haari came in the front door and we all fell silent.

"Don't be quiet on my account. I love to hear the three of you chatting," Haari said, joining us at the table.

I quickly changed the topic to a discussion of the book I was currently reading them.

"We're reading *The Wind in the Willows*. It's about a mole, a rat, a badger and a toad. The librarian recommended it. As soon as we finish lunch I'll take up where I left off, until nap time."

"If you don't mind, I'd love to stay and listen," said Haari. "Nothing is as soothing as being read to."

Haari was spending more and more time with us. I suppose it was good for the children, but I would have preferred less of his company.

***

My mother, for once, kept a promise. She took steps to connect me with her family, sending a letter to them saying I would like to meet them. She also wrote to me; my first letter from her:

Dear Clare, Your relatives are the Hearne's. I was Dorothy Hearne and very glad to leave this behind and become Mrs. Dorothy Kelly. You'll find them, as I said, on the Fourth Concession Road. I have written to tell them to expect a visit from Miss Clare Kelly. I don't know if it was fate that brought us together again, but it would be best for you to let the past go. Move forward with your life. 'Let the dead bury the dead', as they say. I didn't tell you this, but I was struck by how much you look like me. Still, I suspect you have inherited Ned's steadiness and goodness. Who knows who you are? Stargaze.

Despite her advice, I saw the letter as something to save. I was of a naturally conservative nature, determined to hang on to the past and preserve family memories. Dorothy didn't leave a forwarding address, but I was satisfied knowing I could contact her at the Lost Coast Institute. As little as it was, it gave me something to hold on to.

Early on Wednesday morning I went to Lawrenceville, stopping at the first phone booth to call Patrick and let him know my plans. He was awaiting my call.

"Did you know Maureen had been sick? Coughing *all the time* the children said."

"I wasn't aware of that," he said.

"I'm volunteering in the ashram garden to see if I can learn anything. I'll keep in touch."

I felt a need for Mrs. Bergeron. If I was away from her for too long, I began to feel I'd lost my center. I bicycled up the hill to their house, dropped my bike on the lawn and rang the bell. She could see me through the stained glass of the front door and called out, "Clare, where have you been?" This was so simple. How was it possible for such few words to convey acceptance, love and kindness? Although I had said I would not speak to anyone of my mother, the story came pouring out.

"The most astonishing thing happened. My mother turned up at the ashram, dressed like an Indian princess, calling herself Stargaze."

Mrs. Bergeron took hold of my hand. This was very unlike her.

"Tell me about it."

I proceeded to tell her about the evening, my question, Stargaze's response and our encounter in her cottage.

"Oh, and most amazing of all, she has a family I never knew about."

"Do you plan to meet your relatives?"

"Oh yes! As soon as possible. I know this may sound crazy, but I'm hoping there will be a grandmother who's kind and sweet. Maybe even uncles, aunts, cousins." I stopped there, not wanting to sound too enthusiastic.

"You are a good girl. Whatever happens with them you will be able to handle."

This wasn't exactly encouragement.

"I'll let you know how it goes. Now I have to hurry and get on with all the things I have to fit into this day."

I said goodbye and got back on my bike. I bicycled by my old apartment house and dared to take a peek. There were new curtains at the kitchen window. I said, "Jesus, Mary, Joseph, bless these people in their new home." It was the best I could do and lightened my feeling that they were in my kitchen, my bedroom, my home!

My next stop was the library. I wanted to check the newspaper archives to see what I could find out about the Hearnes. I was optimistic but wanted to be prepared. I wasn't quite sure where to start so I mentioned my search to the librarian, who suggested I try the Lawrenceville High School yearbooks.

This was enlightening. I found Dorothy in her Grade Eleven yearbook, sixteen years old, and looking meek. That was a surprise! My father was also in several yearbooks, always looking tidy and smart, but not really standing out. Maybe they were well matched when they met.

There were lots of Hearnes but I didn't know enough about them to know which were my relatives. After that I gave up on the research angle. I realized it wouldn't tell me what I needed to know. Nothing in the library could tell me if the Hearnes were good people.

I had a lunch date with Isabel. She had gone on to Grade Thirteen. It seemed strange for her to still be in high school while I had moved a million miles away from that world. We met at the restaurant across from the school. I told her I had seen her mother but didn't mention Stargaze. Instead I talked about the missing Maureen, and my meeting with her brother, Patrick.

"This sounds right up your alley. You always wanted to be a private investigator. Do you remember our attempts to dig up mysteries?"

"This is different, more like a secret or ... it's hard to put into words. Let's just say I'm not expecting a body to turn up."

"Maybe she's gone to have cosmetic surgery," Isabel offered.

I laughed. "I never thought of that. I've never seen her, but I imagine she is beautiful because the children are so lovely. I'm lucky to have such sweet kids to look after."

"I'm glad you can see the good in this. I worry about you. I hope you can get back to college and continue with your life before too long."

"It's strange but it feels as if I've been led here, and it's right. What about you? How is Joe doing?"

"He's home for the summer. He says university is harder than he'd imagined, but I'm sure he can handle it. He's planning to continue with Engineering in the fall. I'm still not sure what I should do. I've only got a few days of school left. I wish I had a clear sense of direction."

"If you work for a year it may lead you somewhere."

"I'm afraid to end up like Arlene. Her year off led to marriage. Now she has kids, and she and Bill seem like an old married couple. There's nothing wrong with that. Arlene is happy, but I don't want all my options to come to an end so quickly."

"If I hadn't lost Dad, I would have had a hard time ever leaving him. I would have gotten a job in Lawrenceville and stayed home. He would have had to push me out. Did you know he had a girlfriend, our teacher Miss Smart?"

"I knew but I was afraid to mention it."

"I'm starting to think I've lived a strangely blind life. Dad must have deliberately kept it a secret. I guess he thought I couldn't face change."

"Don't be too hard on yourself. I don't think it was public knowledge. I only found out because I saw them together in the city, having lunch. How did you find out?"

"That's too big a subject for today. Will we meet again next Wednesday?"

"I hope so. I'm finished school this week, but I might have a job by then. Hopefully I'll still be able to manage our weekly lunches. I wish we had more time together. Now that it's summer there will be so many great get-togethers; picnics, camping, dances. I hate to think of you missing out on everything."

"It's not as bad as you imagine. Right now I'm trying to save every penny, and looking forward to when I'll be freer. The thing I miss most is our time together; otherwise, I'm a contented spinster."

"You just haven't met the 'right one'." Isabel's tone reflected what I judged to be her happiness in finding the 'right one'.

We had overstayed Isabel's break so we hurried off, Isabel to her exam and I to the ashram. I bicycled back slowly, thinking about how my parents looked in those photos, wondering how Dorothy could have changed so much. I didn't want life to be like that. I wanted the people I loved to stay the same. I hoped Isabel and I would always be close. I could accept her being in love and getting married, but feared changes that could make us grow distant.

I hurried inside to change into my gardening outfit, an old t-shirt and pale blue worn chinos of my father's. I rolled up the pant legs a few turns, and put on my sneakers over a pair of ankle socks, ready for some hard work. I truly hadn't any idea of what to expect. I walked the half mile to the garden, hidden away behind the buildings of the ashram.

There were at least ten people already working on hands and knees beside the raised beds. I went to the first person I saw and asked if I could join in. He was a bearded man with a pony tail and a warm smile. He got up from the ground and extended his hand.

"Hi, good to meet you. I'm Adrian."

Considering how close-mouthed everyone had been with me so far, he was a welcome change.

"I'm Clare. I'm working for Haari, looking after his kids at the house. I thought this would be a great opportunity to learn about vegetable gardening."

"I'm learning myself. You can start beside me. I'm mulching the tomato plants. If you've been watching for long enough you may have noticed there's a lot of reading going on."

I saw what he meant. Mulching involved spreading old newspapers in a layer around the green tomato plants. Many of the gardeners were completely engrossed in the newspapers, oblivious to their surroundings.

"I can understand that. I love reading the paper," I admitted. "I'll have to call up some strong discipline to put these down without being enticed to follow every story."

"A kindred spirit. Here's a stack of papers."

I got started and was finding the whole scene very pleasant, the sun warming my back and the sweet scent of tomato vines filling the air.

"Are you a disciple, Adrian?" I asked, after a while.

"Not exactly. There's a fair number of us who live and work here without paying, but we earn our keep, believe me."

He waited a few minutes, then said, "I'm a seeker, but I can't say I've found the answers here. What about you?"

"I'm the children's nanny. This is my afternoon off. I'm not a seeker. I'm happy with my Catholic beliefs. I'm just here to earn a living until I can get back to college."

Adrian grinned. "Seeking or not, you may be surprised at what you find."

I didn't reply to this enigmatic comment. It was time to get down to my real business.

"The children have been saying how much they miss their mother. Do you know her?"

"Yes."

I waited for more.

"And?"

"Yes, I know her. What else do you want to know?"

"I find it strange. The kids are missing her and don't seem to know when she's coming back. Nobody talks about her."

"I can tell you more, but not here. Let's talk about something else. Do you read novels? Have you read Zora Neal Hurston?"

"I read constantly but I don't know that name."

"Well, you must read her. But come with me, I have something you should see."

He led me away from the others to where they had potatoes growing under piles of hay. "No one can overhear us here," he said. "For most people this information wouldn't need to be kept secret, but Haari is a special case. Everyone believes he's a healer. They come here to have him lay his hands on them, and they go away recovered. So it doesn't look good if his wife is coughing day and night.

It started a few months ago. It was making him look bad. The problem was, nobody knew why. Finally, he sent her away to a clinic in the States. Every time she thinks she's recovered and makes plans to come home, she has a setback."

"How do you know all this?"

"One of my jobs is to open the mail. I've seen her letters to him. They probably should be delivered to the house with his personal mail, but for some odd reason she sends them to the ashram. It's really just about Haari's ego, or his need to preserve his image."

"Those poor kids are so sad not knowing where she is or when they'll see her again. Her family is worried too. Why she doesn't let them know what's up?"

"I don't know. She was very nice the few times I met her, but I had a feeling she wasn't really into the ashram. Haari has created too powerful a profile for himself - healer, teacher, spiritual leader. He's risen so high he can't live up to it. The disciples who come eat this stuff up, but he can't show any cracks in his facade. The strain must be exhausting."

"You think it's a facade?"

"I'm sure of it."

"Thanks Adrian. At least it's not some truly terrible secret. Can you give me the address of the clinic?"

"The letters came in an envelope from the clinic. The return address said, Wilson Institute, Montpelier, Vermont."

"You've helped enormously. I promise not to tell how I got this information."

"You're a good kid. See you in the garden."

The Escape

Although it didn't seem as if I had worked hard in the garden, I was sore the next day. Gardening was not easy, even if it looked like the workers were taking their time and enjoying themselves. I got out of bed and leaned on the sill of the open window. From my room I could see a farm in the distance, with tiny cows dotting the field. Haari's house was well separated from the rest of the world. It was wonderfully quiet in the cool morning, with only birds calling, and the gentle sound of leaves rustling in the Aspens. I heard a tiny voice and turned to see Jiddu.

"Clare, I'm so glad you're back. I miss you when you're gone."

I sat on the rocking chair and Jiddu climbed into my lap. Gita appeared and said how glad she was that Wednesday was over. They were getting very attached to me. Life was so unfair, they needed their mother, but she was gone.

"Shall we get up and start our breakfast?"

The kids loved helping in the kitchen. I got out the bowls, cups and spoons, and they took them to the table and set our places. I poured milk into a Wedgewood pitcher. It looked valuable and fragile. If there had been Melmac, I would have used that, but Wedgewood was all we had, and the children were careful. So far nothing had broken. I measured coffee into the percolator and turned on the gas.

"Would you like oatmeal today?"

I asked this every day, even though I knew the answer was always yes. Gita and Jiddu stood on their chairs and watched as I stirred the oatmeal. The smallest things could make them happy. Were they born this way, or had Maureen taught them to be angels?

When all was ready, I sat with my coffee and toast, while Gita and Jiddu enjoyed their porridge. The first sip of coffee was heaven. I had been drinking coffee since I was child and thought nothing of it. When Haari heard me asking the kids if they wanted coffee, he rushed in and said, "You must be kidding."

That was my first clue that this wasn't considered a child's drink. Haari was usually gone before we were up, but somehow he was still there that morning to catch me in this gaffe. I normally had a cigarette or two with my morning coffee, but this too was prohibited.

The mail arrived and I was surprised to find an envelope addressed to Miss Clare Kelly c/o Haari Devenanda, RR#2 Lawrenceville. It was from Shilta Hearne, one of Dorothy's sisters, inviting me to drop in any time, and saying how happy they would be to meet me. She included their phone number. Dorothy had led me to expect that they would be uncivilized, yet this seemed a very proper and mannerly invitation. I just had to figure out when and how I could get to their place, as it was too far to go by bicycle.

I was thinking about how enjoyable gardening was and wishing that we had a garden close to the house. It would be a great activity to share with the children. I was picturing the three of us with a plot of carrots, cabbage and onions, then realized I was getting in too deep. I was imagining a future here that could not be.

I didn't intend to spend my life raising Haari's children. Even if I wanted to, how did I know that Maureen wouldn't return any minute? I could be out looking for a job next week. This was a good correction to my daydreaming. I tried to refocus on my plan to save money and get back to college.

The rest of the week passed quickly. Haari mentioned that Jiddu should have a haircut. Jiddu's hair was very curly and didn't seem too long, but Haari was insistent that it was time. He arranged for a driver to take us to Lawrenceville. Heinriche, the town barber, quickly had tiny Jiddu into a chair and gowned with a plastic apron.

"What sort of a cut did you want, ma'am?"

I hated to see him lose his beautiful curls.

"As little as possible. Just tidy him up a bit."

I sat in the waiting area with Gita and watched as curls fell onto the floor. It didn't take long. Soon Heinriche had him brushed off and out of the chair. A new boy was revealed. I hugged him and told him what a big boy he was, but I felt a pang of loss.

Gita was detached. "Goodbye curls."

I called Patrick next. He was amazed at how quickly I found his sister.

"You're the best. When this gets sorted out I'd like to get together with you again."

I was all for this. Patrick was the most attractive man I'd ever met.

***

I needn't have bothered with my espionage efforts. The next day, as I was making lunch for the children, I looked out the window and saw a black Mercedes convertible pulling up at the front door. Then I heard a woman's voice saying, "Where are my darling babies?"

Gita and Jiddu jumped up and ran to the front door, throwing themselves into the arms of Mummy Maureen. She was as lovely as I predicted.

She looked at Jiddu and said, "Where is my little boy?"

For a few seconds I thought she would cry. It must have been a shock to see him without his blonde curls, but she pulled herself together and said, "What a little man you are now." Then she saw me and said, "You must be Clare. I've heard a lot about you."

"And you must be Maureen. The children have told me about you. I was just making lunch. Would you like to join us?"

"I want to sit and look at the children."

She was looking at them as if she couldn't bear to take her eyes off them. For some reason, Jiddu suddenly acted shy. He came and hid behind my legs. It was all too much for him.

To break the tension, I chattered about the daily routine I had with the kids, how I had asked to cook breakfast and lunch for them, our reading time before the nap, how well-behaved I found them.

Maureen looked healthy. Whatever her illness had been, it didn't show. I was not supposed to know that she had been sick, so I didn't say anything. It was awkward, as I wasn't sure what my role was to be. Would I have to leave?

Maureen was observing me. Then she said, "I don't have much time. I can see that Gita and Jiddu are fond of you. Do you want to continue to help with the children?"

I didn't have any idea what she meant. I admitted I was very fond of them and was feeling worried that my job was over.

She asked me to come into the den with her and told the children we'd be right back.

"I'll have to talk fast. I'm planning to take the children this afternoon and move to a place my parents bought not too far from here. It's a farm. I have all kinds of plans that I can't tell you about yet, but I'd like you to come with me. I can see you are competent and will be a big help.

I don't want Haari to know. My intuition tells me I can trust you. He will rush over here as soon as someone sees my car. I'll act like I'm home to stay. When he's gone back to work, a truck will come to pick us up and move us to the farm. I know it's sudden, but are you in?"

I had to think fast. I didn't think Haari was evil or dangerous, but there was something about him that made me sympathetic to Maureen's desire to get away. Maureen and the children didn't fit this ashram world. Even though I hadn't spent much time around Haari, I was already feeling I'd had enough of him.

"I'll come with you. Let me know how I can help and I'll get started."

The next few hours I was on a knife edge of anxiety. Haari showed up full of enthusiasm for Maureen's return, saying he would be back at six to spend the evening with her. As soon as he left, we started packing as fast as we could. I piled the kids' things into suitcases and boxes. My own belongings were quickly packed into my trunk, with Toasty stuffed in on top. Maureen said not to worry about getting everything. She was sure that it would be amicable, eventually, and she would be able to come back for the rest. I wasn't confident about any of that.

Patrick arrived with a rental truck. There was a mad rush to get everything loaded in. I rode with Patrick, while Maureen drove off with the children in her Mercedes. She led us down the driveway and through the ashram gate. We sped down the road, bound for parts unknown. As soon as we were well out of sight of the ashram I felt my anxiety lessen.

As we drove along, Patrick told me that almost as soon as I had called to let him know Maureen's whereabouts, she had called to arrange for his help. He knew his sister wasn't happy, but didn't know she was so close to leaving Haari.

"I'm glad you're going to be here to help with this transition. You seem practical."

I guess I was practical, but I was also someone who hated change, and yet here I was, going along with a mad plan without hesitation.

We drove through Lawrenceville and continued west along River Road. The farm was across the highway from the river, down a winding dirt lane lined with poplars. We took a sharp turn to the left and the house appeared; a tall red brick mansion with a full length front porch, furnished with a swing and rattan chairs and a double screen door leading to a large foyer.

I had often driven by this house with my father and remarked on its beauty. To think that I could be living here! I was also realising that I didn't know anything about Maureen and Patrick. How was it possible that her family could own such a place?

Although it appeared to be in perfect shape from the outside, when we got indoors it was apparent that it had been empty for several years. There were dust covers over the furniture and cobwebs everywhere. Nevertheless, Maureen was enthusiastic. She opened her arms wide and said, "Look, how wonderful it is."

Jiddu and Gita were sticking close to me. I was their security at present. We held hands and proceeded together down the hall, peering into the living room and moving on into the kitchen.

"Clare, are we really moving here?" Gita asked.

Maureen jumped in. "Yes, darlings. And I know you're going to love it. There will be a bedroom for everyone."

"I want to sleep with Clare." Gita was trembling.

"Me too," Jiddu said.

Maureen was undaunted. "It will be wonderful. Tonight we may all be in one bed. And gradually we'll get it sorted out. Who wants to help me pick a bedroom?"

My first thought was getting the kitchen in order. I looked around to see if it would be possible to cook in it. Patrick brought in several bags of groceries. The fridge looked like an antique but it was working. I stocked it with the food he'd purchased. There was a big black and white coal stove with pipes going up from it through the ceiling.

"Does anyone know how this works?" I asked.

"Don't worry about that," Maureen said. "Our cook will arrive shortly; she can handle a coal stove. Patrick had coal delivered already. There's a tiny room for it in the cellar."

There was a door in the middle of the hall that led down some steep stairs to the basement. Patrick disappeared down them carrying a black bucket. "Watch for mice," I called. The children stood peering into the darkness from the top of the stairs, relieved when he returned with the coal a few minutes later.

"No mice so far. But it looks like a good place to keep potatoes and carrots. There are shelves for canned goods too. It's going to be very useful," Patrick said.

I filled the sink with warm sudsy water and began cleaning all the dishes, pots and utensils that had been collecting dust. As I worked I looked out the window at the barn. I couldn't imagine that anyone would have left animals behind, but I saw a grey tabby come out from the dark interior, with two kittens following.

I called to Jiddu and Gita to take a look.

"Oh, kittens," Gita cooed. "Can we keep them?"

"They're not pets. They work for a living," Patrick said.

"I'm going to make a trap and catch them." Jiddu had become very adventurous and boyish since his haircut.

I laughed and said, "That will be up to Mummy Maureen."

"What's that about Mummy Maureen?" She had been upstairs checking the state of the bedrooms.

"Look. A cat and kittens!" Gita said.

"I was told they'd be here. She's a barn cat and keeps the rats and mice away. We can get our own house cat, and a dog too if you like."

This was ecstatically good news to the children. I'm not sure where Gita and Jiddu got their ideas about dogs and cats, but they were full of enthusiasm.

"I'm going to have a police dog, and he's going to stay in my room and sleep on the rug beside me, and I'll call him Prince, and he will be obedient only to me." Gita exclaimed.

We all laughed and Maureen said she'd found the perfect bedroom for Gita and Prince. The two went upstairs hand in hand to take a look. Patrick had been helping to clean the cupboards as I emptied them out, but was now sitting at the kitchen table taking a break.

"This is the most amazing turn of events. Saturday I was worried sick about Maureen, not knowing where she could be, and two days later we're here together."

"I didn't even know Maureen until this morning. I've barely had time to think about the consequences of what I'm doing here. What happens when Haari gets home?"

"I'm going to stay here, at least until we know how Haari reacts. Having me in the house will help Maureen feel safe. Not that I expect a problem."

"I can't believe I was so quick to accept her request and come along without knowing more."

"You've made the right decision."

"What about you, Patrick? What do you do when you're not rescuing your sister?"

"I'm at the Seminary in Toronto, studying to be a priest."

This was the last thing I expected to hear. I was embarrassed that I had been thinking of him as a prospective boyfriend. Now I would have to view him in a new light.

"That's lovely," I made myself say. "We need good priests."

He began to chat of this and that. Despite my disappointment, I still felt completely at home with him. Jiddu was sitting on his lap, almost asleep.

"It's past their nap time. Can we find him a place to lie down?" I said.

We went into the living room and pulled the dust sheets off some furniture.

"This will do nicely," Patrick said, uncovering a chaise longue.

I unpacked Jiddu's favourite blanket and his pillow. I read to him from the Wind in the Willows and within a few minutes he was fast asleep.

I heard a car drive up and stop. I went to the front door to see who had arrived. Despite Patrick's assurances, I was still nervous.

"Mrs. Nelthorpe." Maureen had seen her coming and had come downstairs to welcome her.

Patrick and Maureen ran to the porch and greeted her with a hug.

"Mrs. Nelthorpe, this is Clare Kelly. She'll be living here too."

Mrs. Nelthorpe carried a needlepoint covered valise and a large handbag.

"Patrick, I have a trunk full of supplies if you wouldn't mind bringing them in," she said. "I'm familiar with this house, you know. I had a girlfriend when I was in Grade Six who lived here. We played in the attic and all around the grounds. I look forward to getting started. I've longed to be back in a proper kitchen with a coal stove."

I liked her strong forthright look. She gazed at Gita who had followed Maureen to the front door.

"Your little girl? She's so lovely, and so like you as a child."

"Mrs. Nelthorpe was our nanny," Maureen explained.

I felt better knowing Mrs. Nelthorpe was going to be part of the household. She made me feel safe, as if we now had approval for our actions. She radiated moral authority.

"I'm going to get that stove going and supper started. I'd like to have the bedroom facing east, across from the dining room. I remember what a delightful room it is. I brought a cot to use temporarily."

"You're welcome to that room. It has a lot of light. We haven't sorted out where the rest of us will sleep. I'm glad you thought of a cot. The beds are quite worn out, springs poking up through the mattresses. We can make do with sleeping on top of the blankets for now." Maureen was looking tired. "Speaking of beds I'm going to take Gita up for her nap."

"You can take the *The Wind in the Willows* if you like." I showed Maureen where we had left off in the story.

Too excited to rest, I went upstairs to see what the bedrooms were like and wandered into the front sleeping porch. I felt as if I had found a missing piece of myself! It was like the porch on our apartment, and looked over the river from almost the same vantage point. I decided to claim this for my room. It would be wonderfully cool for sleeping in summer.

There was an uncomfortable old daybed on the porch that would have to do. I made it up with the bedding from my room at the ashram and set Toasty on the pillow. I began to feel I had a home again for the first time since leaving Jessup Manor.

There was no dresser, but there was a wicker chair with a flower-patterned cushion, and a small side table with a lamp. I pushed up the windows to let in the breeze from the river, lay down on the daybed, and fell asleep.

I slept for two hours. When I woke up, I could smell roast chicken and pie. I recognized that enticing apple cinnamon scent. Gita was standing beside me, quietly waiting for me to awake.

When she saw my eyes open, she jumped up on the bed and said, "I'm so happy to have Mummy Maureen back and to keep you, too. But where will Baba Haari sleep?"

"You'll have to talk to Mummy Maureen about that. For now he'll stay at the ashram for his work."

Gita picked up Toasty and held him to her cheek. He was soft, even after years of being played with. "Is Toasty happy here?"

"Yes. Toasty picked this room."

"Good, then you'll be happy."

We went downstairs, where we found Mrs. Nelthorpe stirring something on top of the cooker. She told us dinner would be ready in fifteen minutes. She had the table set for six, with blue and white Countryside china.

Jiddu was sitting on Maureen's lap, playing with a string of her beads and some figurines found in the pantry. Maureen and Patrick were talking, and Patrick was making notes on what they would need to take care of in the next few days.

"Gita and I are going to explore the yard," I said.

"You should see the orchard," Patrick said. "Follow the path beside the barn, then go through the gate under the arbour."

Gita and I wandered through the orchard. The apple trees were old, left to become wildly unruly and tangled. It made a wonderful cool grove. We explored to the end and when we returned Patrick had pushed up the windows on both sides of the kitchen and opened the back door so a breeze blew through. The day was becoming increasingly warm and humid. We sat down to our meal and Patrick said the blessing. Mrs. Nelthorpe had prepared a roast chicken, gravy, mashed potatoes and tender green beans; a meal far better than I was accustomed to. My own cooking certainly didn't come close to this.

After supper we all helped to clean up and put everything away. Then Mrs. Nelthorpe taught Gita how to play Old Maid. Jiddu tried to join in, but quickly grew frustrated. Gita loved this game. "Go to the bone yard," she sang out. Before Jiddu could get upset, I found his toy tractor. He was happy pretending to cultivate the floor mat. By nine the children were asleep, and Mrs. Nelthorpe had gone to her room, saying she loved to retire early with a good book.

Except for our voices, it was quiet as darkness fell. I could hear crickets outside, and now and then the faint sound of cars on River Road. Maureen, Patrick and I sat at the kitchen table in a pool of light from the hanging lamp.

Now that we were on our own I was anxious to find out what had led to this flight from Haari. Maureen didn't keep me waiting.

"I want to fill Clare in on what led up to today's move. It's a strange story."

Patrick nodded. "I barely told Clare anything when we met, only that I was trying to find you."

"Harry and I met in high school. We started dating in Grade Eleven and that was it. You may not see it, but his family is Irish, like ours. We both come from Toronto and the same world of private schools. His father is a lawyer. Harry planned to study law and join the family firm. Our family has a shirt factory. Our families got along well and we had lots of friends. We skied and sailed and had an ideal relationship. After a big wedding we set off on a world tour. We planned to be gone for six months."

"But Haari – or rather Harry – looks so much like he's from India. How can that be?" I asked.

"He tans easily, and he accentuates the look by dying his hair black. All of the craziness started in India. We weren't travelling like most young people in the sixties. We were first class all the way. We were staying at the Imperial Hotel in New Delhi. Harry, being dark and soulfully attractive, looked right at home in India.

"We met a couple there from Poona, Maryam and Jatin, who took a fancy to us. They invited us for tea and escorted us to the Taj Mahal. We were thrilled to have them guide us as they knew the place well and made everything easy. Although we had money, finding our way around in Delhi was daunting. They were clearly wealthy and had spent their lives in pursuit of enlightenment. This world of spiritual seekers was new to Harry and me. I wasn't interested, but Harry was fascinated. Within a few meetings they told Harry that they could see his aura and knew that he was the new world spiritual leader. 'You are the world teacher,' Jatin told him. 'It is undoubtable.'

"At first Harry was skeptical but they persisted, appealing to his ego, if not his reason. He became so enamoured of the idea of himself as 'special' that I couldn't talk him out of it. They convinced us to visit an ashram where we learned a great deal about Hindu traditions and Eastern spirituality. The next thing I knew, they made plans for the ashram in Ontario. Our honeymoon was cut short and we moved here.

In the beginning I went along with everything although I didn't believe he was a world saviour, and it caused a lot of unhappiness with our parents. I grew up believing a husband was head of the house, and that I had to go along with his work and way of life, but I wasn't prepared for anything so extreme."

"You must have been lonely," I said. "It's as if you lost the man you married."

"It was. Then I had Gita, and a few years later Jiddu. The children kept me so busy I didn't focus on the ashram. The thing that really brought it to a crisis was this cough I developed. It started about a year ago. I was expected to be present at the meditations and a supporter of Haari's mission. I started to find as soon as I was at the ashram I'd start coughing and would have to leave. It was an embarrassment to Harry because he was believed to have magical powers for healing.

"I would recover completely whenever I was away from Harry and the ashram. I know now I had emotional asthma. While I was away at the clinic I met a wonderful psychiatrist. Finally I was able to tell the whole story to someone who understood perfectly. It became obvious that I couldn't go back there."

Patrick spoke up. "Why didn't you keep in contact?"

"I'm sorry Patrick. I didn't want to be influenced. I knew how strongly you felt. I needed to make the decision on my own."

"What an amazing story," I said. "Until a few months ago I had never heard of an ashram, knew nothing of yoga, nothing of India except that it was full of poor people. It's hard to imagine how anyone could be convinced of such a radical idea so easily."

"That's exactly how I felt," Patrick said. "This has been something I couldn't begin to comprehend."

"I doubt Harry will miss me, he's so full of himself and the adoration of the disciples. He will be embarrassed, and will have to find a way to tell the story so it looks like it was part of the divine plan. I'm not sure about his relationship with the children. I really don't want to share them, because I hate the ashram and the world he's in. So far they haven't been touched by it. Clare, you're brilliant by the way. I couldn't get Harry to let us eat Canadian food. I hope I never see another lentil for the rest of my life."

"That must have been hard. Vegetarianism is so boring."

"It was more than vegetarianism. Certain food was restricted so that our passions wouldn't be excited. No onions. Can you imagine that?"

"That's terrible," I said.

"Maybe so, but there were worse things."

"Like what?" I asked.

"Women were throwing themselves at him. I always told myself he was unavailable to them, but in talking with the psychiatrist, I realized I was fooling myself. Whether he had sex with them or not, he was unfaithful in allowing these women to be so close to him."

Patrick reached out for Maureen's hand. "Thank God you've come through it. Clare is an angel sent to help you."

That made me uneasy. I didn't see myself as an angel. Only time would tell if I had even made the right decision.

Maureen yawned and got up. "I'm exhausted. I put the kids in the big bedroom with me. Tomorrow we can talk about what's next. Goodnight, darling Patrick. Goodnight Clare."

Patrick and I remained behind.

"I don't know Haari very well. What do you think he will do?" I asked.

"The Harry I knew was a great guy, fun and charming. They seemed like the perfect couple. Now I don't know who he is. Maureen left him a letter and told him she would call tomorrow. She wants to get it all out in the open. I understand her taking the kids. Sometimes the only way is to take drastic action."

"How long can you stay?"

"Only a few weeks, then I have to get back to my summer placement at St. Michael and All the Angels."

"I'm not sure what Maureen was thinking about me, but I'm happy to stay for a few months. I'm very attached to Gita and Jiddu. They are loveable children."

"Your help will make this much easier for Maureen." Patrick yawned. "I'm headed off to bed too. I'll sleep on the couch in case Harry shows up."

There was a flash of lightning and a crash of thunder.

"I'm going to wait up and see if this storm develops," I said. "My father and I always got up in the night when there was thunder and lightning."

"I'll stay for a while then," Patrick said, "and see if it comes closer."

We sat in silence, listening and watching, but it soon passed by and all was quiet.

"I guess that's it. No more drama for today. Goodnight Clare."

Buttercup Acres

My first night on the porch was peaceful. I had the windows open, and could hear the breeze in the poplars, and a soft patter of rain on the roof. When I woke up the rain had stopped. I looked towards the river, mesmerized by the morning light as it played on the moving water, steel grey, yellow and sea green.

That morning a telephone worker arrived and a black phone was connected in the front hall. It was a party line he explained, and our line would be two short rings. There were two other families on the line, so we'd have to pay attention and be careful not to pick up their calls.

"Our phone isn't very private," said Maureen. "I'd better go into town to call Harry. It's weighing on me and I need to get it over with."

I agreed to go into town with Maureen, and we took Gita and Jiddu with us. Gita was wearing a colourful skirt over a crinoline, and a blouse with rhinestones sewn onto it, an outfit she chose herself. I helped Jiddu get ready, dressing him in shorts and a t-shirt.

"I hate the idea of having this conversation standing outside at a payphone," said Maureen, "but it appears to be the only choice."

"There's a payphone at the train station," I said, "in a booth with a seat. It's quite private."

Maureen parked beside the old stone train station and I got out of the car with the children.

"We'll explore while you make your call," I said. I knew this area like the back of my hand, every pond, field and rock. "Take your time. We'll have fun."

I knew she faced a difficult conversation. She told me she rehearsed what she planned to say, but it was still going to be hard to get the words out. It occurred to me that I owed Haari a phone call too, but I decided it could wait. I was the least of his concerns.

Gita, Jiddu and I walked up a dirt road and into an open field where tall grass grew higher than the children's heads. They ran exuberantly along trails through the grass, imagining they were hidden from the world in a secret place. I suggested we make a fort by tramping down a patch of grass and calling it our house. This was fun until some big boys with Johnny Seven guns came along and began staring at us. I stood up and they ran off but it made Jiddu nervous. He pulled me to the edge of the field, where we could see the Mercedes. Then we went to a big rock and sat on top of it.

"Clare, what did you do when you were little and played here?" Gita asked.

"I collected pollywogs from the pond in April, and hung around the tracks waiting for the railroad men to give me sugar cubes. Once I picnicked at this big rock with my mother. Best of all was skating on the pond in winter."

"We've never skated. What's it like?" Gita asked.

"It feels like flying, if the wind's just right. I loved to spin in circles, pretending to be a figure skater."

"I'd like that. Maybe this winter I'll be big enough."

41

"You will. And Jiddu too. He can get bob skates to start out."

Jiddu got down and raced around the rock yelling, "I'm on bob skates, I'm a skater, watch me, watch me."

Gita said, "I'll get skates that I can fly with."

I was afraid she may have taken me literally.

I saw Maureen walking towards the car and called out to her. We went over to where she was standing, her face streaked with tears.

"How did it go?" I asked.

"Everything I planned to say was forgotten. As soon as he heard my voice, he started yelling about a trip to India, and how could I pull this when we were scheduled for some big event in Poona, and how he had tickets for the four of us, and how was he going to explain it, and what would he look like to Maryam and Jatin. Not one word about missing me or caring about us. It was all him and the ashram. Then he said he was going to go without us, and stay until December. As soon as he said that I felt a wave of loss. 'I want you back,' I pleaded. 'I want the man I lost on our honeymoon.' I was crying so that I could barely talk, and saying how lonely I was, and... and then, he hung up!"

Now we were all crying. Jiddu, Gita, Maureen and me. Crying beside a train station, on a dirt road, in the midst of fields of milkweed and tall grass.

"I want Baba Haari," Jiddu sobbed.

Then we all cried more, until Maureen said we needed to get in the car and drive to the river and drown our sorrows, which for some reason made me laugh. Soon we were all laughing and crying alternately, but we felt a lot better.

"Let's go out for a Coke," Maureen suggested.

I was surprised to find Maureen was totally unfamiliar with Lawrenceville. She said they almost never came to town. They went to Ottawa or Toronto for anything they needed

"Harry didn't want people in town watching us. He said small town people wouldn't understand the ashram and they'd hate us."

"What's Coke?" Gita asked.

"We could go to Woolworth's lunch counter," I suggested. "It's my favourite spot."

We parked in front of Woolworth's and I realized how out of place the black Mercedes was. People stopping to stare. We sat at the counter, and ordered small glasses of Coke for Gita and Jiddu, and coffee for Maureen and me.

"Bliss," said Maureen, tasting her coffee. "All these things were forbidden at the ashram. Now I'll enjoy them more than ever."

I admitted to her that I had been planning to share morning coffee with the children and she laughed, but agreed it wasn't something she would do.

Gita and Jiddu found the Coke alarming. "Ooh, it goes up my nose. I don't like it." Gita had taken only a small sip. Jiddu was blowing rather than sucking, and hadn't taken any in yet. Straws were also new to them.

"You don't have to like it, darlings. I'll get you some milk."

"Never saw kids turn down soda pop!" said the waitress.

"This takes the pressure off me for now. If Harry goes to India for six months I'll have time to start a new life. But I'm afraid in six months he'll have forgotten us."

"He won't forget you," I assured her. "It will be good for you to have some time to think about what you want."

"You're right. It gives me a breather. I can get on with my plans. One of the first things I want to do is teach you to drive. Let's go home. I want to tell Patrick how it went."

When we got back we found Patrick up on a ladder in the living room, brushing down cobwebs while Mrs. Nelthorpe was wiping down walls with a bucket of soapy water and a sponge. The house had a satisfying, clean smell of lemon.

Maureen said she would like to spend time with the children, as she had been away from them for so long. She took them out to explore the back fields.

I got into my gardening togs to help with the heavy cleaning. It was great to have a clear-cut task. I decided to tackle the upstairs, starting with the bathroom with its old iron claw foot tub. First I swept, getting rid of the accumulation of dead insects and cobwebs behind the fixtures. It felt good to scrub and rinse and bring back a shine to the white ceramic. The black and white tile floor cleaned up beautifully though it was at least fifty years old. I took down the dusty sheer white curtain to have it laundered and the room glowed in the bright sunlight that streamed in.

From the bathroom there was a view of a pond. It had a small dock on the edge, with a row boat tied up to it, like Ratty's boat from the Wind in the Willows. I wondered if it was part of the property.

Patrick came up behind me. "That rowboat looks inviting. We should check that out this afternoon."

He was standing close to me. I wished he would put his arms around me and imagined how good it would feel to lean my head against his shoulder.

Patrick had only come to deliver a message.

"Mrs. Nelthorpe has sandwiches ready. She sent me to gather everyone for lunch."

After lunch, when the children had been settled for their afternoon nap, Maureen, Patrick, Mrs. Nelthorpe and I sat down for a planning meeting. First Maureen talked about Harry.

"I plan to wait until he returns from India before I make any decisions about our marriage."

Then she talked about plans for the farm. She had learned a great deal at the ashram about organic farming. She was convinced this was going to be the up and coming trend and we'd be in at the start of it. I didn't know anything about what it meant to be organic, but it sounded exciting. My brief introduction to the garden at the ashram had awakened an interest in me.

"I also want some animals. We can start with sheep and goats and see how it goes. Mom and Dad are entirely behind me in this, and will help with funds to get it started. We'll need someone to do the heavy lifting once Patrick is gone. Any suggestions?"

I immediately thought of Adrian. He was strong, and not attached to his life at the ashram.

"Maureen, do you know Adrian? He's working for room and board at the ashram. I got the impression he was ready to move on."

"Yes, I spoke to him a few times. He's knowledgeable about gardening and easy to get along with. Patrick, would you see if you can find a way to get a message to him? We'll need a pickup truck too. I can't imagine bringing home feed, manure and goats in the Mercedes. We should take care of that today."

I stayed behind, while Patrick and Maureen went to shop for a truck. Now that I had a moment of quiet I had time to think about all that had happened so quickly. I wondered if my life was going off course, but the more I pondered, the more I thought it was all good. I looked forward to getting together with Isabel, to fill her in on all that had happened. Sharing with her would help me get perspective.

There was also the matter of my newly found relatives. I decided I would call Aunt Shilta to thank her for her letter, and let her know my new address and phone number. This would be my first contact with my family. I dialed Shilta's number with apprehension.

A voice answered on the second ring, "Gurly here."

I was taken aback as it was clearly a man's voice.

"This is Clare Kelly calling. I was hoping to speak to Shilta."

I could hear him call out 'Shilta' and then she came on the line.

"Clare, Gurly told me it was you. It's so good to finally hear your voice."

Shilta was easy to talk to, since she did most of the talking.

"You must come see us," she said. "We're all longing to get a look at Dottie's Clare."

Dottie? That must be Dorothy. I bet she hated that.

"I only have my bicycle," I said, "so I'm not sure how I can get to your place."

"You could take a taxi. We're having a sort of family reunion in two weeks. Why don't you come and you can meet everyone."

"That sounds like a good plan," I agreed. "I'll find a way to get there."

I said goodbye and decided it was a good time to call Haari. He had been decent to me, and I felt guilty for running off without a word.

"Hello Haari, this is Clare."

"Clare." His voice wasn't so much angry as sad.

"I want to explain. I couldn't abandon the children."

"You don't have to explain. I know how attached you are to Gita and Jiddu. Your job would have ended quite soon anyway. I was planning to take the children to India."

I was surprised at how easily I was off the hook. There didn't seem to be any more to say.

I went back to cleaning, starting on one of the small bedrooms. The children were napping peacefully on the big iron frame bed, their cheeks rosy from playing outside.

I was still immersed in cleaning when I heard Patrick call from downstairs, "Come and see the new truck."

Maureen was standing next to an orange and white Chevrolet pickup.

"Stay where you are," Patrick said. "I'm going to get a photo."

Patrick disappeared and came back with a camera on a strap around his neck. I'd seen a few Brownies and one Polaroid but this was nothing like any camera I'd seen.

"That's a fancy camera," I said.

"It's a Leica. A present for my high school graduation. I'm going to leave it here so you and Maureen can use it. I'll show you how it works. Get in the photo, Clare."

I was in my cleaning clothes, but I bravely posed beside Maureen, who always looked gorgeous.

"What a beautiful truck. Is it new?" I asked.

"Not quite. It's a 1966. I fell in love with it. Patrick drove it home, but I'm dying to take it out for a spin. You'll need to learn to drive it, too."

I loved the way Maureen took me under her wing and included me in all her plans. It was beautiful to suddenly feel part of a family. The kids woke up and came out into the sunshine, blinking.

"Mummy, where were you?" said Jiddu, reaching up for her to hold him.

Patrick grabbed Gita and swung her into the back of the truck.

"Here's where you'll sit."

Gita was delighted, but Maureen insisted they sit in the front.

"You can take them for a little drive," Maureen said, "but don't go far."

Maureen and I were left on our own as they drove off.

"We haven't really talked about my job here," I said. "I was working six days a week for Haari, with Wednesdays off. Do you mind if I go to town tomorrow?"

"Forgive me. This all happened so fast I haven't had time to think. Let's start off with the same arrangement for pay, but I want you to have more free time for your interests, like boyfriends and parties. We can be flexible – like family. You already feel like a sister."

"Thanks Maureen, I feel at home with you too. I'll be delighted to have more time for myself, but so far there are no boyfriends and I'm not keen on parties."

"Let's sit down tonight once it's quiet and find out more about each other."

The next day I met Isabel at her house. She was finished school and hadn't yet found a summer job.

"I'm glad you have lots of time today," I said. "I have so much to tell you! You're going to have a hard time believing what's been going on in my life!"

We sat in the backyard at the picnic table, eating dainty chopped ham and pickle sandwiches that Mrs. Bergeron made. She also brought out a pitcher of iced tea.

"First thing I've been wondering about, did you find Haari's wife?"

"Yes. She came back." I told the whole story of how Maureen had arrived, packed up the kids and moved to the farm.

"You're kidding! You've already left the ashram and moved to a farm on River Road!"

"Yes, and that's not all. Last week I met my mother."

Isabel's eyes opened wide. "I can't believe it! After all these years. How did you meet?"

"She came to speak at the ashram She calls herself Stargaze; she's some sort of guru. There's even more. I discovered I have relatives – a big family I've never met."

"This is too much. You must be reeling."

"I was angry and upset at first, but I'm getting used to this new view of my mother. I'm also looking forward to meeting Dorothy's brothers and sisters. I've been invited to a family reunion.

"I'm happy for you. I don't know your relatives but maybe my parents do. Would you like me to ask?"

"No, not yet. It's best if I meet them first, without any preconceptions. Dorothy wasn't very flattering about her family but I'm staying open. Oh, and I'm going to get my driver's license. We have a Mercedes and a truck on the farm. And I'll have more time off, so maybe I can join some of the fun this summer.

"Maureen is nice. Last night we sat down and she told me about her plan for the farm. I told her about my background and said I'm interested in helping for at least a year. Then I'll see. You'll have to meet her and Patrick, and see the house and my sleeping porch."

"What about Patrick? Do you think he'd come to the Regent Hotel on Saturday night? There'll be a band. We could drive to Williamsville together."

"I didn't tell you this part yet. He's studying to become a priest."

"Too bad, I thought you were showing interest in a man for the first time."

47

"It is a shame, but I have to let it go."

"It's possible he'll dance though. It can't hurt to ask."

"Well, maybe I'll see," I replied.

When I got back to the farm, Patrick was at the end of the driveway putting up a sign that said *Buttercup Acres*.

"We found this sign in an antique store in Williamsville. Maureen and I both saw it at once and said, 'That's perfect'."

"I like it," I said. "It speaks of nature and beauty."

Patrick and I walked my bicycle back to the house He led me to the barn to see the sheep and goat and their babies that they had picked up that morning. I could hear bleating and maaaing and baaaing. It was a quick entrance into real farm life. I was overcome.

"Oh, they're so beautiful!"

Maureen was there with the children who were wide-eyed at the baby goats leaping around. The lambs were quieter, nuzzling against their mother.

"We have to get a fence," said Maureen. "They should be in the fields eating grass."

Maureen planned to use the sheep for wool and the goats for milk. She knew that people were developing an interest in homespun wools and that there was also a growing natural food movement which created a demand for goats' milk.

"Could we get some chickens?" I asked. "I'd love to take care of them."

Maureen nodded enthusiastically. "Chickens will come soon. They are essential in organic gardening; giving manure, eating pests. Think how wonderful it will be to get up and have a fresh egg. I will happily turn the chicken care over to you, Clare. There are so many things to do. First, the fence. Next, get some raised beds built for the garden.

"Ideally this should all be dug by hand, but then we'd never get started in time for any crops this year, so I've got equipment and workers lined up. By the end of the week we should be looking like a real farm."

Maureen's enthusiasm was contagious. Gita wanted to help feed and water the chickens and Jiddu wanted to ride the sheep.

"We're going to need a hired man as soon as possible. Patrick has arranged for Adrian to come talk about the possibility of working here. We need to figure out where he can stay."

"There's a guest cottage in a clearing behind the orchard," I said. "Gita and I saw it on the first day."

I led the way through the orchard to the cottage. We peered through small panes of glass on the front door and went in. I was enchanted. Sun poured in through dusty windows. It needed cleaning but was dry inside and would be comfortable, at least until fall. It had a bed, a table with two chairs, a wood stove and a dresser.

"This will be perfect for Adrian," Patrick said.

Adrian had a vision as soon as he saw the cottage. He pictured a greenhouse attached. "It will have a fieldstone foundation with the greenhouse above, made of recycled windows. I'll attach it to the side of the cottage and that will heat the cottage in the cool season. This would be the perfect sunny spot for it. I've had some experience with greenhouse building. It's also likely that when we create the raised beds we'll unearth great mounds of fieldstones, so we'd have a ready supply of them." Adrian looked excited, ready to jump right to work. "I can move in tomorrow, if someone will come pick me up."

"I wish I could stay around to help build that greenhouse," Patrick said wistfully.

We strolled back towards the house.

"Does the pond belong to Buttercup Acres?" Patrick asked.

"Yes, it's ours." Maureen said.

"The rowboat seems sound," Patrick said. "Who'd like to go for a row around the pond?"

"I'm going to take the kids in to get cleaned up before supper," Maureen said. "Why don't you take Clare?"

"I'd love to go," I said.

Patrick was seated in the middle ready to row. I got seated at the prow and pushed off.

"You do swim, don't you?" he said.

"I love to swim and could easily make it across this small pond," I answered. "But I have a fear of weeds and all the squirmy things found in a pond, so please keep us upright."

Patrick laughed. "We won't have to swim in it, but it is charming to look at and to row on. This place is a sort of paradise. I'm going to hate to go back to Toronto."

"This has been an extraordinary couple of weeks," I said, "first meeting you and then Maureen. There's also another even more extraordinary event in my life."

As he rowed I told him about meeting my mother, after not seeing her since I was ten years old. Patrick was a wonderful listener, and sympathetic on hearing of how my father and I had been abandoned all those years ago. I told him about the upcoming family reunion.

Patrick looked concerned. "I can't let you go there alone in a taxi. I'll go with you for moral support and also a ride home, in case it's all too much."

"That is kind. It would make it a lot easier."

As we walked back to the house, I remembered the dance. I felt shy but managed to say, "There's a dance in Williamsville on Saturday night. Would you like to come along with Isabel, Joe and me? I know you can't have a girlfriend or anything, but you still might like to come along for the fun of it."

"Why wouldn't I be able to have a girlfriend?"

"You know, because you're planning to be a priest and ...."

Patrick started to laugh. "You think I'm Catholic, don't you?"

"When you said priest, I assumed..."

"Our family is Anglican. I can have a girlfriend, and later a wife and children. It's almost required for the job, in fact."

"Oh dear, now I feel such a fool," I said, blushing. "Please forgive me, I didn't mean to ..."

"Don't give it a second thought. I'd love to come to the dance!"

The New Age

Evenings settled into a routine. After the children and Mrs. Nelthorpe were in bed, Patrick, Maureen and I sat up and talked. Patrick suggested I tell Maureen about my mother and the encounter at the ashram.

"Stargaze! I know her." Maureen was amazed. "She's been around in these circles for years. I've met her at various ashrams and new age communities."

"What's a new age community," I asked?

"I'm so used to hearing about it I thought everyone knew about it. It's a mix of Eastern religions, marijuana, paganism.... hmmm.... a dash of organic gardening, homeopathy, yoga, hippies and original innocence. I'm excited about the good parts; the love of nature, organic gardening and returning to the land. That's how I developed my interest in it. Otherwise I'd be a city girl and I'd have run home to Mom and Dad to spend my days shopping. I was the person behind the great gardens at the ashram. We didn't have animals there because we were vegetarians, but now I'm been reading everything I can find about animal husbandry."

"It's all new to me. I didn't get to learn much about the ashram. I heard they were meditating and doing yoga, but it was mostly a mystery. The only time I was in the ashram was for Stargaze's talk, and one afternoon at the garden. That's how I met Adrian. I found the people very different from the world I come from. They seemed sort of gullible."

"That's the downside. That's what I needed to get away from. They think they've left convention behind, but now there's even more mind control. I fear that although Harry thinks he's powerful and doing great work, he is the most enslaved to it. I long for him to see through it and get free."

"I don't think the same is true of my mother. She won't be a slave to anyone. She'll take the best for herself and no one will know what she really believes. She loves admiration."

"You seem to be a natural with the children. I'd never guess Stargaze was your mother. Patrick and I were brought up by a mother who was totally dedicated to us. I can't imagine how hard it must have been for you."

"The funny thing is, it really wasn't hard. I'm grateful for everything in my life – even for Dorothy. There was a lot of beauty, and I was mostly happy."

"Tomorrow is going to be a very full day. There will be trucks and workers coming early. Clare, I'd like you to keep the children away from the work areas. I'm going to oversee the raised bed work and Patrick will make sure the fence goes where we want it. See you early in the morning." Maureen headed off to bed.

"Your sister is a dynamo."

"This is a new side to her. I know she has a true interest in starting this business, but I also think she's trying to distract herself from the pain. I'll keep praying for her marriage to work out. They belong together."

***

In the morning I woke up before anyone else. The sky to the east was a blaze of orange and green. I knew it would be a hot day. Not wanting to wake anyone, I wandered outside to sit on the big rock in the front field and look over the river. I lit a cigarette and wished for a cup of coffee. I sat and enjoyed this quiet moment to reflect on the new turn my life had taken.

I received another letter from Stargaze in response to my letter telling her about my change of address and new job. She wrote, *'Do you really want to be a mother's helper? Like in some Gothic novel. Don't you see yourself in a different light?'*

I was angry reading her words. Who the hell was she to tell me what I should do? But she had woken me up to a subject I didn't want to look at. I needed solitude. It was hard having people around from morning to night. I could live with it for now, but I knew it wasn't for me. I missed the quiet life I once shared with my father. I finished my cigarette and went in to start coffee.

There was lots of activity at Buttercup Acres that day. It seemed best to stay out of the way. As soon as breakfast was over, I got Jiddu and Gita dressed, packed up their swimsuits, pails and shovels, and shepherded them down the lane and across the road to the river. There were lots of cottages on the river side, but this spot had a small sandy beach with a willow tree leaning out over the water. We took off our sandals and waded in up to our knees. The water was cool and delightful, but too cold for a swim. Gita asked if I would teach her to swim, and I promised I would, as soon as the water was a little warmer. I wasn't so sure about this beach. I could see there were lots of weeds as soon as the water got a little deeper. The river, once so clear and clean, had become choked with weeds. I no longer trusted it was safe to swim in. This was heartbreaking, as I had spent my childhood summers swimming at the beach in Lawrenceville, but in recent years the water was unhealthy. Maybe I would teach Gita to swim at the pool in town.

Gita and I set to work making a sand castle, while Jiddu was absorbed in digging a large hole. He said he was making a pond for the castle. As the sun got hotter we decided that the castle was finished and moved to the shade of the willow.

"Darling Clare, please tell us a story?"

Gita had picked up the habit of calling everyone 'darling' from her mother. It was charming and I felt no one could refuse anything when asked so sweetly.

"How about Goldilocks and the Three Bears?"

"Yes," they both said.

It was one of their favourites. I told this with some flair, as I'd had lots of practice. When I came to the end I always said, "Goldilocks woke up and saw the three bears and ran away as quickly as she could into the forest." Instead today I said, "Goldilocks woke up and saw the three bears and said, "Darlings, what a charming cottage you have. I could happily live here with you."

"No she didn't," Jiddu said. "She was scared. She ran away into the forest."

"Did you forget the ending?" Gita asked.

They insisted I tell it exactly as they knew it. Then they were happy. Gita told me that Goldilocks couldn't live with bears. They would surely eat her.

"I think the cottage behind the orchard looks like a place where the three bears would live," I said.

Yes," Gita agreed. "Let's called it Goldilocks' Cottage."

Buttercup Acres had lots of new places for them to find and love and make their own. I wished I could see it with their eyes. I glanced at my watch; it was almost time for lunch, and I knew that even a short walk took them a long time. We crossed the road and headed back up the lane.

As summer unfolded there were new things to see every day. The pig's bladder was out, mullein was sending up tall spears, and morning glory was flowering everywhere. We picked dandelions and buttercups to bring to Mrs. Nelthorpe, who was always appreciative of flowers for the table.

Adrian moved in that morning. Patrick picked him up right after breakfast. He was already part of the crew. Mrs. Nelthorpe was busy making lunch for the workers who were there for the day. She set out food on the weathered picnic table in the back yard; plates of sandwiches, a large bowl of cole slaw, and pitchers of bright red, raspberry Freshie. For dessert there was a platter of hermit cookies and brownies. She made many pots of tea. As fast as she could bring them out, they were emptied. There weren't enough lawn chairs to go around, but everyone made do, sitting wherever they could find a perch.

Gita and Jiddu weren't used to being around so many people, having been quite isolated at the ashram. They stayed close to me at lunch, although I could tell they were fascinated by all the big men in their work clothes and heavy boots.

By the end of the first day the fences were finished. By the second day the raised beds were crudely started, with boards hammered together to keep the soil in place. The excavator made quick work of filling the raised beds. There were fifty beds created, each four feet across and twenty five feet long. This was an enormous amount of garden space. Maureen said they couldn't begin to plant it all immediately, but it made sense to get all the digging done while they had the excavator on site. The boards were new and smelled of fresh pine. It was a wonderful sight, row after row of raised beds, where yesterday there had been a field of tall grass. The beds were on a slight hillside and extended almost to the pond.

The garden beds could be seen from the road, and there was a lot of interest from people driving by. The Lawrenceville Times sent a reporter to take pictures and interview Maureen about Buttercup Acres. It was great publicity, although she didn't have anything to sell yet.

On Saturday night, Patrick and I went with Isabel and Joe to the Regent Hotel. I had promised my father I wouldn't drink until I was of legal age. As luck would have it, the age had recently gone down to eighteen, so I could keep my promise and have a drink with everyone else. The group ordered Labatt's 50 and I asked for the same. It was tolerable at the first cold sip, but as it warmed I found it appalling, and wondered how anyone could drink it.

Patrick noticed that I didn't seem to be enjoying my drink and asked if I'd like something else. I told him I had never gone out for a drink and didn't know what I would like. He suggested I try a Tom Collins, which his mother always ordered. I was much happier with that.

The band played one great song after another and we danced to almost every one. This was new to me too, but as it was free form there didn't seem to be much to learn. I just had to move with the beat and imitate what I saw around me. I saw lots of girlfriends from high school. They were looking at Patrick and giving me the thumbs up. The last song they played was Let It Be, and we swayed together in a slow waltz. I enjoyed the closeness with Patrick. When it ended, he kept his arm around me to lead me back to the table. I thanked Isabel for inviting us and told her it had been a perfect night.

"I'm so happy to finally have you join us. Everything is more fun when we're together," Isabel said.

"I hope we'll have a summer to remember."

"Mom wants you to come to breakfast after Mass tomorrow. Could you make it?"

"I'll be there."

Sunday mornings were going to be a lot easier in my new position. I wouldn't have to get up early for Mass and hurry back to work. Maureen and Patrick took the children to the Anglican service and then went out for breakfast, so I was free for the whole morning. It was another good turn of events.

I enjoyed the coolness of the air beside the river as I bicycled to town. I hadn't realized how hard it was to be so tied down to the job at the ashram. Now that it was over, I realized how much I needed freedom to be with friends, ride my bike, and take time over things. I thought about how I was put into the position of being the mother of Gita and Jiddu and realized that once you have children, there's not much free time left for yourself. I felt a twinge of sympathy for Dorothy, but not much.

We met after Mass and walked the short block back to their house. I loved breakfast at Isabel's. All the Bergerons were together, even Arlene who came with Bill and the children. After our wonderful breakfast of bacon, eggs and heaps of toast, we sat around smoking and lingering over coffee.

Mrs. Bergeron said, "I hear you have a man in your life."

"It's not like that yet. I like him, but I'm not sure what direction I want for my life. I don't know if marriage and motherhood are for me. I love Gita and Jiddu, and at the same time I hate being tied down by childcare."

"It's good to take it slowly and pay attention to how you feel about these things. It's hard to turn things around if you go too quickly."

"So far everything is happening too fast. I feel lost without Dad and all the familiar routines. It's good to be here and to remember who I am. My mother is no help. She sent me a letter warning me not to get stuck being a 'mother's helper'."

Mrs. Bergeron surprised me by agreeing with Dorothy. "This is okay for you now Clare, but don't get stuck."

"I've offered to stay for a year to help Maureen get started. I'm planning to return to school the following September, if I can save enough money."

"I have a job for the summer. I start tomorrow," Isabel said. "It's at Dad's factory. It pays lots. If I save everything I make I can pay for college in the fall. If only I could think of what I'd like to study. It seems like we go through all those years of school and at the end haven't a clue what the work world is like or even what's available."

Arlene said, "You're both worrying about nothing. Have faith in life. You'll see. Good things will come along."

I didn't say so, but I still felt it was important to have a plan and not get sidetracked by events.

"Whatever I do, I want to be able to live in Lawrenceville," I said. "I love the river and fields and hills and our dear downtown and the library. Oh and above all, Woolworth's lunch counter."

Isabel said, "I agree with Clare, but I'm afraid there won't be any jobs for Joe in Lawrenceville. What would an engineer do here? We'll have to move to a city I'm afraid."

"I didn't know you were so sure about each other," Arlene said.

I was thinking the same thing. I hated the thought of Isabel marrying and moving away.

"Maybe Joe could start his own company here," I suggested. "Don't we have any engineers in this town?"

Mrs. Bergeron laughed, "It's all a long way off. Don't borrow trouble."

I liked her optimistic philosophy.

When I got back to Buttercup Acres everyone was home. Patrick told me they met lots of nice people and the rector asked if he'd like to give the homily next week. Patrick and Maureen were going to fit very nicely in Lawrenceville. Maureen said the kids had joined the Bible Study.

"Do you know this shepherd, Jesus?" Gita asked, showing me a picture she had coloured of Jesus with a sheep.

I laughed and told her that I did. It was all new to her. Maureen had never taken the children to church when they lived at the ashram. I had a feeling there was going to be no going back to life as they had lived it.

"It felt good to get back to church," Maureen said. "I haven't been particularly faithful. Maybe if I had been Harry and I wouldn't have been so easily pushed into the whole divine world leader thing. I could at least have had a good reason why I couldn't accept it. Not having any strong beliefs left us open to whatever came along. I never really thought about it before."

"Thanks Maureen," Patrick said. "You've given me a great idea for next week's sermon."

Patrick enjoyed talking about his love of theology. He had books of old sermons and loved to ponder theological concepts. He especially admired

C.S. Lewis. I knew nothing of theology except the catechism I'd learned by heart at school. I didn't even know if this counted as theology – it was just what I accepted as truth.

"I have an idea," I said. "Let's read *The Lion, the Witch and the Wardrobe* every night after supper while the kids are still up. We'd all enjoy it. I read it with my father when I was ten and I'd love to hear it again. I still have my copy of it."

We got started that evening, taking turns reading. Gita was a bit young but she loved hearing us read. Jiddu tried to listen but was soon off playing with his truck on the rug. Patrick had a great speaking voice. Mrs. Nelthorpe asked if she could just listen while she knitted. She was making teddy bears for the children. She sat amidst a growing pile of stuffed heads and trunks, ears and noses, soon to be assembled.

Except for meals, Adrian kept to himself. He was an early riser. He mentioned that he had seen me sitting having my early morning cigarette. He told me he got up at dawn and made a big pot of coffee. I was welcome to come over and grab a cup to have with my early morning smoke.

"You must have read my mind," I said.

This began a new routine in which I would get up at daybreak, take my mug to Goldilocks' Cottage, and then return to my rock to enjoy coffee and that wonderful first cigarette of the day. Adrian was always up and out, walking or meditating somewhere on the grounds.

I pondered the upcoming family reunion and decided bringing Patrick along would be too confusing. I needed to be alone to experience my newly discovered relatives.

Family Reunion

The Sunday of the reunion I bicycled to Lawrenceville for Mass as usual, and then to breakfast at the Bergeron's. Mrs. Bergeron told me to consider it a standing invitation. When I mentioned that I was going to call Lorne's taxi to get to the Hearne family reunion. Peter offered me a ride.

"I'm teaching Timothy to drive and that's a good quiet road for him to start out on. We can even bring you home if you're ready to leave by around 3:30."

This was perfect. It gave me a chance to visit for a couple of hours, but also a great opportunity to escape if necessary.

I was filled with trepidation as we neared the Fourth Concession Road. I pictured the property as it had been when I used to drive by with my father. We came to a mailbox that said *Hearne* and a house with several travel trailers behind it. Some old cars were parked along the side of the road and in the driveway. I was happy to see stairs had been built at the front door.

"This must be it. Thanks Peter and Timothy. I'll see you at 3:30."

I must have shown my anxiety, because Peter offered to come back sooner, but I said I'd be alright. I walked up the driveway and saw many tables set up in the back yard, with people everywhere. A pig was turning on a spit over a fire. I saw a circle of chairs with instruments laid across them; guitars, a fiddle and a small stringed instrument I didn't recognize. A woman with dyed blonde hair and a red print dress jumped up from her lawn chair and came over.

"You must be Clare! I'm your Aunt Shilta."

She began introducing me to people. "This is your Uncle Gurly, Aunt Mercy, Uncle Timbo, Uncle Django, Uncle Vano. I know you won't remember all these names so don't worry about it."

She introduced me to everyone as Dottie's daughter. There were many comments on my resemblance to my mother and some said that they had always wanted to meet me. I wasn't able to untangle the relationships. Who was married to whom? Which children belonged to which family? The astonishing thing was the children. They were innumerable.

No one bothered to introduce them and they didn't take much notice of me or any of the grownups. They were busy playing tag, throwing balls, skipping ropes and causing havoc as they raced around tables and lawn chairs. I had never experienced such chaos. I overheard one of the little boys say to another, "Fuck the hell off you little shit." I made sure I didn't overhear any more of their talk.

Someone got me a pink drink, which I sipped slowly, and a plate of crackers, cheese and salami. I was offered a chair. From then on, one relative after the other came over to say who they were and ask me about my life.

"Dottie was the youngest," Aunt Mercy told me. "She was also the smartest. She showed up for school every day and was neat as a pin. We couldn't figure out where she came from. Once she met Ned she kept him to herself."

"I taught Dottie to read the cards," Shilta said. "She was good at it. The best of all of us. I could teach you."

Uncle Gurly noticed my distress as I cowered away from the attentions of some large brown and black dogs. He said, "We must be scaring the pants off you girl," then yelled out, "kids, get those dogs out of here. Tie them up by the barn."

I was happy to have them pulled away. There were also sinister looking cats staring at me, but I suspected nothing could be done about that.

"You're as pretty as a picture," Gurly said. "Your mother was beautiful too, but hard, hard as nails."

"Oh Gurly, don't tell her that. That's not true. She was smart and knew how to take care of herself," said Shilta.

"Just like I said. Taking care of yourself is another way of saying hard as nails."

Gurly was funny. He was full of memories of Dottie and the kids when they were growing up. Before I knew it, Peter and Timothy were back and I was saying my goodbyes. The aunts told me not to be a stranger now that I knew where to find them. One of the older boys said, "She's going to miss the music." I was sorry to leave without tasting that roasted pig too. The uncles had moved into the house to play poker so I went in to say goodbye. Uncle Django had a shy look and called me over. He quietly handed me a package.

"Just wanted to say glad to meet you. Here's a little something. Open it later."

"Thank you," I said. I was charmed.

Peter had taken the wheel again. Timothy was tired out; driving took a lot of concentration. I climbed in the back seat and felt my shoulders relax. I realized I had been terrified of this visit. I was in a daze. I wasn't sure I could come to any conclusions, but I knew I wanted to see more of them. There was so much I wanted to know about their lives. Having broken the ice, I knew it would be easier next time.

When I got back to Buttercup Acres, Patrick was looking after Gita and Jiddu, while Mrs. Nelthorpe was attending to the Sunday roast.

"Where's Maureen?" I asked.

"Harry called early this afternoon, then came and picked her up," Patrick said. "She was nervous and excited. All dressed up as if for a first date. I feel so concerned about her. When Harry came to the door Gita and

Jiddu were all over him. Crying and saying, 'Baba when are you coming to live with us?' It was heart breaking."

Patrick was so distracted he didn't ask about my visit to the Hearne family reunion, and I didn't bring it up.

Maureen called around six to say she wouldn't be back for supper. We sat down to our roast beef and Yorkshire pudding. It was a subdued meal. Patrick kept looking at the clock. I was glad when it ended. Gita and Jiddu were off balance, too. They didn't eat much, and weren't interested in hearing more of the story.

I decided to take them outside to play, as it was a bright warm evening. We went first to the goats and gave them some carrots. Mama goat was a beauty; white, soft and gentle. Her babies frolicked beside her. Then we walked down to the pond and searched for frogs. Being outdoors relaxed the children and they seemed to forget their sadness.

When we came back inside, Maureen was sitting at the kitchen table with Patrick and Mrs. Nelthorpe.

"Mummy, where's Baba?" The children had expected him to return.

"Baba is going to take a trip. Don't worry, we'll see him when he comes back," Maureen sounded sad. She headed for the stairs. "I'm worn out. I'm going to bed."

The children shared a room with two beds. In between was a night table with a clown lamp. I put the children to bed and read from the Wind in the Willows, which always left them relaxed and dreamy. They were quickly asleep. I went downstairs and found Patrick still sitting in the kitchen.

"How do you think Maureen's talk with Harry went?"

"She didn't tell me much, just said he was headed to India soon, and they'd talk again when he returned."

When I went up to bed I remembered the package from Uncle Django. I retrieved it from my purse and undid the pink ribbon. Inside was a box with a square photo, a holy card and a small item wrapped in white tissue paper. The photo was of a baby girl dressed in white wool tights, wearing a rabbit coat and hat. On the back it said, "Here's my little Clare. Named after our favourite Nanny Clare. Love always, Dottie." The photo had a date printed on the bottom. February 1953. I was only eight months old. My mother sent this to her family! Dorothy must have loved me when I was little. When did it all change?

Inside the tissue paper was a wooden statue of Saint Clare, carved by Uncle Django. I placed Saint Clare on my night table and found a candle. I lit it and sat quietly, listening to the crickets and frogs singing in the warm night. Who was Nanny Clare? That would be easy enough to find out. Who looked after all those children? That was unanswerable.

That night I had a dream of Stargaze, dressed in exotic finery, sitting in front of her cards. I was across from her, waiting expectantly for her to tell my future.

The Tao

In the morning I headed to the cottage eager for coffee. There I found a book waiting, with a note from Adrian: *Clare, this is one of my favourites – I think you'll find it interesting.* It was the *Tao Te Ching* by Lao Tsu. The cover had a sepia drawing of an old man riding a water buffalo.

I poured my coffee and took the book to my rock. The morning was slightly grey, with clouds obscuring the sun. I started to read. It was like poetry or scripture, rich with meaning. I felt that it was wise and that I understood it in a deep sense, without being able to say exactly what it meant. It seemed to be saying that there is a natural way to be good, but that we lose our way in rules and laws. I tended to be a rule and law sort of person, so I was going to have to give this a lot of reflection.

Later over breakfast, Maureen talked about the work that needed to be done by the end of the week. She must have been up early, as she had a plan laid out for each of us.

"Darling Patrick, I appreciate the help you've given, but you should get back to your life in Toronto. I have no fears about Harry now."

"I'd like to stay for another couple of weeks. I have a desire to see at least of couple of the beds planted."

Maureen looked strong this morning. "Two weeks. Then you must go. Otherwise we'll never be able to let you leave."

I was longing to get out in garden, but Maureen had me scheduled for looking after Gita and Jiddu.

"We'll need a chicken coop right away," Maureen told Adrian. "You can take the truck. I've set up an account at the Farmers' Supply. As soon as the coop is ready we can get some chickens. I'm planning to work on getting a couple of beds ready for planting. You're welcome to help with that Patrick. This is where we'll start to get those piles of field stones."

Maureen also had lists of supplies she needed and asked Adrian to pick them up while he was at the Farmers' store. The truck was going to be full.

"When we were at the ashram, I was able to do some housework in the morning while the children watched Romper Room. Maybe we should get a television," I suggested.

"I don't want Gita and Jiddu watching TV." Maureen was firm. "It's better for them to be playing, and learning from the real world."

That was easy for her to say, but I was the one she was leaving with their care.

Gita and Jiddu were agreeable to anything I came up with, so when I suggested we play near the raised beds, they came along happily. Jiddu brought his trucks and filled them with dirt, making tracks in the heaped soil. Gita brought dolls and made chains of wildflowers for everyone's hair. I still had to keep a close eye on them, making sure they didn't wander off, but I also spent time sifting soil and separating out a pile of field stones. I wondered if there were children on neighbouring farms. I wasn't sure how to go about meeting the neighbours. There wasn't anyone closer than half a mile.

While I was wondering about this, Mrs. Nelthorpe came out to say, "You have visitors. Mrs. Nye from up the road has come over with fresh muffins and her three little ones. She wants to welcome you to the neighbourhood."

"Blast, I wasn't expecting this. Darling Clare, could you handle it?"

I was delighted, almost wondering if I'd conjured Mrs. Nye and her children up with my thoughts.

"I'd be happy to."

"You should go, Maureen," Patrick interjected. "You're the one who needs to make friends and allies with your neighbours."

"I hate to leave when we're just getting started, but you're right. Let's go and meet Mrs. Nye."

This proved to be a fortuitous meeting. Mrs. Nye brought her three and five year old sons and six year old daughter, and soon the children were having enormous fun playing in the living room together. I asked her if there were other children close by. It seemed there were plenty of kids on nearby farms. I'd definitely need to get my license soon, so I could take Gita and Jiddu on visits. They needed companions. Walking to the neighbours would be too far for Jiddu's tiny legs, and in any case, it wasn't safe to walk on the road.

Adrian returned before lunch, the truck piled high with wood, fencing, chicken wire, nails, manure, starter plants and seeds. Patrick helped him unload. They decided to build the coop right beside the barn, with an opening to the barn to allow the chickens to go inside at night.

After lunch, while the children were napping, I came out to thank Adrian for the book. He said I was welcome to work along with him, then we could talk. Together we put up the wood structure for the coop. I mostly held things, while he sawed, hammered and measured. He talked about Chuang Tsu and Thomas Merton and R.D. Laing. Our conversation wandered from enlightenment to psychoanalysis to the possibility that we have no self.

"David Cooper thinks that families cause schizophrenia by giving mixed messages to children. Putting them in a double bind where everything they do and think is wrong. Laing is on the same track. Both of them suggest that to be sane is to be mad."

"How can that be?" I countered. "Families make us strong and healthy. Mothers are where we learn to love and be virtuous. Glorifying madness can only lead to more madness."

Our conversation flowed. Adrian had a wealth of fascinating ideas, and didn't seem attached to anything. He had read something from every possible discipline, and threw it all out there for discussion. He was talking about A.S. Neill and free schools, when Patrick came along.

"You two seem to be having a lot of fun building that coop."

Patrick sounded jealous.

"We are having fun, but now it's time to go in and see if the kids are awake," I said.

When we got inside, Patrick suggested we take the children for a walk to the beach. They loved being with Patrick. He carried Jiddu on his shoulders and swung Gita around until she was dizzy.

As we walked along, Patrick said, "I'm sorry I didn't ask about your family reunion when you returned yesterday. How was it?"

It was good to have someone to talk it over with. "It's a big family. Lots of aunts and uncles, and countless children. Uncle Django gave me a photo of me as a baby, with a beautiful inscription from my mother. It made me wonder if I really knew her at all. Whatever I thought I knew about her keeps on changing."

"Maybe we never really know anyone. I mean, we can't pin them down as this or that, and leave it frozen. Not even our own selves. We're always changing."

"Do you think you're changing?"

"Clare, you're very perceptive. I'm wondering if I'm cut out for priesthood. I've only been here a couple of weeks and I'm already tired of Maureen's problems. I'm impatient instead of loving."

"It seems to me that just showing up is good enough."

I was a big advocate of people who stick around, no matter how they're feeling.

"I worry that I'm a resounding gong," said Patrick.

"What does that mean?"

"As in First Corinthians, 'If I speak in the tongues of men or of angels, but do not have love, I am only a resounding gong or a clanging cymbal'."

"It's funny you should say that. Adrian gave me a book today about that very thing. The idea is; those who think they have virtue, don't. Those who act righteous, aren't. I'm trying to get my mind around it. It's as far as possible from what I have always been taught."

Instead of engaging with this thought Patrick said, "Be careful of Adrian. He's liable to lead you astray."

I decided not to defend my friendship with Adrian. I had a feeling Patrick wanted to put me in a box, even at the same time as he was saying that life is all about change. Still, Patrick did have a sweet smile, sparkling blue eyes and a winning way. I wanted to enjoy our time together, so I didn't argue.

It had been an overcast day, but very hot. We reached the water and I said, "Let's get wet." I sat down in the shallow waves close to the shore. Gita and Jiddu joined me and called for Patrick to get in too.

"But we're not in our bathing suits," Patrick protested.

"Our clothes will dry, come on," I urged.

Patrick again refused.

"Come on, Uncle Patrick," Gita said. "Come stand in the waves. It feels great."

Patrick removed his sandals and walked in up to his knees. Two seconds later he was splashing everyone. Soon we were all soaked from head to toe.

As they walked dripping back to the house Patrick said, "I don't know what came over me, but it was fun."

Dating

As Patrick was going to be around for a few weeks, I asked if he could teach me to drive. Maureen decided I should learn on the truck. Patrick was a methodical teacher and made sure we covered everything. I would be taking the driver's test in Lawrenceville, which had only two stop lights and very light traffic.

I still had my day off on Wednesday but Isabel didn't have a long enough lunch break for us to get together. She took her lunch to the factory, and ate with the other workers in the cafeteria. We decided instead that I would meet her after work when she got out at three and go to the pool together. She was always hot and frazzled after a day in the furnace-like heat of the factory.

We put on our two-piece bathing suits, hers a pink stripe, mine black with polka dots, and our flower covered bathing caps. Isabel ran to the pool's edge and dove in. The pool was filled with frolicking children, so there wasn't much room to swim. I thought about the beautiful river, so close and inviting, yet so polluted we didn't dare go in. After our swim we lay on our towels on our stomachs.

"How did it go with your new relatives?" Isabel asked.

"They're a whole different world from the people we know." I described the scene.

"Lots of kids. Sounds like our house."

"It isn't really. It felt more like chaos, as if no one was in charge. I'm not sure I could stand to be around it much. I have such a longing for order. At the same time, I loved how friendly and welcoming they were. They were surprised that I'm not married yet. They told me I'd better hurry up."

"What do your uncles do?"

"I couldn't tell. They could be mechanics. There were old cars around, and car parts. No one talked about work."

"Is their place a farm?"

"Not that I could tell. There were scary dogs and cats, but I didn't see any sign of gardens or farm animals, not even chickens. Funny. I think they have land. They talked a lot about my mother, and what their childhood was like. I loved that."

"I'm glad you've got relatives. Even if you're not sure how you feel about them."

"How about you?" I asked. "What do you think of your first week at work?"

"It's unbelievably terrible. I'm hot. I'm bored. I'm fed up. But I have to last for eight more weeks."

"I'm feeling a bit fed up too. There's lots of good in my job; the kids are loveable, the farm is wonderful, my room is spectacular; but I find it hard to spend so much time looking after children. It's crushing in a way. I was hoping I would have more variety. Maybe share the childcare fifty-fifty. So far it's more like eighty-twenty. On the other hand, I'm getting driving lessons from Patrick, and there is an interesting man working for Maureen. I'm having long discussions with him about everything under the sun. I really shouldn't be complaining."

"I'm feeling sympathetic to my father. I don't know how he puts up with factory work. He never complains, so I'm not going to say a word about it at home."

"Let's get back in the water."

We went back and dove, over and over, into the blue water. This was heaven. On the way back to the Bergeron's, Isabel asked about Patrick.

"He's okay. I find him attractive. I can tell he likes me a lot, which is flattering, but he's got his life mapped out. I don't see how I could fit into it."

"Joe and I liked him a lot. He's easy to be with. I love it that he didn't drink too much, and that he was so attentive to you. He's not a flirt."

"The thing is, if I was his wife, that would be my job description; the Anglican priest's wife. I'd have to host afternoon tea parties, and arrange bazaars. I'd be an extension of his work. I'm not sure I can see myself in this. I'm coming to realize I'm very solitary. Not that we're anywhere near this level of closeness – I'm just worrying in advance. Also, how can a Catholic girl be an Anglican Priest's helpmate?"

"I hadn't thought of that part of it. Lots of our group have girlfriends and boyfriends who aren't Catholic, but this is an entirely new dilemma."

"Why do I have to break new ground? Are you and Joe going out tonight?"

"He's going golfing, which means a long game and then drinks at the club. I can't stay up that late, now that I'm working. The best I can do in the evening is to play cribbage with Madeleine and Mom, and then I'm off to bed."

I returned to pick up my bike at Isabel's. Peter was sitting on the porch steps when we arrived and asked me if I'd like to go to the movies that night. This was a surprising invitation. He had never taken any notice of me over the years, nor I of him.

"We could stop at A&W for supper on the way," he suggested.

I loved Teen Burgers, Coney fries and root beer, and the fun of being served food right in the car.

"Sure, I'd love to go." I thought he must be including his brother and sisters in the invitation but it was just me.

"Throw your bike in the trunk and we'll drop it off on the way past."

I popped in to the kitchen at Buttercup Acres to tell Mrs. Nelthorpe I wouldn't be in for supper.

Patrick said, "Who's waiting for you outside?"

"Isabel's brother. See you later."

Peter and I watched *Little Big Man*. Everyone in the audience seemed to love it. We all stood at the end, cheering and clapping.

Peter dropped me off at Buttercup Acres.

"I had a great time tonight," I said.

Peter was staring at me intently. "You've changed."

I realized he had too.

"Well, see you later." I jumped out. He was making me nervous. I wasn't used to so much attention.

Peter laughed. "I guess you haven't changed that much!"

The house was dark and quiet when I came in. Patrick was sitting in the living room reading by candlelight.

"What are you doing?" I asked.

"I love to read old books by candlelight, as if I was back in the time when they were written."

"What a romantic notion."

"I'm a romantic guy. Haven't you noticed?"

I didn't know how to respond to Patrick's invitation so I escaped to my room. I was thinking of Mrs. Bergeron's advice, not to go too quickly. I wasn't in danger of that; rather I was at a standstill. I decided to write to Dorothy, if only to clarify my thoughts.

Dear Dorothy, I can't bring myself to call you Stargaze, I hope you don't mind. I need some advice on how to deal with men. For the first time in my life I am being sought out. One is Maureen's brother Patrick, who is very honourable and planning to be an Anglican priest. He is staying here for a brief time to assist Maureen, but I now think he is prolonging his stay because of his interest in me. The other is Isabel's brother, Peter. He is home from university for the summer. For some reason he asked me out tonight. I haven't made any sort of promise to either. I'm afraid of both of them. Any advice? Yours, Clare. PS Who is Nanny Clare?

The New Consciousness

In the morning when I went to get my coffee, Adrian had left another book with a note: *Clare, I don't want to overload you, but I just finished this one and you must read it!* This must-read was *The Greening of America.* The cover talked about the coming revolution. From my perspective, revolutions were things that happened in the past. I acknowledged some problems in the world, but believed we had found the best possible systems to live by. This book was sure to spark some lively conversation between us.

I thought back to the wonderful evenings with my father, sitting and reading as the sun set. Neither of us talked much. I was comfortable with our silences. On the other hand, I didn't have a clue how Dad felt about most matters. Was he conservative, liberal, a free thinker? I didn't have much evidence to go on. I wished I had asked more questions.

Now that some of the seeds and seedlings were planted, there was watering to do in the garden. This was something the children and I could help with, although we had to do it before the heat got too intense at mid morning. All the water came from a well. We had running water in the house and a pump in the yard. Gita was just tall enough to pump water into a watering can, which we would then take in the wheel barrow over to the plants. Jiddu ran alongside. We made countless trips back and forth, bringing water to the emerging crops. Patrick said we needed an irrigation system. Maureen agreed. She said she would soon get sprinklers installed at the raised beds.

In the meantime the children and I found it fun. I strongly identified with the little marsh hen in the Tao Te Ching, who happily ran back and forth, gathering materials for a nest. I enjoyed watering the garden and would be sorry when it was automated.

I loved this verse from the Tao, "A small country has fewer people. Though there are machines that can work ten to a hundred times faster than man, they are not needed." It expressed so well how I felt about many things in life.

The chicken coop was now ready and Maureen asked if we wanted to come with her to pick up some chickens. We piled into the truck and headed to the Farmer's Supply. We bought Rhode Island Reds and Leghorns. We picked them because one gave brown eggs and the other white. While we were there we also got chicken feed, oyster shells, pine shavings, a feeder and watering station, and last, a government booklet on how to raise chickens. We looked at all the wonderful farm clothes. Maureen said we should all have jeans, a denim shirt and rubber boots, so we came out with a full set for everyone.

"What about Patrick?" Gita asked.

"Darling, Patrick's going back to Toronto. He won't need farm clothes." Maureen grabbed a straw hat. "This will be perfect to keep the sun off."

"I need one too," Jiddu said.

We all got one. Once again the truck was piled high when we returned to Buttercup Acres.

We were a cheery group at lunch. The chickens were released into the coop and could be heard exploring their new home, making little talking sounds. I was now in charge of them. I added that to my early morning routine. I studied the government pamphlet. I was disconcerted to learn about how aggressive they could be with each other. I hoped ours would be peaceful chickens.

In the early afternoon when the children were napping, I sought out Adrian to join him in his tasks. We worked side by side while he told me about Esalen in California. It was there that he learned about all the changes that were taking place in people's consciousness.

"Reich has captured this perfectly in his book."

I told him I would read it, but I felt we were in a pretty darn good world, and wondered why people thought it needed to change.

Adrian scoffed. "Do you think you have as much freedom as Patrick, or any of the boys you went to school with? Do you think any of them would do the work you're doing for so little pay?"

I hadn't thought about this. I imagined that I was perfectly free but suddenly realized there were a lot of restrictions in my life that wouldn't be there for a boy. A young man in my position, left without family, would

69

have an apartment of his own, a job that paid well, and probably even a car.

"I'm trying to save money for my future. That's why I'm doing this. Do you think that I should have looked for something else?"

"I'm not criticising you. Even if you had looked, no job in Lawrenceville would have paid enough for you to have what a man could have. That's what I'm saying. There's a movement coming in women's rights, in freedom from conformity, in saying no to war and industrial pollution and the established order."

"What about you? You're working here for a small amount of money."

"I've made choices based on my desire to be free of the rat race. I'm looking for inner peace instead of things. But I can see you feel oppressed."

I was horrified that it showed. "I admit I long for more free time, some solitude, and more challenging work, but I see all this as temporary. By next year I'll have moved on."

"This work can be what you need it to be for you now. Just keep your goals uppermost in your mind. I want you to see there are lots of possibilities so you don't start closing down options."

This reminded me of my mother's letter. Did everyone see me as oppressed? I realized it was more than being female. It also had a lot to do with wealth. Maureen had freedom because she had her family's money. Without that, I wondered if she could ever have left her husband and taken the children.

"You are powerful now. Make sure you see it, and don't let it slip away," Adrian said.

This was mysterious, but I knew he wasn't giving me an empty compliment.

On my next trip to the library I saw a notice of a meeting about pollution in the river. I thought it would be good for me to get involved. I loved the river and was heartbroken at how quickly it was deteriorating. This was the sort of thing Adrian was telling me about. We can't go along with factories pouring their poison into our beautiful river.

The meeting was scheduled for Monday night, which I could arrange if I traded off my Wednesday night. My free time so easily got booked up. I wished again that I had a regular job that left me free on weekends and evenings. The talk with Adrian was helpful though. I realized that it wasn't just me, it was hard for any young woman to make enough money to be independent. I doubled my resolve to get an education.

Adrian said he wanted to go to the meeting too, so we travelled together. He knew a lot about organizing citizen's groups. At the end of the meeting, he brought up the idea of starting a recycling centre for paper, tin cans and glass. No one had ever heard of this, but he sparked a lot of interest. There was a feeling of excitement at this first meeting, as if we were pioneers.

One of the town councillors attended, a woman who had moved to Lawrenceville recently, and who wanted to bring about improvements. Her name was Dolores Black. She spoke up in a way I wasn't used to hearing. She had a biology degree and knew many things about the ecology of the river. She pointed out biological markers that I noticed, but didn't realize were all connected to pollution; the fact that we had almost no more cardinals, no ospreys, few herons, the growing weediness of the river, the dead fish on the river banks. I knew this was all true and had seen these changes happen in my lifetime. The degradation was happening fast.

After the meeting I went over to speak to Mrs. Black. She was friendly and asked me to call her Dolores. I told her I had grown up on the river, and that it was important to me in ways beyond expressing. She said she was pleased to have someone with my youth and energy. I said it was true, I was young, but I didn't have a lot of free time. "I'll do what I can though," I promised.

Before he left for Toronto, Patrick told me he hoped I would come for a visit and stay with their family. "I'm sure Maureen could spare you for a weekend. I'll show you my favourite parts of Toronto."

I said I would enjoy that. We arranged for a visit in September.

Dorothy wrote back promptly.

Dear Clare, You seem to be stuck. Everything isn't an all or nothing proposition. You can enjoy both of those guys and you don't have to marry either one. It took me years to learn this so don't feel bad. I come from a family where you married the first guy you met, no kidding! Nanny Clare is my father's mother who came from Ireland. She married a traveller (gypsy to you) and together they came to Canada and the rest is our family history. She was kind and gracious - a lady. I wanted that for you. Not the kind of world I was brought up in, which you have now seen for yourself. PS You are too attached to Lawrenceville. Haven't you noticed it getting dumpy? The bandstand is gone, the beautiful old post office is gone, there's a horrible grocery store where the historic town hall used to be. Before long there'll be nothing left. The river is dirty. Somebody has to point this out. Stargaze

I wished I could take things lightly with Patrick and Peter. I had such a scrupulous conscience that it made it difficult to make any moves towards romantic experience. I was terrified of finding out that I was like Dorothy, capable of loving and losing interest. I thought it would help to talk this over with Isabel. She seemed sensible when it came to romance. While we were walking back from Mass that Sunday I told her how afraid I was to have a boyfriend.

"Peter mentioned you are hard to pin down. He likes you. He said he would love to go out with you."

"That's the thing. I'm afraid to start down any road. What if I lose interest?"

"That's the chance anyone takes. Not every romance turns into a lifetime commitment."

"But yours has."

Isabel started to cry. "I think Joe has found someone else."

"Oh no! How could that be?" I felt as sad as she looked.

"He's always at the golf club and that's a richer crowd than our family. I saw him in Jane's convertible when I was walking home from work. I went by way of the river to cool off and they drove by – I don't think he saw me. I thought he would have been at work. She's rich. And fast. I think I've lost him. I'm so sad I can't eat, I can't think. I'm always crying."

"This isn't the Joe you met and fell in love with. Being away at university must have changed him."

"Ever since Christmas I thought he was different. I'm afraid he has a girlfriend at university too. I didn't want to face it."

"Did you talk to Arlene or your mother?"

"Arlene said Joe has moved on and I'll have to face it. She tells me she's certain I'll get over it and find someone new. She has been a great listener."

My problems seemed small by comparison. Isabel's broken heart was written all over her. She had even lost weight and looked exhausted.

"I have moments when I can talk about it and think of it as something that happens in life, and then I almost go crazy with despair and feel like I can never get over my love for Joe. I have one of his sweaters that he forgot at our house – sometimes I hold it because it smells like him."

I was crying too. Her words called up the heart-breaking memory of packing up my father's clothes and giving them to charity. It felt like his presence was in them.

"Let's stop crying before we go in to breakfast. I don't want to make everyone upset," Isabel said.

There was such a big crowd at breakfast, with everyone talking at once, and the grandchildren playing around, that it seemed Isabel's sadness wasn't noticed. Before I left, Mrs. Bergeron called me aside and said, "Did Isabel and Joe break up?" I told her that I thought it was coming. "That will be hard to get over." She meant for herself as well.

Peter was there and invited me to see what he'd been working on. It was an old bike that he was fixing up for Arlene's five year old. "I had fun going to the movie with you."

"Me too," I said.

"So, how about it? Couldn't we see each other now and then?"

I laughed and said, "Okay, but I have almost no free time."

"Well, when are you free?"

"Sunday afternoon is it. Why don't we go to the quarry for a swim? See if Isabel wants to join us?"

"That's not exactly what I had in mind, but that's a good idea. It will get her mind off Joe."

It seemed that Isabel's problems weren't a secret.

The quarry was an abandoned limestone pit that had filled from underground springs. It was the turquoise of the Caribbean. We weren't officially allowed to swim there, but it was a favourite hangout spot of every young person in the region and always full of swimmers. It was so deep no one could ever reach the bottom. We dove off the cliffs into the clear blue water then clambered up the steep rocky sides to do it again.

We hurried back to town so that I could be at Buttercup Acres in time for supper. My heart ached for Isabel. I told her to call me if she needed a friend, but warned her the phone was on a party line.

"I'll be okay. I know I have to get up every day and go to work. That's turning out to be a good thing, as it's a complete distraction from my problem, and wears me out."

At Buttercup Acres we were still reading *The Lion, the Witch and the Wardrobe*. It felt strange to continue without Patrick. His reading brought the characters to life. Gita and Jiddu missed him and complained about his absence.

"Darlings, Patrick can't live with us. He has work to do. He just came for a visit."

"I want him to stay. And I want Baba. Why is everyone always going away?" Gita, who was always so agreeable with me, could become very upset around her mother. She turned away from us and said she didn't want to hear the story.

Jiddu then got upset and cried, saying, "I want Baba, where's Baba?"

This day had been full of tears. I hoped the coming week would be easier.

***

The next day there was a new book and a note waiting for me by the morning coffee. *Clare, just one more. It's essential reading. Silent Spring* by Rachel Carson. This time I was ahead of him. I'd read it in Grade Twelve.

Now that Adrian and I were part of the new group that was forming to take action on cleaning up the river, we had even more to talk about and our afternoon chats had become the high point of my day. Adrian also liked to sing, and was teaching the children Pete Seeger songs. They were quick learners. In the morning if we were out playing by the gardens we would all end up singing, Maureen as well. We soon knew the words to *We Shall Overcome, Where Have All the Flowers Gone, If I Had a Hammer* and the children's favourite, *Abiyoyo*.

Maureen bought a record player in Williamsville that week. She owned a collection of records and had no objections to my entertaining the children with these. She had lots of great folk music. Her records were mostly from her teen years, but she said she wanted to find out what was happening in the music world, and get more up to date. She had a box of 45's from her childhood too. No one I knew had records when they were little and I was fascinated by them. Some of her records were red and you could see through them. The sleeves were colourful and intriguing. Now Jiddu and Gita and I had another enjoyable thing to do when we tired of playing outdoors.

There were stories and comedies and songs for marching around the room. It was a treasure trove. Maureen's childhood was privileged. When she talked about it, I was always astonished at the wonderful things available to her and Patrick. They had been given every kind of lesson, trips around the world, and the best of everything. I liked hearing about her childhood and imagining how happy it must have been. I began to look forward to meeting her parents when I went to visit Patrick in September.

"You'll love Mom and Dad," Maureen said. But I didn't have to wait until September to meet them. Out of the blue they drove down and stayed for a few days. At lunch one day we heard a voice call, "Where are my beautiful grandbabies?"

Mrs. Anderson was tall and blonde. She smelled wonderful. Gita and Jiddu jumped up and ran to her. "Grandma." They hung on to her and led her into the kitchen.

Mr. Anderson followed behind. He had a cigar in his mouth and a puzzled air. They brought presents for the children; *A Child's Garden of Verses* for Gita and *Tommy Caboose* for Jiddu. There was a bottle of wine for Maureen and a bottle of scotch for the house. As soon as they were settled in the living room Mrs. Anderson said, "Clare, we've heard so much about you from Patrick, we had to meet you."

When I heard this it occurred to me that they had come here to check me out. Patrick's parents were involved in his life in a way I hadn't seen before. The families I knew would not take such pains. I saw this with Maureen as well. She planned her children's life carefully. After the first visit with the neighbour's children, she let me know that she would need to meet people before she would let the children play with them; she had to make sure they were the right sort of companions. They wouldn't be allowed to drift into whatever came along; Maureen would be guiding and teaching them. This was a revelation. Although she was leaving me with the children's care most of the time, she was also very particular about how I looked after them. They were coached in good manners, and explicitly told the right way to behave in every situation.

What habits had marked me as a child who grew up with almost no supervision? Now and then in my youth, I would learn from other children some bit of my missing parenting, such as when I discovered that I should be brushing my teeth every day. My parents never taught me that. Dorothy assumed I would learn this on my own. My hair was a tangle of snarls when Mrs. Bergeron noticed one day and helped me to comb it out. Patrick and Maureen however, had been explicitly trained in all that would lead to success in life. That had been missing for me.

Despite Mrs. Anderson's meticulous parenting, something had gone awry with her plan for Patrick. Neither parent approved Patrick's choice of profession. They had expected him to go into business administration, and eventually take over running the shirt factory. Mrs. Anderson could envision Patrick as a bishop possibly, but not as a lowly priest.

"Don't you think God is directing his choice?" I asked.

Mrs. Anderson didn't have an answer for that.

I had expected Maureen's parents would be staying with us as there was plenty of room, but they booked a suite at the Skylane Hotel in Williamsville.

"The hotel has a lovely pool. I thought the children would enjoy it," Mrs. Anderson said.

I hoped I would be invited too. I had often looked with longing at that turquoise pool. Maureen said we would come up later that afternoon for a swim and also have dinner with them at the Skylane, in the restaurant on the top floor. She seemed to be including me in this plan, so I was thrilled. This restaurant was the best in our region and most people went to it for special occasions only.

When the children got up from their naps, I helped them get ready for the trip. Maureen had thought it all out. They would travel in casual clothes since they would be swimming before dinner, but she packed a blue smocked dress for Gita, and a sweet little jacket and tie for Jiddu to change into for dinner.

She oversaw my dinner costume as well and told me, "You can call my mother Mrs. Anderson and my father Mr. Anderson." I was okay with that, although I found it amusing and realized she was coaching me just like the children. She couldn't trust me to do the appropriate thing. If I had been in love with Patrick, I might have been nervous at all of the fuss, but as it was, I was happy to go along for the ride without worrying how they would evaluate me.

I enjoyed myself at the Skylane. I played in the pool with the children until Mrs. Anderson said we must be getting along. Mr. Anderson swam too, floating back and forth on his back, looking at clouds. I decided he would be easy to like. Maureen and her mother sat beside the pool, looking elegant. Neither of them would ever get their hair wet, so swimming was out of the question.

I wondered about Maureen's decision to start a farm. How did that fit with her upbringing and her values? Maureen saw it as a good business decision; getting in at the beginning of what could be a goldmine. She may have been right. I admired her for her willingness to dive into something new, but I suspected her long-term plan was to have others doing the hard work while she managed things and collected the money.

The dinner was elegant beyond anything I had ever experienced. The dining room tables had crisp white table cloths and heavy silver cutlery. We sat by a bank of windows looking out over the hills to the north. Everything was hushed and the staff were courteous, helpful, and unobtrusive.

The children seemed to have done this before. They were on their best behaviour, sitting up and beaming with pleasure at being in this grown up sanctuary. Maureen kept Jiddu beside her as he was the most in need of reminders. I was beside Gita, who looked like a doll in her blue dress.

Mr. Anderson ordered trout, which was served with the head on. I was astonished, but knew better than to remark on it. I ordered roast beef and Yorkshire pudding. Mr. Anderson looked with longing at my plate

"I'd love that, only I'm on a diet," he said.

Maureen ordered for the children. They had seafood too. I wondered if I had made a faux pas, but then Mrs. Anderson ordered tiny little chickens, so I relaxed. I discovered they were called quail. Mr. Anderson ordered two bottles of wine, red and white. I still wasn't used to drinking but allowed myself a small bit of the red. I didn't have much knowledge of wine but it tasted good.

From the conversation, I gathered that the Andersons would have preferred to have Maureen come home to stay with them, but they were willing to support her in this business as they wanted to help her get free of the ashram.

"Harry's parents were over last week. They're going to try to talk some sense to him," Mrs. Anderson said.

"That will make it worse," Maureen said, looking annoyed. "He has to see for himself."

I learned that the in-laws and Harry's parents had been upset about Harry's 'capture' by Maryam and Jatin and had done everything they could to try to bring him back to the family fold.

"I don't understand the hold those people have over him!" Mrs. Anderson was raving. "But at least there's a chance now that he will see the light."

I thought about the ideas Adrian had been discussing with me; the new consciousness, the refusal of young people to go along with convention, the openness to Eastern spirituality, and the coming revolution. I realized all of these things were going on with Harry's life, possibly as a pawn in the midst of it, but maybe he was a true believer. Of course, I didn't say any of this.

Mr. Anderson looked at me. "What do you think of all this nonsense? Karma, world teacher, Harry/Haari as a realized being?"

I hesitated a moment before blurting out the truth. "I'm a Catholic. To me all this is wrong."

There was a moment of embarrassed silence. Mr. Anderson cleared his throat as if to make a pronouncement, then turned to the nearest waiter to ask for the dessert list.

Mrs. Anderson broke the silence. "The children are very fond of you, Clare. We think you are a God-send. Do you have brothers and sisters that you helped to look after?"

"I'm an only child. I didn't even do any babysitting. It's going well because Gita and Jiddu are such wonderful children. There are some I recently met who are a different story."

I was going to tell them about the Hearnes. Maureen may have suspected this and cut me short.

"Clare is too modest. She's patient and generous and does of all kinds of great things to keep the children happy."

How much of my real life would be unspeakable to the Andersons? At least Patrick seemed to accept me as I was.

When we left everyone hugged, something I was not accustomed to. It made me slightly anxious. Mr. Anderson said, quietly, "You're a good girl."

When we got home Maureen was talkative. The kids were in bed and she asked me to sit with her on the porch. It was a warm night with a crescent moon hanging over the river, reflecting silver on its surface.

"One thing that gives me hope about Harry is the kids. When they were born, he gave them Hindu names, but he wouldn't let them be brought up around the teachings of the ashram. He was afraid of it for them. That's why I figure, on some level he's not really convinced."

"Was Harry brought up as a Christian?" I asked.

"Yes, but he's what Patrick calls a functional atheist. I guess I am too. The funny thing is our family was Anglican, but it was more or less a social club. Then this thing with Harry and the ashram got Patrick interested in religion, and led to the path he's on now. He said he became devout because of all his prayers for me. He was terrified of losing Harry and me to the ashram. He's been praying for a miracle to bring it to an end."

Suddenly, Maureen turned to me and said, "Don't hurt Patrick."

Before I could think of a response, she had gone in the house.

***

At the next Save the River meeting in Lawrenceville there was a new member, a woman in her mid thirties with long brown curly hair, bare feet, shorts and strikingly blue eyes. She came into town in an old truck. She told us she was part of an intentional community living on the land near Copper River. Her name was Viviana but said we should call her Viv. It seemed appropriate; she was full of life.

Viv didn't take over the meeting, but she had a lot to say and brought tons of enthusiasm. She told us her community was looking for a big project, and the cleanup of the river would be a good match for their skills. Adrian couldn't stop talking to her at the end of the meeting and I finally had to remind him that I needed to get home. I heard him ask her to meet for coffee.

When we were outside on the street I pondered how she could drive a truck in bare feet, but then I saw her pull a pair of construction boots out and put them on before she drove off. There were peace stickers on her bumper.

I was jealous. Not because I thought of Adrian as a boyfriend, but because I thought of him as my exclusive companion for stimulating conversation and knew how valuable this was. Why was this so rare? If I didn't have Adrian, where would I go to learn anything new?

Meanwhile, I was brooding over my mother's criticisms of Lawrenceville, saying it was going downhill. I hated to agree, but she was right. Whenever anything new came to town, it was inevitably ugly and replaced something beautiful. Was this going to be the tragic direction for everything in life from now on? I shuddered at the thought.

Dorothy's suggestion that I be detached and move on to new places was not right for me. I intended to stay and fight the decay. Maybe I would even become a town councillor, like Dolores. What good would it do if everyone moved on from their home town? We would all become rootless. There would be no one who remembered the beauty that used to exist.

I planned to fight. I had always known I was committed to my town, but now I could see it on a new level. I had assumed I would stay here, and it would be more or less the same place I had always known and loved. But now I saw that without a conscious effort to hold onto the beauty, it would slip away under the forces of economics, indifference and ignorance.

The next day as Adrian and I were having our afternoon conversation and weeding the garden, I told him my thoughts on needing to preserve the beauty of Lawrenceville.

"You should read Jane Jacobs, *The Death and Life of American Cities*," Adrian suggested. "She's all about preserving what's good, the things that make a city work, such as sidewalks, people knowing their neighbours, and having stores and businesses close to where people live. She's been a real thorn in the side of heartless developers."

"But I'm worried about this small town, not a city, and not the U.S."

"Doesn't matter, her principals apply anywhere. She lives in Toronto now. Maybe you could meet her?"

"Me?" I immediately felt that I couldn't possibly introduce myself to someone who had written a book.

"I'll lend you her book. You don't give yourself enough credit. I'll bet if you were to call her up and tell her how passionate you are about Lawrenceville, she would be happy to meet you."

Our conversation continued on to a discussion of Murray Bookchin, Kropotkin, anarchism and utopian communities.

"Viv mentioned living in an intentional community. What did she mean?" I asked.

This opened the floodgates. I had no idea there were people around the world forming communities based on shared beliefs. He told me about the Catholic Worker. He said maybe I should visit; see what it was like to meet committed Catholics who really put their lives on the line for their beliefs.

"They impressed me. I stayed for a few months in New York and experienced people who truly believe Christ's message. They were feeding the hungry, housing the homeless, and visiting the sick. They weren't afraid to dive right in and help."

"So, why didn't you stay?" I asked.

"Partly because I'm not a Christian, but mostly because I need solitude. There wasn't much privacy in those packed houses. I was sleeping in a room with five men. There were bedbugs. It smelled like garbage. Only a saint could survive."

I understood that. Community living wouldn't satisfy me. I looked forward to having my own place someday.

I was thinking about how complicated life was. It seemed as I grew older there were competing demands and calls for loyalty. It was important to know where to draw the line, so I wouldn't end up on someone else's path. For most women I knew, their lives were in complete abeyance to the path their husband was on. Was that going to be my life too? Did I have enough passion to demand my own path?

When I was younger, I had pictured my adult life as one in which I had a job as a secretary, living with my father and carrying on the life I had known. I believed Dad needed me and that I didn't need anyone else. I was consigning myself to life as a spinster, but I didn't think of it that way. It was more that I already had a life, and there was no room for another man.

Now, although I wasn't seeking men out, they were finding me. I had become attractive. I was surprised to find that I drew looks from men everywhere I went. My hair was shiny and thick. Despite the fact that I continued to wear it hanging to my shoulders, it looked elegant. My figure was shapely. My skin flawless.

I had inherited Dorothy's good looks and maybe even some of her sexiness. Adrian talked about 'my power'. I know he meant more than this, but I suspected beauty was part of it. Beauty gave people power. I had seen it. I needed to make sure I didn't squander this.

Isabel and I met again on Wednesday after she got out of work. It had turned into a cool damp day so our visit to the swimming pool was out. She suggested we go to the tavern in Lawrenceville's only hotel.

"You're kidding, right? I wouldn't even consider it," I said.

"I thought it might be interesting. Peter and his friends go there."

"It's no place for women. You can't even go in without a man. How about a Coke at Woolworth's?"

As we sat with our coffee at Woolworth's lunch counter I tried to interest Isabel in the cause of saving the river. It was hard to find anything to draw her out. I was worried; if Isabel couldn't have Joe, did she think there was nothing else in life? I told her that I had been thinking about, women having their own priorities and goals. She didn't take it the way I expected.

"Leave my brother alone if you're going to be so heartless."

I was speechless. Two warnings in one week. Did my exploration of freedom sound cold and hard, cruel even? Did we owe it to men to comply with their needs?

"Isabel, do you think your devotion to Joe for the past three years has been worth it? You could have been meeting people and finding out all sorts of things about life, instead you were doing whatever interested him."

"You've changed. You used to be kind; you used to be on my side."

I tried to explain to her all the things I was learning in my discussions with Adrian, in the Save the River group but she wasn't interested. Isabel was in too much pain. I wanted her to get through this and come back to an awareness of herself as a wonderful, smart young woman.

"I am on your side, Isabel. I'll always be your friend."

She cried then and said, "I'd better go home. I'm not fit company for anyone these days."

I bicycled back to Buttercup Acres, worrying and hoping that Isabel would soon get over this heart break. I was learning it's possible to love someone and not be able to help them at all.

The Pessimists

When I went to get my coffee early the next morning, I was embarrassed to find Adrian still in bed. What's worse, he was with Viv. Shocked, I closed the door quietly, hoping I hadn't woken them. Was this the free love I was reading about? The revolution in consciousness encouraged people to jump into bed as soon as they felt the urge.

It continued to be grey and drizzly, so the children and I played inside. I was enjoying Maureen's childhood records. I had a favourite that I played over and over. The children and I never tired of it. It was a Jerry Lewis recording of a skit called *The Noisy Eater*. Gita got the humour, and Jiddu laughed because he liked to join in. Sometimes he would come over and say to me, "Let's laugh."

The Andersons returned to Toronto. Maureen said, "They like you," confirming my suspicion of the purpose of their visit.

Maureen and I were talking about how we would spend our time in the fall, when it occurred to me that Gita should be starting school in September. I asked Maureen if she had given this any thought.

"It is on my mind. My mother asked me about it, too. The school bus could take her to public school in Lawrenceville, but I can't bear to send her off on a bus every day when she's still so little."

"I know what you mean. It feels like too big a jump from home to being out in the world on her own."

Patrick was writing me letters, at least two a week. They were warm and witty, and showed a new side of him. He talked about the work he was doing at St. Michael and All the Angels, and said it didn't inspire him. He asked me if I could recommend any good books, as he was feeling in an intellectual desert.

I suggested *The Seven Story Mountain* by Thomas Merton. My father had read it and told me it was the most inspiring book he knew of. I proposed to read it at the same time as him, so we could discuss it when I came for my visit.

I answered Patrick's letters regularly, telling him about Isabel's broken heart, the Save the River group, and how the goats, sheep and chickens were doing. Although our life was simple, I found lots to tell him.

Maureen had been adding to her record collection whenever she went into town. There were two special albums that we both grew to love. One was *Wildflowers* by Judy Collins; the other was *Joe Cocker,* with a black and white photo of the singer on the cover. Maureen and I had gotten into a new routine after the kids were in bed. She would pour us both a glass of wine, put on a record, and then we would sit in the living room on the antique sofa and talk. We would light only one small lamp that gave a red glow to the room.

She talked about the farm, and whether it was going to be possible to turn it into a successful business. The markets for what she wanted to produce were far away. Maureen had learned to milk the goat and we were getting a good quantity of goat milk, but none of us at Buttercup Acres liked it. She wondered if she should try making cheese. She wasn't discouraged, but was seeing that there could be barriers to success. She talked a lot about Harry, how much in love they had been, and what he was like before his transformation. She also talked about Lawrenceville not being the right place for Gita and Jiddu to go to school and find friends.

"Please don't think I'm a snob, but I want them to have the opportunities I had, and it's not possible here. I'm still trying to figure it out, but time is short. My mother suggested sending Gita to live with them, but I don't want that."

"Adrian has been telling me about alternative education, free schools he calls them. He also told me about people who teach their kids at home, so they get a more rounded education, and aren't indoctrinated by the state. Maybe that would be a way to start Gita's education, and give you more time to decide what's best?"

"Do you think you could teach her?"

"Me?" The idea surprised me. "I suppose I could teach her to read, and whatever else they do in Grade One. My Grade One teacher was a monster. I could definitely do better than that. But what about her having friends? Don't you think it's a lonely life with no playmates?"

"I'll give it some thought, but I'll have to decide soon."

These night-time talks while listening to music were something I looked forward. Maureen wasn't an intellectual like Adrian, but she was smart in a different way. She understood society and business.

I avoided Adrian for a few days. The next time we got together to work in the garden he said, "Don't be judgmental."

I felt embarrassed and defensive. "Is it judgmental to have moral standards?"

"It is, if you expect the world to live by yours. What gives you the right?"

"If I look upset, it's not because I'm judging you. It's because I've never met anyone I enjoyed talking to more than you. This may sound crazy, but I'm jealous of you finding someone else to talk to. No one else has ever shown me that there are so many ideas in this world."

I started to cry, much to my embarrassment.

"Clare, I love our conversations, too. You don't have to worry about losing me, but you really need to meet others who are interested in ideas."

"I'm so confused. It feels like for every thought I have now, I also have a counter thought. I can't figure out what's true. I'm exhilarated about life, but I seem to have lost the certainty I thought was my centre. I'm afraid if I change too much, there won't be anything left from the world I knew."

"You'll change as you learn new things, but you'll still be you."

We resumed our friendship and I continued to learn new things from our discussions. We talked endlessly about natural farming and the devastation caused by plowing. We both read a book on permaculture by

Masanobu Fukuoka. Fukuoka became our guide to perfection, both in agriculture and in living. We also talked about Christopher Alexander, Buckminster Fuller, Alan Watts, and Joseph Chilton Pearce. We couldn't talk fast enough. I was getting the benefits of Adrian's insatiable appetite for knowledge and his love of talking. As much as I had loved my father, I didn't want a man who was as silent as Dad. I began to wonder if my father had been depressed, or if he just didn't have anything to talk about.

In August we had a large harvest of tomatoes and cucumbers. Mrs. Nelthorpe enlisted everyone's help in canning whatever Maureen hadn't been able to sell at the market. It was hot work and it took hours from vegetables to canned goods gleaming on the shelves.

Mrs. Nelthorpe was a good organizer and figured out what job each of us would do so it could go smoothly. I was astonished at the sheer volume of vegetables from each raised bed. Maureen clearly had a green thumb!

The amount of zucchinis taken to market was amazing. I took photos of Maureen with bushel baskets of zucchinis, wax beans, tomatoes, carrots and potatoes. She said that it would have been even better, had we started a month earlier.

The winter squash and pumpkins were still developing, but it looked as if there would be a mountain of them to sell. I was taking good advantage of Patrick's Leica. My photos turned out very well as Patrick had given me lessons on composition and lighting and especially on what not to do. In my innocence, I didn't realize what a fabulous camera it was, casually carrying it around the farm.

Maureen waited until we were sitting with our evening glass of wine to tell me she thought Harry was going through a big change. She brought out his letter and read from it:

I look in the mirror and see my father. My hair is going grey. I'm getting those red veins on my face like his. I see Toronto and English and even Anglican looking back at me. I'm not Haari. I don't know what to do about it. I miss you and Gita and Jiddu more than I can say. For the first time, I miss our old life. I feel homesick for the world we grew up in which I've thrown aside. I feel ashamed. Every day I have to face people who think I have answers. I'm trapped.

Maureen put down the letter. "For the first time I feel optimistic. Maybe he's coming back to us. I'm worried about what the strain will do to him. He was becoming arrogant and hard in being revered as world teacher, but that's not who he is. He is also sensitive, and I don't think he can keep on lying to himself."

"That is good news," I said, but thought to myself, if he comes back, where will they live and what will he do? They lost the life they were embarked on when first married, and I wondered if they could return to it.

***

I dropped in to visit with Mrs. Bergeron that Wednesday. We chatted about this and that until finally I got to the point.

"I really want to talk about Isabel. Is there anything I can do to help her through this?"

"It will just take time, and maybe finding another boyfriend. She's already starting to come around. She ate breakfast this morning without throwing up; that's an improvement."

"Love doesn't seem worth all the trouble."

"Don't get cynical. It's the only thing that is worth the trouble. You'll see."

With time to browse around town before I met Isabel for a swim, I walked around Woolworth's looking at everything; rabbit's foot key chains; salt and peppers shakers shaped like windmills, ducks, bees, and chefs with white hats; painted ceramic salad bowls with "Made in Japan" stamped on the bottom; flannelette pyjamas in pastel shades. I loved all this stuff. I had spent many hours of my life examining these goods.

I ran into Mrs. Dell, an old neighbour from Jessup Manor. We chatted about the weather and how I was doing on my own. I told her I missed my father, that I was working, and about my plan for returning to school eventually. She said, "God bless you, you are still a good girl."

Isabel and I had our swim. While we lay on our towels, I told her about my day. Isabel seemed less anxious and I said, "You seem more like your old self. Are you feeling better?"

"I am. Mom told me I have to pull myself together. She's right. It still hurts, but now that it's clearly over with Joe I can stop having false hope. That's worse than anything. I'm sorry for what I said to you about staying away from Peter. You're right; I need to have a life of my own, stop living as if I'm nothing without a boyfriend. This may sound dumb, but I'm going to try to find someone to date as fast as possible. This time I won't let it take over my life."

"Do you have anyone in mind?"

We talked about various boys she might be interested in, and then we lay quietly soaking up sun and heat. I could never get enough of summer.

***

After the next Save the River meeting, several of us went out for coffee. We sat in a booth and continued our discussion.

"I don't plan to have children. The world is so close to nuclear annihilation."

"The big problem is the coming ice age. I have it on good authority that each year is getting colder."

"You can't trust food in the grocery store. There's no vitamins and minerals left in the soil."

"Acid rain, that's the problem. All those coal factories."

"Nuclear power, that's what worries me. We're probably poisoned for miles around from the Pickering plant."

"If we go on like this," I said, "we'll be too depressed to do anything. Wouldn't it be better to focus on the river and figuring out how it can be cleaned up?"

"It's all connected. Capitalists are ruining everything."

"Money's behind it all. Greed. I don't trust anything or anyone."

Despite their gloomy words, everyone in the group appeared to be healthy, well-fed, even glowing. I didn't intend to spend my life worrying about all of these things, but I knew this group couldn't be talked out of their dark thoughts. We were living in what was probably the best of all times, and they had no appreciation of it. I didn't want to throw the whole system over; I just wanted the birds to come back, and to be able to swim in the river again. As far as I could tell, a carrot was still a carrot, even if it came from the grocery store.

***

After Patrick returned to Toronto, Adrian took over as my driving instructor and by September I was ready to take my test. I passed with no difficulty. Now that I could drive I was able to take on lots of tasks at the farm that Adrian had been doing. I could also take Gita and Jiddu with me on errands.

I asked to borrow the truck to visit to my relatives and drove out to their place on my first free Wednesday. There were fewer people there. The children were in school. Uncle Django was the only uncle around, but both my aunts were home.

When I drove up I was afraid to get out of the truck because the dogs had come out. They were barking fiercely at me. I honked the horn to let them know I was there. Uncle Django came out and said, "Come on in."

"I'm afraid to walk past the dogs."

"Oh, they wouldn't hurt anyone." Thankfully he led them away and tied them up.

Uncle Django came back and we went inside, winding our way around the clutter in the yard; headless dolls, bicycle parts, filthy stuffed toys. My aunts, Mercy and Shilta, were seated at a card table in the living room with two other women, laughing and joking as they played cards.

"Welcome. Glad we didn't scare you away," Aunt Shilta said.

I sat on the couch and listened to their banter while Uncle Django sat across from me, whittling a small figure and dropping wood chips on the floor. He was a very silent man. I thanked him for the carving of Saint Clare. He was too shy to reply.

"Do you play Euchre?" Aunt Mercy asked.

"I played in high school. I love it," I answered.

"Sit in for me. I'm going to see about lunch."

I saw the kitchen on my way in. The table was piled with laundry. The counter was covered with dirty dishes and containers of food and, to my horror, cats were up on the counter eating their food from what appeared to be the same dishes the family ate from. I felt huge trepidation at the thought of lunch. I knew I could not swallow a morsel of food from that kitchen.

Aunt Mercy called from the kitchen, "How about a fried baloney sandwich?"

I thought she was joking until Shilta yelled back, "Sounds great."

"I ate before I got here, sorry if I put you to any trouble," I said.

"No trouble at all," Aunt Shilta told me. "This is just our usual."

I played Aunt Mercy's hand until she came back with the food. The five of them dug in happily. The sandwiches actually looked tasty, but it was too late to change my mind, and I was still feeling leery.

Uncle Django was watching a game show on TV at high volume as he whittled. I wondered why no one asked him to turn it down, but it didn't seem to bother the others. A girl of about seven or eight wandered into the living room.

"What are you doing home," Shilta grabbed her daughter and put a hand on her forehead. "Are you sick?"

The girl was wearing a dirt-stained dress and her tights were covered with cat hair. She appeared to have been sleeping in them.

"Nobody called me to get up this morning."

Shilta didn't seem surprised. "Too late for school now."

The child settled down in front of the TV. I finished my coffee and said my goodbyes.

"Don't be a stranger," Aunt Shilta said as I was leaving.

I realized that I wanted to be a stranger. Being around them was too painful. I could see why Dorothy had left them behind, but not why she left Dad and me. We had an orderly, pleasant home. Dad was kind. He was making a living. Dorothy wasn't burdened with a house full of children.

Maybe having left one home behind made it easier for her to walk away from another. I cried as I drove along the dirt roads. I couldn't tell if I was crying in sorrow for the Hearne children, or for myself. I only knew I felt bereft. By the time I got back to Lawrenceville, I stopped crying. And decided it would be a good time to visit Mrs. Bergeron. She was home making pies for supper and invited me into the kitchen.

"Tea?"

"Yes, I'd love some. I just came from seeing my relatives. Now I have a clear picture of where Dorothy came from." I described the disorder at the Hearne house to Mrs. Bergeron. "As far as I'm concerned that's the last I want to see of them."

"I knew all that, but I thought it would be best for you to find out for yourself," Mrs. Bergeron said.

"At least it helps me understand Dorothy better," I replied.

"They say to understand all is to forgive all," Mrs. Bergeron suggested.

"I wouldn't go that far."

***

September brought more change. Isabel finished her factory job and we celebrated at the bar in the Regent Hotel. Isabel even had a date; a boy she met at the factory who was heading back to university. Peter came too. We danced and drank and life felt perfect. Isabel was starting school in a few days at the community college in Williamsville. She decided to study Early Childhood Education. Peter was heading back to his studies in Ottawa. I wasn't going to school, but I was looking forward to teaching Gita.

Right after Labour Day I started home schooling Gita. Maureen bought school supplies and texts and found out what the Grade One curriculum was. Gita was quick to learn; we sped through the lessons. If she continued at that rate, she'd be ready for Grade Two by November. Jiddu's fourth birthday was coming up in December. He had a short attention span, but he often joined us at the table. Before long I could see that he was also learning to read. I was amazed at how easy it all was. Why had my Grade One teacher been so cross?

Toward the end of September I caught the train to Toronto on a Friday evening. Patrick met me at the station with flowers.

"First, dinner, then I'm taking you to the Riverboat Coffee House."

The act at the Riverboat that night was Arlo Guthrie, who I knew little about. He sang *Alice's Restaurant* and the audience went wild with appreciation. He had a wonderful style of telling stories and fitting them into music.

"Would you take me to a record store tomorrow? I want to bring Arlo's music back to share with Maureen," I said, when there was a lull between sets.

"I'm so happy you love his music too," Patrick said. "He's the real thing!"

Our evening together had been perfect. I went to sleep feeling content in Maureen's old room.

The Anderson's house was in Rosedale, on a street lined with tall trees. All the houses were behind gates and hedges. The neighbourhood was truly grand. In the morning, Mrs. Anderson came to my room with a cup of tea which she brought to everyone on Saturday and Sunday mornings. I preferred coffee, but found this tradition pleasant. I was glad I had met the Andersons before, so that I had some idea of what to expect.

On Saturday Patrick took me to his favourite haunts. We walked on the boardwalk at the Beaches and wandered around Kensington Market. He showed me where he studied at Trinity College and it was exactly what I would have expected were he studying in England. We discussed Thomas Merton's autobiography. Patrick was totally captivated. He said if it wasn't for me he would have been sorely tempted to join a Trappist monastery.

"Joking aside, Merton's passion for religious life makes me realize that I'm tepid about it. I wasn't enthused about working this summer for St. Michael and All the Angels and I'm starting to think it's not for me. I need a Plan B." We talked at length about what else he could study. "It's good to talk to someone who isn't trying to push me in any particular direction."

Patrick's parents took us out to a French restaurant. Mrs. Anderson was full of questions about Gita and how her lessons were going. She was pleased to know both grandchildren were quick learners. On Sunday morning I got back on the train.

Before I left Patrick said, "I had hoped for more time with you. It seemed to slip by before we even had time to talk."

"It was too short, but we can do it again."

"I'm glad to hear you say that."

***

September was here, the swimming pool was closed, and the days were growing cooler. We stopped wading at the beach across the road from the farm. I still had my coffee and cigarette at the rock in the early morning, watching fog rise above the river in the cold air. Maureen gave me a hand-woven blue-green poncho from Ireland, which I took to wearing when I got up. One morning I saw a heron sitting on the shore and prayed for flocks of herons to return. I felt hope that a time would come when they would be again as common as robins.

Isabel's college life kept her busy with travelling, full days of classes, and studying every night. I saw her only on Sundays. On my free Wednesdays now, I often packed a picnic lunch, bicycled to Lawrenceville in the morning, then kept going north of town to a place where I could leave my bike and walk into the hills. I always brought a book. When I got to my special spot by the creek, I would sit and read and daydream. I thought a lot about Patrick, wondering if he was 'the one'. Our lives were both so open-ended that I couldn't picture what our life would be like together.

I wandered around the streets of Lawrenceville with the Leica, taking pictures of old stone houses, yards with vegetable gardens, sheets on clotheslines blowing in the breeze, a front yard full of coloured reflective balls, factories old and new, churches, and the waterfront from varying perspectives.

As soon as the library opened in early afternoon, I went to do research in the Lawrenceville history section. I was looking for descriptions of Lawrenceville before industry arrived. Mostly I wanted to know what sort of birds, fish and other animals lived on the river. I thought people would be more interested in cleaning up the river if they knew what had been lost.

The Wind in the Willows had surely brought the Thames to life for generations of readers. If only someone like Kenneth Graham would write a children's story that would give readers a love for my river. I wasn't a writer, but wondered if I could do something like that. Could I invent a few animal characters and tell the story to Gita and Jiddu?

I always found time to go to Woolworth's lunch counter before heading home to Buttercup Acres. Around four o'clock I bicycled downtown and leaned my bike against a parking meter. Father Belfast was standing by a meter, searching for change. I offered him some pennies. He took them and filled the meter. Despite a lifetime of attending Mass, I didn't know him well. Over the years he came to our class a few times a year, and even though I had gone to confession to him countless times, we still we weren't really acquainted, so he surprised me by saying, "You're Ned's daughter. Sorry to lose such a good man," and continued on his way.

I still loved my chocolate covered donut, but now I ordered it with coffee, instead of Coke. I sat at the counter with my book and lit a cigarette. Madeleine came in, joined me and ordered coffee.

Madeleine was teaching Grade Six at our old school. After she recovered from her mononucleosis she went to Teacher's College in Ottawa and got her teaching certificate. She looked very professional, wearing a tweed skirt, a blouse with a cardigan and shiny brown loafers, truly elegant.

It was early for her to be out of class. "Aren't you teaching today?" I asked.

"I usually work until five or six, but when I looked up from my papers and saw how beautiful it was I decided to get out and walk. I saw your bike out front so I came in to look for you."

We saw each other almost every Sunday at brunch but it was fun to be together on our own so we could really talk.

"I'm getting my own place," Madeleine said. "There's an apartment available in Jessup Manor, on the second floor at the back of the building so I'll have a view of the river. It's close to school and to Mom and Dad's. I can just afford it."

My old home! I was dumb-founded at the thought.

"Congratulations. That's a big step in your life," I said.

"I'll invite you over as soon as I get settled."

I wondered if that would be too painful for me.

"How is the teaching going?" I asked.

"Those kids are sassy. I don't think we were like that. I promised myself I would never give anyone the strap – and I haven't – but you know, it's good to be able to have the threat of it."

"I never pictured you as a teacher, but it seems to suit you."

"I remember the good teachers and the bad ones. I try to be like the best. For instance, the kids love art class and I make sure they get it every Friday afternoon. I remember how disappointed we were when instead of art, we'd get more math. I also remember how the day used to drag and how often I would look at the clock, so I try to make it fun. The world of teachers is changing. All the young teachers are studying in the summer to get bachelor's degrees. So much for my dream of lying around by the pool!"

"I saw Sister Mary Margaret today. She was a tough one."

"I never want to be like her. I have nightmares about Grade One."

"I got over it, but I don't know why she had to be so hard on us."

"The world is changing for the better."

"You should talk to our Save the River group," I suggested. "You wouldn't believe what pessimists they are. Worrying about the fate of the earth is making them crazy. One thing is, they won't have any descendants. They all think it's a crime to bring children into this polluted, corrupt world."

"I hope they don't become teachers," said Madeleine. "The last thing we need is people weighing children down with despair."

"Actually, two of them do teach at the high school." I sighed. "I hope their students are mature enough not to be swept into their teacher's bleak world view."

Madeleine looked sad. "Can you imagine a world where all the young people thought there was no future?" she said. "I hope I never see it."

"You know the verse, 'better to have a millstone around your neck than to harm the little ones' or something like that. Maybe I should mention this at our next meeting. I want to work towards a better world, but not if it means I have to always be with people who are enraged and filled with hopelessness."

"I haven't had experience with that type, but I'll watch out for it."

"You know, Madeleine, I still don't have any idea what I want to do with my life. I was so certain when I was nineteen! Now, after the past months of working and meeting new people, I am totally confused."

"There's no such thing as vocation in my opinion. Just do what you like, even if it's not perfect. Thinking too much can leave you stuck. I had too much time to think when I was sick that year. Now I try not to over-think."

"That's the first time I've ever had that advice. I've been thinking like mad about all sorts of things and feeling more and more in a quandary. I'll try the Madeleine method and see how that goes."

We laughed and headed our separate ways. As I bicycled home, I thought about the things I liked to do; talking to Adrian about ideas; reading; everything to do with looking after a household. I liked everything we did on the farm; the animal care, the gardens. Could any of this translate to paid work?

Maybe Madeleine was on to something. I should stop thinking so hard, see where life took me. After all, I hadn't planned any of the things that had happened in my life, and yet here I was, happily living in a beautiful house, surrounded by good people. I needed to trust more and worry less. This left me feeling buoyant.

That night I wrote to Dorothy. I decided not to tell her about my latest visit to the Hearnes. She knew exactly how it was. She didn't need any reminders of how she'd suffered in childhood. Instead I told her about my weekend in Toronto and my day in Lawrenceville. I felt the need to write and let her know what I was up to, whether she wanted to keep up a connection or not. Having found her, I wanted to stay in touch.

Cooking Lessons

One evening while Maureen and I were having our wine and conversation, I told her about life after my mother left. I described how I took over the cleaning and cooking, and the sorts of dinners I made. To my surprise she started laughing. I couldn't get her to stop long enough to tell me what was funny. Then she said, "We're going to have to do something about that. I want you to start learning about cooking from Mrs. Nelthorpe."

"So you don't think much of what I used to make for my father and me?" I was amazed. I thought it was good, healthy food, not that different from what I had when I visited friends.

"I'm sure it was fine, but Patrick and I grew up with a lot more variety, and a lot more fresh fruit and vegetables. Of course, we had the Kensington Market and all the great things Toronto could offer."

I suspected Maureen was preparing me for my role as her future sister-in-law.

As Thanksgiving approached Maureen said this would be a great opportunity for me to learn to make some wonderful new things. Her parents were coming for the weekend and would be staying again at the Skylane. Patrick was coming too, and would stay with us. Harry's parents were going to come for dinner. It was to be a family gathering such as I had never experienced.

One of my first lessons was how to make pastry. Mrs. Nelthorpe lent me an apron. She showed me how to work the lard and butter into the flour, and to add ice-cold water a bit at a time until it felt just right. She tended to work by touch and by look, with a minimum of measuring. It was a lot harder than I expected. She rolled her pie crust out first on the pastry cloth, with neat, quick moves. Almost in seconds, she had a round thin pastry that she grabbed up onto the rolling pin and popped into a pie plate.

"Now your turn," she said.

I had my pastry rolled into a ball. I laid it on the floury pastry cloth.

"Put a little flour on the rolling pin."

This I did. As soon as I attempted to roll the pastry out, it began cracking at the edges and pushing the cloth to the edge of the table.

"Start again. It takes practice."

I started over several times and was feeling frustration but determined to get it right. Finally, I had a more or less round pastry and laid it in a pie plate.

"That's lovely dear. Now we'll make the top crust."

I had to do it all again! I was hot from the effort. The second one was equally difficult, but Mrs. Nelthorpe promised that with practice I would find it easy.

We filled one pie with sliced apples, sugar, cinnamon and a little flour for thickening. The other had blueberries with sugar and tapioca flour. I asked why we used tapioca in one and flour in the other.

"Because my mother did it like that."

That was good enough for me. The top crust was left whole on the apple pie, and we made slits for the steam to escape. Mrs. Nelthorpe showed me how to make dainty leaf cut-outs from a bit of leftover pastry which we laid on the top crust to make a pretty design. We made a lattice crust for the blueberry pie, cutting the rolled out pastry into ribbons and weaving them across the top.

Both pies were beautiful. Mrs. Nelthorpe had the oven ready. It had a temperature gauge on it but she said that she did this too by feel. She opened the door and put her hand in and said, "You want a good hot oven to start." I thought that I was unlikely to have a coal stove in my life but I put my hand in too, to get the feel of it.

The pies took a long time to cook and cool. That was a good lesson too. I realized this was no last minute dessert. When they came out of the oven, she placed them on the counter. I went up to my room for the Leica and took a picture of her with the pies.

Mrs. Nelthorpe had a twenty-five pound turkey in the fridge, ready to be cooked on Monday. She had a lot to say about turkeys and all the preparation and timing. Again I was surprised at how much work went into it. I had no idea it took all day.

Mrs. Nelthorpe told me that anything that could be made ahead would make the day of the big dinner easier. On Sunday, after we had the pies ready, we made cranberry sauce. This was simple, just cooking fresh cranberries with sugar and water for a short time. We also peeled and cut up sweet potatoes and placed them in a casserole dish, with butter, brown sugar and orange juice. This cooked for about an hour. Again Mrs. Nelthorpe said to go by how tender they were, and how much the juice was absorbed, not just by the clock. These things couldn't be learned from a book; it was essential to have a teacher to show what to look for, how it should feel, and how it should smell.

On Thanksgiving morning we started cooking as soon as breakfast was over. First we made the stuffing. We chopped onions and gently cooked them in the iron frying pan with lots of butter, sage and savoury. Mrs. Nelthorpe cut the crusts off some white bread and we sat and tore the bread into small pieces that we put into a large bowl. Then we mashed some boiled potatoes. Eventually the onions, bread and mashed potatoes were all stirred together in a large yellow ceramic bowl and allowed to cool. We peeled more potatoes and set them aside in a pot of cold water. We cleaned and prepared a mound of Brussels sprouts.

The turkey was placed in the roaster. We spooned in the stuffing and Mrs. Nelthorpe sewed the opening closed with black thread and a huge needle. She rubbed the turkey with butter, sage, savoury, salt and pepper, and tied the wings and legs so they would stay close to the turkey, and not get dried out. She said it needed a moderate oven, and again demonstrated what that felt like.

Patrick spent a lot of time with us in the kitchen, observing the process and at the same time, studying for exams that were coming up later in the month. Now and then he read to us from his notes.

"Chambers is getting to be my favourite theologian, listen to this, 'All your circumstances are in the hand of God so never think it strange concerning the circumstances you're in.' I find that fascinating. Oh, and this, it's perfect for today, 'To be shallow is not a sign of being sinful, nor is shallowness an indication that there is no depth to your life at all— the ocean has a shore. Even the shallow things of life, such as eating and drinking, walking and talking, are ordained by God.'"

Patrick's enthusiasm was catching, but only to me. Mrs. Nelthorpe was not impressed.

"Give me good plain preaching," she said. "Now, let's get that giblet gravy underway."

That weekend Patrick and I talked about his growing awareness that he wasn't cut out for the priesthood, yet he still had a great desire to study theology. He joined Maureen and I in our evening ritual and shared his doubts with her.

Maureen said, "You and I have been so lucky. We always know we can fall back on Mom and Dad. They've given us freedom to try things out. That's what I'm doing now. I appreciate it so much. If this farm had to start showing a profit right away, it would be impossible."

I was glad to hear she was aware of her good fortune. Patrick and Maureen were the only people I'd ever met who had the luxury of exploring life in this way. On the other hand, I had been forced to find work quickly, but ultimately what I was doing was also exploring. I wasn't stuck. I could try things out and move on. I too felt thankful for my good fortune.

"Maybe your studies won't help in your work life, but they will make you a better person," I suggested.

"That's just it though, it doesn't reach my heart. I'm still the selfish person I always was. I thought I could study religion and become good. It seems I was under an illusion."

Maureen said, "At least you're honest with yourself."

When I met Patrick, I thought he was going to be a Catholic priest. Then I thought he would be an Anglican priest. Now it seemed he might not go in the direction of a religious vocation at all. He was kind, considerate, scholarly. What sort of career did that suit him for? I knew so little of the world of academia that I couldn't advise him in any way. I feared that if he didn't have a strong sense of direction, his mother's powerful influence would have him working in the family business.

I thought about my own religious upbringing. Did that make me a good person? I sometimes wondered how deep it went. Without my father and my connection to the Bergerons, would I continue to go to Mass? There was something sterile about it. The Latin was gone. The music had changed. It felt pedestrian. Father Belfast didn't seem particularly joyful or loving. It had always been an accepted fact of my life, like the colour of my eyes, but now I was seeing that there were all sorts of ways of being religious.

How could anyone make up their mind what was the right way? It was easier when everyone in one's world belonged to the same church. I had recently read *Franny and Zooey*. I sympathized with Franny's plight. She had been taught all the world religions and traditions and she was left adrift, not knowing what to believe. I couldn't see how faith could survive in a world of multiple choices.

I told Patrick and Maureen what I was thinking.

"I know what you mean," Patrick said. "You can't shop for your faith."

Maureen said, "Being Anglican is what fits my life. I mean, I want the kids to have the good teaching I had, whether it's true or not. I want it to be there for Christmas and Easter."

I was surprised that she could be so business-like about faith, but was I any deeper?

Gita and Jiddu had a wonderful weekend with their grandparents. The Andersons again brought presents, this time hand knit sweaters. They took the children to stay with them overnight at the Skylane Hotel, where they swam indoors and were treated to an afternoon movie in Williamsville. I thought they would feel lonely being away from home, but they returned full of enthusiasm.

The Lynches, Harry's parents, arrived Monday at noon. They brought presents for everyone, plants for the house, wine for the table, and boxes of Laura Secord chocolates. It was thrilling!

We sat down to dinner in the dining room, which we had never had an occasion to use before. There were twelve of us at the table, including Mrs. Nelthorpe, Adrian and Viviana. We put the leaves in the mahogany table to make it as large as possible. Luckily there were twelve matching chairs with needlepoint seats. The dining room had two tall windows facing west. The sun was low in the sky as we started our meal, casting an orange glow on everything.

Mr. Lynch said, "Patrick, would you say the grace?"

The family joined hands. "We give you thanks, O Lord, for the food we are about to receive, for the hands that prepared it, and for all gathered at this table. Make us mindful of the needs of others and strengthen us in your service."

"Amen."

The meal was perfect. Mrs. Nelthorpe was a master of timing. I had a new appreciation for her skills now that I had helped in the kitchen. We had champagne with the meal. The children were both given a tiny amount in sherry glasses. Like the wine, Gita and Jiddu were sparkling from the excitement of having the family together. We all shared a rosy glow.

Sophie the Cat

As the nights grew cooler I couldn't continue to sleep in the porch, which had no insulation and single-pane windows. The second floor still had unoccupied bedrooms, so I took one that looked out to the river and the rising sun. It was almost as good as my sleeping porch.

Adrian, Maureen, Patrick and I retrieved the storm windows from the basement on Thanksgiving weekend. We polished them, recaulked the edges, and between the four of us, managed to get them installed. It was heavy work, especially carrying them up the ladder to the second story. This made an immediate improvement in our comfort. We could get up in the morning without feeling it was too cold to leave our beds.

The mice were having similar thoughts and started invading the kitchen. Maureen said it was time to get a housecat, so we went to the Williamsville SPCA where there were lots of cats to choose from. We told them we wanted an indoor cat to catch mice. The attendant suggested a two-year-old female tabby, named Sophie. "She's very alert and easy to pick up and cuddle." We decided she was the one after Jiddu held her and she didn't scratch him or run away.

She turned out to be an excellent mouser. Within a week, Mrs. Nelthorpe stopped finding signs of mice. Sophie loved the kitchen and chose the rocking chair near the stove as her favourite seat. As this was also Mrs. Nelthorpe's favourite seat they often had to share.

"My grandmother always had a cat in the kitchen," Mrs. Nelthorpe said. "It makes me feel relaxed having Sophie here with me."

Patrick was still excited about Thomas Merton and had moved on to more of his writings. He wrote me letters full of quotes, '*Love is our true destiny. We do not find the meaning of life by ourselves alone - we find it with another.*' Patrick wondered how a celibate who lived in a monastery could say such a thing. In Patrick's view finding love could only be about finding a life partner. Everything Patrick read and learned that fall was about love and he wrote about it endlessly in his letters.

The pumpkins had turned bright orange and stood out clearly in the garden once the vines died back. We gathered all of them on the last Saturday of October and Maureen took them to the market for Halloween sales. We kept a few for ourselves, and made enough Jack-o-lanterns to line the front stairs. With a flickering candle in each, it was a glorious sight. When I described it to Patrick he said he longed to be with us to share all these wonderful things.

I was trying to live as Madeleine had suggested, not over-thinking everything. I was living more in the moment, trusting that life would work out, putting thoughts of what I'd like to do with my life on hold.

Adrian continued to share books and ideas with me. There were many things in the world I had never had the slightest notion of. I discovered that Adrian had been a Catholic in his youth, but had left it behind. However, I could see that he wasn't happy without a belief in something. Leaving his faith had left a vacancy that he was trying to fill through his explorations. He meditated and did yoga, and would often be trying some new discipline, such as fasting, or trying to stop living by habit, or wearing shorts into the cold season.

Adrian read a book by Wilhelm Reich, a psychoanalyst who had invented a machine called the orgone box. Adrian described it. I thought it sounded mad, but Adrian was hopeful of someday going to a clinic and trying it out. He also would have liked to be much more radical in our approach to farming, but Maureen kept him restrained. He set up pyramids as an experiment in some of the plots, believing this had beneficial effects on the plants.

Adrian made a start on the fieldstone wall for the new greenhouse and I helped whenever I had a spare moment. I loved collecting stones and wheeling them over to the cottage. We made so many trips we wore paths between the cottage, gardens, barn and house.

Adrian and Viviana were spending a lot of time together. Once I got over my jealousy, I enjoyed her company. I had never met anyone so free of convention. She was consciously trying to live as if she were the first woman on earth and could define life for herself. She told me she had been a teacher for a few years, but after she tried LSD she couldn't go back to what she called *straight thinking*. She felt that school was designed to train youth to follow orders and she wouldn't be part of that. She taught the children and me how to tie-dye. We did it outside on the picnic table where it wouldn't make a mess. We made t-shirts for everyone and put them away to give as Christmas presents.

She also taught us macramé. We made plant hangers for every window, then kept going and made macramé presents for everyone. Viv had left behind a husband and children. I wondered if she ever planned to go back to them. Her husband was a dentist. She had a home in the suburbs, awaiting her if she returned, but she said suburban life was killing her spirit. I told her my mother had left me when I was ten and that Dorothy may have felt similar longings.

"You were lucky to have a mother who followed her heart," Viv commented.

She was kind to the children, but I could never plan anything around her. She wouldn't be limited to a schedule, but when she was there we enjoyed her.

In early November, Maureen got a letter from Harry that left her upset. "He's sick. He has had fevers for more than a month and he isn't eating. He's too proud to ask but I know he wants me to come to him."

She called the Lynchs and asked if they had heard from him. They too were worried. It was easy to get sick in India, but this had been going on for too long. Mrs. Lynch thought he was lonely.

"Could you handle things here without me?" Maureen asked. "I'm not sure how long I'd be gone."

"We'll be fine," I said, "but this time you must tell the children what's up and let them know you'll be back."

A week later, Maureen left for India. I soon received a letter on the thin blue paper of international airmail.

Dear Clare, My first sight of Harry was frightening, so thin I barely recognized him. He has been clinging to me, talking endlessly about the nightmare he endured. After a few months in India nothing in his life made any sense. He woke up knowing he was an imposter. It made him sick to think of how he had played a game. Then he started to speak of this openly at gatherings. Maryam tried to keep him away from the disciples. She tried to convince him he was just having a crisis, a dark night of the soul. She swore he would come out of it absolutely assured that he was the world teacher. Harry couldn't be convinced any longer. He told enough of the disciples so word spread that he no longer believed himself to be the world teacher. Maryam and Jatin became barely civil to him. Harry was too sick to leave, and no one was caring for him. I arranged for a car to take us from the ashram to the city, then took him to a doctor. Right now he's in the hospital, dehydrated and depressed, but his condition is turning around fast. It's a miracle. Patrick's prayers have been answered. We'll be home as soon as Harry is strong enough. Tell my darling babies that Mummy misses them and will be home soon. Yours, Maureen. PS I'm so grateful you're there to look after them.

While Maureen was away, I started telling the children a story about a mink and a muskrat who lived by the river.

> *"It was a bright yellow sort of day on the riverbank. Morris, a shiny sleek dark brown mink was sitting on his favourite lawn chair at the entrance of his house on the riverbank, waiting for Martha to come by with her sailboat. Morris had a dock where the sailboat could tie up. Martha, a furry light brown and dark brown long-haired muskrat came sailing along and spied Morris gleaming in the morning light.*
> *"Ahoy!" Martha called out.*
> *Morris went to the end of the dock, leaped aboard the sailboat, and they sped away. Morris was clinging to the edge with glee, but then realized that might not be the best place to be.*
> *"Should I be sitting in the boat?"*
> *"Well, I rather think so," answered Martha. "That is, if you don't want to get knocked over by the sail."*
> *The swells were huge. The waves were washing over the edge. The cool water felt refreshing.*

"Where are we headed Martha?"
"I know a lovely spot where we can have a picnic."
"But where is the picnic basket?"
"I thought you were bringing it?"
"Well, I thought you were bringing it."
"Well I thought you were bringing it!!"

Jiddu laughed. "They don't have a picnic basket, what will they do?"
"We're going to find out," I said.

"I have an idea," Morris said. "Let's stop at Sheila's house. She always has lots of food stored up. I'll bet she would put together a picnic basket for the three of us."

Sheila was a flying squirrel, grey and fluffy, with a marvellous plume of tail. She lived in a tree by the riverbank. They sailed close to her tree house and Martha called up to her, "Sheila, Ahoy!"

Sheila came out on to her porch and shouted down, "Ahoy, mates. What are you up to?"

"We're planning a picnic," said Morris, "and somehow we forgot to bring provisions. Is there a chance you could rustle up a basket of lovely picnic foods and come along with us?"

"I'd love to," said Sheila. As quick as you can imagine she put together a basket with a loaf of French bread, a jar of potted shrimp, a salami, a selection of fresh fruits, a large slice of brie, and a bottle of fine wine.

"I say," said Morris, "stopping for Sheila was a great idea."

Sheila, grabbed the basket and glided from her porch onto the mast, then slid down beside Morris."

"That sounds like a lot of food for a picnic," Gita said.
"That's all for tonight. We'll find out tomorrow how the picnic went." I said good night and turned out the light, but left the door open so that they could see the light in the hall.
"Promise you'll tell us more?"
"Yes, I promise."

***

As soon as Harry regained strength, they flew home. The Lynches and the Andersons met them at the airport. The Lynches begged Harry and Maureen to stay for a few days so they could enjoy having Harry back and get caught up after years of absence. They were overjoyed to see the son they had lost.

There was a feeling of snow in the air the day Maureen and Harry arrived at Buttercup Acres. The children had been playing outside in the chill. Their cheeks and noses were rosy. We were picking dried goldenrod from the front field to make a bouquet when we saw the black Mercedes pull in and hurried to meet them.

"Darlings." Maureen hugged both children at once.

"Jiddu, Gita," Harry knelt down to hold them, "I'm home."

"Baba, you're back."

They were all crying.

"Yes, I'm back. I'm going to live with you now."

Mrs. Nelthorpe came to the door to greet them. She said she had the kettle on and would have tea ready in a minute and wasn't it a cold day and they must be tired after that long drive. It was comforting to have her talk of small things. It took away some of the tense emotion of the reunion.

Harry looked different in western clothes, much thinner than I remembered. He had lost his sleek, plump, guru look. Maureen was smiling, and happily handing out presents to the children from the grandparents.

Harry was not fully recovered. For the first week home he didn't go far from his bed and the couch. Mrs. Nelthorpe made nourishing soups for him. He had been away from meat for a long time so she gradually snuck it back into his diet.

"No one can thrive without meat," she said.

I tended to agree.

Maureen and I returned to our evening ritual. It was good to have her back. There was a lot to discuss about how they would proceed with their life now that they were a family again.

"I hadn't looked ahead to this," Maureen confessed. "I don't know what Harry will want to do. I'm not even sure we'll stay here. I feel like all my plans are completely upset."

"Madeleine and I have talked a lot about how she learned not to over-think life. Her approach is to trust that life will bring good things and that she'll know how to respond as opportunities arise. I'm trying to live this way. This would be a good practice for you and Harry. You don't need to have it all figured out."

"How were the children while I was gone? Did they miss me?"

"They asked about you every day. Whenever we got a letter from you I told them what you were doing. They made a calendar and crossed off the days. I've been telling them a story about a mink, a muskrat and a flying squirrel who live on the riverbank."

"I'm sorry I missed that."

***

Now that the cold weather had set in the gardening was finished, but there were still chickens, goats and sheep to take care of.

Adrian was working full time on the greenhouse, hoping to complete it before the snow arrived. As soon as Harry felt well enough, he joined Adrian. Harry said he had never done any kind of construction, not even a tree house, and he found it wonderful to be outdoors using his body.

Adrian found a building that was being torn down in Lawrenceville and he arranged to have all the windows and a door delivered to Buttercup Acres. They were old windows with wood frames in various sizes, painted green. They had the original wavy glass in them and a few even had stained glass. With Adrian and Harry working together, the building went up quickly. They had it framed and the windows and door installed by mid December. It was cold but there had been no more than a dusting of snow.

I continued to teach Gita her lessons, Jiddu too, as much as he wanted to learn. By the end of November, Gita had learned everything on the syllabus for Grade One. Maureen said we would start Grade Two in January and would take December off. She thought it would be fun to spend a week in Toronto with the children, visiting her parents and shopping. After her gruelling trip to India, she felt the need for a holiday.

Maureen and the children took the train to Toronto, while I stayed behind to look after the animals. Mrs. Nelthorpe decided it would be a good time for her to visit her sister in Copper River, so she was also gone for the week.

Harry and Adrian had become friends while working together on the greenhouse. One night that week they drank some beer with dinner, then went out to the cottage to do some planning for the greenhouse shelves. They must have had a bottle of whiskey. From indoors I could hear them laughing and singing, then arguing. I went out to see what was happening.

Adrian was cutting, "You're a phony. I knew it at the ashram. All that crap about world teacher. How can you live with yourself?"

"Phony! What about you? Pretending to be part of the ashram? Disappearing when there was so much work to do?"

Accusations went back and forth. Phony! Hypocrite! Liar! Poser! Adrian attacked Harry over and over. I had never seen anything like it when he was sober. I couldn't understand how he could be so cruel.

I was afraid their argument would turn to physical violence and shouted, "Stop this, both of you."

They took no notice. I had never seen drunkenness like this. Adrian was barely standing. Again he called Harry a phony. Then Harry started to laugh, saying, "You're right. I am a phony."

Just like that it was over. They were both laughing and friends again.

I went in the house disgusted. "Men!"

The next day they were both hung over and quiet. That night after supper, Harry and I sat at the table and he told me that, as stupid as it had been for them to have that argument, it left him feeling better.

"It's good to get it all out in the open. I was a phony in that whole thing. It doesn't help to pretend it didn't happen." Harry was thoughtful. "I hope I won't be weighed down with shame for my whole life. I want to move on. But it was so public I'm not sure how I'll get free of it. I don't know if I can go back to law school. Those doors may be closed to me."

***

College was winding down for Christmas, so Isabel and I had more time to spend together. I came into town in the truck and we went to the Santa Claus parade one afternoon. Appropriately, it began to snow as the parade came down the main street. At the end, Santa came in his sleigh, throwing candies to all the girls and boys.

We wandered around downtown, enraptured by the Christmas decorations and coloured lights that glowed in the early dark. Isabel was enjoying her courses. She talked a lot about child psychology and the best ways to raise healthy children, and how they needed a good start in life. I could have used some of that knowledge before I started my work with Gita and Jiddu, but I was kind to them, and they already had a great start.

We met up with my Aunts Mercy and Shilta, who had two little girls with them. I introduced Isabel.

Pulling the girls forward, Aunt Mercy, said, "This is Dottie and this is Bella."

I recognized Bella as the little one who had not been woken up for school. They had come to town for the parade. I asked if they would like to warm up in the coffee shop. We all went in, and I bought hot chocolate for the girls and coffee for the women. They seemed quiet and out of their element. Isabel talked to the girls, asking them about school, and how they liked the parade. They spoke very little. They both looked frozen, and their noses were running.

"Dottie was named after Dorothy," Shilta said. "She's not much like her though. Dorothy's type don't come along every day."

After parting from my aunts, Isabel and I went to her family's house for supper. The lights shone from every window, and the house was cozy. Mrs. Bergeron made spaghetti and meatballs. I told her I was learning to cook from Mrs. Nelthorpe, and how Maureen thought my cooking experience had been extremely limited. Mrs. Bergeron said she thought I had done amazingly well cooking for my father, and it wasn't that different from what anyone ate in those days. "We'd never even heard of pizza then," she said, "and now that's all Arlene's kids will eat."

***

That night Harry and I sat up late talking, drinking wine and listening to records.

"I don't know what to do with my life now that I'm not at the ashram. It was so easy going along day after day, knowing exactly what I needed to do. Being admired. Did I let it go too quickly?"

"If you stayed with it, I'm sure you would have lost Maureen. When I helped her move out that day, I never dreamed it would turn around. I thought your marriage was over. I know she loves you, but she's had enough of you as great world teacher."

"I may have been a fraud, but there were lots of good things I did, like teaching yoga and meditation. I helped people."

"Are you regretting you came back to her?"

"No. It's just that I want it all."

"You were close to losing her. What pulled you back?"

"Being sick left me helpless; full of self doubt. My usual strength disappeared. It was terrifying."

Harry refilled our wine glasses.

"Now that I've recovered my health, I'm seeing my life in a different light. The ashram wasn't all corrupt just because I was I was faking it, in some sense."

In some sense? Didn't Harry see that pretending to be from India was completely fake? Didn't he see the role he played as world teacher fake?

"Is it power you miss?" I asked.

"You're as bad as Adrian. And you're not even drunk."

"You're not going to get another chance with Maureen and you probably don't have a chance of resuming your life as revered world teacher."

"I can't tell Maureen this, but I loved being important and respected."

"Don't worry, she knew."

"I feel I can tell you anything. You're the kind of woman who understands."

"Harry, it's never good to hear a married man say 'you're the kind of woman who understands'. It's right next to 'my wife doesn't understand me'."

"You're right. I love your honesty."

Harry pulled out a ragged hand rolled cigarette.

"Adrian got me some pot. Want to share?"

We were listening to The Moody Blues, the lights were dim, snow was falling softly.

"Why not?"

We passed it back and forth. Slowly. Meditatively. There was a sweet, heavy smell. I thought, 'nothing is happening', until I realized I was full of the thought 'nothing, nothing, nothing'. It was soothing as snow. I relaxed into the couch and felt no surprise when Harry leaned over and kissed me.

"Adrian is right. You are a phony. A charming phony."

I got up and went to bed.

Snow

I woke up to white light and snow piled in the corners of the windows. My first thoughts were of Harry and our evening together. I wasn't angry with him. He had a sort of lightness that made it hard to take him seriously.

I eased out of bed into the cold room, found my wool slippers and bathrobe, and went downstairs to put on coffee. With Maureen away, I felt free to smoke in the house, and I noticed Adrian did too. It was funny how the dynamics changed when certain people were away. Adrian was in the kitchen and coffee was perking on the stove. Harry must have smelled the coffee. A minute later he was down too. We sat at the table in sleepy silence. Hands warmed by mugs of coffee. Smoke curling up. A peaceful quiet.

"There's a lot of snow."

"Yup."

"A good day to stay in and read."

"Yup."

"But somebody has to feed the animals."

"I'll do it," I said. The snow looked inviting, and I loved the smell of the barn in winter, loved gathering the eggs, loved the sweet way the sheep and the goats came to greet me.

Viv came in from the cottage, brushing snow from her hair.

"I'll make pancakes when I finish the chores," I said, then went up to change into my barn clothes.

Viv called up the stairs after me, "I'll get breakfast. It will be ready when you come in."

The four of us spent the day reading, listening to records, and making macramé plant hangers. I suggested we sell them at the market, since we'd already made presents for everyone we could think of.

Now and then Adrian would read aloud some striking bit of wisdom from his book.

"Listen to this: '*Happiness is the absence of the striving for happiness.*'"

We talked about Chuang Tzu, and whether it was possible to live a life without striving, without pretensions.

Harry said, "Let's have a party tonight. Before everyone gets home."

Again I thought, 'why not?' The snow made me feel as if we were outside time; protected from the rest of the world.

That week revealed a new Harry. He wasn't the guru, or the repentant husband; he was swinging bachelor Harry.

We were saved by the return of Mrs. Nelthorpe, who waltzed in carrying her suitcase and found us lounging in the living room. Sophie ran to greet her, meowing loudly as if to complain that we hadn't looked after her properly.

"My nephew was driving in this direction and I thought I'd catch a ride. Save the bus fare. The driveway's not cleared."

This was all it took to get the household back to work.

I was glad of her return. Those few days when we felt like unsupervised teenagers were heady, but I welcomed order. The ashtrays were emptied and put away, old routines resumed. It was good to have

Mrs. Nelthorpe in the kitchen again. I felt safe knowing she was knitting by the stove with Sophie staring up at her, waiting for her lap to be free.

Harry and I sat up late again, talking and drinking wine, but there was no more marijuana. He spoke of how he loved the new consciousness; freedom, exploration of new ways of being. I could hear Adrian's enthusiasms seeping into Harry's world. I told him that it was one thing for a single person to pursue this, but quite another for a parent. Harry was definitely getting inspired. He said families would change too. Everything would be more open. I was pretty sure Maureen was going to hate this. I began to wonder if it was in Harry's nature to follow whatever strong voice came along. I began to worry about what was ahead for Maureen.

The next day Isabel came out to visit with Peter, who was home for the Christmas vacation. They brought snow shoes, and we went walking over the snow covered fields. Isabel and Peter talked about school, how much work they had to do, and how great it was to have a couple of weeks free. If we had been on our own I would have talked to Isabel about Harry. I wanted Isabel's advice on whether I should tell Maureen about Harry's behaviour while she was gone.

It snowed while we were out, the sun a dim white ball in the sky. When we were completely frozen, noses and cheeks red, feet aching, we went in and sat in the kitchen by the woodstove. Mrs. Nelthorpe got out fruitcake and I put on the kettle for tea.

"I helped make this fruitcake," I said proudly. "You cannot imagine how much preparation went into it. We chopped mountains of dried fruit, cooked the batter for hours, then left the cakes for six weeks in cheesecloth soaked in brandy."

Isabel said, "Nothing could taste better after coming in from the cold."

Peter asked if I would show him the animals. Isabel stayed inside by the stove. When we were alone, he asked if I would like to go to a party on the weekend. I realized that things had changed since summer.

"I can't. I'm not the kind of person who can have two boyfriends at once."

"You're a good catch. Patrick is a lucky guy." Peter didn't seem too disappointed. I suspected he would easily have another date by Saturday.

Maureen and the children returned at the end of the week. Harry drove to Williamsville to pick them up at the train station. Gita and Jiddu were thrilled to come home to a snow covered farm. As soon as they got home, we all went outside and made a snowman. They told me with great excitement about everything they had done in Toronto. They saw a big skating rink and a giant Christmas tree at City Hall. They went to see The Nutcracker Ballet and had a special box to themselves and ate chocolates. They shopped and shopped. Maureen looked relaxed and happy. She took many shopping bags upstairs to hide until Christmas.

"Patrick and Mom and Dad are coming on Christmas Eve. I'm so excited. I dreamed of this, of us all being together, but didn't expect it to come true. Harry's parents want us to come to Toronto for New Year's Eve. It's all planned. I bought the most beautiful black dress for their New Year's party."

I decided then not to say anything to Maureen about Harry. I couldn't bear to spoil her happiness.

The week before Christmas we had another baking session. Mrs. Nelthorpe got out her recipes and we made many cookies: hermits, shortbreads, ginger crinkles, chocolate chip, coconut macaroons and date filled turnovers. We also had another pie session, this time making mincemeat and pumpkin pies. I still struggled with pastry, but it was getting easier.

"Are we going to hear more about Morris and Martha and Sheila?"

Gita and Jiddu hadn't forgotten my story. They were lying on their beds ready for their afternoon nap. Gita was getting too old to nap. She was raised up on her elbow talking to me, and didn't look the least bit tired.

"Where did we leave off?" I asked.

"You know, they ate their picnic, got back in the sailboat, and the wind carried them to an island."

"Oh yes. Morris was telling Martha off."

> "Why didn't you check the weather? Didn't you know it was getting too windy?"
>
> Martha sadly replied, "I was having too much fun. It felt like we were flying. I didn't want to stop." She sniffed and a tear rolled onto her pointy snout.
>
> Sheila said, "As long as we've run aground here, let's get out and see what we can find."
>
> Morris looked sadly at the empty picnic basket. "No food either. What are we to do?"

"First things first." Sheila, ever resourceful, ran up a tree and acted as scout. "I see something interesting on the other side. Shall we take a walk?"

The three friends climbed a rise and came over to the other side of the island, where they spied a field of cows. They were brown and white and had a large earring in each ear.

"How did they get here?" Martha asked. "Do they swim?"

"How did the cows get there Clare?" Gita asked. "Why do they have earrings?"

Jiddu was already asleep.

"I'll tell you more next time."

I picked up a novel and lay down on my bed to read, but instead of reading, I found myself thinking of my life. This was my first Christmas without my father. It didn't seem possible that I had been on my own for less than a year. I could never have imagined the changes that had taken place. Nothing that was in my consciousness last year, whatever it may have been, my plans, my dreams, none of it counted for anything now.

Was I even the same person? I wasn't sure what to do with this thought. Did it mean that life was a dream, like Chuang Tzu's speculations about his dream of being a butterfly? One thing still made me feel connected to my father, to my past, to all that I thought was the real Clare; Sunday Mass. It was the anchor in my fluctuating world, yet I found myself questioning it too. I had moved away from a world where almost everyone I met shared my beliefs. I hadn't gone far from home and yet the world around me had completely changed.

Christmas Presents

I started thinking about Dottie and Bella after seeing them at the Christmas parade. I wondered what sort of Christmas they would have. I phoned the Hearne home and Uncle Gurly answered. I told him I wanted to bring presents to Dottie and Bella, and asked him how many other children there were.

"Just Tim, that's Timbo's son, and Little Django, Mercy's son."

"When I was at the reunion I got the impression there were countless children," I said.

"It can sure seem that way," he said. "They're busy little devils."

"I'll come on Christmas Eve to deliver the presents if that's okay."

"We'll be home and glad to see you."

I called Isabel and asked if she'd like to shop with me for the kids' presents. I told her I'd come by in the morning.

Mrs. Bergeron met me at the door and said Isabel would be right down. She asked how I was doing. I loved the fact that she kept track of where I was in my life; I didn't think anyone but her would notice, but she knew it was my first Christmas without Dad.

"I'm grateful for all the good things that came my way this year, but also slightly lost. When Dad and I were together, I always knew exactly who I was. Now I'm not sure."

"Lots of things are changing," Mrs. Bergeron said.

She looked sad. I knew she was thinking of her best friend, Maisie Dennis, whose husband had deserted her for a woman he met at work. Mrs. Dennis was left with seven children and little money.

"Who ever heard of anyone doing such a thing in middle age?" she said, and I could hear both anger and sadness in her voice.

The snow had been coming steadily for weeks and the streets were lined with snow banks. Isabel and I started our shopping at Woolworth's. I bought dainty pocket handkerchiefs for Dottie and Bella. They were pale green and had a circle of pink dancing fairies on them. For the boys, I found red kerchiefs with cowboys. I didn't think I should buy clothes as it was hard to know exactly what size they were. I bought each of them a lucky rabbit's foot key chain. Even if they didn't have keys, we could all use some luck. Toys were more difficult. I wasn't sure what would interest them. Isabel said she thought model airplanes would interest the boys, and cut-out dolls would be good for the girls. I only needed wrapping paper and ribbon, and we were done.

"Let's have coffee at the lunch counter." It was busy with Christmas shoppers but we managed to squeeze in.

"Do you want to come to our place for Christmas dinner? Mom mentioned it today."

"Thank her for me. I'll come over for a visit sometime over the holiday, but I'm having Christmas dinner at Buttercup Acres."

"Peter told me Patrick won. Are you a couple now?"

"Patrick and I saw each other a few times in the fall, and he's been writing to me. I'm open to seeing what happens. Madeleine and I talked about not over-thinking life and I've been trying to follow her advice."

"You don't sound swept away."

"Let's just say I'm cautious. What about you? How are you feeling without Joe?"

"I'm glad it turned out this way. I feel free. I was too young when we met. It was keeping me from meeting new people, from exploring what I wanted to do with my life. He was too powerful."

"How can we keep that from happening? I think about this a lot. It may be the price you pay for being a couple. Maybe we could be like Jean-Paul Sartre and Simone de Beauvoir, and keep it loose."

"Who?"

I realized how much I had changed. In my new life, knowing the French existentialists was a given. At Buttercup Acres we talked about Jean-Paul and Simone as if they were our next door neighbours.

"French philosophers who were lovers. They never lived together and always had lots of other partners. I wouldn't recommend their life though."

"I should think not! What's come over you?"

I laughed and said, "Nothingness."

"You seem to have learned more this year than I have," said Isabel, "even though I was the one in school."

"What I've learned about schools from Adrian might be true. They teach you to conform, not to think."

"Don't let Dad hear you say that."

I laughed. Her father barely spoke, but lately he'd been complaining about hippies and free love and crazy radicals. He was furious about the Dennis's breakup.

"He won't talk to Mr. Dennis now, and they used to be friends. It broke up their poker group."

"I'll make sure I don't upset your father. I love how solid he is. I'd hate to see him change."

Christmas Eve was going to be busy. As soon as I was up I was hurrying, taking care of the chickens then grabbing a quick breakfast before I set out with the presents for the children. I was nervous about winter driving, and drove the truck with great care on the country lanes. The snow had been pushed into great banks that towered above the road, creating a white tunnel. Thankfully the lane was cleared at the Hearne home and I was able to drive into their yard. Uncle Django came out when he heard me arrive and said, "I put the dogs in the barn." I appreciated his thoughtfulness. It was still early, but everyone was up and drinking coffee, even the children. I knew where my coffee habit came from.

Their tree was decorated with popcorn strings, lights, and carved figures whittled by Uncle Django and painted by the children.

He handed me a paper bag and said, "For you." It was a bag of his carvings. "Your little ones can paint them."

I was warmed to think of him carving all these for me. I placed the presents I'd bought under their tree. I had also wrapped a box of our Christmas cookies to give to the family. Uncle Timbo was sitting with his guitar and Uncle Gurly had a mandolin.

"Let's have some carols while you're here. Do you sing?"

They played and everyone sang. It was the carols I'd heard all my life, but the first time I'd ever realized the sweetness of them. After a while, Gurly and Timbo started playing music such as I had never heard. Uncle Django now joined in with a banjo. Little Django was leaning on my knee and tapping his foot in rhythm. Tim, although he appeared to be only about eight, also had a guitar. He played fast and hard, keeping up with the others.

Aunt Mercy got out the cards. Aunt Shilta, Uncle Vano and I joined her for a few hands of euchre. The little girls played in the corner with a baby doll and a walking doll. The walking doll seemed to be looking after the baby doll, but she was terribly bossy.

"I hate to run off but I have to get back."

I said my goodbyes and this time when I left I felt better about my connection to them.

On the way through Lawrenceville I stopped at Bergerons to drop off a present for Isabel, a copy of *The Mandarins* by Simone de Beauvoir. It would give us lots to talk about.

Late in the afternoon as dusk had fallen and blue shadows lay on the snow-covered field, the Andersons arrived in their new Cadillac. It made me think of my father, and how much he would have loved to own such a car. I wished he could be here to share this with me.

The house was welcoming, with Christmas lights in every window. The Andersons came in laden with suitcases and packages. We greeted each other in the front hall that was decorated with evergreen boughs, red ribbons, and holly. There were hugs for everyone. Patrick looked handsome in his leather college jacket and his hair fashionably long.

Adrian had gone to visit his parents. He seemed uneasy about it, and I was surprised. Generally he was cool about everything. He admitted that despite all his years of travel, learning and growth, when he got back to St. John, he became a miserable, sullen teenager.

"I can't help it. I keep thinking this time I'll be different, but as soon as I come in the door, and see my father sitting in his lounger and my mother looking so anxious to please, I go crazy."

Mrs. Nelthorpe was staying until after Christmas, then she and her sister were going to Florida for a month. This was fortunate because we couldn't possibly manage the Christmas dinner without her.

Wine and whiskey flowed freely that evening. I wished we could sing carols together, but there weren't any musicians in this family. I told them about my visits to the Hearnes, and of how the men all played instruments. Mr. Anderson said, "Sounds like gypsies."

Mrs. Anderson laughed in a pained way and said, "They must be very charming."

"It was beautiful," I said. "I've never met anyone quite like them. Although I suppose my mother must be like them."

"I've never heard anything about your mother, I thought she must have passed away," Mrs. Anderson said.

I had never spoken of Dorothy to them, although I was sure Patrick and Maureen knew of my mother.

"She's very much alive. She calls herself Stargaze and travels around raising money for a community of mystics and magicians."

Harry looked shocked. "Stargaze! That's your mother? I had no idea."

"I was reunited with her because of her visit to the ashram."

"What a strange world. To think that if I hadn't suggested you go to that talk, you might never have known where she was."

Mrs. Anderson seemed uncomfortable with the topic, but Harry was fascinated. I didn't want to be any more fascinating to him than I already was.

"I'm not like my mother," I began, and then thought of how disloyal this was so I changed the subject.

The Anderson tradition was to go to Midnight Mass. My father and I always went to Christmas Mass in the morning, but I was willing to join them and see what an Anglican service was like. I didn't know how I could possibly stay awake after my long day of visiting, cooking, and getting ready for visitors. I was almost saved when Maureen said it would be too late for the children to be up. I gladly volunteered to stay with them; then Harry jumped in and said he'd stay too. Maureen said there was no point in both of us staying, so I was back to going with the group.

At eleven we piled into the Cadillac, and Mr. Anderson drove us to Lawrenceville on roads slick with frost. The car smelled of perfume and whiskey. Mrs. Anderson had on a fur coat with matching hat. She looked elegant and warm, while the rest of us were frozen.

I was surprised to find the Anglican service identical to a Catholic Mass. I sat close to Patrick and leaned against him to enjoy his warmth. I wished Harry was there for Maureen. It felt like he should be with her, after years of neglect.

I decided that someday I must have a fur coat like Mrs. Anderson's. Lots of the mothers in town had fur coats, mostly lamb and muskrat, but Mrs. Anderson's was different. It looked more alive than any of the coats I'd seen. It was gleaming and stripy and rippling. It looked expensive. I never had a great desire for clothes, but her coat created a deep longing in me. Later, I asked her about it and she seemed very pleased.

"Wild mink. A present from Daddy," she explained.

When we got back to Buttercup Acres, I fell asleep instantly and dreamt of my father. He was driving a Cadillac, smoking a cigar, and wearing a big fur coat. He said, "I'm your Daddy." A silly dream, but Dad was still on my mind when I woke up. I wished I could walk across the hall, wake him up, and share our usual Christmas morning.

Our ritual had been to open one present each and go to early Mass. Then Dad cooked a big breakfast of pancakes, bacon and coffee, and we opened the rest of our presents. The presents were mostly for me, but I made sure there were a couple for him.

I thought about our last Christmas together. He looked healthy. There were no signs of what was to come. I said a prayer for him and decided I would not allow sadness to ruin the day. I would focus on the present and be grateful.

The children were awake, waiting in their beds for someone to get up. It was almost eight o'clock so they were being very patient.

"Clare, can we get up now?"

"Yes, let's go downstairs and see what Santa brought."

They jumped out of bed and held my hand. We went downstairs to the living room in our robes and slippers. I could smell the coffee Mrs.

Nelthorpe had perking on the stove. She was setting the table and slicing bread for toast.

"Let's wake everyone up," I said.

I put on a Perry Como Christmas record and turned up the volume. The sweet sounds of Perry Como and the Ray Charles Singers filled the house. Soon everyone came down, even Mr. and Mrs. Anderson, who had stayed overnight so they could be with us for Christmas morning.

There were heaps of presents under the tree. Mr. Anderson took command. He proceeded to hand out presents to each of us. He did so in a deliberate, relaxed fashion so that it wasn't a free-for-all, but went along very efficiently, as one would expect from the manager of a factory. He asked Mrs. Nelthorpe to bring coffee for the grownups. The children were too excited to think of anything but presents. At my suggestion, Maureen bought skates for Gita and Jiddu.

"Can we skate today?" Gita asked.

"Yes, the pond is frozen," I said. "We'll just need to shovel a clear patch."

There was a toboggan from the Andersons for the children and snow shoes for Maureen and Harry. I had knitted a scarf for Patrick, to match his leather jacket. Mrs. Nelthorpe taught me to knit. It was my first accomplishment. Patrick bought me a gold bracelet, very simple, with a heart clasp. It was beautiful and exactly right. The children got the most presents. By the end of the gift opening they were dazed.

I had a present from my mother, the first since I was a child; a blue and white, enamel coffee pot from Norway. The card said, for your hope chest. Unlike most young women, I didn't have a hope chest, but this could be the start of one.

Mr. Anderson said, "I wanted to buy a colour television for Buttercup Acres, but Maureen asked me not to. She said it would ruin the beauty and order of life. I can't see what's wrong with the occasional football game on a Sunday."

I could see both sides of this, as a former television addict. Maybe I would be all the better for not having spent so many hours gazing at the screen. Still, I had fond memories of the shows I loved so much.

Gita said, "I miss Romper Room. Couldn't we get one Darling Mummy Maureen?"

Maureen just laughed. She was always firm on decisions about what was best.

After breakfast, I helped get the dishes cleared up so we could start the dinner preparation. I knew from my Thanksgiving experience that it would be an all-day affair. This time I made the stuffing on my own, but allowed the children to help me tear the bread into small pieces.

Patrick and Harry spent the morning clearing snow from the pond. They brought down a bench where we could sit and put our skates on. Patrick came in and asked when I'd be free to come out and skate. Mrs. Nelthorpe said, "I can manage here, go ahead."

I helped the children get into their snowsuits and I dressed in my warmest clothes. We took our skates and went to the pond. I helped them get their skates on first. Patrick was ready before us. As soon as Jiddu had skates on Patrick was shepherding him across the ice. I got Gita ready and quickly laced up my skates before my fingers froze. I held her hand and we wobbled along. She wasn't worried about falling, and it didn't take long before she could glide along without support.

The snow was banked along the edge of the pond, and provided a good place to fall into. Maureen, Harry, and the Andersons came down to watch. The Andersons said they would bring their skates next time. Maureen said she thought she'd better not skate.

That afternoon everyone was tired from the late night, the Christmas excitement and the fresh air. There were naps for all. The house was silent.

At three I woke up. Gita was standing beside me.

"Darling Clare, I'm awake."

I couldn't help but laugh. If she continued to be so sweet the world would give her anything she wanted.

"Could you tell me more of the story? Is Martha still sad?"

I sat up and Gita got up beside me. I continued with my tale of the sailboat adventure.

> The cows wandered over to the three friends. They introduced themselves. "This is Clara and Sara and Farrah. I'm Tara."
>
> Morris jumped in, "I'm Morris, this is Martha, and that's Sheila. We were wondering how you got here and why you have earrings, if you don't mind me asking."
>
> The cows all started talking at once and it was impossible to understand a word they were saying. Mooo, moooo, mooo! What a din.

Sheila, who was excellent at bringing order to chaos said, "One at a time, please."

I felt a small hand on my leg. "Me too, can I come up. I don't want to miss the story." Jiddu was awake. I went over what he missed and continued.

Tara, who was the boldest of the cows, said, "We came over on a raft. Farmer Scott brought us two at a time. It was a wild ride, believe me. Our yellow earrings were a gift from Farmer Scott. We think he put them on us so we'd look beautiful. Now we're alone over here. We are pleased to have some visitors besides the seagulls. And how did you get here?"

The three friends told of how they had been flying along in the sailboat when a big wind picked them up and left them on the shore. Martha was feeling better. She told them it was her sailboat, and that she knew the river like the back of her paw.

"We'll just visit a bit," Martha said, "and then we'll be heading home. It's safe now that the wind has died down."

Morris still wanted to be cranky. He looked for reasons to be a grump. As beautiful and sleek as Morris was, he often had a sour, pinched look on his face. In fact, it was hard to picture him with a smile. Why was that? Sheila was always smiling. Martha was always smiling.

"Maybe they're happy," Jiddu suggested.

I could hear everyone stirring. We went downstairs and found Maureen had set up a card table in the living room. She and Mrs. Anderson were working on a jigsaw puzzle. The children ran over to look at their presents, and were soon playing with a toy gas station that had been given to Jiddu. It had gas pumps, a lift for the cars, little mechanics in coveralls, and vehicles to be serviced.

Christmas dinner was a triumph. At the beginning, we were all given a Christmas cracker to pull. Inside was a tiny present, and the paper from the cracker was then put on as a crown. For dessert, Mrs. Nelthorpe brought in a flaming plum pudding with silver coins hidden in it. Finding one was good luck. These were the Anderson's traditions, all new to me.

For the next few days we skated, snow-shoed, played games, and ate turkey sandwiches. It was wonderful although different from the quiet holidays I had shared with my father.

I was delegated to stay and take care of things at Buttercup Acres for New Year's, while everyone would be in Toronto for the Lynch's party. Patrick said New Year's Eve would be no fun without me, so he decided to stay and keep me company.

Mrs. Anderson wanted to know if I felt that it was improper. I told her it would be fine. I don't think she was really worried. She already seemed to see me as a potential daughter-in-law.

Isabel invited Patrick and me to spend New Year's Eve with her family. It was a simple affair. We had snacks and coffee and watched Guy Lombardo on television. Arlene and Bill and the children were there. They left at ten, and Patrick and I decided to leave then too. We drove down the snowbank-lined roads back to the silent farm.

We had a bottle of champagne ready for midnight. It was a silvery night, with the moon shining on the snow. We sat in the living room and played records. Just before midnight, Patrick counted the seconds until the clock struck twelve.

"Happy New Year Clare." He poured the champagne into our glasses. It fizzed, bubbled, and winked. We laughed with the sheer joy of being young and healthy in this beautiful world.

"Just think, a year ago we hadn't met. I feel lucky and blessed. I hope you share some of my happiness," Patrick said.

"I can't think of anyone I'd rather be with." I told him about a game Isabel and I used to play with the Simpson Sears and the Eaton's Christmas Catalogues. "We would look through the men's clothing section, and pick a date for New Year's Eve. I'd pick you if you were in the catalogue."

I wasn't trying to flatter. I meant it. Patrick was everything I could want; dark hair, deep blue eyes, gentle, and considerate. With his tight jeans, loafers and leather jacket, he was my picture of the perfect college guy.

We drank all the champagne. We talked about many things; our pasts and our dreams. It was the first time we were completely alone.

"I'm so in love," I said, without even thinking.

"Do you mean it?"

"I'm in love with life, with everything, with you too.... although I may be drunk. Ask me again tomorrow and we'll see."

We went off to our rooms.

Patrick called down the hall to me, "I won't forget to ask you."

It was fun to wake up the next morning, just the two of us alone at the farm. I got up and put the coffee on. I didn't have a cigarette. I decided I would quit as New Year's Day was the right time for resolutions.

I went out to the barn to feed the animals and collect the eggs.

Patrick joined me and said, "We need to bring in a sheep and a goat. It brings good luck for the New Year."

We managed to get them into the kitchen, causing the cat to jump up on the counter and hiss with great agitation. They wandered once around and then we shepherded them back to the barn.

"That's good enough," Patrick said. "We have our luck."

A New Year

In January life returned to routine. I started teaching Gita her Grade Two lessons and Adrian returned from Christmas with his family. He and Harry finished the inside of the greenhouse. Although it was cold, it would soon be time to start seedlings. The greenhouse was an architectural marvel with its many shaped panes of glass, to which Adrian had added an artistic touch in their arrangement. It also kept the cottage much warmer.

Adrian and I talked about his trip to St. John.

"I've read David Cooper, R.D. Laing, all the new psychologists, about getting free of family, free of the hang-ups they leave us with, but none of it seems to apply in the real world. I mean, my father is cold and my mother is neurotic, but I still love them. I would be rudderless without them. Of course, I do stay at least a thousand miles from them."

I laughed, but I agreed. Family, even one as skimpy as mine, was important.

While Mrs. Nelthorpe was away in Florida I did all the cooking. It was fun planning meals, looking through her cookbooks, and trying new things. I attempted roast beef with Yorkshire pudding, which was more than I could manage. The pudding was flat and greasy, the roast beef not up to Mrs. Nelthorpe standards. As soon as she was home, I planned to have her show me how she did it as hers was always perfect. I suspected the pudding involved precise timing and exactly the right heat, something that could only be learned from experience.

Adrian started play-reading sessions for our Saturday night entertainment. He borrowed multiple copies of plays from the library or the high school, and we would each take a part and read aloud. Now and then, one of our friends would join in. I had never seen live theatre, and knew only the Shakespeare we read in high school. It was amazing to experience plays from this perspective, and I began to develop an appreciation for theatre. We didn't practice or memorize anything; we just dove in and read. One of the first plays was *A Thousand Clowns*, which became my favourite. All of us were indignant at the social worker in the play, who tries to take the young boy away from his unconventional uncle.

Patrick was back at school for his final semester. His philosophy class was reading Heidegger, Husserl and Gadamer. He included quotations in his letters. These led me to think I would never understand one word of what he was studying. On his own he was reading Samuel Beckett. I advised him to read P.G. Wodehouse as an antidote.

Maureen gave us a big surprise in February when she returned from a doctor's appointment with news that she was pregnant. Gita was thrilled and talked constantly of helping with the baby. Jiddu said he didn't want any more babies in the family. I too was slightly leery, wondering if their marriage was solid enough for more children.

Realizing how much I had changed and grown in being exposed to new ideas at the ashram and the farm, I decided it would be good for my little cousins if I were to take some part in their lives and introduce them to new experiences. I asked Aunt Shilta if I could take the girls to a play in Ottawa. There was to be a production of *The Emperor's New Clothes* I thought they would like. We could see the afternoon showing and be back by supper time.

I took the girls to Nate's for lunch before the play. They were silent on the drive to Ottawa and I was fearful they were bored. They sat quietly through the production, but on the way home, they were completely animated. I was amazed at how much they remembered. It made an enormous impression on them.

When we went in the house, Tim said, "Are Little Django and I next?"

I was somewhat apprehensive of the boys, as Tim could be rough, but I knew children needed to feel the world was fair, so I agreed to do something with them too.

I had promised myself I would return to college in September, but now I was wondering if I should stick to this schedule. I still didn't know what I wanted to do with my life. Being a secretary had stopped being my only option. I didn't think it would be a bad job, but I had developed a bigger perspective. Adrian talked a lot about avoiding a career. He talked about the Tao and the importance of being useless, like a turtle in the mud. I could see his point. Work could take over one's life; leave one used up. I didn't want that. I also loved the life I had. I hated to quit and move on, when it seemed as if every day was full of enjoyment. I didn't want to leave Gita and Jiddu and the farm. Dorothy told me not to get stuck, but now I wondered why. What was wrong with this life and with taking things as they come?

In March, Patrick suggested we go away for a weekend to Ottawa. He knew if we met in Toronto his mother would take over and we wouldn't get enough time together. He took the train from Toronto, and I took a bus from Lawrenceville and we met at the Lord Elgin Hotel where he booked a suite.

We wandered by the canal on a damp, misty night and eventually made our way to the Bytown Market, looking for a restaurant. We settled on one with dim lighting and a cozy look. Patrick asked if I'd like him to order for us. I found that romantic. He ordered a bottle of Pouilly-Fuissé. I couldn't imagine it was possible for wine to be more delicious. We had scampi as an appetizer and Quiche Lorraine for the main course. We sat in the window, looking over the street.

Patrick talked about how well his studies were going, but that he still didn't see a career in it. I told him of my thoughts about school and work, and of how much I loved life just as it was. I told him about our most recent play reading of Eugene O'Neill's *The Iceman Cometh*. As I described the play he told me that I too should read P.G. Wodehouse as an antidote. I had to agree. I loved O'Neill, but found him ridiculously stark. We spent a long time over our dinner. We finished the wine, then had coffee. It was great to have all the time in the world to talk.

We left the restaurant and walked through the dark city, under street lights shedding small, dim circles in the mist. As we walked, we talked about Quakerism, which I had been reading about. I said I found it to be honest, in a way that I didn't think my religious upbringing had been.

"I love the prominence of the spirit in their belief. It's about experience, as opposed to accepting dogma. I also love their marriage tradition, which is simply to clasp hands, and say that it is so. It seems very romantic, but I suppose it could get you into trouble."

We got back to the hotel chilled from the dampness. Our suite had a cozy living room where we sat on a fluffy sheepskin rug and leaned against the couch. There was only the murmur of the downtown traffic. I felt electrified by joy.

Patrick turned towards me and began kissing me, with soft warm kisses. We were relaxed, unselfconscious. He slowly undid each tiny pearl button on my blue peasant blouse. There was only the light of the street shining in.

"You are beautiful." He breathed shallowly with excitement. "I could never have imagined anyone as perfect as you."

I pulled away. "I'm not ready for this."

A Change in Plans

"Good morning, Patrick."

"Good morning, darling."

"Are you terribly disappointed?"

"I didn't really have expectations."

Patrick was good-natured and a gentleman.

We spent the weekend enjoying the luxury of being on our own in Ottawa; ordering breakfast in our room, enjoying the silver carafe of coffee and the elegance of the breakfast service, wandering the streets of Ottawa, looking in store windows, going to the Chateau Laurier in the evening to hear jazz. The love songs seeped into my bones.

On Sunday we rented skates and went the length of the canal, from the Chateau Laurier to Dow's Lake. It was a sunny, mild day. We were lucky there was still ice. We bought hot chocolate and sat on a bench in the sun, feeling warm through and through.

Our conversation was foolish and delightful. We couldn't stop looking at each other and touching. I thought, this must be love.

When I returned to Buttercup Acres, Gita greeted me with, "Darling Clare, are you going to be my aunt?"

"Maybe someday."

Maureen said, "We have news. Harry has decided to go back to law school. We'll be moving to Toronto in the summer. I'm afraid it's going to mess up all the plans for the farm."

I was shocked. I didn't know what I would do if they were planning to leave. I went out to the cottage and found Adrian sitting beside the stove, reading.

"Did you hear that Maureen and Harry are moving to Toronto?"

"They told me today."

"I wasn't expecting this."

"I tried to convince Harry to stick around, try it here for a year, but he misses the city and being a big shot."

"What will you do?"

"Trust in the Universe."

"Everyone told me not to get stuck here, but I like this life. Why does it have to change?"

"You can marry Patrick and stay here." Adrian looked peeved. It was his turn to be jealous.

"I'm not ready for marriage. I've barely lived."

"Everything is a gift, even this. The Universe takes care of you too."

"I call it providence, but I believe in the same thing. Still, I'll have to make some decisions."

"Remember the Tao, 'stay still until the stream clears'. Give yourself some time."

"Thanks Adrian. It's good to know I don't have to make a decision right away."

I went back to my room and wrote to Dorothy. I told her what had happened, and that I would soon to be free to move on whether I liked it or not.

Gita and Jiddu came in and said, "Could we hear more about Morris and Martha and Sheila?"

"Come on up."

After they had a wonderful long chat with the cows, Martha noticed that the wind had died down. "Well we must be moving on now. Goodbye Tara, Sarah, Clara and Farrah"

"Good mooo Bye mooo, Mooo mooo," said Tara, Sarah, Clara and Farrah. Their earrings clinked pleasantly as they swished their heads back and forth to show how much they had enjoyed the visit.

Martha and Morris got back in the sailboat. Sheila pushed off from the shore and jumped in. The wind caught the sail. They were soon propelled in the right direction, headed back to shore.

"I envy those cows," said Morris. "What a peaceful life. Nothing to do but look pretty and eat grass. No one to disturb them at all."

"Wouldn't you miss all your friends if you lived like them?" Sheila asked.

"Wouldn't you miss the picnics?" Martha asked.

"Okay, I have to say we have a very nice life," Morris admitted. "I guess it's just that the grass is always greener on the remote island."

When they got to Morris's dock there was a friend waiting there for him. It was Mr. Heron. As was his usual habit, he was standing on one foot, gazing into the water.

"Ahoy Mr. Heron," the three friends called.

"Ahoy."

Morris said quietly, "You see what I mean? I never get a moment's peace. Always someone visiting."

"Ahh, you know you like it. Get out you old grump," Sheila said. "Look, he's caught you a nice fish."

And so he had, but Mr. Heron quickly swallowed it down before he could share it with Morris. Morris gave them a look that said, "I told you so!" and jumped onto his dock.

Martha and Sheila said goodbye to Morris. Sheila climbed to the top of the mast and shouted gleefully into the breeze, "Let's go." Sheila loved the thrill of danger. "Let her rip!" Martha steered out to the deeps and the sails filled with wind. The spray flew around them and they laughed with delight.

"I'd like to climb to the top of a mast," Jiddu said.

"Mummy Maureen says we're going to get a sailboat when we move to Toronto," Gita said. "Will you come with us Clare?"

I was too sad to answer.

"That's enough for today. Let's go downstairs and see if Mrs. Nelthorpe is making anything interesting we could help her with."

Madeleine called that day and invited me to her place for supper on Wednesday.

"It won't be much, whatever I can whip up after a day of teaching."

"That's exactly what I need. I'll see you Wednesday."

***

I found it strange to enter the lobby of the apartment building where I had spent so much of my life, and to knock on Madeleine's door. The building had a particular smell that I remembered well, a combination of cigarette smoke and laundry detergent.

"Come on in. It's not locked."

Madeleine was peeling carrots in her kitchen overlooking the river. She hung yellow curtains to match the counters, table top and chairs. The sight of the white ceramic sink like the one I had so lovingly cared for in our old apartment brought a fleeting sense of loss.

Madeleine set out pork chops, mashed potatoes and carrots, and sat down across from me. She poured ice water from a pitcher.

"Tell me how you've been," she said.

"I just came back from a weekend with Patrick at the Lord Elgin in Ottawa."

"That is amazing news. And...?"

"There really isn't an and. We had a wonderful time. It's still early days. I don't want to move too fast."

"Spending a weekend in Ottawa sounds fast to me."

I told her the details of my weekend and then moved on to my present dilemma.

"I'm going to be out of a job soon."

"How's that?"

"Maureen and Harry are moving to Toronto."

"I know you've been happy there since Maureen came along, but you knew you'd have to move on sometime."

"I knew it, but would have liked more time."

"Now what?"

"The thing I've missed most is being alone, having my own schedule. I'd like to have an apartment, a job and an ordinary life. I want time to think about who I am, what I'd like. Being responsible for children and in the midst of people all the time has its rewards but has also been hard."

"Let me know if there's anything I can do to help."

After dinner she showed me the rest of the apartment. Her bedroom looked over the river and led out to a porch. I thought of how wonderful this would be once the weather warmed up. She had a cozy living room with a stereo and some records she kept in a gold wire stand.

"Here's my newest acquisition. Leonard Cohen."

We sat and listened. His voice was deep and dreamy.

"You've made this apartment really lovely," I said. "I was afraid I'd come in and feel sad, but your place is entirely you, not full of ghosts from my past."

"I feel so lucky. I've got family and friends close by, a good job, and best of all, I can come to this wonderful apartment, close the door and be completely free. I don't even bring work home. I make sure I get everything done at school."

"You're not lonely?"

"No. I'm happy with my own company. Do you think that's selfish?"

"It's something to aspire to."

I noticed she had a few jazz recordings. "What are these?" I asked.

"My jazz collection. I'm starting to really love it. I'm going to New York in April with the Grade One teacher to see Bobby Short at the Café Carlyle. You're welcome to come along."

"New York!" I said, "Count me in." I needed a treat.

"We're taking the overnight train from Montreal. It will be great to have you along."

Cheered by my evening with Madeleine, I drove home singing show tunes.

***

Gita continued to learn at an incredible pace. Jiddu was not as likely to sit through the lessons as he did in the first few months. Now he preferred to be active, but he was still going to be far ahead of any of the other children when he started school in September.

Now that Maureen knew she wasn't going to stay at the farm, there was less to do. She didn't see any point in planting or in continuing with the animals. She sold off the animals except the chickens, which continued to provide us with eggs every morning. She didn't show her pregnancy yet, but she seemed different. She moved as if she were in a separate universe, a protective bubble. She told me that this was how she always felt when she was pregnant, as if nothing could touch her.

Maureen asked me about my plans and I told her I was hoping to find an apartment and a job in Lawrenceville. She said I was free to move on as soon as something came along.

Our late night discussions ended. Maureen was in bed early each night.

Adrian moved out at the beginning of April, off to join the community in Copper River, and get a job in construction. They had a huge acreage and he was planning to build a cabin on it.

"Are you going to live with Viviana?"

"She's gone back to her family."

I was glad to hear that. I hoped it would work out, and that she wouldn't leave her kids again.

"I can live in a trailer while I'm building my cabin. I'd like you to visit."

"I hope we always stay friends," I said.

"We will. There will always be shared books, and I'll keep on coming to the Save the River meetings."

"Knowing you'll still be around helps."

Before he left we had one more great literary conversation, about Dostoevsky's *The Idiot*. Adrian found Prince Myshkin infuriating while I found him exhilarating and beautiful.

"What good did he do? He's a saint. So what? Everything was chaos around him. He wasn't helping anyone with his saintliness."

"The story makes no sense if you don't believe in the resurrection," I said. "Only a mystic, or someone who can at least accept the consciousness of a mystic, can appreciate the prince. Otherwise you only see the darkness. I'd love to live in a world where everyone goes around having incredible, intense conversations like they have in *The Idiot*."

"You and I belong in a Dostoevsky novel," I said and suddenly it hit me. We were moving on. Our time together was done. I turned away to hide my sadness. My throat was closing with the longing to cry, knowing how much I was losing.

***

Mrs. Bergeron called a few days later to tell me about a job in the Miss Lawrenceville Restaurant.

"I mentioned you were looking for work. They said you should come by and talk to them. With tips, it pays well."

I thanked her. Before I knew it, I was hired. They asked me to start in May. Maureen said I could take the truck to work until I figured out where I would live. She was making it easy for me and even suggested I could stay with them in Toronto and help with the new baby, but I felt this would be a dangerous path to take. I loved Lawrenceville and didn't want to lose my ties to it. I also didn't think it was good to continue living in the same house with Harry. He hadn't tried anything lately, but he still paid too much attention to me, and tended to get a little too close.

Gita and Jiddu clung to me. They had changed so much in one year; it was hard to believe how much bigger and more knowledgeable they were. They had almost been babies when I first looked after them.

I found an apartment on the top floor of a big, stone house near Sacred Heart Church. It had been an attic but had been converted by adding a bathroom and a small kitchen. The ceiling sloped, as to be expected in an attic and reminded me of a Paris artist's garret. The house belonged to an elderly woman, Kate Murphy, who had lived there for her entire life with her family but was now the only one of her family left.

The apartment wasn't available until June. I spent May learning my new job and driving back and forth from Buttercup Acres. I had a regular day shift from 7 until 3. Gita and Jiddu were waiting for my return every day, wanting to know what it was like to be a waitress.

As the date approached for my move, I was sad to think of leaving them. I continued to tell them the story of Martha, Morris and Sheila. They wanted to make sure they heard it to the end. We sat together on the front porch swing.

The three friends spent countless hours sailing through the summer and had many adventures. They were all freckled and tanned and ruddily windblown after four months of sunshine and spray. Even Morris had become a seasoned sailor. He hardly ever complained now. Early in October, Martha and Sheila came to Morris's dock.

He came out holding a mop. "I can't go with you. My basement is flooded," he said. "I'm going to be mopping all day."

"We'll help." Sheila jumped off the mast and started to tie up the sailboat. "This will be our last sailing day. We don't want you to miss it."

The sun was shining brightly on the water. The previous days of rain seemed far away, but Sheila was right as usual. The days for sailing had come to an end. The darkness was growing each day and the mornings could be frosty.

Martha grabbed her swabbing mop and a pail of rags and they went inside to help. Morris's basement was soon put to rights. Sheila suggested that Morris should move higher. "This was just the beginning. We don't want to find you floating in your bed."

"I'd better move soon," Morris admitted sadly. He was attached to his cozy spot and had everything just the way he liked it.

Martha was prepared with a picnic and they set off for a few hours of fun. They sailed around the island where they had met the cows but there was no one there.

"The cows must have gone back to the farm for the winter," Sheila said.

They all agreed that was the most likely thing.

Martha dropped them off at their houses and said she was putting the boat to bed until the next warm season.

"Goodbye little sailboat," Morris and Sheila said. "We've had a wonderful summer.

"No tears now," Martha said. "We'll have a lovely winter of naps and coziness. We'll be back out on the water before we know it."

"Will they still see each other?" Gita wanted to know.

"Oh yes, they'll get together whenever they have a bright sunny day and the snow's not too deep. They'll sit by the fireside and talk about their adventures."

"They will have a good sleep." Jiddu said. "Adrian told me that some animals sleep all winter."

"Morris will still be out in the snow, but Martha and Sheila will hibernate," I said.

"Morris will look beautiful in the snow," Gita said.

***

In June I moved to my new apartment. Harry, Maureen and the children helped me carry my things and get settled in. There wasn't much to it. Within a few hours we were finished. I made tea and we sat in the filtered light of the afternoon at my kitchen table. Maureen was now almost completely in her own world, dreamy and elusive. Gita and Jiddu were even more attached to me because of their mother's state. Harry's attachment had grown too, but I refused to pay attention to that. Gita wanted assurance that I would visit in Toronto.

"Don't worry. I'll come and stay with your grandparents. We'll all go sailing. It will be just like Martha and Morris and Sheila's adventures on the river, only we'll be on Lake Ontario."

The first night in my own apartment was bittersweet. I finally had the solitude I craved, but I missed the world I had come to know. I feared life was always going to be like this; moving on, living with loss, finding new loves. I was determined to find out what I needed to be faithful to. I was willing to accept change, but not annihilation.

An Apartment of My Own

When I awoke I wondered for a moment where I was. Sunlight peeped through a small gap in the curtains. Toasty was on the pink satin slipper chair, along with the clothes I'd worn yesterday. It wasn't like me to leave anything out of place, but the previous night I was so tired I went to bed while it was still light, and fell into a deep, dreamless sleep, worn out from all the emotional goodbyes.

There had been so many changes over the past year that I was hoping to come to an unchanging period, long enough to get oriented to where and who I was. I got out of bed, put on flip flops and found my way to the bathroom, thinking "Finally, solitude!"

It was a small bathroom, with white walls, white floor tiles, and an iron tub on claw feet. I was happy to see there was a shower in the tub with a curtain on a ring. A window looked over a side yard full of ferns, lily of the valley, and lilac bushes on their last blooms. I could also see the moss-roofed garage belonging to Kate.

I filled the aluminum percolator with water, spooned some coffee into the basket, and set it on the stove. Sophie came over to wind around my legs, reminding me it was time to feed her. I was the only one at the farm willing to keep Sophie and I was happy to have her. Sophie was not only great at keeping away mice, she was also affectionate, a rare quality in a cat. "Remind me to get you a brush," I said. Sophie had been beautifully groomed by Mrs. Nelthorpe and I hoped to continue to take good care of her. She was a long-haired tabby and needed a lot of brushing.

I thought about how perfect it would be to sit and have a cigarette right at that moment. I'd quit smoking on New Year's Day and was not going to start again.

The clock on the stove said 7:30. I turned on the radio on the kitchen table and tuned it to the Williamsville AM station. The Sunday morning Scottish show was on; lilting music redolent of the heathery hills of

Scotland, or that's how it was described by the announcer. I didn't need to hear the weather. The sun was shining and I knew it would be a fine day.

As it was Sunday, I was going to breakfast at the Bergeron's after the 10 o'clock Mass. Isabel and all her family would be there for the usual hearty breakfast and endless coffee. We would sit for an hour or two, reviewing the week past and the week to come, deciding what to do with our afternoon. It wasn't hard for Mrs. Bergeron to decide, she always cooked a great Sunday dinner, which took up a good part of her day. Mr. Bergeron also knew what to do; go to the garage to tinker. He had a workbench and tools and was always finding something to fix.

Isabel and I decided to ride our bikes to the hills north of town. When we got to the tracks we heard the train whistle in the distance and got off our bikes to wait for the train's approach. It came thundering by, whistling and clacking, setting our hearts beating faster to its rhythm. When it had passed Isabel said "So exciting." We paused for a brief moment then jumped back on our bicycles.

Within a half hour we reached the sand hills where we leaned our bikes on the split rail fence and climbed over to begin our trek. I carried apples in my satchel and had the Leica around my neck on a colourful strap. When I moved out of Buttercup Acres I offered to give the camera back to Patrick, but he insisted I keep it. He said he enjoyed the photos I'd taken for the past year. I suspected he felt it kept me connected to him, as if it were an engagement ring.

We chatted as we walked along. Isabel was worried about what she was going to do next with her life.

"I only have a month of college left and I'm in the same position as last year at this time; looking for work, and uncertain of what I want. I should have thought this through before I started."

"Don't you want to work in a daycare?"

"It was fun learning about it, and I could probably do it for a few hours a day, but a full eight hours a day, week after week. No thanks!"

"I know what you mean. Childcare is hard," I said.

"In some ways it's harder than working in the factory but I don't want to do that either. I'm completely at a loss."

"Waitressing isn't so bad, and it's paying the bills. It's always busy, which I like. I'm getting to know the customers. Mostly they're friendly and polite. When it's over at three, I'm free. You could do worse."

"I know you'll hate this Clare, but I'm thinking about moving to Toronto."

"I do hate it. Why Toronto, of all places?"

"I've run out of possibilities in Lawrenceville."

I was saddened. "Do you mean work or romance?"

"I admit I mean romance. In my deepest self, I feel my real life and work is to be a wife and mother. I don't care about work, except to hold things together until I get married. Do you think that's dumb?"

"Oh Isabel, I would never think that! That's what we learned, even if it wasn't explicit, but I'm afraid that hope is an illusion. You need to be prepared for the possibility that you will work for your whole life, even if you do marry and have children."

"I've been afraid to tell you. I've already made plans. I'm going to share an apartment in Scarborough with two girls from the course. I'm leaving at the end of this month."

"I'll miss you," I said, "but I'll see you when I visit Patrick in Toronto and you'll come home for visits. It's not that far away." I thought sadly of how the pool would open in July and how much I would miss swimming with Isabel.

Just when I hoped life would stop its constant change. I was learning this was an impossible request.

We walked as far as the stream and sat down. We took off our sneakers and put our feet in the cool water. Small fish came and bumped against our ankles. The sun was hot. Despite sadness at the prospect of Isabel's move, I felt excited by the promise of summer to come.

Kate

When Isabel told me she was moving to Toronto I thought of Marian and Ainsley, characters in Margaret Atwood's novel *The Edible Woman* depicting a Toronto full of desperate single women looking for husbands and working at pathetic jobs. I wouldn't dare mention it to Isabel, but I hoped her life there wouldn't be as depressing as that.

When I got home, Kate was sitting on the porch and she invited me to join her for tea. After walking and biking all afternoon, I was happy to accept. She brought out a tray with a beautiful orange china tea set, with white and black bands and an orange flower.

"I love this tea set. Does it have a story?" I asked.

"It was my mother's. The pattern is Richelieu. She kept it for good but I use it every day."

I told her about the Countryside set we used at Buttercup Acres and how I missed it.

"That's Wedgewood too. I have some old pieces of Countryside left over from our family's set. I'll send them up to you."

"I would love that."

"I wish I could offer you cake, but I'm not up to baking anymore." Kate held up her hands to show how arthritic her fingers had become.

"I don't have enough equipment to bake," I said, "but if you'd like I could do some baking for both of us in your kitchen. I'm a beginner, but I could manage a tea cake."

"I'd love that. I'll get out my favourite recipe for Madeira cake. I can coach you."

After tea I went up to my apartment. Sophie was sitting on the kitchen window sill, watching for birds. The air was still and silent. At the moment my apartment was Spartan, but I liked that. It had one large window, which was in the living room and faced north, and small windows on the other three sides. At this time of year there was plenty of light and even in winter, when the trees were bare, it would still be bright.

The living room had a love seat, excellent for reading, upholstered in soft maroon velvet in a fern pattern. There was a lamp on a table beside the couch, and a matching upholstered armchair. The wood floor was painted creamy white. I planned to get a plush rug for the living room, and a sheepskin for my bedroom, so I didn't step out onto a cold floor.

I decided to organize my bedroom. I hung my skirts, blouses and dresses in the wooden armoire, placing the rest of my clothes, neatly folded, in a blue chest of drawers. There was plenty of room for my few things. The room had a single bed with a white painted metal frame. On this I placed a quilt that Maureen gave me. She called it the Primrose quilt and said it had been made by her great aunt. It was white with a pattern of pink flowers, green stems, and yellow stamens. Soft and pleasant to lie under, it carried a faint scent of cedar.

I felt the need of a desk and a bookcase, but decided I could write at the round pine table in the kitchen. It would be better not to get cluttered. A bookcase though, was essential. I suspected Kate had one she could lend me. There were generations of Murphy family possessions stuffed into unused bedrooms.

Kate's father had been the town doctor for sixty-five years, until his death at the age of ninety. His surgery at the back of the house was still intact, with a skeleton, rows of pills in glass bottles and an ancient scale. I spied all this through a dusty window when I was parking my bike behind the house. Kate was the only one of the ten Murphy children left.

Mrs. Nelthorpe sent a box of groceries to carry me over until I got settled. She provided me with the makings of an omelette and salad, as well as coffee, bread, milk and cereal. She was so thoughtful. I had taken her for granted when we were all together at Buttercup Acres and now I realized how much I had come to count on her. She was going back into retirement, returning to live with her sister in Copper River.

I decided to try out my new table by writing a letter to Patrick. I got out the Waterman pen he gave me and sat, looking around at the simple kitchen, thinking of what I wanted to tell him. He had written to say he was going to work for his father for the summer, while he tried to decide what to pursue in the fall. *I'm a scholar, or maybe I just like being a student. I could happily go on studying classics and medievalism and more theology. But what for? Is it enough to do it for enjoyment?*

I found Patrick's scholarly interests wonderful, maybe the thing I loved most about him. I didn't see why he couldn't keep on studying until he had a PhD, then spend his life at the university teaching and writing.

I wrote, *Darling Patrick, I'm not sure why it is such a problem. Why don't you keep on doing what you love? I have been reading Barbara Pym novels and discovering the world of academics in England. They all seem to spend their lives researching arcane subjects and getting together at conferences to discuss these things. It's a perfectly legitimate way to live.* I went on to describe my apartment and new landlady and how I had taken Sophie to live with me. I sealed it and decided to walk to the post office before dinner, as it was only a skip and a hop away. How good it was to be back in town! I felt completely happy.

Miss Lawrenceville

The next morning I was up at six. I perked some coffee, ate some toast, fed Sophie, and put on my uniform for work. I loved having a uniform. It simplified my day. It was pale pink and had a tiny white apron. I wore it with white sneakers. These were the best shoes for spending the day on my feet and on the run. I was getting familiar with the routines at work and it was easier every day. The owner, Mr. Smith, was the cook. His wife also worked in the restaurant, mostly sitting at a high stool by the cash register, as her legs were sore and she had a hard time standing.

I liked that there was always something to do. As soon as I arrived at seven, there were customers waiting. Most of them I had seen before and knew exactly what they wanted. Mr. Smith had several pots of coffee ready on the Bunn heaters. I started by filling cups. Tea drinkers were rare in Lawrenceville. From seven until nine it was a steady stream of bacon, eggs, and toast, with the occasional orange juice. As soon as it got quiet, I started filling salt and pepper shakers, putting sugar cubes and creamers in bowls, emptying ash trays, and cleaning the booths. For the rest of the morning there was a trickle of customers coming for coffee and conversation.

Lunch was challenging. The menu was more varied, but I soon grew comfortable with that. The most popular items were hamburgers and fries, or soup and a sandwich. It was three o'clock before I knew it. Mr. Smith was very fair and insisted I leave on the dot.

I stopped at the post office every day after work to check for mail. It was wonderful to have my very own box. Would the excitement of finding a letter ever wear off?

On Friday I was in an exuberant mood as I headed home from work. My first weekend on my own beckoned invitingly. At the post office I found a slip in my mailbox telling me I had a package waiting. I retrieved my package at the counter and saw that it was from Patrick. I hurried home. Inside was an aluminum coffee pot in three pieces; a reservoir at the bottom for water; a basket in the middle for the coffee, and a top piece with a handle and lid that said STELLA ESPRESSO. On the bottom was stamped ALLUMINIO PURO 99.5%. It had a copper ring in the middle. Every part of it was beautiful, but I had no idea what it was. Patrick included a letter explaining that it was an Italian moka pot to make espresso with. He bought it when he travelled with his family to Italy in 1968. He promised to take me to Toronto's Little Italy when I came for his graduation and buy me some Italian espresso grind.

I accepted Madeleine's invitation to join her and her friend Marty for their regular Friday night trip across the bridge to Nilsonburg on the American side of the river, to have pizza and draft beer in one of the town's many taverns. I knew Marty from our weekend in New York City. She was the driver on these outings.

I had a few hours before we were scheduled to meet so I filled the bathtub and relaxed, reading my new Doris Lessing novel. It was called *Martha Quest*, the first novel in a series of five. This would keep me busy for quite some time. Adrian was also reading the series. We had promised to continue to share books and ideas, even if we didn't see each other often.

The evening with Madeleine and Marty was enormous fun. Marty had some quirky religious fixations. She had us riveted with stories of her over-scrupulous conscience. This led to our own stories of our strange obsessions and misunderstandings arising from the mysteriousness of Catholicism.

We sat at a round table drinking draft beer, talking and laughing, feeling at ease in the midst of the happy chatter and juke box music around us. We ordered pizzas; thin, hot, and perfect with American beer. I was entranced by the revolving Schlitz globe and the variety of neon signs in the window and over the bar. When I got home and climbed the stairs to my apartment I was tipsy from beer and laughter. It was a perfect start to my new life.

Jessup Manor

On Monday night we had our regular Save the River meeting. I was beginning to find the meetings dispiriting. Some of the group were loudly angry at the existence of factories in Lawrenceville, and by extension, disparaging towards those who worked in them. I don't know how they thought people could live without jobs. We needed legislation to clean up their processes, but I didn't want the factories to pack up and move away.

It had been over a year since I'd become involved and I couldn't see that we had accomplished anything. It helped that Dolores was endlessly optimistic. She understood the political process better than anyone else. Her presence made me feel we weren't just wasting time.

Adrian came for the meeting, but said it would be his last. He was working in construction and it left him too tired to drive to Lawrenceville after a day of hard labour. How long could he keep up this pace? He never wanted to be what he called a 'wage slave', sucked dry by the end of the day. He told me he didn't have enough energy to read anything but detective stories. Even meditation was out of the question.

I invited Madeleine for supper on Wednesday. I didn't have great cooking facilities, but I was able to manage a salad and a roasted chicken from the grocery store. As soon as she arrived I could see something was disturbing her.

"Take a look at this."

She handed me a letter. It was an eviction notice from Stoneleigh Developments.

"It says I have to be out by August 31. The building is going to be torn down. I'm not just upset for my loss but for the other tenants. Some have been there for twenty-five or thirty years. It's their home. They love their apartments."

This was devastating news.

"There must be something we can do? We need to find out who owns it and talk to them. I could ask Dolores. She's on the town council. She might have more details."

I hated to think that my old home was going to disappear, and for what? Jessup Manor was in good repair. The town didn't need a new apartment building, nor did it need more stores. There were always several standing vacant on the main street.

Madeleine and I were shocked to discover the building belonged to Father Belfast. After Mass the following Sunday we asked him if we could come over to the rectory to discuss it.

"There's nothing to discuss," he curtly told us. "It's entirely in the hands of Stoneleigh Developments."

"Do you mean they own it now?" I asked.

He wouldn't give me an answer.

Madeleine called Stoneleigh's headquarters in Montreal. She spoke with a receptionist who told her Mr. Stoneleigh would get back to her. It was all we could do for the moment.

***

Patrick's graduation was scheduled for the third Saturday in June. I arranged to take Friday off and caught the morning train to Toronto. Patrick met me at Union Station and took me directly to Little Italy where as promised, he bought me ground coffee for my Stella pot. I found out from the woman in the shop how it worked. We had espresso while we were there but I found it too strong, so Patrick ordered me a cappuccino.

The barista gave me a lesson on how to make Italian coffee. I was full of energy afterwards for the full day Patrick had planned for us.

The graduation took up the entire afternoon. Afterwards there was a lot of picture taking, almost like a wedding reception, with photos of Patrick in cap and gown with his parents, his sister, the children, and of course with me. Then we went to Mr. Anderson's favourite restaurant, a famous steak house. The booth was big enough for the eight of us. There were pictures of celebrities on the wall, taken over the years with the restaurant's owner, and signed lavishly; Love Zsa Zsa, Rock, Elizabeth, Cary, Shirley. All the glamorous stars of the Forties and Fifties had eaten here.

Gita and Jiddu were delighted to see me and they sat close on either side of me in the booth. It had only been a few weeks since I'd seen them, but they already seemed more grown up.

Maureen and I had a few moments on our own in the powder room. She looked beautiful as always, but slightly anxious. She said she missed life at Buttercup Acres.

"I'm stuck with the Lynches for now, until we get a place of our own. My mother wants us to change the kid's names. What should I do?"

It wasn't like Maureen to be indecisive.

"Those names are part of your shared family history. You can't just wipe it out by calling them Suzy and Tommy and pretending it never happened."

"I sort of agree, but I can see my mother's perspective. She says they'll always raise questions with those names."

We didn't have time for a longer discussion, but I hoped that Mrs. Anderson didn't get her way. On the sidewalk in front of the restaurant there were goodbyes and more congratulations to Patrick.

"Why don't we drop the kids off and head to a club? We've barely started to celebrate," Harry said.

Patrick grabbed my hand and said, "Sorry, Clare and I have plans."

After they had all headed off I asked Patrick what our plans were.

"I just wanted to have you to myself. This is a momentous occasion and I don't want to drink my way past it. I want to sit on a park bench, hold your hand and just be in the present. Do you know what I mean?"

"I like your way of celebrating. We've had the speeches and the toasts, now it's time to let it sink in."

"Exactly. This moment will never come again. Starting Monday I'll be working for my father. I know he's always hoped I'd take over the business. I'm going to give it a chance, although I doubt it will be my path."

We sat for a long while watching the crowds of Torontonians enjoying the evening light; walking dogs, throwing Frisbees, dangling their bare feet in the fountain, keeping cool before the hot darkness descended.

Edgar Visits

I was happy to get back to Lawrenceville Sunday evening. The walk home from the train station was a joy. The evening was still light and children were playing Hide and Seek. I could hear their excited calls as they ran to their hiding places behind shrubs, under porches, and in back yards. There were parents out too, sitting on porches and front steps. The summer heat had arrived.

That week Madeleine got a call from Edgar Stoneleigh, architect and owner of Stoneleigh Developments, the company that was planning to tear down Jessup Manor. He said he would be in Lawrenceville and would be happy to talk to her. She asked me to join them.

I hadn't any notion of what to expect, but was surprised when I saw what a handsome man he was, and what elegant manners. He told Madeleine he could see how much she loved her place, and how charming he found it. It was hard not to warm up to him. When we got down to the business of talking about the building, he told us it belonged to Father Belfast, and was entirely the Father's to do with as he pleased.

"The plan is to put in a parking lot and a building with a few storefronts."

It sounded grim.

"I don't understand why anyone would do this when there isn't a need for more stores," I said.

"Development isn't about what a community needs, it's about what the owner can make money with," Edgar said.

This was the sickening truth.

Madeleine and I tried to speak with Father Belfast again. He cut us short. I managed to get a few minutes with Dolores to discuss it, and she told me there wasn't much the town council could do.

"He's not breaking any laws. We may not like it but we can't stop it. The building isn't old enough to be considered historic."

One lesson I learned in this conflict was that parish priests took vows of obedience and celibacy, but not poverty. Father Belfast was free to do whatever he liked with his own money. As it turned out, he had long been a real estate speculator. Mr. Bergeron told me about it.

"You shouldn't judge Father Belfast," he admonished me. "It's not a sin to make money."

"But what about the people who are losing their homes? Doesn't that matter?"

"Don't worry Clare. Madeleine will soon find another place. And she can always come home if she needs to."

Madeleine's perspective was changing too. She and Edgar had gone out for dinner to the Skylane. After this she was under his spell.

"He ordered the most divine Cabernet Sauvignon," she gushed.

"That doesn't mean he's trustworthy. Don't jump into this too fast."

I hated to see Madeleine lose her balance.

I wrote to Patrick and told him about Madeleine's eviction and how we were going to try to prevent the building from being torn down. He wrote back saying it was unlikely we could do anything. *It's just business. The way of the world.* I was disappointed with his response. Those weren't the words of a sensitive theology graduate. After only a few days working for his father he sounded like a businessman.

Madeira Cake

On Thursday after work I fulfilled my promise to bake a Madeira cake. Kate was waiting for me with her recipe card, a bottle of Madeira wine, and an assortment of ingredients and bowls on the counter. She handed me an apron. I got started while she talked of her life and family.

"You may think this strange, but my father, Dr. Murphy, didn't really believe in science. He was a great healer, but he had other methods."

As I levelled off a cup of cake flour, she explained what those methods were.

"Faith, good food, exercise, right living, ... and sugar pills. He was a great believer in sugar pills. That's what he made in his surgery, but he never told anyone what they were. He would hand them out in different sizes, shapes and colours, along with an aspirin. His patients loved him."

"What about when they didn't get better?"

"Hardly ever happened." Kate pointed to the lemon and said, "You need to zest the peel."

"You must have known everyone in town."

"Oh, those were good days. We were well respected. Now the Madeira. Give a full measure."

I buttered and floured the spring form pan and filled it with the batter.

"Father wouldn't have approved of this, you know."

"You mean the cake?

"Yes, he was very strict about diet. No sugar. No white flour. No alcohol. But mother could always get around him. We had lovely tea cakes at least once a week."

We sat on the porch while the cake baked. Kate brought out a photo album which kept us amused until the timer bell rang. I tested the cake with a broom straw. We put it back in for a few minutes as it was slightly wet due to the full measure of Madeira.

I left Kate with the cake cooling on a rack. She said it would take a day or two to develop flavour, so we made plans for tea on Saturday afternoon. She asked me to bring my friends.

A letter arrived from Dorothy telling me how glad she was I had moved on from being a governess. I had to laugh. She told me when she was a child she remembered seeing Kate Murphy in town. *Kate was stylish and beautiful. I envied her. I always wondered why she never married.*

Maybe I would find out. Kate loved to talk about the past. When she was in her early twenties she lived at home and had many boyfriends. She spent several years travelling in Europe between the wars, and then a few years living in Montreal, where she owned a dress store on Saint Catherine Street.

***

Patrick was working full-time at his father's shirt factory. He was given an office and was instructed to shadow Mr. Anderson's second in command. It was a chance for Patrick to learn what went on at the factory and see if he would like to be part of it. Mr. Anderson very much wanted to pass his legacy on to his son. Patrick wrote to say he felt useless, but was persisting. He was spending his free time at the yacht club. They were having great weather for sailing and he was getting his sea legs again. Despite my children's story, I had no experience of sailing, or of yacht clubs. I imagined everyone there would be rich and attractive.

***

On Saturday Madeleine and Marty came for Kate's tea party. It was a hot afternoon with a sultry breeze, perfect for sitting on the porch. I helped Kate serve the tea and slices of Madeira cake. Kate was delighted to have new women to talk to. She told many stories of her life and the early days of Lawrenceville. She spoke of the many men lost in the Great War. I suspected that was why she never married. I discovered she owned several buildings in town.

We told her about Madeleine's apartment, and how it was to be torn down. Kate gave us an insider's picture on what it was like to own property. She said she was often approached to sell her buildings on the main street by developers who wanted to tear them down. She always refused because she knew they were heritage treasures. She was worried about who would protect them when she was gone.

Madeleine reconciled herself to moving. She found an apartment to move into in August. I knew the building; built in the 1960's of white and grey ornamental brick, with wrought iron balconies. I was sure it would be comfortable, but it didn't have the charm of Jessup Manor. It backed onto the railroad tracks and she would have a longer walk to work. She said she might buy a car.

I too was reconciled to the loss of my childhood home, although I still felt sad. I talked to Adrian about it when he came to town for a medical appointment. We met for coffee at Woolworth's lunch counter. We discussed it in a more philosophical sense, talking about what sort of society we wanted, and whether it was worth it to give up some freedoms, such as property rights, in order to have certain social goods, such as housing. It helped me put it into context. I had no desire for a communist state in which Father Belfast wouldn't be allowed to proceed, but I still had a desire for beauty to be preserved. It was a quandary. Adrian said he would happily live in a centrally controlled state in which the collective good was given higher priority.

I was hoping Patrick would come for a weekend visit, but now that he was working he seemed to want to stay in Toronto. I had pictured a summer in which we saw each other every few weekends, and maybe even took a holiday together. It seemed odd that it was now July, with no plans on the horizon.

The pool was open. I carried my bathing suit, towel and bathing cap with me to work every day so I could have a swim before I went home.

Now and then Madeleine joined me, but she was talking a course towards her bachelor's degree and was busy studying and writing papers. She said studying was torture in the heat of summer. I brought a book with me to the pool and read in between swims. It would have been more fun with Isabel or Madeleine, but I still enjoyed it.

Weekend With The Girls

Isabel was now living in an apartment in Toronto and had found a job in the office of a car dealership. She said she filled in forms, made coffee for the salesmen, and filed things. She invited me to visit for a weekend, saying I could sleep on the couch. I decided it would be interesting to see that side of life. One night on a couch would be enough, so I arrived on a Saturday and would return on Sunday.

Her apartment was in an old red brick building in a shabby part of town, but it had a certain charm. It was unbearably hot however, and the only relief was a fan in the window. Her roommates were very cheery, like soldiers in their acceptance of their crowded apartment. They joked about keeping their underwear in the freezer.

Isabel and her roommates went to a tavern every Saturday night, where they listened to loud music, drank a lot of Harvey Wallbangers, then slept late on Sunday. With little choice, I tagged along.

I woke up early Sunday morning with a headache and a longing for my own bed. I made a big pot of coffee. Gradually the girls got up, and sat blearily drinking coffee, smoking, and browsing through the weekend newspaper. This visit didn't inspire me to move to the big city. Isabel walked me to the train station. I asked if she was happy with her decision. She said she felt that at least she was taking control of her life, and she knew she would meet someone, she could feel it in her bones.

On the way home I reflected on what I'd experienced over the weekend. The Toronto I saw when I was with Patrick was nothing like the Toronto Isabel was living in. There was a much bigger divide between the world of the rich and the world of the struggling than was apparent in my small town. As the train headed east I looked back and saw the city covered with a haze of yellow, but ahead all was blue. I was glad to leave it behind.

***

Patrick wrote that week, inviting me to visit. He said if I could get a few days off, he would too. This sounded promising. Had I been worried for nothing? I was soon able to arrange a three day weekend. I travelled to Toronto on a Friday and Patrick met me at the station. As usual, he had many plans.

He wanted to introduce me to the yacht club. Mrs. Anderson told me there was a dress code, and asked if I had packed good Bermuda shorts, a sleeveless cotton blouse and a light cardigan. I hadn't. My summer wardrobe was denim shorts with a t-shirt or a short sleeved red checked shirt, although I did bring a mini dress and ballet flats to match, in case we went out to dinner.

Mrs. Anderson lent me the appropriate outfit. It wasn't my size, but I made do. I shuddered to look in the mirror as it made me look so matronly. Mrs. Anderson seemed cooler than usual but Mr. Anderson was still jovial and kind. He was especially happy because he had Patrick working with him.

Patrick seemed slightly off balance when we got to the yacht club. Too bright. Too cheery. He took me into the lounge and looked around. Spying some young men at a table, he took me over and made introductions. He said he'd need a few minutes to make some arrangements, and left me with them. They were all tanned and fit, with perfect white teeth. They chatted about sailboats and waves and winds. I grew restless and wondered how long it had been since I'd seen Patrick.

I decided to take a look around. I went out the glass door to the docks and saw Patrick standing with a beautiful young woman who seemed to be hanging on to him. She was tall and blonde, like Mrs. Anderson. She was wearing tight cut-off shorts; so much for the dress code!

I got closer and heard her say, "Well why didn't you tell her already?"

Patrick saw me then. As soon as he looked from her to me, I knew he was in some sort of relationship with this woman. There was no mistaking this picture. I turned and ran, caught a taxi back to the Andersons, returned her suitable clothes and took the next train home.

I was in shock. I couldn't tell if I was heart-broken or angry. My mind was a tempest. How would Patrick explain my flight to his family? What if I had been mistaken about what I had seen? Had I acted too quickly? No. I knew in my heart something was going on.

I told Kate I came home early because I didn't feel well and wanted to be in my own place. I went upstairs to hide away. I took out the Leica and stared at it. Would I have to mail it to Patrick? I became obsessed with how I would return it. Wasn't it too valuable to put in the mail? And what about Gita and Jiddu? When would I ever see them again? I couldn't read or eat or settle at anything. I went to bed and watched the sun's rays fade. Eventually I slept.

Since I was supposed to be in Toronto I had no plans for the weekend. I walked downtown in the morning and sat at Woolworth's lunch counter, lingering over coffee, my mind a jumble of conflicts. I walked out into the bright sun. The glaring reflections in store windows felt painful. My eyes hurt. My head ached. Maybe I was sick. As I passed the meat market I ran into Mrs. Bergeron.

"Weren't you going to Toronto for the weekend?" she asked.

Then she noticed how terrible I looked.

"Oh goodness, you're not well. I'll drive you home."

She parked in the shade of a large maple in front of my place.

"Now, tell me what happened."

I told her my sad story and she said, "There's got to be more to it. Everything you've told me about Patrick doesn't add up to this behaviour." I hoped she was right.

On Saturday night I sat at my table, feeling miserable and wondering if there was anything I could do to take my mind off my sadness. I decided to write a letter to Father Belfast. I might not change his mind, but I could at least tell him how I felt.

Dear Father Belfast, I would like to have a chance to tell you how I feel about Jessup Manor and also, by extension, how I feel about our town. I grew up in Jessup Manor, first with my parents, then, when my mother left, with my father. It was a wonderful home but I was forced to leave when my father died last year.

On top of losing him, I felt the loss of our home very deeply. It's not just real estate. That building is the sort of place people can grow to love. It has a wonderful balcony at the back that gives a view of the river and provides cooling breezes in summer. It was built with kitchens one can eat in; kitchens for real families who sit down together for meals.

The fixtures, the many touches of beauty, the wood floors, the windows, the solid walls which make it so soundproof – these were built to last for a hundred years. Probably more than a hundred years. There was love and care put into this building. It may not be made of stone or so old that you would raise the ire of historians, but it is a treasure if only you could see it.

I worry about the loss of Lawrenceville's downtown. I have seen it decline over the years, yet I still love it and have hopes for its recovery. But how can it recover if the beautiful historic stores on the main street empty and we put up flimsy new stores and strip malls? I'm not an economist. I don't know how it is that things that are unnecessary and ugly can be profitable. All I know is it's important to save what I love.

Respectfully,
Clare Kelly

By the end of the letter I was overcome with grief. I felt the loss of everything at once; my father, Patrick, the children, the wonderful times we'd had at Buttercup Acres, the hopes and dreams of a farm. All the grieving I had pent up over the course of my life hit. I was sunk for a night and a day.

On Sunday evening I realized I'd have to work in the morning so I had a shower, set out my uniform and went to bed. Monday I arrived on time at the restaurant, although I knew I looked haggard. Mrs. Smith was very concerned. I told her I had a summer bug but I was sure it wasn't contagious. I made it through the breakfast crowd, then when it was slowing down, I dropped a mug of coffee on the terrazzo floor. I heard it smash and was in tears again. Mrs. Smith led me to the kitchen.

"It's all right; you'll be okay, just sit quietly."

She held my hand. Her sympathy left me more aware of my pain.

Finally, I went to wash my face and came back saying, "I'll be fine now. I can make it through the day." I didn't want to go home. I knew it wouldn't be good to go to my apartment and brood. "Really, I'll be fine."

I made it through the day and knew that I would make it through the week. When all else fails, there's always routine.

When I got home I saw the letter I'd written to Father Belfast. I threw it in the garbage. I went to the liquor store to ask for a box. I needed one to mail the Leica. When I came in with the box, Kate stopped me and said,

"Can I do anything to help?" I realized I was surrounded by kindness. It was good to be in a world where people noticed and cared.

"Thank you for offering. I'm going to be fine. I just need some time. It looks like Patrick and I are through. It was a rough weekend."

"Come and have a nice cup of tea. We'll talk about whatever you want."

We sat in Kate's kitchen at the table. I told her about the yacht club and found that I was feeling extremely angry about the clothes.

"Imagine Mrs. Anderson telling me what to wear!"

Kate laughed and said, "The world has lots of Mrs. Andersons. It's good to steer clear of them. I always made my own rules. If people didn't like it I'd find others who did. How about a tiny glass of sherry with our tea? It's just the ticket at a time like this."

Kate was full of colourful stories. She had lived in Toronto in the days before the Gardner Expressway and the towering buildings. It sounded like a decent place then. She told me about men she had loved, particularly a man she met in her mid-thirties.

"He was the one for me. He had sparkling eyes and curly hair and made me feel like a million dollars."

"What happened?"

"Nothing. He was already married. I wouldn't ever go down that road."

Being with Kate helped me to get perspective. She had been through a life of joys and losses, and at eighty-two was still strong and joyful.

"I have a strong belief in Providence," I said. "If Patrick is meant for me, we'll be together. If not, I can let him go. I even believe that my old apartment building is in the hands of Providence."

"Maybe so, but you still need to take action. Providence needs us to do our part."

I went upstairs and thought about Kate's words. I retrieved the letter from the wastebasket, smoothed it out, and mailed it.

I went to my Save the River meeting that night, glad I had something to keep my mind occupied. This cause was bigger than me, and I was happy to focus on it. We were planning a campaign to lobby Members of Parliament about pollution standards.

I went back to my routines; books, swims after work, and comforting strolls through the aisles in Woolworth's, but my heart was heavy. Madeleine and Marty invited me along on the Friday trip to the tavern but I didn't feel I could be a good companion.

"I'll come next week. I need a little time."

At home after work on Friday, I thought of how I needed a project or a new interest, something to pull me out of my sadness. I sat at the table with the boxed up Leica in front of me, wondering if I should include a letter. I was at a loss for words.

Kate called up to me, "You have a visitor."

I heard footsteps and Patrick appeared at the top of the stairs. "May I come in?"

He looked ravaged and immediately said, "Can you ever forgive me?" He reached out and I went to his arms. "I should have come sooner, but Maureen had her baby on Friday, the day you left, and the week was chaos. I know I have a lot to explain."

We moved to the living room and sat side by side on the couch.

"What is going on? Are you going out with that blonde woman?"

Patrick proceeded to tell the whole story of his mother's campaign to take over his life.

"The pressure was intense. Linda, who you saw on the dock, is the daughter of my mother's best friend. Both mothers had long planned to bring us together. Linda's family are part of my parent's social circle; you know what I mean?"

I nodded.

"It felt as if the time I spent with you, and the whole world of Buttercup Acres, was some kind of illusion. Like a dream that was over. I suddenly saw myself going off day after day to run the factory, having cocktails with people from my parent's world, sailing in the summer, going to Florida in the winter. It was rolling out in front of me. I had no choice. Linda is a steam roller. It sounds like I'm saying I'm not responsible; I know I'm responsible, but I honestly felt I was being led to my fate. I couldn't escape. When we went to the yacht club and I saw you in that setting, I felt I was in the midst of a nightmare. Even you weren't you anymore. When I looked at you I saw my mother. What the hell were you wearing?"

"That's a sad story too."

"You were right to run away. You could see through the falseness. How could I subject you to that world?"

Patrick was finding it hard to speak. I got up to get us water.

I returned and said, "I knew when we were in Ottawa that I loved you and I believed you loved me."

"Loving you is the truth. I've spent the last week trying to get my thoughts straight. Trying to get out of the spell that was being cast around me. Can you forgive me? Can we move on?"

"I want that more than anything." I felt we had to get everything out in the open. "Patrick, I have to know I can trust you. I can't live with unfaithfulness."

"I never cared for Linda. You were on my mind the whole time."

"It was so painful, seeing her act like she owned you."

"I'd been sailing and partying with her, and I admit I hadn't told her about my relationship with you, but I promise you, I will never behave like that again."

I took a leap of faith. "I believe you. I'm ready to move past this."

"I see my life more clearly now. I want us to be together forever." Patrick knelt in front of me. "Will you marry me?"

I needed a few deep breaths before I could answer.

"I will."

"I want to suggest something totally mad. I've been thinking it through all week, and talking to Dad about it. I'm completely serious."

"What is it?"

"I want to make Buttercup Acres a Tourist Home. A farm vacation sort of thing. We'll get married and move back in. We can get the gardens going, get some more chickens, maybe some cows...."

"Oh Patrick, that would be a dream come true."

We were laughing and crying now. I felt I had gone from despair to perfect joy and hope within the span of a few minutes.

"What about Maureen? Did she have a boy or a girl?"

"Both. She has twins."

Happiness

The next day we were worn out. We wandered around town in a dream and found ourselves at Woolworth's lunch counter.

"Do you remember the day we met here?"

"Yes, you had on a green dress. I thought you were sweet."

I sat silently, thinking about all that had happened since we'd met, and how I was always in a quandary about what sort of life Patrick and I would have. I could never see myself living in Rosedale, going to cocktail parties and giving dinner parties for wealthy couples.

As I was pondering this Patrick said, "I could never imagine a life for us in Toronto. I knew I wanted to marry you, but couldn't see how we'd live. As soon as I had the farm vacation idea I felt it all come together."

There was a lot to plan and discuss, but we said very little that day. Patrick had Maureen's pickup truck, so we drove up River Road to Buttercup Acres. It had a deserted air but I knew we would soon bring it back to life. We sat on the porch and watched the ocean liners going up and down the river.

***

On Sunday Patrick came with me to Mass and then to breakfast at the Bergeron's. We told them of our engagement and basked in their warm congratulations. Mrs. Bergeron took me aside and said she was thanking God for this turn of events.

"I was so worried about you last week that I made a special Novena."

Peter shook Patrick's hand and said, "So, you're the lucky guy. I wondered who could possibly catch Clare."

After breakfast, Patrick got ready to drive back to Toronto. He wanted to give the news to his father and mother.

"It won't be a big surprise. My father knows how I feel already, and my mother could see her plans for me were falling apart."

"Will you go back to work for your father?"

"No, I was just filling time at the factory. I'm not suited to it and my father knows it. We had a good heart-to-heart talk this week. I'm going to pack up and move here. I want to get started on our new life."

When I went back to work on Monday morning I felt like a new person. Mrs. Smith noticed immediately.

"Looks like you're feeling a lot better. I've never seen you so happy."

I told them the news of my engagement. They were happy for me, but hoped I wouldn't be leaving right away. I said I would give them plenty of notice. Now that we were engaged, I wanted to enjoy this time of my life, and not rush through it.

I phoned Isabel that night. She told me she was planning to come to Lawrenceville for the weekend. She needed to get out of Toronto as it had been unbearably hot in her apartment. Lawrenceville would be heaven to her after a few months in Toronto. We made plans to celebrate by going to The Regent on Saturday night. I told her I'd let Madeleine know, and would see if Peter and some of our other friends would like to come along.

The next day, Joe came in to the restaurant for lunch. He asked if I would have time after work to talk. It had been a year since I'd seen him. We agreed to meet later at Woolworth's lunch counter. Joe and I arrived together and found seats at the counter. He was looking deeply tanned and strong.

"You must be working outdoors," I said.

"I've got a construction job for the summer. It's hard work, but it's good for me after so much time studying and sitting all through the school year. You look great, Clare. Life must be treating you well."

I told him about my engagement.

"I want to ask you about Isabel. I know I was a cad, but do you think she would ever be willing to go out with me again. I've stopped seeing Jane. Or, rather, she's stopped seeing me. She found someone who fits her family's expectations better. It was rough but I've learned some lessons."

I told Joe about Isabel's move to Toronto, and what I knew of her life there.

"Why don't you come to the Regent on Saturday? See what happens."

"Could you let her know I'm not going out with anyone? Sort of set the stage?"

"I'd be glad to."

Kate asked if I would like to take a picnic to Williamsville that evening to eat in the park. She still drove her old red Studebaker, although she didn't take it out of the garage very often. We stopped for fish and chips and took them to a picnic table looking over the river. It was still light and there was a gentle breeze. She told me more about her father and his interesting beliefs.

"He was always ahead of his time. Now I hear people talking about exercise and not eating sugar, but he knew all that long ago. This generation thinks they've found a new consciousness. Hah. They're far from the level of understanding he had of the mysterious connection between mind and body. He didn't hold with crystals, though. He was no crank. He believed you could control fertility. He said you would only get pregnant if you were ready and wanted a child. That is, if you followed his method."

Kate gave me a burning look.

"Why are you looking at me?" I was blushing.

"You need to know these things. He talked to young brides and gave them excellent advice."

"Did he explain it to you?"

"It's the principle of mind over matter. You tell your body what you want it to do. It's more powerful than pills."

"I would like us to have children, maybe even as many as the Bergeron family, but not yet. I want to wait for a few years."

"Just tell yourself that. Your body will cooperate."

I was fascinated. I'd never heard such advice. I thought it would be great it if was true!

Kate added, "It also works the opposite way. No matter what method of birth control a couple uses, if a baby is truly desired, a baby will soon be on the way."

"It sounds like my belief in Providence."

***

Patrick was back in Lawrenceville by Thursday. He came into the Miss Lawrenceville around 2:45 and sat in a booth. I came over with my tiny order pad, surprised and delighted to see him. He had never seen me in my pink uniform. He whistled.

"You're the cutest waitress I've ever seen. Would you marry me?"

I held up my tiny order pad and pen. "I will, but first I'll take your order."

He had a Coke while he waited for me to finish work.

The orange and white Chevrolet pickup truck was loaded up with Patrick's possessions, ready to take to Buttercup Acres. It was Patrick's truck now.

"Dad's giving me the same chance he gave Maureen. He'll keep us going for a year until we can make a living."

"I'm glad to have the truck back. I had good times with it."

"Do you want to come help me unload my stuff?"

We spent the next few hours getting things organized in the house. I was pleased to see Maureen had left the record player and records. Except for a bit of dust, things were pretty much in order, although we didn't have Mrs. Nelthorpe to take care of us. That would be a big change. She had the knack of bringing order and sanity.

Patrick called from the front porch.

"Let's sit and talk about what comes next. I have all sorts of things on my mind, but first we should decide when to get married."

"I've given it some thought this week. I'd like a November wedding. I'll continue with my job and my place at Kate's for a few months. It will give us a chance to spend time together and talk about all sorts of things, make sure we know what we're doing."

"I'd like to have you here with me now, but your plan sounds good. Why November?"

"It's my favourite time of year, when the trees are bare and the first hint of snow comes. There's an air of excitement. November is full of promise. I'd like to get married at Sacred Heart, with our families and a few friends. Would that suit you?"

"That sounds good. I'd like to have the reception here; it's such a beautiful place. If we don't have too big a crowd we could manage it. It's also good to have it where my mother won't be able to take over."

"How did your mother react when you told her we were getting married?"

"She accepted it. She respects you. I'm not sure how to explain her. She's a good loving mother, even though some of the very things that make her good also make her too controlling. Ultimately, she wants the best for me. Can you understand that?"

"I understand, and I appreciate that she brought you up well. I will always welcome her in our lives, but it may take time to warm up to her."

"I'm starved. Do you realize I've never had to cook for myself or do my own laundry or even make my bed? I'm embarked on a whole new life. It feels exciting."

"I'm glad you see it in that light. I'm starved too. Let's go back to town. I'll make us something at my place."

The next morning as I got ready for work, I wondered how Patrick was faring on his own. I'd never had to go through this, as I had taken care of myself since I was a child. I was looking forward to seeing how he handled all the small details of life.

On Saturday night there was a big crowd celebrating with us at the Regent Hotel. I called Isabel as soon as I thought she'd be home and told her about meeting Joe. I couldn't tell how she felt about it. She was quiet. Maybe she wasn't sure herself. Madeleine came and brought Edgar Stoneleigh and Marty. Peter came with May, who was home for a visit from England. She was studying art at University College London. It had been a long time since I had seen her. She was no longer the boy-crazy girl she was in high school, but she was still flamboyantly attractive. She looked every inch the artist.

May brought presents for me and her sisters; Mary Quant tights in striking colours never seen in our stores. Mine were bright yellow. They would look great with my ballet flats.

To my great surprise Arlene and Bill came too. They almost never went out to bars, and couldn't stay late because the kids were with Mrs. Bergeron.

We all arrived before the band started, which gave us a chance to talk before it became impossible to hear over the music. After we had all been up dancing, Edgar asked me to dance. While we were on the floor he said, "Could we go where it's quiet for a minute? I want to talk to you."

We stood outside in the warm night air, away from the noise and the smoke. Now that I wasn't a smoker, I found the dense smoke in the bar appalling, and was glad to get a breath of fresh air.

"You seem to know Kate Murphy well."

"I'm getting to know her. I have an apartment in her house."

"She seems to be quite a hold-out on development in your town."

"What are you talking about?"

"There's a group of businessmen who want to buy her buildings on the main street and she won't sell. She's unreasonable. She won't even consider it!"

I felt the gulf between my perspective on life and Edgar's. How dare he use this occasion to try to talk to me and influence Kate?

"If I have any power with Kate it will be to encourage her to protect what she loves."

I quickly turned and went inside. How could Madeleine date him? Didn't she see what he was? We should be chasing him out of town with tar and feathers.

Patrick saw me come in and grabbed me for another dance.

"You look great tonight."

He held me close in a slow dance.

"Where were you?"

"I'll tell you all about it later."

While I was outside with Edgar, I missed seeing Joe's approach to Isabel, but now I saw them dancing together. My imagination raced ahead. What if things worked out for them and she moved back home?

The next morning there was a huge crowd at Bergeron's for breakfast. What a lot of work it must be for Mrs. Bergeron! Maybe because I was moving into a life more like hers, I had a new awareness of how hard she worked to take care of us.

I was longing for a heart-to-heart talk with Isabel. After breakfast we made plans to meet at the pool for a swim. The pool was busy with the weekend crowd. We had a quick dip and went to lie on the grass on our towels. Isabel was pale since she didn't spend much time outdoors. Her work days were long and she spent a lot of time travelling on the subway and bus. She had changed her hairstyle. It was now short, and what she called 'frosted'. It didn't suit her. I didn't think it would suit anyone.

"How did you and Joe get along last night?"

"He told me what he told you, that he's on his own and has learned a lesson. The problem is I'm seeing someone in Toronto. He's a salesman at the dealership. It's early days but I don't want to mess it up. Why does Joe's timing have to be so bad?"

"Do you really like this guy?"

"I'm not blown away. He's the right age, he's working, he's good looking. My roommates say I should grab him. He's taken me out almost every night since we met. He sends flowers and even brings chocolates. I came home this weekend to have a break from it all. I feel he's on the verge of wanting a commitment."

"I wish you would move home."

"I can't. I've only been in Toronto two months, even though it feels like forever. I have to confess, I'm afraid I'd get married just to get out of that suffocating apartment. There is something joyless about the life, and yet we are frantically trying to have fun. You've never heard so much laughing!"

I was quiet. I could hear Isabel telling me that she wanted out, but wasn't ready to admit it to herself. It was clear she was in the wrong place. Everything shouted it; the job, the boyfriend, the hairdo. I wasn't particularly fond of the roommates either. They were both desperate, and it was rubbing off on Isabel.

"Let's dive for rocks."

Isabel gave me a funny look and said, "We haven't done that for years. I'm game."

I found a spotted, pinkish rock and we spent the next twenty minutes dropping it in the deep end and challenging each other to be the first to grab it on the bottom of the pool. I felt ten years old again. Isabel whooped with glee whenever she grabbed the rock first. By the time we got out our fingers were puckered and our eyes red from the chlorine. We went back to our towels to drip in the sun.

Isabel lay on her back and stretched her arms over her head with catlike abandon, then staring at the sky said, "I'm coming home."

Edgar

Patrick was settling in to his new life and thinking about all the possibilities open to him.

"I can keep on studying, I can write, I can even paint, which I also love. It's amazing how much there is to do. It's too late for the garden this summer but there are lots of other things to get started on. I'd like to get a new flock of chickens. I'm having fun learning to cook. I'm going to make a special dinner for you next Saturday."

I loved his enthusiasm. He was also getting to know Lawrenceville. He went to the Lawrenceville liquor store in search of Pouilly Fuissé. He didn't find it on the wine list and asked at the counter

"How about some Baby Duck? That's our biggest seller."

Patrick had to make do with a bottle of Blue Nun.

I told him about my conversation with Edgar. Patrick was suspicious of the Jessup Manor project.

"Edgar thinks of this as a place where he can make lots of money, but he doesn't live here and doesn't have the town's best interests at heart."

I was amazed. Only a few weeks ago Patrick had said "it's just business" when I complained about Jessup Manor being torn down for a parking lot and stores. He saw a different side of it now that he was living here.

"Do you think I should talk to Madeleine about it?" I asked.

"That may not be good for your friendship. Madeleine will have to see for herself who he is," Patrick advised.

I also talked to Kate about my conversation with Edgar. I thought she should be aware that there were people plotting to buy her properties.

"As long as I'm of sound mind that's not going to happen. I appreciate you telling me about Edgar. I know his family from Montreal. His mother used to buy clothes from me and we stayed friends after I closed the shop. She visits now and then and always sends me a Christmas card. The last one mentioned Edgar's fiancé. I don't think Edgar knows about my connection to his mother."

"I wasn't going to say anything to Madeleine, but if he's engaged she needs to know."

"I can find out. Maybe he's already married. I'll call her."

Right then and there, Kate picked up the phone and called Mrs. Stoneleigh.

"Betty! It's Kate Murphy. I was just thinking of you. Yes, it's been a while since our last visit. Have you been kept busy with Edgar's wedding? Hmm hmm, hmm hmm. Next weekend. So soon. Well, you must have your hands full. I hope to see you before too long. Me too. Good bye."

Kate hung up the phone. "Edgar's getting married next weekend."

"Now I have to tell Madeleine."

I called Madeleine that night and asked her to walk to the library with me after supper. We walked and chatted. A lot of her conversation was about Edgar this and Edgar that.

"We were planning a trip to New York, but Edgar called to say that he's going to Vancouver for a few weeks on business."

"He's not going to Vancouver on business. Edgar is getting married this weekend."

"That's not funny."

"I'm not joking. Kate knows Edgar's mother and that's how I found out about his engagement."

"I can't... I can't believe it. How could he be such a liar? How could I be so taken in?" Madeleine sat on the bench by the library doors. "I'm stunned."

"I'm sorry. I can't stand to see you hurt."

Madeleine stood up. "I'm going to return my books. Then I'm going to go home, call, and let him know what a cad he is."

Madeleine looked angry. That was good, better than tears.

"Do you want to talk about it? I'm free all evening."

"Thanks Clare, but I need to be alone."

***

Isabel was serious when she said she was moving home. She gave two weeks' notice at the car dealership, packed up her possessions and was back home by the end of August. Letting go of the salesman was easy. As soon as she told him she was moving back to Lawrenceville and breaking off their relationship, he asked if she was okay with him dating one of the roommates. It was a win/win. Joe drove to Toronto to help her move.

***

On Saturday morning Patrick and I went to Williamsville for the farmers market. Afterwards we strolled around the tree lined streets admiring the waterfront mansions and the beautiful old stone homes. We walked further than usual and came to an area with factories and car dealers. We saw a row of empty shops with a 'for rent' sign. It had a shabby, down at heels air. Patrick noticed that the owner was Stoneleigh Developments.

"Could that be our Edgar?"

"That's the sort of building he wants to put up in Lawrenceville. It's an eyesore and obviously not even profitable. Father Belfast should be told."

"I'm glad it's Father Kelly who's marrying us. I wouldn't want to be taking marriage preparation from someone you are at war with."

"It's not war. I respect Father Belfast. He may have good reasons for what he's doing, but it's not too late to point things out to him."

I was sure this would change Father Belfast's mind, but I wondered how I could get him to see it. Luckily, I was carrying the Leica. I took a picture of the shabby building to show how ugly it was.

"Let's head back downtown and see if we can find presents for the twins."

Patrick and I were planning a weekend in Toronto to visit his family. I wanted to bring presents for Gita and Jiddu too, so they wouldn't feel left out.

Patrick bought corn, tomatoes, and lettuce at the market, and napoleons and Hovis bread from the bakery. On the way home we stopped at a farm where he'd heard they sold meat. We pulled into the yard beside the farmhouse and saw the shop.

"This is almost as good as the Kensington Market, except we have to travel a bit to find everything."

I was glad he was resourceful at finding the good things the area had to offer. I wanted him to love Lawrenceville as much as I did.

Patrick planned a special dinner. When we got to Buttercup Acres he told me to relax, he would take care of everything. I went upstairs to my old room on the porch to read. It was wonderful to be looked after. I must have slept, because suddenly I realized the light had turned gold, and I heard him calling from downstairs. When I came down candles were lit and a George Shearing record was playing on the stereo. It was romantic music, perfect for tonight.

"I bought the record this week. You can't believe how many George Shearing LP's I had to choose from."

I had told him about listening to the Shearing Trio at Madeleine's. Patrick was very observant.

Patrick poured two glasses of wine. "Here's to us," he said, holding his glass up in a toast.

"Are you happy here?" I said.

"Happier than I could have imagined. Don't worry; I'm not a city mouse. Even before I knew I wanted to be with you, I loved this place. Don't you remember how I hated to leave?"

"I remember, although last summer seems a long time ago. So much has happened."

"My mother gave me Joy of Cooking when I told her I needed some recipes. I used it for the supper tonight. I hope it's good. I tried to find something that didn't look too demanding, especially with the coal stove to figure out."

"I'm glad I got instructions about that stove from Mrs. Nelthorpe. Who knew I'd ever need to know how to use it?"

Patrick made pan-broiled steak with a sauce of Maitre d'Hotel butter, Franconia potatoes and a tossed salad.

"I'm impressed. You have a talent for cooking." Patrick glowed. "Maybe we can have Isabel and Joe over soon, and you can make it for four."

"Good idea. I'll keep making it until I perfect my technique!"

The potatoes had a crisp, brown crust.

"These are perfect." I loved potatoes in all forms but recognized this as high art. "Crème de la crème."

"When you move in with your beautiful coffee pots, life will be complete."

"I still haven't used the Norwegian coffee pot from my mother. I'm saving it for when we're married. I can picture how smart it will look in this kitchen."

Dinner was a memorable success. Patrick was always amazing me. He only had to have a desire to do something and was able to pull it off with elegance and style.

***

It was great having Isabel back. One afternoon we met at Woolworth's lunch counter after I finished work. She was looking more like herself, although her hair was still 'Toronto'. Thank goodness it would grow out eventually.

"I'm helping Mom paint the kitchen. Then we're going to put new wallpaper in the rest of the downstairs. It's fun. We need to finish the kitchen as fast as possible so life can get back to normal. Right now she's cooking on the camp stove, and we're eating on the picnic table. As long as it doesn't rain we're okay. My mother is a hard worker. I can barely keep up with her."

"Patrick and I will need to do some painting and wall papering and I haven't got a clue. I'm excited about all the new things we'll have to learn."

Isabel spun on the red stool to look at me. "Thank you, Clare."

"What for?"

"You saved my life. It's hard to explain the drugged feeling I had when I saw you a few weeks ago, as if I were under a spell and had lost my power. Somehow being with you, hearing you say I should come home – it made all the difference. I was on the edge of disaster and you made me aware of it. Does that make sense?"

"That's what Patrick went through. He described it as being under a spell. That feeling clearly is a sign that something is wrong. If you experience it again, you'll know you're going in the wrong direction."

"I hope I recognize it if it happens again. If it's a spell, I probably won't."

"True. The problem is that it's unconscious. That's a scary thought."

"We'll watch out for each other. Hopefully we won't both be under a spell at the same time."

"It's a deal!"

After our conversation I pondered what it meant. What happened when we entered a state in which we were pushed in a direction not in our best interest, yet fell into line as if programmed? Whatever it was, I didn't believe it was inevitable. I knew that if one stayed close enough to one's highest principles, it would prevent these lapses. Still, it was all very mysterious and I didn't know anyone who could explain it.

The Shadow World

I had my film developed and my pictures clearly showed the ugliness of the empty stores. Stoneleigh's name was in black letters on the rental sign. I rushed over to the rectory where Father Kelly answered the door.

"What can I help you with Clare?"

"I'm looking for Father Belfast."

"He's out. Is there anything I can do?" Father Kelly always had a warm smile and never seemed to be too busy.

"I wanted to give him these photos. I'll add a note, and leave them for him."

It was in the hands of Providence. I had done what I could.

***

I walked by Jessup Manor and saw it was now empty. All of the tenants had moved and the windows had a blank look without the usual colourful curtains and plants. Father Belfast was standing on the other side of the street, gazing at the building, just as I was. I crossed the street to speak to him. He saw me coming and gave me a rueful smile.

"Miss Kelly, you certainly are persistent. Do you have more information for me to consider?"

He sounded gruff but he was smiling.

"Good morning Father. No, I've told you everything I feel about it. I'm leaving it in God's hands."

"I've decided to sell it. Edgar Stoneleigh backed out. He said the development plan didn't make economic sense after all."

Could Edgar's decision have had something to do with Madeleine? I never found out.

***

I told Mr. Smith I would continue to work until mid-October, and asked if he would consider hiring Isabel to replace me. He suggested I send her in for an interview.

Isabel and I had discussed it. She thought the restaurant job would be perfect. It would leave her weekends free so she could spend them with Joe. She wasn't going to let him get away again. She was light-hearted about it, confident and unconcerned about the future. She was placing her life in the hands of Providence too.

I wanted to take advantage of the coming weeks while I still had my apartment and solitude. On the other hand, I loved spending time with Kate, and wanted to make the most of this as well. Life was full of good things. It was hard to find time for them all.

I thought about how it would feel to be the owner of a tourist home. Would I be resentful at having strangers in my house? I had learned a lot at the Miss Lawrenceville about how to serve people so they felt satisfied, and I stayed cheerful and upbeat. I would need to have clear boundaries.

Patrick and I held business meetings to discuss the tourist home; ideas for how it would work, what we could charge, and whether or not it was a viable business. Patrick had the benefit of his father to discuss this with. I wished Maureen could be part of it. She had such great business sense.

Our visit to Toronto to see the twins was wonderful. They were plump, rosy and darling. They were named Patricia and Robert, but were called Patty and Bobby.

Harry and Maureen were still with the Lynches. Now that the babies were born Maureen was glad of the help. Mrs. Lynch had a cook and a gardener, and had engaged an au pair from Sweden to help with the children. When I heard about it, I hoped that the au pair wouldn't be too attractive, knowing Harry's proclivities.

It was clear there was tension between me and Mrs. Anderson. I didn't know how to get past it, but she approached it headlong, never at a loss for how to behave.

"Clare, I know you're upset about me trying to bring Linda and Patrick together. That was a mistake, and I want you to know I'm happy to have you for a daughter-in-law. I want you to feel welcome in our family."

I hadn't expected such directness.

"Thank you Mrs. Anderson, I appreciate having it brought into the open. I'm willing to leave it in the past."

That was the best I could do. It eased the tension, but would I be calling her Mrs. Anderson for the rest of our life? I wasn't sure what other people called their in-laws. I decidedly could not call her 'moms' as Patrick and Maureen did.

That weekend I met a friend of Patrick's who had just been ordained a priest in the Anglican Church.

"Mike, or should I say, 'Father Mike, meet Clare, my fiancée."

Father Mike was well over six feet tall and ruggedly handsome. He took my hand and looked into my eyes.

"It's a pleasure to meet you. Patrick has spoken of nothing but you for the past year."

Patrick laughed and said, "Was it that obvious?"

"It was obvious but beautiful. I have big news for you. I'm invited to be assistant pastor in Lawrenceville. I expect we'll see a lot of each other. Oh, and you can still call me Mike. It's a shock to be called Father. There's just a small problem about where I'll live. As soon as that's settled I'll be there."

"I'm alone in a huge house," said Patrick. "Why don't you come and stay with me until you get a place?"

"That would solve a lot of problems. I'll take you up on it if you're serious."

"It will be fun. You can share my last bachelor days."

We brought Father Mike and his few belongings home with us.

***

I rarely saw Adrian as he was working hard and staying close to home, trying to build his cabin before winter. He didn't have a phone, so I wrote a letter telling him about my engagement. He wrote back to say he'd love to get together for coffee. Adrian had never seen my apartment. I invited him to drop in as soon as he could get to Lawrenceville.

Adrian came after supper one evening. He admired the apartment and my moka pot, and gave a warm hello to Sophie. I made cappuccino and we sat at my kitchen table.

"You look healthy and happy, peaceful even," he said, "like you've stopped needing to question everything."

"I don't know if I'd go so far. I am happy though, especially about getting married. I'm enjoying this time in my life; the restaurant, having my own place, being in town. It's all good. You don't look like you're enjoying life so much. What's going on?"

"I wish it wasn't so obvious. I'm not in a healthy space. The Copper River community is full of people who talk about health and spiritual awakening. The reality is they're a bunch of pot heads. Unfortunately I've been joining in on the scene. It's work all day and stoned the rest of the time. I know better, but I'm not sure how to get out of it."

"What's keeping you stuck?"

"Desire. Desire to own land and a house. The same desire that keeps people stuck everywhere."

We sat quietly for a few minutes. I didn't have any answers for Adrian.

"Will you keep on working in town after you're married?"

"No, we're going to make Buttercup Acres into a tourist home and pick up where Maureen left off with the farm."

"Don't let work take over. Leave room for your soul. It's good advice, even if I'm not living it at the moment."

***

Kate planned a wedding shower for me. I agreed to do the baking. First we made ice box cookie dough, formed it into two long rolls wrapped in waxed paper, and refrigerated it. On Saturday I cut them into thin slices, baked them, and made jam-filled sandwich cookies. Kate also wanted an Imperial Sunshine cake, which called for a lot of separated eggs, with precise amounts and instructions for each step. It turned out beautifully, golden yellow, which explained the name. We also made cucumber and cream cheese sandwiches, and plenty of tea. The party was in her front living room which was seldom used. I helped get everything dusted and polished.

As we worked together, Kate talked about the secret of a healthy life.

"Habits. A good life is all about habits. There's no point in following trends, going on diets, taking up yoga. All of that will just be a disruption. What you need is to have routines to follow that are conducive to health. If you start something and you and find it unhealthy, don't ever do it again."

This sounded almost too simple, but I could see that it worked perfectly for her. Starting with her father and mother's training, she carried on with a life of moderation; keeping busy, positive thinking, kindness, and keeping her house and her work in order. All these formed her life.

"Discipline must become second nature. It can't be something we wildly grab at when everything is sliding out of control. Father taught us all to meditate. We sat down after breakfast and counted our breaths for ten minutes. Even the little ones. Then he said a prayer of thanksgiving, and we started the day. He wouldn't allow any disorder. Mother taught us to keep our possessions and rooms tidy, but he inspected regularly, and insisted on immediate action if anything wasn't up to snuff."

"What would he do if you disobeyed?"

"Look sternly at us. That struck terror into our souls."

Dr. Murphy obviously had moral authority oozing out his pores, like Mrs. Nelthorpe. I couldn't see Patrick or I as that sort of parent, but I hoped we would have a peaceful, loving home that brought out the best in us.

"Father knew what went on in people's homes because he did a lot of home visits. He learned from these intimate views into people's lives what creates health and what creates sickness. He spent a lot of time talking to patients, giving advice. He was a doctor of the soul as much as the body."

I thought about the Hearne house. They were warm, welcoming people, but I felt that if I were to grow up in such a house, I would need to flee. It was painful to be around such disorder. I thought of life with Dorothy and Dad. I wasn't given much encouragement to learn and expand my horizons. I was left to my own devices most of the time. Luckily I didn't fall into bad company and dangerous habits. I felt it was the Grace of God that had protected me, but maybe I was just inclined to follow the middle road, never straying far from the path.

"Father also kept strict control of what we read and on our entertainments. He was appalled at comic books. We didn't have a lot of spare time to get in trouble. We all had responsibilities and lessons and that kept us busy."

I liked to imagine Kate's family, especially as they looked at the turn of the century. Kate had wonderful family photographs that helped me create a vivid picture of their life.

"You are the luckiest person I know."

"Anyone who follows my father's philosophy will have a grand life."

"What would you think of someone writing your family history, focused especially on your father?" I asked.

"It would be a fascinating piece of history."

"I'm going to talk to Patrick about it."

"Why not you?"

"I'm not an academic. I can't see myself sitting in a study all day. I'd go mad."

"You seem scholarly to me."

"Well, that's just pursuing things I'm interested in."

When I approached Patrick with the idea, he loved it. He immediately arranged to spend time with Kate so he could find out as much as possible about Doctor Murphy and the family.

The weekend after the bridal shower I had a visit from Dorothy. She was coming to give another talk at the ashram, and asked if I could pick her up on Saturday morning. Kate lent me her car. I was at the gate of the ashram by ten. I was glad she hadn't suggested I come to the previous night's talk, as I felt uncomfortable at the ashram.

I was startled by Dorothy's changed look. Her hair was dyed red which made her black eyebrows look even more dramatic. She had on tight jeans, an Indian cotton blouse, and a suede jacket. She was wearing odd looking sandals. I asked her about them.

"Birkenstock's. Great for your health." She settled in beside me. "I want to go by the old Hearne place."

We headed through Lawrenceville, north to the Fourth Concession Road.

At first she was quiet, saying she needed time to clear her mind as she had been up late. We passed an old country store and she said, "Stop here." She got out and came back with cigarettes and coffee for both of us. "Now I'll revive."

We sat in the car in front of the store, drinking coffee, Dorothy smoking.

"I only have a few hours and a lot I'd like to tell you."

How strange that when I had given up on ever getting explanations from Dorothy, she should turn up and offer them!

"You need to know more about me before you get married. When I met Ned I saw him as my way of getting away from a life of squalor. I liked him and thought we would have a life of adventure. He seemed open to travel and trying new things. But it didn't go that way. Almost as soon as we were married he became his father. Everything was routine, order, safety. I was unhappy but blamed myself. I decided that if I had a child it would make me normal, like other women. I would have a purpose and would start to love being a wife and everything would fall into place. After you were born, I did love you. For almost a year or two I was content. But it didn't last. I started to go through the same moods. I felt Ned was a weight on me. I couldn't stand to have him around. I pushed him into taking the job travelling to get him out of the house. He felt like a second child, needy, so clinging. I longed for my own room. How I hated sharing a bed. Does this horrify you?"

"It's what I remember. I'm not surprised."

"I tried to be good to you, but I felt so unmotherly, almost allergic to motherhood, and finally, I knew I wasn't doing you or Ned any good."

"Why are you telling me this now?"

"I want you to know who you are before you marry. When you were little you were my shadow. Following me everywhere until I felt I'd go mad. You were so black and white. Constantly telling me I was doing the work of the devil. Quoting the catechism to me. But now I'm your shadow. Maybe you became this conventional good girl in reaction to me, but what if I'm lurking in you?"

I started to protest the craziness of this thought, but Dorothy stopped me. "I know it sounds mad but I keep being led to tell you this. It is always in the cards."

"I don't believe in any of that."

"But I do. I've seen how it makes sense of life. This is the shadow world too. You can't pretend it's not there."

We finished our coffee and she asked me to drive on.

"What do you think of your relatives?"

I told her about my visits. "Patrick and I took the boys to a football game in Ottawa a few weeks ago. They loved it. I don't fit with them, but I feel it's good to keep a connection."

"How do you think they make a living?"

"I thought they must be on relief. I don't know."

"See Clare, you don't want to look at things. You are trying to avoid the shadows."

"I couldn't ask them."

"They made moonshine when I was a kid. It's a wonder they didn't kill anyone with it. Now it's probably growing pot. You're right about the welfare, of course."

She lit another cigarette. "How do you think you're going to feel? Waking up every day beside Patrick. Serving him, serving children, serving guests. Won't you go mad?"

"How can I know? I haven't lived it yet. I love Patrick. I don't see why I would go down the same road as you. I expect to be happy."

"But I can tell you don't know."

"Why are you doing this? Are you trying to throw my life into chaos?"

"It's in the cards."

We were close to the Hearne home now. Dorothy said, "Don't stop. I just want to drive by and see that nothing has changed."

The yard was a mess as usual, but I couldn't tell if anyone was home. Dogs trotted out from under the falling-down porch and chased the car.

"I want you to see it Clare. We all have a shadow."

"Is this some kind of Stargaze nonsense?"

"It's Carl Jung. I believe it to be absolutely true."

"Dorothy, you grew up in chaos and ugliness. I didn't. I had stability, good moral teaching, and the church behind me. I like solitude, but I don't expect to spend my life alone. I want to create a family. I love to work and to be a part of the community. I believe in faithfulness, staying around, and preserving beauty."

"Well, if that's not shadow talk I don't know what is. You're just staying on the bright side. Let's head to Williamsville for lunch." She could see that I was looking miserable. "Don't be upset. You have to look inside your own heart, that's all I'm trying to say."

I dropped Dorothy off at the ashram in the middle of the afternoon feeling like I had been cursed. I didn't know what to think about all she had told me. I wished I had told her about the wonderful, kind, faithful mothers I had met. I wanted her to feel guilty, show her she could have done better. I didn't care about Carl Jung. This was just another way for Dorothy to avoid responsibility for her heartless actions. I didn't want to judge her, but it was impossible not to see her as an unrepentant sinner.

One thought ate away at me. What if I hated sharing a bed with Patrick? It was something I worried about but hadn't spoken of to anyone. It wasn't sex that worried me; it was the loss of a room of my own. I wanted to wake up alone, read in the middle of the night if I felt like it, get dressed and undressed without someone watching me, have my morning coffee alone, have an inviolable space. Maybe Dorothy was right. How could I be a good wife and mother when I had this longing for solitude? Maybe I wasn't capable of intimacy. I had been accused of being a prude by Adrian in one of our discussions, but maybe that wasn't the half of it. It's possible I was incapable of true, intimate love.

I called Patrick to cancel our evening together. I told him I wasn't feeling well and needed to rest. I didn't feel up to being in anyone's company.

I fell asleep early and dreamt that Dorothy was marrying Patrick. I woke up in the dark feeling horror and confusion. I didn't know who I could discuss this problem with. It seemed too arcane for Isabel or Mrs. Bergeron. Adrian and I had discussed Jung; the anima, the animus, the shadow, but this dilemma was too personal to bring to him. Maybe Father Kelly could help.

The next morning I caught Father Kelly after Mass and asked if I could talk to him.

He must have seen the desperation in my eyes as he immediately invited me into his study. I told him about Dorothy and Jung, the shadow side, and my fear that I was incapable of being a wife and mother.

"What if I turn out to be like my mother?"

Father Kelly listened. When I stopped talking, he sat quietly for a minute.

"The real test in this is whether or not you can share this concern with Patrick. Can you tell him your fears; let him know what you need in order to be happy? Maybe you need assurance that you can have your own space. That's not unreasonable."

Wedding Plans

Father Kelly's words made me realize my desire for solitude was not such a big thing. I over-reacted, knocked off balance by Dorothy's presence. She was a strong force, and I would have to be alert to avoid being pulled into her orbit. The idea that I was incapable of being a wife and mother was nihilistic and cruel. I wanted to think that Dorothy was capable of love and kindness, but maybe it wasn't in her to be generous, or to have faith in people. One thing I was sure of, my fate was not subject to Dorothy and her card reading!

When I got home, I found Kate sitting at the kitchen table doing a crossword puzzle and drinking coffee in her sunny spot. I told her about my conversations with Dorothy and Father Kelly.

"Shadow! What bosh! I was in analysis briefly, in my forties. I did some reading then about Jung. I concluded it was an ersatz religion, a complete dead end. Jung lost his faith and made up a new one based on mythology and his desire to make sense of the world. Of course he has some insights, but he could have gone a lot farther if he'd stayed with Lutheranism."

"Dorothy left me feeling I was doomed."

"Her dramatics cause you to give too much weight to her words. Remember, that's how she makes her living; she's a persuader. If anyone else told you that you would have dismissed it."

"Something good did come out of it. Father Kelly made me realize I need to be honest and speak up for what I need. It's too easy for me to just go along with things."

"It's good to have balance in everything – both in getting what you want and learning when you need to compromise. No one ever had a good life by getting everything their own way."

"I'm going to hate leaving you. I don't think I've ever met anyone I felt so happy with."

"See, you're not a loner. Sure, you like order, and time to read and reflect, but you are open to people and to loving in a way that is rare."

I knew Kate was right. But I also knew that Dorothy was touching on something in me that I needed to pay attention to.

Kate jumped up. "I almost forgot. I have something to show you." She led me to a bedroom full of boxes and furniture. "Here it is." She pulled a garment bag out of a closet. "Now you don't have to say yes, but if you like it, I would be honoured for you to have it."

She unzipped the bag and revealed a lace wedding dress.

Isabel came over just as we were examining the dress.

"Try it on," Isabel said.

I quickly changed into the dress and stood in the mirror, turning to see it from all angles.

"It's perfect," Isabel said.

Kate agreed. "It looks like it was made for you."

I stood, looking at my image in the mirror, bemused at seeing myself as a bride.

Kate said, "I'm glad you're both here. There's something I want to talk to you both about. This is the perfect time. It's about sex."

I was surprised and Isabel looked worried.

"Let's sit down in the kitchen. We'll have tea and I'm going to tell you things that I learned from my father, and from life; things you both need to know."

As we sat with our tea she told us that sex was as essential to a healthy marriage as good habits, discipline, and high moral standards. She said she could not over-emphasize how crucial sex was to keeping love alive and the family united.

"What I'm going to say now may shock you. Right now it will seem impossible to believe, but within ten or fifteen years of marriage, maybe even sooner, many of the couples you know will stop having sex at all. They won't divorce. They won't tell anyone. But it will be over. That's what I want to prevent. The biggest stumbling block is lack of communication about sex."

Isabel started to protest. "Sex is all anyone ever talks about these days."

Kate stopped her. "That's not the kind of communication I mean. What I'm talking about is much more difficult to begin and maintain. It is about being honest with your husband about what you want. And above all, realising that love will be destroyed if sex is used for power. If you use sex as a bargaining tool, if you withhold sex because you're angry, if you think of it as something you are holding over him, it will poison your life."

I immediately thought of my parents; of my father, sleeping on his own.

"This is about the communication you have at all times. If you're angry, don't hide it from yourself. Take a look at it. Don't build resentment. If you need to make a change, talk about it. Be open. You have probably been told at school that men and women are very different in their approach to sex. Don't dismiss this because of some feminist ideas that are being promoted. It is fundamentally true. Men are stimulated by what they see. They are much more easily aroused. But they also need to feel that they are appreciated, that sex isn't just something tolerated. They also need warmth, love, acceptance. There may be more that I should say but I'll leave it for now. It's a lot to think about."

Isabel and I left together. As we walked down the sidewalk Isabel laughed nervously and said, "I was afraid she was going to tell us not to have sex before marriage. Or to warn us about men and their wily ways. I wasn't expecting to hear that sex is a good thing."

"She's right; it's a lot to think about."

We said our goodbyes and I headed off on my bicycle to Buttercup Acres. It was still warm for September. The leaves were just starting to change colour. The breeze from the river carried a chill. Patrick was in the back yard with a pen and a notepad, making a list of things that needed to be done.

"Clare, I'm so glad you felt well enough to come out today. How are you?" He held me close to him.

"I'm fine, now that I'm with you."

Father Mike called to us from the barn, "I see a way this could work."

"Mike and I were talking about making a space for cows and a dairy. I'd love to make cheese."

"You're always surprising me!"

Mike came out and grabbed the notepad from Patrick, then sketched his vision of how the barn could be renovated. They debated back and forth about the plan. I basked in the warmth of the slanting sun. Life seemed to hold endless promise and happiness. How could I have been so quick to fall into the depths of despair yesterday?

"I met a friend of yours," Mike said.

"Who's that?"

"Madeleine. I was walking through the school yard and saw this lovely woman, talking two boys out of a fight. I introduced myself and she told me she'd heard all about me. She's coming over for supper."

"I'm delighted to hear you've met. And that you're bringing her over for supper. Who's cooking?"

"I thought it would be fun if we all cooked together," Patrick said. "I have a menu planned. Your contribution will be apple cake, I'm making roast beef with Franconia potatoes and Mike is making his specialty, cole slaw.

"I'd better get started now so my cake will have time to cool."

"I've been to the market. I bought Macintosh apples, fresh from the tree," Patrick said.

He had the coal stove fired up already. I peeled the apples and laid thin slices in a delicate pattern on the bottom of the buttered cake tin. I topped this with a mixture of brown sugar and butter. I let this cook a little in the oven while I made the batter. I poured this on top of the hot apples, then sat watching Patrick prepare the potatoes while the cake cooked.

"I have something I want to talk to you about," I told Patrick.

"Let's go for a row on the pond, I have something to discuss with you too," he said.

As soon as we were out in the middle Patrick said, "My mother wants to have the reception at the Skylane."

"Did you tell her we already have plans?"

"I said we would think about it."

"What is there to think about? You wanted it here specifically so she wouldn't take over."

"She just wants to help."

"That's exactly it."

"Maybe we should try to see it from her perspective?"

"What about what you want? Is it impossible for you to say no to her?"

"There's one more thing. She wants you to go to Toronto next weekend, so she can help you find a wedding dress."

"I have my dress already. She doesn't get to decide on that."

"I can see you're annoyed."

"Do you know anything about Jung?"

"What does that have to do with anything?"

"It's too complicated. There's no time to have this discussion. What I need to say can't be rushed. We've got to get back and take care of supper. Let's make a date to talk seriously this week."

"But I don't know what to tell my mother?"

"You'll just have to live with being uncomfortable."

"Clare, you're so stern."

"I love you darling, but we still need to work some things out."

Despite our tense talk in the row boat, we managed to leave it behind and the evening was a success. Madeleine arrived with a Miles Davis record she wanted us to hear. It was apparent she and Mike were compatible. Although they'd just met, they were standing together, arms around each other's waist, as we gathered in the kitchen to watch Patrick make the final preparations. Madeleine looked stunning in a fall leaf-patterned silk dress that clung to her beautifully. I put all conflicts out of my mind and enjoyed the perfection of the four of us together.

We talked for hours that night. Mike was funny. He had a lot of interesting stories, but he didn't take over. Either he was on his best behaviour, or he was truly a perfect gentleman.

After dinner Madeleine took me aside and said, "Thank you for tipping me off about Edgar."

I hadn't seen Madeleine since that night and I was relieved to know she wasn't angry with me.

"I'm so happy to see you here tonight. What a great surprise to have you and Mike find each other, just by chance," I said.

"Chance? What happened to Providence?"

"If you're speaking of Providence, that tells me you see good things from this encounter."

We moved into the living room and Patrick put on Miles Davis. At the end Madeleine said she had to be up early for school and said her goodbyes. She offered to drive me back to town with her and I happily accepted. I too had to be up early for my shift at the Miss Lawrenceville.

In the car I told her that the Jessup Manor project wasn't going ahead.

Madeleine smiled and said, "That's good news."

Whatever she knew, she wasn't telling. She asked me about Mike and I told her the few things I knew about his university years with Patrick, and his new career as an Anglican priest.

"Father Mike or would it be Father Michael? Both sound so impressive." Madeleine was finding everything about him fascinating, even his name. She ruminated about Mike for the rest of the trip. I was glad to see that she had moved on so quickly from Edgar.

I went quietly up the stairs to my dark apartment. I felt Sophie rubbing against my legs and heard her low purr. I hoped she would be happy when we moved back to the farm.

I went to bed exhausted but had a hard time sleeping. I wished that Patrick and I had been able to talk about my encounter with Dorothy, and Patrick's with his mother. Unless we could stand up to them, we weren't adult enough for marriage. I needed to have this conversation as soon as possible. It was weighing me down. I found myself imagining a life of Mrs. Anderson picking my clothes, naming our children, and deciding what our lives would be.

Finally I fell asleep. In the morning, I felt more optimistic and told myself I was being overdramatic. Mrs. Anderson wasn't that controlling.

Patrick picked me up after work.

"It's just you and I tonight. Let's go to that wonderful German restaurant in Williamsville and have a long talk."

I moved close to him on the bench seat of the truck and he put his arm around me. I stopped at home to change out of my uniform and put on my rust coloured corduroy jumper, yellow turtleneck, Mary Quant tights and matching ballet flats. I added my gold chain belt, grabbed a cardigan and ran down the stairs saying, "Sorry Sophie, I'm out again tonight."

Patrick had installed an eight track player in the truck. As we drove we listened to The Who. Patrick liked loud music while driving, while I preferred to listen to something soothing on the CBC.

"My mother called again this morning. I told her we hadn't had time to talk about it. She made an appointment to get your hair done in Williamsville before the wedding."

I felt sick and outraged. How could he calmly tell me that? What kind of a person thinks she can make such decisions for a daughter-in-law?

"Let's go to the park first. We need to have this talk right away."

We parked at the top of the hill and walked through the pines to the beach. It was still light but the summer's heat was gone.

"I gather you're not happy about the hair appointment?"

I had to pull myself together. I didn't want to take my anger at Mrs. Anderson out on Patrick, but I had to be absolutely clear with him about how I felt.

"I don't plan to have anything done to my hair for the wedding. But the real issue is why didn't you tell your mother that you had plans already; plans that you made yourself, that you were happy with, that we were both happy with? Why can't you stand up to her?"

"I thought you'd be happy about the hair appointment. It seems like she's taking an interest in you and trying to be kind."

"Oh Patrick, you have no clue."

I was so frustrated by how far apart we were that I didn't know how to proceed. If we couldn't even talk about this and make ourselves understood, how could we ever talk about anything important? Was this a matter of social class? If I had grown up in his world, would I accept his mother's influence and find it normal? This was no time for self doubt. I needed to state my case.

"If it was up to your mother, you would have married Linda. You'd be working for your father. If you really want to get free, this is your chance. You have to tell her that you have a different vision of the wedding, that it's our celebration. If you can't do this it will poison our start. And it's not going to end there. She will continue to interfere in our lives. You need to find this strength or you won't ever be free of her control."

Patrick sat looking thoughtful, then said, "What was it you wanted to talk about?"

I told him about my visit with Dorothy.

"She tried to convince me I was incapable of being a wife and mother, incapable of loving. She almost succeeded. I was shattered after our talk. I saw myself as someone who would never be able to share my life, who would run from intimacy. I couldn't even talk about it with you, so I went to Father Kelly and he was able to put it in perspective. He made me see that I do have a love of solitude, but that's not all I am. He advised me to speak up about what I need to be happy. We both have to get past our mother's power over us."

"I'm afraid of my mother," said Patrick softly. "Can you understand that? Saying no to her makes me sick. It's not rational. I don't even know what it is I fear. I thought my actions this summer had freed me, but it's still there. I didn't have the courage to speak of it to you."

"I've never told anyone this before, but I always assumed it was my fault that my mother ran away," I said. I thought I was unlovable, or that I hadn't loved her enough. I was afraid she knew I wished for a different mother. I tried not to think about her over the years but I always felt guilty."

Patrick reached for my hand and said, "I have fears about marriage too, about losing independence, about having to compromise, about being so close to one person. We both have a lot to learn about how to love."

"Let's promise to be honest with each other," I said, "no matter how scary it is."

Married

October brought frosty mornings and trees blazing with colour. Our invitations had gone out. All was in place for the wedding. Isabel agreed to be Maid of Honour. Mike was standing up for Patrick as Best Man. I told Isabel I would be happy with whatever she wanted to wear. She chose a pale gold gown in soft jersey that flattered her figure. It looked beautiful with her blonde hair.

Kate told me the romantic but sad story of the dress, and how she had expected to wear it. She said it was completely free of all sad associations now that I would be wearing it. I felt that her gift was a talisman of faith and hope in love itself.

To my happy surprise, Mr. Bergeron offered to lead me down the aisle. He was not a man to make such gestures. I was deeply touched and accepted gladly.

Patrick told his mother that our plans were made and the reception was going to be at Buttercup Acres. She offered to make all the arrangements to have it catered and we both agreed that would be a good thing. She even talked it over with me, suggesting a string quartet and a waiter in tuxedo serving champagne and handing out canapés. It was the most beautiful wedding reception imaginable, and not just because it was ours.

Kate wanted to show me one more thing before I moved out.

"My mother always made her own marmalade," she said. "I still have all the canning equipment and jars. It will be a great thing for you to serve at breakfast."

She sent me to the store to buy oranges, grapefruits and lemons. We spent half the day peeling, cutting and chopping. Isabel came over to help. Kate kept us entertained with stories of Lawrenceville in the early part of the century.

"There were two big hotels, and lots of taverns. This town was a going concern. My father was the only doctor in town for a number of years, so we saw everyone come through these doors. My mother served as receptionist, and sometimes my older sisters helped. They knew how to stitch wounds, assist with putting on casts and taking them off. They could have treated patients themselves after all the time they put in."

We boiled the fruit in a heavy stainless steel pot until the peels softened, then added great quantities of sugar, boiling and stirring until it thickened.

When we finished we had twenty jars of beautiful marmalade, glowing orange in the sun that streamed in the kitchen window. We covered each jar with a ring of checked gingham and fastened it with a rubber band.

***

Dorothy didn't come to the wedding. Her travel schedule was booked six months in advance, and she was in Scotland that week. She sent a card with a picture of Carl Jung smoking a pipe, and below it a quote, "Knowing your own darkness is the best method for dealing with the darkness of other people."

I thought about throwing it out but I showed it to Patrick and he said, "We'll keep this in our wedding album."

There it stays, amongst the photos of happiness and hope.

Clare Anderson

After the excitement of the wedding died down, Patrick and I found ourselves face to face with a new life, happy and open to whatever came along. It was time to move from dreams to reality, exciting but also challenging.

"Clare, we should do some work on the dairy. It's cold but we could work outside for part of the day."

I was sitting beside him in bed with my tea. I hadn't been up yet and was hesitant to put my foot out of the covers onto the cold floor. I must get some sheepskins for the floor, I thought dreamily.

"I've never felt so lazy and content. After two weeks of sleeping in, walks, shopping, treating ourselves to wonderful meals, and driving down country roads, I don't know if I can ever go back to work," I said.

Patrick looked at me with wonder before he spoke.

"How is it possible for life to be so good? Would we ever get bored? This has been the best honeymoon any couple has ever had. Still, it's time we got down to work."

"The cows won't be here until April, what's the rush?"

"What would you rather do today?"

"Let's have a business meeting. Plan our schedule for the next few months. That way we'll be working, but not diving in at the deep end right away."

"It looks like snow today. It would be nice to be inside and cozy."

I got up and put on flannel lined jeans, a soft denim shirt and a heather-gray, ragg wool sweater I inherited from Maureen. She left it behind when she moved back to Toronto. I discovered all sorts of other wonderful clothes left by Maureen. When I mentioned it to her she said, "Keep them. They're only good for the farm."

Patrick had stoked the coal stove and the coffee was perking. Sophie was sitting in her favourite chair beside the stove. She immediately reverted to her old habits as soon as I brought her back to live at Buttercup Acres. I wondered if Sophie missed Mrs. Nelthorpe.

I put the iron frying pan on the stove and reached for some eggs from the hanging basket. They were fresh from our chickens, light brown and slightly mottled. The hens had slowed down in the cold weather but there were enough eggs for the two of us. I thought of all the baking I wanted to do for Christmas and realized I needed to start saving some.

"Mrs. Anderson," Patrick called out.

I felt a momentary sense of alarm. Was my mother-in-law here? No, of course not, I was the Mrs. Anderson he was referring to. This would take time to get used to.

"Here I am."

I went to see what he wanted. He was using Mrs. Nelthorpe's room for a study, a porch with windows on three sides. He was standing at his desk which held his sea foam green Herme's 3000 typewriter.

"What is it darling?" I asked.

"Nothing, I just wanted to see you."

I went to his side and we stood wrapped in each other's arms in the cool room. It shouldn't have been a surprise that we were so incredibly happy, but it was.

"Have you gotten far with the Murphy family history?"

"Still just notes towards it, but I feel excited about beginning."

After breakfast we sat at the kitchen table and made lists of things we needed to get a start on. We discussed priorities and debated possibilities. After a few hours of this I got up to stretch. I went to the window and saw snow falling softly.

"Let's go for a walk," I suggested.

After we came in it was too cozy by the woodstove to start any projects, so we lazed away the rest of the day.

On Tuesday I said, "Maybe we could visit Kate today. She told me she has more photos to give you and I'm sure she will never run out of stories about her father."

"Good idea. It's time to reconnect with people, although being alone is heaven. Let's invite Mike and Madeleine over for dinner."

"Don't forget Isabel and Joe. I'll ask Isabel what weekend he'll be home."

When we arrived at Kate's she had a visitor, her great-niece, Deborah Murphy. I had heard of her, but we had never met. Deborah seemed pointedly unfriendly. I almost thought she was trying to get rid of us. In light of this, I declined Kate's invitation to stay for tea, telling her we'd come back in the afternoon.

***

Patrick and I dropped in to the Miss Lawrenceville for lunch. I wanted to see how Isabel was doing. She wasn't wearing the pink uniform that I felt so happy in, but instead chose a black check, with the same white apron, and low black pumps. It suited her well. She didn't have time to chat but agreed to come for dinner on the weekend with Joe.

"I'm enjoying this job. You're right, the Smiths are wonderful employers and the day flies by. See you Saturday." Then Isabel was off, notepad in hand, serving other customers.

"Isabel looks great," I said. "I'm so happy she moved home from Toronto and that she likes the job. It's amazing how well it all turned out."

"Thanks to you," Patrick said.

Kate greeted us with enthusiasm when we returned after lunch.

"Now, you two are people I welcome a visit from. I can see that marriage agrees with you. You're both glowing."

"Life is more wonderful than I could ever have imagined," I admitted. "How have you been?"

"Better, now that Deborah left. I was dreading her visit. She is a major interferer. She imagines herself inheriting all that I have. I can almost see her rubbing her hands together in glee."

"I noticed she was cool towards us."

"She was trying to convince me that living in this house is too much for me, suggesting I move to Montreal and live in her granny suite. Not just suggesting it but almost trying to force it on me. She doesn't take after any of the Murphys. None of us were so pushy. She never learned to live by my father's wonderful rules for life."

"I hope she doesn't visit too often if she's so upsetting."

"I have a remedy for that. I'm going to make sure she knows exactly what she's inheriting, which is to say, almost nothing. I've worked it out with my lawyer. That will be the last I see of her. I don't like her and I don't trust her."

Obviously Deborah had pushed too far. Kate may have been eighty-two but she was still entirely sure of herself and wouldn't put up with interference in her life. "I've asked him to send her a letter. Make it official."

"You've handled it already? That was quick!"

"My father always counseled taking care of matters as they arose. Not letting things hang over one when it's clear something must be done."

Patrick opened his notebook. "That's what I'm hoping to hear today, more like this about your father. I like it best when you bring him up in the course of conversation. I also brought some questions to keep ideas flowing. I'd like to start meeting with you regularly so you can hear what I'm doing and help to fill in the story. Could we start our week with a meeting?"

"Monday morning is best. As per father, get the important work done in the morning."

After we left, Patrick said he'd need to do a lot more research into the history of Lawrenceville. "We will have to go to the archives in Ottawa. Our local libraries won't be enough."

"I'd love that. Maybe we could go when the canal is frozen and make a holiday of it."

"I have another treat for you."

"What is it?"

"You'll have to wait until we get to Williamsville."

He parked in front of the Williamsville sports store and we went in.

"This is the surprise," he said.

Patrick had arranged with the owner to fit us with cross country skis, boots and poles. We bought matching sets in a shiny black and green design, as well as Jack Rabbit wet and dry wax, which the owner told us was the simplest wax system.

"I have one more surprise. I signed us up for beginner lessons at the Williamsville YMCA. They start mid December as long as there's enough snow."

"I've never been on skis."

"That's why we're taking lessons."

"What a wonderful surprise. Thank you darling!"

"You two newlyweds?"

"Yes," Patrick answered.

"Easy to tell. After folks have been married a while they don't jump so happily into new things together. It's beautiful to see."

When we got back in the truck I said, "We won't change."

"Promise."

"Yes."

St. Matthias Christmas Bazaar

When we got home we unloaded the skis and the groceries and I put the kettle on for tea. Mike called and I heard Patrick talking to him in the hall.

"A bazaar. I could help with that."

"Baking, sure."

"Old skates, toys, clothes. Not too sure about that. I'll ask Clare. Great. See you Saturday."

Patrick came into the kitchen. "That was Mike. He's arranging a bazaar at St. Matthias. He asked for a few things from us. They never talked about this stuff when we were studying theology."

I was familiar with the bazaars at Sacred Heart Parish. We had one every fall. Ours was called a Tea and Sale. The Catholic Women's League organized it and did all the work. Dorothy never helped out, although I once suggested it.

"Nah. I'm not their type," she told me.

I should have asked, "Whose type are you?" but I wasn't quick enough.

Dorothy was on my mind a lot these days, but not in a worrisome way. I found myself thinking about her and her strange beliefs, and wondering if we would ever be able to really communicate.

"We could do some baking," I suggested. "I heard you mentioning skates and such, but we haven't been together long enough to accumulate extras."

"He asked us to drop our things off on Saturday morning, early. Oh, and he asked me if I would handle the fishing booth."

"That sounds like fun. I could help. I'll let you know what little girls would like to catch."

On Saturday we arrived at the Anglican Church hall at eight o'clock with brownies and blondies wrapped in saran and tied with ribbons, ready for the sale. Mike didn't need us until ten so we took a walk. We passed Jessup Manor and I saw that people had moved back in. Once again there were curtains on the windows and philodendrons on the sills. I felt good about that, but wondered if any of the old tenants were back, or if it would be a whole new group.

We walked up to the train station and sat on the bench, waiting for the next train to pass. Within a few minutes we heard the whistle. We counted one hundred and thirty cars, racketing and rumbling and shaking our bones as they went by. From there we walked to the park by the river, then back to the bazaar just in time to get into position behind the fishing booth.

The children knew what to expect. There was quickly a line of boys and girls eager to see what they would catch. There were boxes of crayons, colouring books, sock monkeys, tiny Kewpie dolls, toy cars, skipping ropes, marbles in a Crown Royal bag, a doll's tea set, and more. The Anglicans certainly did a great job of donating for the bazaar. I was impressed. It was heart-warming to hear the excitement in the children's voices as they saw what they had caught.

Madeleine was helping at the clothing stall. She made a sign that said Jumble Sale, as she was a great lover of English novels about curates. I took a break and went to see how she was doing. There were two boys looking through the pile, saying they needed hobo clothes. Halloween was a long way off but it was already on their minds for next year.

"St. Mathias really knows how to put on a bazaar. There's some great stuff here," Madeleine said.

"The fishing is great too. Don't tell anyone I said so, but this is better than Sacred Heart's Tea and Sale."

"Mum's the word."

"Oh look. I'd swear that is a cashmere sweater with a mink collar."

"It is. I was hoping to buy it myself and give it to Mom."

"Take it now, before someone else grabs it."

"Do you think I dare?"

"If you don't, I will."

I came away from Madeleine's jumble table with a fisherman knit pullover for Patrick and a reversible kilt for me. Not in style, but I liked it. At the table of handicrafts made by the church women I bought a quilted tea cosy to give to Kate and couldn't resist buying a poodle tissue box cover.

As I turned towards the tea and sandwiches area I saw Adrian sitting at one of the card tables. He called me over and introduced me to a woman who was with him.

"Clare, this is Harmony."

Harmony looked grumpy. She appeared to be pulverizing an oatmeal cookie to crumbs on her plate. She had a large bag of clothes on one of the chairs which Adrian moved to the floor to allow me to sit down.

"How is married life?" Adrian asked.

I told him about how happy I was to be back at Buttercup Acres.

"I miss my refuge in Goldilocks' Cottage. I'm still in a trailer."

Harmony's attention was caught by his mention of Goldilocks. "Where's that?" she asked.

Adrian told her about the year spent at Buttercup Acres helping to get a market farm going. "Unfortunately, it didn't last forever."

"I'm helping Patrick with the fishing booth so I'll have to get back to give him a break. Why don't you come for a visit one of these days?"

"I'd like that. We have a lot to catch up on."

I went back to relieve Patrick. I saw Adrian leave with Harmony and her bags of bazaar sale treasure. I hoped he wasn't saddled with her.

Another Wedding

Mike and Madeleine arrived first for the dinner party. They handed me a bottle of red wine and hung up their coats on the hall tree. They were excited about how well the bazaar had gone. It was Mike's first event of this type and it left him feeling part of a warm community. Madeleine was glowing too.

"Did you see how much stuff we sold? I thought I knew everyone in Lawrenceville, but I met all sorts of new people today. I got a good view of how much work it takes to put on a day like this. When we left there were still five women in the kitchen washing dishes, putting things away, straightening up. I'll bet they didn't get out of there until suppertime."

Mike playfully ruffled Madeleine's hair, "Can you see yourself with that group?"

She suddenly looked serious. "There was one sad note. I saw a little girl, around eight, waiting and looking worried. I heard her ask one of the women if her mother was ready to go home and this woman gave the most horrific answer. 'Go on home. Your mother's busy.' That may not sound all that harsh but it was getting dark by then and I could see that the little one was upset. People don't realize how easy it is to break a child's heart."

"Thank goodness you're a teacher," Patrick said. It's good to know there are some who really care."

We were talking about children and their sensitivity when Isabel and Joe arrived. It had begun to snow and they came in brushing off fluffy flakes from their clothes.

"It feels good to get inside. It suddenly turned stormy," Joe said. "What were you talking about? You all look so earnest."

"We just got into a discussion about children and how sensitive they are," I said.

Isabel turned pink and said, "That's a good lead in for us."

"A lead in to what?" Patrick asked.

"We're getting married and we're expecting a baby."

There was a moment of silence before everyone began talking at once. Madeleine didn't seem surprised. Isabel must have told her family already. I was only slightly surprised.

There was a lot of hugging and congratulations, but it made me cry. It was such a big leap from girlhood to wife to mother. I could hardly take it in.

Joe brought a bottle of champagne which he insisted we open immediately. We toasted to their happiness.

"When is the wedding?" Patrick asked.

"Over the Christmas break. Joe will have time off and we can have May home for Christmas and the wedding with one trip. It's going to be low key."

"That's the best kind of wedding," I said.

"Mom is happy about it, but Dad is upset," Isabel said. Dad never says much about anything directly but he's grumbling. Right after I told Mom and Dad, he gave this rant about Trudeau.

"That damn Trudeau with his 'no place for the state in the bedrooms of the nation' nonsense. What room does he think the state belongs in?"

"I know that was directed at me. He was so full of anger and disgust!" Isabel had tears running down her cheeks.

Mike agreed. "You caught his tone exactly. I was waiting for Madeleine to come down. I heard it all."

"Dad will come around, Isabel. He finds any kind of change hard."

Madeleine was right, but it was painful for Isabel to live with her father's disapproval. I thought of how kind Mr. Bergeron had been over the years, but I always knew where he stood on issues, and how disappointed he would be if I transgressed.

"The important thing is that you love each other and are ready to have a family together." Mike was speaking in his pastoral counselling voice, trying to make Isabel feel better.

After he said this I thought, what if they're not ready? But I didn't say anything. There was much to say, but not in this setting.

Joe took Isabel's hand and said, "I'm happy you're having a baby. I'm thrilled we're going to be together for life. I know your father is upset, but he'll come around. Even the timing isn't too bad. I'll be graduating in a few months and ready to take on the world."

It was reassuring to hear Joe say all this. Whether he meant it or not, Isabel needed to hear it.

Isabel looked at him with devotion. "I know I can count on you."

Our party went well after that. Everyone seemed to relax and let go. We sat around the large dining room table, eating plates of spaghetti, drinking Italian red wine, and laughing at everything. We could hear the wind rising and snow hitting the window now and then. It felt cozy to be together in the midst of the storm.

By the time our guests left the moon had risen and the snow stopped, revealing a clean, bright world. When we went back in the house Patrick said, "I found something special for you at the bazaar. Come and look." He led me by the hand to the office. "What do you think?" It was a blue and white Underwood portable typewriter. It said "Underwood 315" on the top.

"It looks new. Did you get this at the sale?"

"It is almost brand new. I can't imagine who would have donated it. It was probably the best thing they sold today. I thought maybe you could write down your story about Martha and Sheila and Morris. We can both have a writing project."

"I love it. I never considered having my own typewriter. It's so elegant. I can hardly wait to start."

"I could see you were sad about Isabel. I hope this cheers you up."

"I'm not really sad, more worried. They belong together and love each other, but it's not the best way to start."

"It's the beginning of a lot of marriages."

"I want life to be perfect for Isabel. I don't ever want her to be hurt or disappointed."

"You'll see, this will be the beginning of a great life for Joe and Isabel."

"I'm her best friend. I'd better start planning for her bridal shower."

The Santa Claus Parade

The next morning we went to Bergeron's for the big Sunday breakfast and I had a chance to talk quietly with Isabel and plan a date for the wedding shower. This was now such a big crowd I wondered how Mrs. Bergeron could handle it, but she was always welcoming and never flustered. Mr. Bergeron seemed to be coming around to acceptance of Isabel's pregnancy. Not that he said so, but at least he didn't have any rants about Trudeau and how far Canada had sunk into depravity.

I told Isabel I would help her in any way I could, for the wedding and for the baby. She said she would like one favour, to have her reception at Buttercup Acres.

"Our wedding is at eight in the morning so it will be a breakfast reception. There will be about twenty all together. Is that too much for you?"

I assured her it would be fine. "What would you like us to make?"

"I seem to have lost my appetite for breakfast. I'll leave it to you. As simple as possible. Except we should also have champagne."

"Of course! We'll also have plenty of our homemade marmalade and hot scones. This is going to be fun."

"And I'd like you to be my Matron of Honour. Joe's brother will be his Best Man."

"I'm delighted to do that."

***

Adrian came to visit that afternoon. He looked tired. The ebullient, interested in the world, friendly, warm Adrian I met at the ashram seemed to be gone. I made coffee for us and we sat at the kitchen table.

"You haven't seemed happy since you moved on. I know you've been working hard for a house, but it seems like this life doesn't suit you," I said.

"You're so right. I'm happiest living a life where I'm free from a lot of responsibility; with time to read, to be present to people, to experience joy in the moment. Life now feels like it's all towards a goal. It's all about 'getting there'. I've known this about myself for a long time. It's why I never married and had children. I knew I wouldn't be a good family man. I practically wrote the book on how to escape the treadmill, and then, wham! I get caught in it."

"You've gotten away from what you know to be your true self. You're right. You have written the book on this. It's all we talked about for months together. I see how fast you've lost your way. I may be able to help you to turn it around. Patrick and I are going to need help. Would you consider coming back?"

"I never expected this. Are you sure Patrick would want me?"

"We talked about it after I saw you at the bazaar. He knows the work you did for Maureen and said you would be perfect for the kind of help we need."

"In that case I'd love to move back. When would you like me to start?"

"As soon as you can. Then we can start moving forward with our plans. You have skills we need."

"My construction job stops in a week. After that I just have to pack up my things and say goodbye. It will be good to get back to my life in Goldilocks Cottage."

"I've missed our great talks about life and literature."

Patrick came in from the barn where he had been cleaning out the chicken roost.

"Adrian. Good to see you."

"Clare invited me to come back to work here. She said you discussed it." Adrian said this with a questioning note. I could see he didn't want to jump into something if Patrick wasn't on board.

Patrick was being up front about this too. "I know you and I had our differences. I was jealous of your friendship with Clare. That won't be an issue now. I'll be happy to have you on the Buttercup Acres team."

Patrick and Adrian shook hands. It was a deal. Within a few weeks Adrian was back in the cottage, keeping the stove going, surrounded by his books, with a pot of coffee always ready.

On Monday morning we went to Kate's as soon as we finished breakfast. She was an early riser and ready to work on the family history with Patrick. Kate had prepared a genealogical chart of the family. It had been such a large family that it was amazing to see how it could dwindle down to just Kate and Deborah.

I mentioned this to which Kate said, "Never take anything for granted. You don't know what's ahead. You can't assume life will continue in the patterns you're used to. The Great War followed by the Spanish flu changed everything. Until then our life felt like a series of blessings; healthy children, a safe town, a comfortable life. After that I knew that suffering and loss were possible. But let's start with 1867. That's when my father hung up his doctor's shingle on this house. He bought it from an old man."

I sat and listened as Patrick took notes. Kate had a good memory and knew many details about her father's start as a doctor. She had gotten up to his marriage to her mother and the first child and said, "It's time for tea."

This became the pattern of our Monday mornings. Kate would talk for an hour or two, then tea, after which we would hurry home so that Patrick could start writing as soon as possible, while it was fresh in his mind.

I called Shilta to ask if she would be coming to town for the Santa Parade that was coming up that Saturday. She said the kids wanted to go but she was working on Saturday and Mercy didn't drive. I offered to come and get them, although it was a tight squeeze with me and the four of them on the bench seat of the truck.

I picked them up mid afternoon and we got in place just as it was beginning. The high school band came by playing Rudolph the Red Nosed Reindeer, the baton twirlers managing to do their twirling even with frozen hands. Luckily the parade was only a few blocks long, not miles as it would be in a city. Like magic, as Santa's sleigh came along it started to snow a few light flakes, creating the perfect feeling of Christmas. Santa threw candies and the kids scrambled after, gathering them up.

I took them to the Miss Lawrenceville for hot chocolate afterwards and asked them how things were going. "Your mother said she's working on Saturday. Did she just start?"

The children looked blank. Then Dottie said, "What do you mean?"

"Your mother told me she couldn't bring you to the parade."

I saw more blank stares and realized I shouldn't ask questions about their life at home. Better to wait and see what they offered.

The boys were punching each other and laughing hilariously. Bella was poking at the marshmallows in her mug. Dottie was glued to my side, feeling my scarf and rubbing the soft wool against her face. I dropped them off at home and spent a few minutes visiting with Mercy and Uncle Django. They had already put up their Christmas tree, and the house was cheerful. I wished them Merry Christmas and headed home, thinking what a mystery their household was.

Patrick was happy to see me come in. "I was looking out the window at the snow. It's starting to pile up. I hate to think of you out on those dark country roads by yourself."

"I'm glad to be home. It isn't slippery yet, but it is dark and lonely out there on the Fourth Concession. I wouldn't want to live so far from town. We're in just the right spot."

"We are in just the right spot."

I told Patrick about how funny the kids were and how mysterious.

"Kids live in their own world with their own rules. We eventually lose the ability to join in."

"Do you really think that? Jiddu and Gita seemed to be different."

"They needed you. They accepted you as a mother."

"Is it that simple?"

Patrick had dinner ready. The kitchen was cozy and smelled wonderful from the apple crisp he was cooking. Sophie wound herself around my legs, meowing loudly. She too was glad I was safely home. Life was perfect.

Another Happy Couple

The snow came and stayed and was soon deep enough for cross country skiing. We went to our lessons in Williamsville and quickly learned all we needed to know. We skied across our fields almost every afternoon, coming home when the shadows slanted and turned the snow blue in the setting sun. We would come into the kitchen, rosy and exhilarated, take off our snow covered mitts, gaiters and long ski socks, and sit by the stove to relax. A feeling of peace and contentment would descend. I wanted to share this great thing we'd found.

"We need to convince Mike and Madeleine to take this up. It would be fun to go together."

"It's funny how quickly they became 'Mike and Madeleine'."

"They seem to be made for each other."

"Mike is full of charm."

"Madeleine is elegant and smart."

"How wonderful for us."

We laughed at how marvellous everything seemed.

"Seriously, I find it amazing how quickly they have become an established couple. Doesn't it amaze you?"

"I've known Mike for a long time and I am never surprised at how easy it is for him to find love."

"Oh." That made me somewhat uneasy. "Does he also walk away just as easily?"

"Don't worry. He hasn't been breaking engagements and hearts. I mean he's easy to love. You must have noticed."

"Yes, it seems entirely natural to have him around. Almost as soon as I met him I felt I'd known him forever."

"That's exactly it."

"I want everything to be perfect for the people I love. I need to let go and trust more."

As it turned out, they were delighted to take up skiing with us. We went together to the Williamsville sports store and helped them get everything they needed. We discovered a cross country skiing paradise north of Williamsville, on a farmer's property. It had miles of groomed trails; across fields, through wooded areas, and over hilly terrain. This was our favourite skiing destination.

We gradually got to know the farmer and his sheep, who came over to greet us as soon as we parked. We skied there almost every Saturday through that winter. Often we would go back to our place and make dinner together. We did it so often we developed a routine and could work around each other with ease. Mike always had to be up early on Sunday for church services so they would head back to Lawrenceville early. Sometimes he still had to write a sermon. I wondered how he could stay awake to write after a day of skiing in the fresh air and a wonderful supper.

Patrick sometimes went to services at St. Mathias, especially if Mike was preaching. Other times he came with me to Sacred Heart. When we had our marriage instruction from Father Kelly, Father talked to Patrick about converting. I would have loved that. It seemed best, especially if we had children. Patrick never said much about it. He may have been contemplating it. Given his background as a candidate for the Anglican priesthood, I expected that he would give it a lot of thought. In fact he had been debating it, but his conclusion was that I should join the Anglican Church.

"Think about it Clare. It's not much different from the Catholic Church. And you'd be part of my family's religious celebrations."

"Your family only goes to church for weddings, Christmas and Easter."

"They aren't a sterling example of Anglicans. I got a little scared by Father Kelly's instruction. Being Catholic seems hard. So many rules and so few ways to get around them."

"Then you understand why I couldn't possibly leave it. The church is who I am. It is the only unchanging and unfaltering institution in this world."

Patrick didn't look convinced. "Let's drop it for now."

Which we did.

***

Mrs. Anderson, now 'Evelyn' to me, invited us to stay with them for Christmas. She said it was easier for me and Patrick to travel to Toronto, than for all of them to come to us. We decided to travel by train and not worry about driving through winter storms. As soon as Isabel and Joe's wedding was behind us we set out for Toronto, laden with presents and luggage.

It was my first time staying with the Anderson's as a daughter-in-law. I wondered what room we would be given. On previous visits I had stayed in Maureen's room, which was very girly, and still had her stuffed animals, dolls, and books. I liked that. It gave me a glimpse into her past. Patrick, of course, slept in his own room, which had bunk beds for a sleep over with a friend.

This wouldn't do now. Much to my delight we were given the guest room with its own bathroom, a comfortable queen size bed, and a beautiful view of the back garden. It was built over the garage, separate from the rest of the house. I had never seen it on previous visits.

Gordon and Evelyn. I said these names to myself as we neared Toronto. My in-laws. I wasn't used to calling any middle-aged person by their first name. That's why I was practising. It didn't feel natural.

It also seemed that our usual complete understanding of each other was draining away with each mile we got closer to the city. I knew I was getting tense, and I felt it was understandable given my last visit to the Anderson's house, but why was Patrick growing cold and losing his sense of humour?

The Anderson's met us at Union Station. "Moms, Dad." Patrick hugged his parents in turn.

"Clare." Mrs. Anderson turned towards me. "How's our girl?"

"Evelyn. So good to see you."

She hugged me and I felt the softness of her wild mink coat that I so admired. We drove straight back to their place. As soon as we got settled Gordon asked us to join them for drinks in the living room. The setting was impressive. They had a large Christmas tree in the corner of the room and the fire was blazing.

Gordon asked us what we'd like. He turned to the sideboard covered with crystal decanters, glasses, ice and a black and silver soda siphon. He passed around our drinks and said, "Here's to many happy Christmases together."

Evelyn raised her glass and added, "And to your first Christmas as a married couple. It is very special." She clinked glasses with me.

We were being given the royal treatment. I wondered why we had been so uneasy about this visit. I suppose Patrick was worried about the possibility that his mother and I would not get along, but it seemed we worried for nothing.

We stayed for four days that were a constant round of parties, dinners and presents. Gordon and Evelyn were popular. There was barely ever a space in their social calendar.

Christmas day we spent at the Lynches. We went early to enjoy seeing the children open their presents. The twins, Pattie and Bobbie, were barely six months old, but were bombarded with gifts. I doubted presents even registered in their infant minds. We took turns holding them, giving them bottles, and handing them off to the au pair when they cried.

Gita and Jiddu were happy to see us. They were still young enough to be open in their affection, constantly holding my hand, sitting on my lap, and saying they wished I would move in with them.

"What about Patrick? We're married now."

"Oh, he can come too," Jiddu assured me.

It had snowed overnight. Patrick and I went out in the yard and made two large snowmen with Gita and Jiddu after breakfast. It was cold. Our feet were soon frozen, despite winter boots and warm socks. We went back inside to do puzzles by the fire while we warmed up.

Gradually everyone went off to their own corner. The Lynches had a library where I found a book to keep me amused. Patrick and his father went into the den to watch American football with Mr. Lynch. The twins were not in sight; they were probably sleeping in the nursery. Maureen was sitting, staring at the puzzle pieces, her hand hovering aimlessly over the pieces. We were alone.

"Are you happy?" She spoke this quietly.

"I'm as happy as possible on this earth."

"It looks like it. Why are you so lucky, Clare?"

"The way you say that, it sounds like you are saying you are unlucky. What's going on?"

"I'm so tired all the time I barely feel alive. I can't think straight. Nothing interests me."

"Did you go to the doctor?"

"He gave me pills. I'm full of pills. But I don't feel better."

I came over and sat beside her on the couch.

"We got to know each other pretty well at Buttercup Acres. You were full of energy. Confident. Smart. What's changed?"

"The doctor says it's hormones, brain chemistry, some crap. I know that's not it."

Before she could continue Mrs. Lynch came back in the room.

"How's my girl today. You didn't eat much breakfast. I brought you some toast."

It was true. Maureen only picked at her food.

"Thanks Betty, I'm ready for it now." Maureen smiled at her mother-in-law, held the toast up, and took a bite.

Mrs. Lynch turned to me. "I hope you can talk to Maureen. I don't want her starving herself."

As soon as she left Maureen pushed the plate aside.

"I'm not starving myself. Betty is kind, but she doesn't understand what I'm feeling. I need to get away."

"Get away from what?"

"That's something I can't quite put my finger on."

Gita and Jiddu returned to the puzzle. Maureen put her hand on mine, "Help me," she whispered.

We couldn't continue our discussion.

We had our Christmas dinner mid-afternoon. It was elaborate. The Lynches followed the English tradition of Christmas crackers, flaming plum pudding, and the hidden, lucky coin. We were back at Patrick's family home by early evening. It had been a tiring day.

Before we left I took Maureen aside. "I'll come over and get you in the morning. We'll go out by ourselves for lunch."

"I'll be ready."

Maureen suggested a restaurant she knew well. It was in the midst of a street of boutiques and gift shops. We were led to a table through a maze of hanging plants and wicker furniture.

"This feels cozy. These macramé hangers make me feel right at home."

"I come here to be quiet." Maureen lit up a cigarette.

"You never used to smoke. What's going on with you?"

"I did for a while in high school. It calms me down. Helps me think."

"I know what you mean. I used to feel completely at peace with the world in that few moments when I sat with my cigarette and coffee in the morning. At no other time did life make so much sense."

"I don't smoke at home, so I'm not going to get addicted. This is temporary, until I can get my life sorted out."

"You look better today."

"Yesterday was rough, knowing that I'd have to spend the day surrounded by family. That I'd have to try to look happy. After all I've gone through, getting free of the ashram, getting Harry back from all the craziness, having beautiful, healthy twins, you'd think I would be on top of the world. Instead, I feel like I've lost all reason to live. I have so much, and I feel so impoverished. Can you understand any of this?"

"I've been through some rough patches but I don't think I've been where you are now."

"The doctor says it's post-partum depression."

"That could be but Kate says nothing is ever just biological. Our spirit is intertwined with everything. Every health crisis, no matter what the physical diagnosis is, is also a spiritual crisis."

"That's more respectful of how big this feels. It isn't some chemical that's out of whack. I feel like I've been shaken out of orbit. I'm not at home anywhere. I need to find out what my purpose is, beyond being Harry's wife and a mother."

"You could find meaning in those things. It's enough for lots of women."

"The happiest times I've ever had in my life were those months at Buttercup Acres. I felt so alive. It seemed as if there were consequences to my actions. People were counting on me. I had real responsibility. I need that. I feel like an ornament in the life I'm living now."

"Does Harry know how you feel?"

"I tried to tell him but he doesn't get it. He wants me to take my pills and get over it."

"You asked me to help. What can I do?"

"I'd like to be involved with the farm again. I don't mean that I plan to run away from Harry and move in with you, but I'd like to work from Toronto. Create a market for whatever you produce. It might bring me out of this."

"A great idea! I would love to have you back in our lives. I miss your business skills. Let's get together with Patrick and talk it over. We're heading home in two days and the social schedule here is packed. Can we manage to find some time together?"

"We'll make it happen."

***

"Home again." I sighed with happiness. "Isn't it great to be back?"

Patrick agreed. "There are so many things I want to do, I hardly know where to start. I want to skate, and ski, and lie on the couch and read, and say hi to the chickens, and see our friends...."

I laughed. "All of those are calling to me too."

"Let's never go away again."

"What could possibly be better than life here?"

We dropped our backpacks and packages on the floor in the hall and went out to see how the chickens were doing. The sun was slanting through the dusty barn window onto a patch of straw covered floor. The chickens hurried over to greet us when we walked in, moaning and lamenting. I think they were pleased we had returned. The eggs, collected by our neighbour over the past few days, were in a wire basket by the door.

As we unpacked from our trip we talked about Maureen's proposal. Patrick was on board with having her as a business partner. He too recognized her skills. The fact that she was in Toronto could be a positive thing, leading to markets we'd never thought of. After all, Toronto was full of rich people who were longing for the world they'd lost; nature, innocence, fresh air. Maureen was planning to sell that.

"New year's Eve is coming up. Do we have plans?" Patrick had already handed over our social life to me.

"Last year was the best," I said. "Just you and I welcoming in the New Year."

"It was an unforgettable night."

"I'll call Isabel and see if she has any plans. They're staying with Joe's parents over the holiday. Not much of a honeymoon."

"You were right; it's not the best beginning for their life together. It's easier to see now that they're in it, having to make quick decisions about work and where to live, knowing that in a few months there will be a baby to look after."

When I called, Isabel told me there would be a band at the Regent Hotel on New Year's Eve and they planned to go with all the rest of the friends we knew. She said to arrive early before it filled up. I asked her how it was going at Joe's place.

"For the first time I've had some good talks with Joe's mother. She's happy to have me in the family. That's a big help, but the next few months will be hard. I'm going to stay with Joe in Ottawa, in the apartment he shares with two other students."

I could easily imagine it. Poor Isabel, in a two-bedroom apartment with three men!

"I visited in the fall. It's crummy. Remnants of cast-off furniture, a bathroom you don't want to think about, a stale sweaty smell that doesn't go away except when it's replaced by the smell of hot dogs and Kraft dinner."

"Are there no other options?"

"It would be too disruptive to find a place now. Joe needs all his energy to finish up his degree. I'll be there all day, so at least I can keep it clean. Maybe cook something besides hot dogs for the guys."

"You'll come through it," I assured her. "When you and Joe have your own place, it will be all the more special."

Did I really believe this? Her next few months sounded like a nightmare.

The next day we skied with Mike and Madeleine. It was a crisp, sparkling day. We were out for hours and came home glowing. We sat around the wood stove, basking in the warmth, feeling lassitude spread through our bodies.

"Would anyone mind if I took a nap? I don't think I can cook until I've had a rest." I went upstairs.

When I woke up an hour later it was dark and I discovered everyone sleeping in the living room. I could hear the clock ticking in the kitchen it was so quiet downstairs. I went around the house lighting candles in the windows, thinking how blessed we were. I was grateful for where I found myself; in this beautiful home, with such wonderful friends. It was a miracle. There was no question about it.

A New Year Begins

Adrian decided to take a vacation in January. He went to Mexico after visiting his parents at Christmas. He sent post cards every week, saying he was getting back into meditation and reading as if his life depended on it. He had many books to catch up on after having spent the previous year working too hard. "Never again," he wrote.

It was funny to have our hired man letting us know he wouldn't want to work hard again, but I knew exactly what he meant. He was not going to let his life become unbalanced. I agreed completely. There must always be time for reading, for beauty, for aimless meandering around the aisles of Woolworth's. These things kept us sane.

Maureen said she would like to come and stay for a few days so we could talk in depth about a business plan. She planned to bring the children and the au pair, Inger. We were going to be a full house. I reminded her to bring the children's skates and lots of warm clothes. I looked forward to playing outdoors with them in the snow.

The pond was well frozen and I knew Gita and Jiddu would be longing to get out and skate. It also gave me the motivation to start writing down my children's story, and to add to it so that I could continue the tale when they arrived. I was excited about their visit.

I remembered the wonderful evenings spent with Maureen the first summer we met, sitting up late, listening to records, drinking wine, and talking. I hoped we could recapture some of that.

Maureen borrowed her father's Cadillac for the visit. It had lots of room for the six of them and their luggage. The twins, despite their small size, had the most luggage; diapers, bottles, snow suits, wool hats, mitts, socks, rompers, sleepers, undershirts, face cloths, soothers, stuffed toys, rattles, baby blankets, and more. As soon as they came in with their luggage, the house, which had always seemed like a vast mansion, became crowded.

They arrived in time for lunch. I had a large pot of homemade chicken noodle soup ready, along with a platter of sandwiches. While I was getting the food on the table, Patrick helped get them settled in their rooms upstairs. Luckily, we had room for everyone. It felt good having a full house and hearing children's voices.

Gita brought her school books and proudly showed me her reader and math book. She told me she brought work with her since she would be missing a week of school. She clearly loved being a student. Jiddu was in kindergarten. As far as I could tell, he never gave it a thought. He was immediately immersed in the world of Buttercup Acres, longing to be outside.

"I want to see the chickens and skate on the pond and visit Goldilocks' Cottage." Jiddu remembered well the things he had loved. "Where's Adrian?"

"He's on vacation. But you'll get to see him on your next visit. He lives in Goldilocks' Cottage again."

Maureen's visit helped to clarify what we would be doing for the next year at least. She had been doing research, and thought we should drop the tourist home idea.

"The money is going to be in organics. Organic everything. Food, cosmetics, fabric. You name it; it will be worth triple if it's organic. Patrick's plan to make cheese could be a real winner. I have a feeling this will sell really well. You should still have the organic garden, but the big focus should be the dairy."

I was relieved when she said that. I was dreading the idea of having paying guests, but hadn't really admitted it to myself. I could much more easily see myself working with the garden and dairy cows.

Maureen was going to contact cheese markets and specialty shops in Toronto. She wanted us to get started as soon as possible, even before the cows arrived.

"We'll need to learn cheese making," Patrick said.

"I've already been looking into that. There's a business for sale near Toronto, owned by an older couple, from France. They want to retire. They're willing to pass on their skills to the new owner."

"Sounds perfect," Patrick said.

By the end of her visit Maureen had us on track for starting a small organic cheese business.

The au pair was delighted to be out of the city. She borrowed my skis every day and went for a long trek over the fields. She told me she felt at home at Buttercup Acres.

"For the first time since I arrive in Canada, I lose my loneliness."

I remembered how lost I felt when I went to work at the ashram, and realized how much worse it would have been in a far away country.

When Maureen left at the end of the week, she was transformed from the depressed woman I saw at Christmas. She was now full of energy and confidence. On the morning they were returning to Toronto she called me into the bathroom.

"Watch this." She took the pills that had been prescribed for depression and flushed them down the toilet. "That's what I think about my doctor's advice."

Patrick realized we would soon have all our time taken up with farm work. He decided he needed to get as far as he could on his book about Dr. Murphy. He asked Kate if she could make time for him a few mornings a week. He then spent every afternoon typing up his notes at his desk.

I went with him for most of these mornings. I loved being with Kate and enjoyed the stories about her family. On one of these mornings, she told us about her father's belief about living always in the presence of God.

"He tried to convey it to us. He said it was a state in which there was only joy, no fear. I have experienced this myself. When I'm outside of it, life is hell."

Kate was not religious in the conventional sense. I wasn't aware of her having any connection to a church. Her description of this experience of being in the presence of God sounded like a profound belief and faith in Providence. Like the state I would imagine a saint to be in.

"In everything my father did, he started with an acknowledgement of the presence of God. From there all things flowed easily. He knew what to do. God himself was instructing him. Nothing was work. It was all joy. Do you think you would dare to write of this? Would it seem like madness?"

"Your father must have been a profoundly holy man. I don't have any experience with such things, but I can accept that such a state is possible. I went through a religious conversion which led me to think I had a calling to be a priest. I met many good and holy people through this exploration, but nothing to compare with this," Patrick said.

I thought of my own life, of how important the church had always been to me, and of the religious people I had known. I had to admit, none of them seemed to be in this exalted state. This talk left me with a desire to know more. I wanted more than ritual; I wanted an experience of God.

"I'm planning to write a chapter on your father's philosophy, his wisdom. I think it will be the last chapter, but maybe it should be first. It might help make sense of all the rest."

While Kate and Patrick talked about the structure of the book, I was lost in a reverie. What did it mean, to live in the presence of God? I longed to find out. I knew Kate was unlike anyone I'd ever met. Her honesty and integrity were unshakeable. I might describe her as 'real'. Real in a way I had never before encountered. She wasn't swayed by the currents around us. She didn't need to be liked.

I said, "How do you get there? I mean, into the presence of God?"

Kate's answer was simple. "You must pray unceasingly."

Simple. But impossible.

***

Adrian returned from Mexico looking relaxed and peaceful. He was excited about having discovered the writings of Krishnamurti, and could speak of nothing but this.

"Krishnamurti says truth is a pathless land. No guru can take you there. You must find it for yourself. Truth is, when thought stops."

This was an even more daunting teaching than that of Kate's father. The more I learned of Krishnamurti, the more my head ached with trying to understand. But it was having a transformative effect on Adrian. He was spending a lot of time in silence. He said now he could see clearly the danger of alcohol and pot. He was completely freed of the desire for it.

"It's like seeing a dangerous snake. I know not to go near it. There's no conflict in me. I just stop," he said.

I wasn't sure how much I was going to like this reformed Adrian. I hoped he wouldn't also give up reading. I wanted to continue our shared love of literature.

"Truth is a pathless land."

"Adrian, if that's true then why read Krishnamurti?"

"I know, his message is confusing and difficult. Even contradictory. But I'm sure reading him is good for me. Krishnamurti has been called a 'spiritual window washer'. That's how I see it. He is clearing away all the crap, all the things I've learned that programmed me and prevent me from seeing what it."

Adrian lent me some of Krishanmurti's books. I enjoyed the beginnings of his essays, which were always grounded in a reflection on nature and beauty. As soon as he started to talk about ending thought, I would entirely lose the thread.

A Weekend with Children

On our first free weekend in January, I fulfilled my promise to the four Hearne children. I picked them up after school one Friday and brought them to Buttercup Acres for the weekend. They just barely fit in the truck. I threw their few belongings in the back and drove carefully down the snow-lined roads. I asked Shilta to make sure they had their skates with them.

I had reservations about entertaining the kids and hoped Patrick would have some ideas on how to keep them amused. Before this I had only spent a few hours with them. I still didn't know them well. The girls, Dottie and Bella, were easy as I wasn't that far away from being a girl myself. The boys, Tim and Little Django, were more rambunctious and foreign. I hoped to tire them out with skating.

Patrick planned to play hockey with the boys. He also had his table top hockey game from childhood which he set up on the table in the summer kitchen. It didn't matter that it was cold in there as they'd be working hard at playing.

I expected the girls would bring Barbie dolls and thought we could make them some clothes. I met with Mrs. Bergeron and told her about the upcoming weekend. She gave me a box of remnants, as well as a collection of pin cushions, needles, thimbles and oddments.

"I remember how happy you and Isabel were playing together with Barbies, making evening gowns from bits of old silk scarves."

"We'll see if Dottie and Bella find this fun. It's hard to know what to expect. I'm terrified."

Mrs. Bergeron laughed. "It will be fine. How could they not love a weekend at your place?"

As soon as we got in the house with all their bags and skates I took them up to their rooms and then gave them a little tour of the house.

"Where's the TV?" Tim sounded upset.

"We haven't got one," I said.

"We'll miss Kojak, and the Price is Right." Tim was getting worked up.

"What will we do in the morning? We always watch cartoons on Saturday morning," Bella said sadly.

I sympathised. I wasn't that different when I was a kid. I could barely tear myself away from the screen, except that my father kept strict control over it, and curtailed my television time in a way that I thought was entirely unfair, but now greatly appreciated.

"We have lots of things planned. You won't miss TV, you'll see," Patrick said. "We're going to have fun."

Dottie took control. "Mom told us to be good guests. That means doing whatever Patrick and Clare want! Say you're sorry, Tim."

Tim didn't look sorry, but he quietly said, "I didn't mean it, about Kojak and all."

"Apology accepted," Patrick said. "Now, let's go out and skate!"

The two oldest, Dottie and Tim, were strong skaters and raced quickly around the pond. Bella and Little Django were a different story. Bella could stay up and skate a bit, but Little Django's ankles weren't strong enough to keep him from falling over constantly. I held hands with Bella and Little Django and soon my arm was sore from his weight on me.

"Let's sit for a minute," Patrick said to Little Django. "Let me take a look at those skates."

They were definitely too big. "I've got an idea. Mike's got lots of skates left over from the bazaar. Let's go there in the morning and see if he's got something that will fit better."

After supper we got out a jigsaw puzzle for Dottie and Tim, and I played "Old Maid" with Bella and Little Django. Around 8:30 I took the little ones up to get ready for bed.

"We stay up as late as we want at home. I always fall asleep on the couch," said Little Django.

"Yes, then somebody carries us to bed," Bella agreed.

"Let's try it my way tonight. We'll see if you manage to fall asleep," I said.

I put them in the room that Gita and Jiddu had shared. I told them the story about Martha, Morris and Sheila and they listened quietly. After about ten minutes I realized they were both asleep. I left the door open so they could see the light in the hall and went to join the others.

Patrick had a Miles Davis record on and they were engrossed in the puzzle. I took up my book and sat with my feet up on the couch. It was wonderfully peaceful. Looking after children isn't that hard, I thought.

"What kind of music is this?" Tim asked.

"Jazz," Patrick said.

"I hate it."

Dottie gave Tim a frown.

I knew they were used to hearing the hit parade on the radio, as well as the lively music they played on their instruments at home.

"When this ends we can look for something you'd like better," I offered.

***

We made it through the night with no disturbances, and to my surprise, no tears or homesickness. Patrick took the boys to town after breakfast and returned with well-fitted skates for Little Django. Mike and Madeleine followed soon after. Mike came to join the hockey game.

"I brought beads," Madeleine said. "I thought it would be fun to make jewellery."

That was a great idea. We made bracelets, and then worked together in the kitchen on two batches of cookies.

The guys came in for lunch, glowing from their game.

"Little Django is doing great with his new skates. He can skate like anything now! And he's a natural with a hockey stick. Tim, too!"

"We play hockey at school," Tim said, "but the little ones aren't allowed. Don't go thinking you can play with us next week," he said to Little Django.

"I will if I want to!"

Mike distracted them with a story about meeting Gordie Howe and getting his autograph.

I took them home early Sunday afternoon, wanting to get back to Buttercup Acres before a winter storm that the radio predicted. The children ran into the house, anxious to tell all they had done, to show off their bracelets, new skates, and for Tim, a Hardy Boy novel that he'd found on our bookshelf, and immediately got hooked on.

"I hope they weren't any bother," Shilta said.

"It was great." I meant it. I was exhausted, but they had been cooperative and cheerful.

As I drove off I turned on the radio and heard the opening of Cross Country Checkup. Canadians calling in to talk about whether or not there is a Canadian identity. I turned it off and enjoyed the silence.

Patrick was working in his study when I got home. I could hear him typing and humming softly, as he tended to do while he was concentrating. Coming home to Patrick was absolute heaven. What did I do to deserve such a wonderful life?

Patrick came out, holding a sheet of paper.

"Here's a start on my chapter about Dr. Murphy's prescription for a good life. Would you like to take a look and tell me what you think?"

'Doctor Murphy practiced medicine in Lawrenceville for over 60 years. His medical practice was as much about the philosophy he imparted, as the pills he prescribed.

Here are some of the ideas he readily shared with his patients:

- *Health starts with an orderly household*
- *Good habits and good attitudes lead to a good life*
- *Health requires faith in God and in yourself, which will radiate out to all around you*
- *Always see yourself as 'the luckiest person on earth'*
- *Never look for a person or event to blame – look within and accept responsibility*
- *Never try to reform others, if you haven't first put your own life in order*
- *No guilt, no obligation*
- *Live consciously*

"I don't understand all of them, for instance, what does 'live consciously' mean?" I asked.

I'll have to ask Kate. I wrote it down and now I'm not sure myself."

"The things I understand seem like great advice."

"I'll leave it for now. It needs lots of clarification. How was your trip to the Hearne's?"

"Quiet. They were all talked out."

"We gave them a weekend to remember, at least insomuch as it was different from what they're used to. Dottie reminds me of you. You're very alike. Had you noticed?"

"I hadn't. Do you mean her looks?"

"Partly, but it's more. Her mannerisms, the way she looks after the others. She's has a winning way about her."

"I'm glad to be back on our own. Let's ski to the far hills before the storm starts."

We set off in a light snowfall. By the time we returned we could barely see a few feet ahead. The wind was howling and snow was falling heavily. We came in chilled and sat by the stove, reading, listening to the storm, and taking turns petting Sophie, who moved from one lap to the other.

The storm continued all night. When we came downstairs in the morning snow was piled up to the middle of the windows, creating a spooky, cave-like feeling.

"I'll have to start shovelling. The chickens can't be left," Patrick said.

He was headed out the back way, but quickly returned. "The back door can't be opened. There's too much snow against it."

"I'm going to help," I said.

Together we forged a path around the side of the house, cleared away the snow from the back door, then made our way to the barn. It was still snowing and blowing and I feared within a short while our path would disappear. The chickens grumbled and murmured in the dim light and chill of the barn. I gathered a few eggs while Patrick filled up the feeders, then we struggled back to the house. In the back kitchen we shook off the snow and left our boots and damp clothes.

"We're snowed in," Patrick said.

"Did you have plans?" I asked.

"Kate was expecting me. I'll give her a call."

Luckily we still had electricity. I built up the fire in the kitchen stove and started the coffee.

I went to the window and peered out the top panes. All the landmarks had disappeared, no fences, no road, no river. There was only white.

I felt strangely stimulated, as if on the verge of a tremendous adventure. I loved being shut in by the storm. I could think of a million things to do. Baking, writing, going through the attic to see what treasures had been left over the years, lying on the couch listening to records and reading. I embraced the day.

Patrick was agitated.

"In Toronto during a snowstorm city workers would take care of everything. Now it's all up to me."

The phone rang. It was our next door neighbour calling to say he'd be over to plow our driveway as soon as it let up.

"I expect I'll be over around noon. Everything else okay with you?" he said.

"What a relief!" Patrick said. "I was wondering how I'd ever be able to shovel all that."

We sat in the warm kitchen, drinking coffee.

"Not being able to get out the back door was a shock. It's suddenly made farm life seem more real. Soon we'll have cows and more responsibility. What if the power goes off? How could I handle all that?"

"We'll learn from our neighbours. People help each other. You'll see."

"We've only been snowed in for an hour and I already have cabin fever. How am I going to survive storms that last for days? I'm longing to jump in the truck and go to town, stop at the restaurant, run into the hardware store."

Patrick truly looked like he wanted to flee. He was sitting on the edge of his chair, scowling. I didn't know if I should tell him how much I embraced this stormy weather.

"It could be you're only now realizing what it means to be in the country. It does call for a lot of self-reliance. We've been in a honeymoon phase for weeks, but reality may be setting in. We'll both have a lot to learn. Being responsible for animals and a business is going to make us grow up fast."

"I think that's it. This storm suddenly made it all real. We'll be here, stuck, with animals that we can't leave."

"What are you saying?"

"I'm anxious about everything. It feels like too big a responsibility. I have no background in all this."

"There will be new responsibilities for both of us but I'm sure we can handle it. We're far more able to succeed than others, given all the support we have from your family."

"It's not about money. It's whether I've got what it takes."

Patrick got up. "I'm going to the study."

Within a few days the world was back to normal. The roads were cleared, our driveway was ploughed, the sun was shining, but Patrick's gloom continued.

Lent

Lent began in February that year, when we were still deep in snow. One bright spot in life was Adrian's return from Mexico at the end of January. He came back even more enthused about Krishnamurti, who he had taken to calling 'K'.

"At first K's writings were just words, but while I was away I experienced being outside thought. It truly gave me a new insight into everything." Adrian pressed several of K's books on me. "You must read these."

I was on a different spiritual journey. I was concerned about Patrick, feeling that we were on a strange road where I didn't have any signposts, and needing the familiar. I made an effort to go to Mass every day in Lent, even if it meant driving on slippery roads in the early morning. I got up in the dark, before Patrick was awake, and headed off in the cold. I had an idea that only prayer and fasting could help in this situation.

I spoke to Father Kelly one day about what was going on with Patrick.

"Patrick won't talk about what's bothering him. He's distant and always busy, all the playfulness and joy has gone out of him. What can I do?"

"You're still getting to know each other. You may not have seen him like this during your courtship, but it may be something he returns to again and again. I hope not, but it isn't uncommon. You'll need patience. Only love can make it past these things. Don't clam up. Let him know how you feel."

"I'll try to keep communication open. It's hard when I feel so hurt."

Maureen had Patrick and I scheduled for a week of training with the Augsbergs, the couple who were selling us their cheese business. They lived north of Toronto in a farmhouse, with the cheese factory in a small metal building in the yard. We stayed with them, sleeping in a small room in the attic under the eaves of the sloping roof. It was charming, although somewhat chilly.

We worked all day with them, following the procedure from raw milk to curd to cheese. They were easy to be with and very organized. They had planned out the week so we would learn enough to get started. When we left, they promised to visit us in the summer and help with questions that were sure to arise after we'd gotten our own cheese started.

Patrick went straight from this course to an intense training session on dairy cows at the Agricultural College in Peterborough. I returned home on my own, feeling a lot more confident about being a cheese maker.

I was glad of a break from Patrick. He'd been pleasant over the week at the cheese factory, but there was always an uncomfortable distance between us now. I resumed my Lenten routine, morning Mass and fasting. Father Kelly asked how it was going.

"Patrick's away for two weeks. I'm hoping that time apart will make a difference."

Adrian had been looking after things while we were away. He'd made progress on the renovations in the barn where we planned to have the dairy set up. The Augsbergs equipment would soon be sent to us. The floor where we planned to work was concrete; the walls were uninsulated barn board. One of Adrian's tasks was to get this section insulated and put up drywall. He was also making a window in the south wall, over the area where we planned to have big sinks. We had a plumber coming to get running water in the barn and the piping necessary for production, and an electrician to install heavy-duty wiring.

I helped with the renovation in whatever way I could, and in between I studied the cheese making manuals the Augsbergs had given me. In our free time, Adrian taught me to play Botticelli, which he'd learned in Mexico. It was a guessing game, like twenty questions, but much more complex.

"The letter is S," Adrian started.

"Is it an island in Italy?" I asked.

"No, it is not Sicily."

"Is it a sea?"

"No, it is not the Sargasso."

The game could go on for ages given how circuitous the questioning was. It was enormously entertaining to us, especially as we had a large store of shared knowledge of famous people. Strangely, we often guessed the answer within a few questions. We played while we ate supper, since we were alone.

The cheese manuals had charming pictures of small cheese factories. Many had black and white ceramic tiles on the walls. I decided I wanted tiles like these and ordered some to be delivered immediately. Adrian said he could put them on as soon as the window was in and the drywall done.

Mike visited to see how it was going. He loved helping out with construction and had been involved with the plans since the start. He had wonderful suggestions for how it could be laid out.

"How are you doing without Patrick?" Mike asked.

"Let's take a coffee break," I suggested. "It's easier to talk inside."

I made coffee and we sat in the kitchen at the table.

"Patrick has been acting strange since the big snowstorm. He's been doubting this whole farm project, doubting himself, and worse, not talking to me about what's going on. I'm at a loss. I'm hoping that while he's away he'll see things in a new light and maybe it will blow over."

"When we were at school together he had periods of depression. He'd stop talking. He'd race from class to the library so there was no time to be together. I never was able to have a good discussion with him about it. He kept it hidden. I tried, but he wasn't letting me in. Then he'd return, his old sunny self, and we'd be back to usual."

"What do you think it is? It scares me."

"I'm no psychiatrist. I would put it down to moodiness, without knowing more."

"My father was too silent. I'd hate to live with that again," I said.

"Some say we pick husbands and wives who repeat the patterns of our family," Mike said.

"That's a crushing thought. I barely had a family. No, I don't really mean that. My father was good to me. I know he loved me, but we never talked. After he was gone I realized I hardly knew anything about him. It left me wishing I'd paid more attention, tried harder to get him to talk. I felt it was my failure."

"You shouldn't blame yourself. Although I didn't know your father, I doubt you could have changed him. You were a child. Children aren't responsible for their parents. It has to be the other way around. It's a recipe for disaster when children take care of their parents."

"After my father died, I found out he had a girlfriend. I didn't know if he kept it a secret because he thought I couldn't handle it – or what? Why would he do that? I find it hard not to think it was some failing in me."

"Clare," Mike took my hand, "you've carried too much."

We sat without talking for several minutes.

"I've struggled with the same things," Mike said. "I grew up in a family where I felt responsible to keep everyone happy, to make sure anger didn't erupt. Of course, it never worked. It may have been what led me to be a priest. It wasn't a healthy, loving attitude; it was me trying to be God."

"I say I believe in Providence, yet I act as if it's all up to me," I said.

"Exactly."

"You're a great counsellor Mike. I feel better. Patrick is coming home this weekend. Maybe he'll come in all smiles, if not, I'll deal with it."

"I'm here for you and for Patrick, if he decides to share."

After Mike left I sat and thought about how I had been approaching this problem with Patrick. I'd been racking my brains trying to think of what I could do to help him, wondering how I could change to make things better, asking myself what I'd done to make him so silent. After talking to Mike I could see it clearly. I was blaming myself. Where did this come from? Was it because I was a Catholic that I was so quick to take on guilt? I urgently needed to know why. It wasn't helpful, it didn't change anything, and it made me miserable. I was determined to pay attention and move away from this behaviour.

I had a new thought. Maybe I was starting to see what Dr. Murphy meant by 'living consciously'. Could it be a level of awareness in which we saw deeper into our motivations and decision making? I decided to take it up with Kate. I was excited about exploring this further.

I got my pen and notebook and started writing down my thoughts on this matter: *'If there is conscious living there must also be unconscious living, which is to say, an unexamined life, one in which we are programmed from our past, and react constantly out of habit. My immediate leap from being upset at Patrick's behaviours, to my explanation that it was my fault, was a perfect example of unconsciousness. Unconscious living clearly is painful, but what about conscious living, would it be any less painful? Possibly not, but I want to find out.'*

I called Kate, told her I was on my own and wondered if I could come for a visit.

"Come right away, I haven't had a tea party in ages."

"I made a pound cake," I said. "I'll bring some with me."

The streets of Lawrenceville were lined with dirty snow banks and there was a thick layer of salty sludge everywhere. I got out of the car and walked carefully to Kate's door, trying not to fall.

She had tea ready and we sat down in the kitchen, the warmest spot in the house. There was no sun but it was still pleasant to look out on the backyard with its pine trees amid pristine snow.

"I've been thinking about your father's prescriptions for living, in particular the live consciously rule. I didn't know what it meant, but I'm getting a glimmer of an idea. I wanted to see if you could help me understand it."

"That one isn't obvious. It's definitely subject to interpretation. Father did elaborate on it somewhat. Would you like to know how he explained it?"

"Yes, very much."

"He used to use the example of someone who was bad-tempered. When they would get upset they would simply lash out without thinking. It was an instinctive reaction. But if they had learned to live consciously, they would experience the anger, but then there would be a space between the anger and the action. A time of consciousness in which to decide how to act. The anger could be useful, but probably not. In most cases a conscious person would decide to let it go."

"Hmmm," I said. "I was thinking of how I automatically respond to those I love by taking responsibility for their moods, feeling I am somehow responsible. If I know this is my habit, I can see it and get some distance from it before I go down the road of feeling guilty and responsible. Do you think that is living consciously?"

"Definitely, but there's more. Father also tied it to the idea of being aware of the road you're travelling, and asking questions about how you got there. He told us it was important to know if it was our own chosen path, or the well-trodden path someone had laid out, not necessarily in our best interest. This was quite insightful for the time."

"I was following the well-trodden path when my father died. Since then I've had to find my own path. This is the first time I've seen it in this light. I've decided to keep a journal to explore this sort of idea. I started it today."

"An excellent way to clarify your thoughts! I've kept one for years. Although I have to say, when I look back through them I realize I tread the same ground over and over."

Before I headed home I decided to browse around Woolworth's. It seemed like ages since I'd done so. Their stock didn't change much but I was happy to see the same things I knew and loved. I wandered amongst the children's pyjamas, feeling the soft flannelette and imagining myself buying these for little boys and girls. I was in a sort of reverie, a deep relaxation.

I heard an angry voice, "I see what you've got. You're not going to get away with stealing!" I turned around and saw a saleslady holding Dottie by the arm.

"Dottie, what's going on?" I said.

215

"She yours?" the saleslady said.

"You weren't trying to take something, were you?" I asked Dottie.

"I was going to pay," Dottie said. "I just didn't get to the cash register yet."

"I'll go with her and make sure everything is paid for," I said.

"I'll let it go now, but I'm keeping an eye on her."

Dottie and I walked to the cash and I saw that she had a lipstick and a tiny makeup mirror.

"Do you want me to pay for these?"

"I don't want them. I was only walking around with them, imagining I could buy them."

"Where's your family?"

"I'm alone. I hitched a ride."

I was surprised. Dottie was only 12.

"Would you like to have a coke at the Miss Lawrenceville?"

"Okay."

Dottie didn't say much as we walked down the street, but as soon as we sat down she started talking.

"I'm running away."

"Why?"

"They're not my family. I don't belong with them."

"What happened?"

"I overheard Shilta and Vano talking. My real mother left me with them."

"What exactly did you hear?"

"My real mother is Aunt Dorothy. She left me with them and never came back. I'm your sister."

I was shocked, but it was strangely believable.

"Where were you planning to go?" I couldn't imagine how Dottie could set off on her own, in the middle of winter, with nothing.

"I was thinking I could stay with you. You have a big house. I wouldn't be in the way."

"Dottie, it's not that simple. Your family loves you, they'll want you back."

"They're not my family!"

"Did you bring any clothes?"

She had a paper grocery bag with her.

"Just this. I couldn't carry much."

"You can stay tonight. We'll call Shilta and let them know where you are. It will all work out, don't worry."

But I could see Dottie wasn't worried. As far as she was concerned it was settled; she was living with me.

Dottie Hearne

It was late afternoon by the time we got to Buttercup Acres. It had been a grey day and light was disappearing without a sunset. I wished I could be alone to think, but I'd have to look after Dottie, find out what else could be going on to lead her to run away. Could she truly be my sister? It was very confusing.

Adrian was in the kitchen. He called to me when he heard us come in, "I started supper. I hope you like tofu and brown rice."

Dottie and I went into the kitchen.

"What's this, a visitor?"

"Adrian, this is Dottie." I didn't say, 'my sister Dottie'. I couldn't bring myself to do so.

"Good to meet you, Dottie," Adrian said, giving her a warm smile.

I was glad he was with me. He was great with kids and would take some of the tension away.

"First things first. I'm going to call Shilta and let her know where you are."

I went to the hall and called their house.

"Vano here."

"Vano, it's Clare. I have Dottie with me."

"Oh."

"Didn't you know she was gone?"

"Let me get Shilta."

"Hi Clare, what's this about Dottie?"

"I found her downtown. I brought her home with me for the night."

"Well, for heaven's sakes, I thought she was in her room. What's going on?"

"She says she's run away."

Shilta was silent for several seconds. "What else did she tell you?"

"She says she's Dorothy's daughter. Is this true?"

"Oh hell, we should have told her, and you, a long time ago. I didn't want her to find out by accident. Is she upset?"

"She must be if she felt she had to run away. I'll keep her here tonight. Tomorrow we'll have to talk. We'll come out in the morning."

"A night away may be all she'll need. See you tomorrow."

I could tell Adrian had heard our conversation. He was looking from me to Dottie.

"Dottie is my sister." There, I'd said it.

"Wow Clare, your life is full of good surprises."

"It is a good surprise."

Hearing this, Dottie looked cheerful.

"I belong with you, don't I Clare?" she said.

This was going to be heart-breaking.

"Let's have supper and later we'll sit and talk."

I was surprised to find the only things Dottie brought with her in the paper bag were her skates and one of Uncle Django's carvings.

"Could we skate in the morning?" she asked.

She really had planned ahead and knew exactly what she wanted. Truly, Dorothy's child!

After supper we sat in the living room, in the soft light of the lamps. I kept expecting tears or some sign that Dottie was upset, but she wasn't the least bit distressed. She was calm and talkative, full of plans for her life with me.

"Were you unhappy at home? Why don't you want to live with them?"

"No reason. Are you saying you don't want me?"

"It's just that they're your family too. More than me, because they've had you since you were a baby. Don't you see that?"

"I can still go and visit them."

Dottie was being perfectly reasonable, while I was become unhinged. What would Patrick say about all this? I wished he had been home so we could have responded to this together. I was starting to think having her come to live with me was completely reasonable, maybe because I had a longing for family. Whatever it was, I knew I couldn't decide without Patrick.

I lent her some soft pyjamas and ran a bath for her. I told her to call me when she was in bed and I would come say good night. After Dottie was asleep, Adrian and I sat in the kitchen talking about the events of the day.

"What am I going to do?"

"Normally, there wouldn't be any question. She obviously belongs with her family, but are you getting the feeling they'd happily pass her over to you?"

"I don't know. They're not ordinary people. I guess I'll have to see what tomorrow brings."

***

Shilta called in the morning and asked me to delay my visit.

"I'm busy tomorrow. Could you keep her for a few days?"

"I could," I conceded, "but this can't go on." I was shocked at her delay.

Dottie was up early and ready to skate before I'd even had my coffee.

"Not yet," I said. "We have to have breakfast and I have to feed the chickens. I never do anything before coffee."

"I'm excited. I woke up a long time ago and I've been waiting for you for ages."

"What about school? You should be there this morning."

"They won't be surprised. Bella, the boys, and I go to the same school. They don't get too concerned if we aren't there."

I remembered the day I visited and saw that one of the little ones had slept through the morning and no one had noticed.

"If you lived here you'd have to go to school every day."

"I know that. I wouldn't expect to stay home and play every day."

This sort of conversation was dangerous.

I needed to talk to Dorothy, but that was impossible. I decided to write to her and hoped she would get back to me quickly. I had to know the truth.

I had been clearing space in the barn for the cow stalls. There was years of junk accumulated that I was sorting into three piles; discard, save, and sell. I left Dottie in the house with a book while I continued with the work. It helped to be busy. Part of my mind worked on the matter of Dottie, while another was completely engaged with sorting.

Around four o'clock I was surprised to hear Patrick's voice. He came out to the barn to find me.

"Patrick, darling. I didn't expect you until the weekend."

"Clare." He held me close. "We finished the course early and I came right home."

"It's good to have you back." I meant it.

"What's Dottie doing here?"

As soon as I heard his question, I lost my tentativeness about the situation. I knew what I needed to do. If she really was my sister, she was my responsibility.

"Something amazing has happened." I told Patrick the whole story.

"My God! I'm glad I came home early. This is too big to handle on your own. Funny, I was just saying how much she resembles you. We'll sort it out."

I didn't get together with Shilta and the family until Sunday. Dottie didn't want to come with me, afraid that she would be forced back to her old home. This alone made me feel that something was very wrong. I decided it would be easier to talk it over if she wasn't present.

"We should have told you sooner," Shilta said, as soon as we sat down to talk. "But when we first saw you, you were working as a babysitter. We didn't see how you could possibly look after your young sister.

"When the kids came home from their weekend with you, and talked about how great it was, we started to think it would be a better place for Dottie. We hadn't made any decision, we were talking it over, and she must have overheard."

"You mean you don't want her?"

"Now, don't put it that way. It's just that we're poor, and you're not."

"I won't make any decision until I hear from Dorothy. I want to know exactly what happened. Do Dottie and I have the same father?"

"Dorothy will have to answer that."

"She can stay with me for now," I said.

"I've packed a few of her things," Mercy said, handing me a small suitcase.

The uncles stayed silent while we were talking, but Shilta and Mercy seemed to have already made up their minds that Dottie was my responsibility now.

Uncle Django looked downcast. He was fond of Dottie, but he never made a fuss.

As I was getting in the car, Vano came out with a puppy in his arms. "We've had another batch. Would you like one?"

I declined. The last thing I wanted was one of their terrifying dogs. What a family I came from!

A Sister

Dorothy called when she got my letter. I was glad for a chance to ask her questions.

"I knew you'd find out sooner or later. I should have told you myself, but it all feels so far in the past. Like it happened to someone else. Do you know what I mean?"

"Of course I don't. I can't imagine having a child and leaving it behind and saying 'it felt like it happened to someone else'."

"You're self-righteous and angry again. I can hear it."

"I'm trying to be calm. I want to know the story. Especially who Dottie's father is."

"I was pregnant when I left Ned. It's probably what pushed me to go. I knew I couldn't go through it all again. I went to stay with my sisters until the baby was born, and then I slipped away. I didn't even know what they called her. I'm shocked there's another Dorothy. How unimaginative!"

"So she's really my sister?"

"Yes."

"She looks like me."

"Lucky girl!"

"What about Dad? Didn't you think he'd want to know about his own daughter?"

"Ah Clare, it's all in the past. Let it go."

"It's not the past for me. It looks like she's going to come and live with us. I hope I never drop people the way you have."

"You may be an exception."

"What's that supposed to mean?"

"Look, I'm thrilled for little Dottie moving up in the world. I know you'll be good to her."

That was it. Dorothy was still surprising me, even after all the previous surprises. I would never get used to her hardness.

As Mike had suggested, when Patrick returned home he was his usual happy self. I was preoccupied by Dottie and almost forgot how strange he had been. When we finally did speak of it he dismissed it, saying "I was a little moody. I needed some time to sort it out." Maybe Mike's evaluation was right and it was something that would come and go. I was glad to have Patrick back to his old self, especially as he was so supportive of my decision to take care of Dottie.

When I told Dottie she could stay with us she surprised me by saying she wanted a new name.

"Dottie isn't dignified. Would you call me Ellen? It's my middle name."

I was amused by this.

"I'll try to remember. You'll be starting in a new school next week, so it's a good time to have a new name. We must go to Williamsville and shop for some new clothes for you too."

The clothes Mercy sent in the suitcase were too shabby for Ellen to go to school in.

"I know exactly what I want," Ellen said. "Howick jeans and a black cotton turtleneck."

"You'll need skirts or dresses for school. You can't wear pants."

"I know, but I'm most interested in the right jeans."

Where did she get her fashion sense? Since she'd arrived she'd been wearing my clothes, rolling up the sleeves and pant legs, not at all interested in her own things. She especially liked the clothes that Maureen left behind. She had an innate appreciation of fine things.

"I won't ask for a lot."

"I'm happy to get you what you need. It's going to be fun. I never had a little sister before."

"Please, don't send me back."

***

I made a date to get together for coffee with Madeleine. I wanted to talk to her about Ellen.

"She'll be in Grade Seven so I won't have her in my class, but I can watch out for her," Madeleine offered.

"I don't know what sort of student she is. School wasn't a priority in the family. It sounds like she stayed home as much as she went. She may be far behind. I know she can read, but I don't know what else she learned. One thing she knows well is how to play cards. She's a whiz at Euchre. We've been playing with Patrick and Adrian. Everyone wants to be her partner. She's unbeatable."

"She may have some gaps, but I'm sure she can catch up. If she's a good card player it means she has a good memory and good thinking skills," Madeleine said.

"She loves fashion," I said. "I took her shopping and she was very precise about what she wanted. Nothing flashy, just a few good things. I can't figure out how she came by this. Is it possible to be born with style?"

"I'm intrigued. I noticed when we made the jewellery together that she was intent on getting it right. Bella sort of slapped hers together, but not Dottie. I'll have to remember, from now on, she's Ellen. The name change is a smart decision on her part."

"She also asked to have her hair cut. It was the first time in her life. She used to keep it pulled back in long braid. Now it's like mine, hanging to her shoulders."

"How are you feeling about this, Clare? Madeleine asked. "It must be a shock."

"At first I was confused and unwilling. I couldn't bring myself to believe she was my sister, and even if she was, I didn't see why she should come to me. I was struggling with it and out of the blue, I saw clearly that she belongs with me."

"I know a lot about young girls. I'm happy to help if you have any problems. Mom is also a great help. She loves girls and she knows how to keep them in line."

"Speaking of girls, have you seen Isabel lately?"

"Mike and I are going to Ottawa on Saturday to visit. Why don't you and Patrick come along?"

"You're forgetting Ellen. Could we bring her too?"

"Sure, Mike has use of a big, black sedan, belonging to the rector. We can all fit in that."

"The canal is still frozen. Would you and Mike like to skate while we're there?"

"Great idea!"

***

On Monday Patrick and I drove Ellen to school. We went early so we could go to her classroom and speak to her teacher, Sister Mary Francis.

"I've put Ellen here." Sister pointed to a seat in the front row. "She's between two girls. A good quiet spot."

Ellen sat at her desk and opened the lid. There were books inside for all her subjects. Sister gave her several blank notebooks and a pen and pencil.

"I'll pick you up at four," I said.

"Thanks Clare. Don't worry," Ellen said, "I'll be good."

Ellen seemed to read my mind. I would be glad when she had a few weeks of school behind her; she was such an unknown quantity. I hoped she would make friends and be a good student.

Patrick and I went straight to Kate's after dropping Ellen off. It had been a few weeks since he had gotten together with Kate to talk about her father. She invited us into the kitchen.

"Clare, tell me about your sister."

"It's such a strange story, but I've heard it confirmed by my mother, so I accept its truth. Dorothy left the baby with her family and disappeared. They simply accepted it. I don't know if they even contacted my father. They may not have known he was Dottie's father."

"What a life your mother has led!" Kate said.

"I got upset talking to her about it. Her selfishness is beyond comprehension. I'm excited about having a sister. Dottie wants a new start and a new name, so it's Ellen from now on. I'm optimistic about having her in my life, but I know that there will be challenges. She's come from a tough world, the same world that Dorothy was so anxious to escape. She's smart and appreciates the chance she has to live a better life with us. She's conscious of her new advantages. I'm enjoying getting to know her."

"What a turn of events! I look forward to meeting her."

We moved on to making notes on Dr. Murphy's life.

"What did Dr. Murphy mean when he said, 'no guilt, no obligation'?" Patrick asked. "I've added it to his list of rules for living but I couldn't figure out what it means."

"Father gave this advice when presented with someone who was entirely weighed down by obligations, mostly to in-laws, but it could be to immediate family, friends, and church. The basic idea is that all action should be motivated by love. If it grows out of guilt and obligation it will be corrupt, and will lead to wrong action. This is a difficult rule to comprehend and live by, especially for anyone caught in a tissue of obligation and having no idea what they would do without it. It's also terrifying for those who fear no one loves them, and count on pulling the strings of guilt and obligation."

"But if we didn't have obligation, wouldn't it be impossible to keep families together?" Patrick asked. "This sounds a lot like people just following their own inclination, and the hell with everyone else."

"That's the devil of it," Kate admitted. "It is close to Saint Augustine's statement; 'Love and do what you will.' This too seems dangerous."

"We fear this because we know how little love there is. In the absence of love we need guilt and obligation as motivators." I was thinking out loud. The proposition troubled me too.

"What about compromise?" Patrick asked. "Isn't it possible that when a situation arises where we are called to do something we don't truly want to do, that we might do it to keep peace? Isn't that a kind of love?"

"What sort of loving relationship is it that makes you fear a breakdown of 'peace'? It sounds more like a tyranny of some sort. Or a war being fought underground," Kate went on, "My father gave people a lot of credit. He thought we could be loving; he wasn't afraid to aim for perfection."

"I can apply this right away to the situation with Ellen," I said. "If I take her in out of a sense of obligation and not love, it will be terrible for both of us."

"Exactly," Kate said.

"As Divinity Students we talked about this sort of thing, but I couldn't really apply it to life," Patrick said. "Speaking of it so clearly now, I fear I come from a family run by guilt and obligation. I hate to say this, it seems so disloyal. Not that there isn't love there."

"This still worries me," I said. "How do you keep people faithful? I mean, people don't feel loving all the time. What's to keep us from falling in love constantly with new people, and moving on, as the hippies are doing?"

"Well, it belongs in context. It is advice for people who have been crushed by guilt and obligation. Father also believed in honouring commitments. Faithfulness to marriage and family were uppermost in his rules."

"I could write pages and pages about this one," Patrick said. "It puts me in mind of what I told Clare when I first met her, that I feared I was a resounding gong, which is to say, all words, no heart. I agree, love needs to be at the centre of everything; relationships, work and play."

Patrick was excited to get home and set to work on his notes from the morning's discussion. I sat at the kitchen table and opened my journal. I wanted to put down my thoughts on guilt and obligation. I was thinking mainly of Dorothy. Would my life have been better if she had stayed around out of a sense of obligation? It would have been a very different life, with two parents and a sister. I couldn't help thinking that obligation would have been a good thing in this case, and maybe she would eventually have come around to loving all of us.

I seemed to be more on the 'obligation' side of the spectrum. I wanted to think that I was motivated by love, but I definitely felt comfortable taking refuge in rules. I appreciated the direction I got from my faith and didn't trust myself to live without this guidance.

When I picked Ellen up from school she was waiting by the gate, talking to two girls. She looked lovely in her new red plaid coat and knee high winter boots. She called goodbye to the girls and jumped into the truck.

"How was it?" I asked.

"I made two friends. They asked if they could come and skate at our place. Would you mind?"

"I love the idea."

"I have homework. Math."

It was a reassuring start.

Euphoria

We were a cheery group travelling to Ottawa on Saturday morning. It was a bright, crisp day and the roads were clear. Mike loved to sing in the car and had us all joining in. "The bear went over the mountain, the bear went over the mountain, the bear went over the mountain, to see what he could see." This was one we all loved. It was new to Ellen but she caught on fast and liked to sing.

"I wanted to play guitar," Ellen told us, "but it's only for boys."

"That's not true," Madeleine said.

"Well, that's how it was at home. Tim and Little Django learned, but Bella and I weren't allowed to."

"When we get home I'll put on a Joni Mitchell record. She plays guitar, sings, and writes songs," I said.

We reached the apartment where Isabel and Joe lived, a high-rise far on the outskirts of Ottawa, in the midst of fields of snow. Madeleine pushed the button and we heard Joe's muffled voice over the intercom.

"It's us," Madeleine said.

"Take the elevator to the eighth floor. I'll meet you."

The halls and elevator had a stuffy, dusty smell, and were stiflingly hot.

Isabel was starting to show her pregnancy. She invited us into the living room where we squeezed onto a brown couch, while Isabel sat in a green armchair with Joe balanced on the side. At first it was awkward, there seemed to be nowhere to leave our coats and bags. The couch was so worn it was hard to stay upright and I found myself sprawling over Madeleine and Mike.

"I've got coffee on," Isabel said, "and I made muffins. I'm sorry it's such a tight squeeze. Joe, bring some chairs from the kitchen."

We relaxed after this. Isabel talked about her latest doctor's appointment and how the pregnancy was going.

"I'm feeling great now that I'm not sick every morning and I've gotten into a routine. I feel like Snow White, living with all these men. They're happy to have a good supper every night and it gives me something to do besides taking walks and shopping. You may have noticed we're in the middle of nowhere. I have to walk a couple of miles to the nearest grocery store, or wait for the bus in the freezing cold, with the wind tearing across the fields."

"I find it strange," I said. "It's an odd place for a high rise."

"It was meant to be the first of several buildings. For some reason, the rest never got built," Joe said.

Isabel was curious about Ellen. I told her a bit on the phone before we came.

"It's uncanny, as if we have young Clare with us. Do you see how alike they are?" Isabel asked.

"I noticed it, even before I knew they were sisters," Patrick said.

"Clare and I have been best friends ever since we were little," she told Ellen.

"I've never had a friend like that," Ellen said. "We were too far away from other families for me to have a best friend. I've always wanted one."

Isabel beckoned me into their bedroom.

"Isn't it a scream?" she said.

"The apartment?"

"Yes, look at the view from this window. It's like the Steppes of Russia."

"Toronto was worse."

"Are you okay about taking Ellen in?"

"It is turning out to be wonderful. Are you okay, I mean with this apartment and all?"

"I'm so focused on being pregnant that it hardly matters where I am. I know it sounds crazy, but it's all encompassing. I've never been so completely and utterly happy."

We asked Joe and Isabel if they wanted to join us on the canal but Joe had to study and Isabel said she didn't think it was safe for her to skate.

We parked near Dow's Lake and skated the length of the canal to the Chateau Laurier. We stopped to have hot chocolate and rest for a few minutes, basking in the warmth of the sun before skating back to our starting point.

"I've never skated so far," Ellen said. "I didn't know it was possible."

"It's hard work. I'll be sore tomorrow," Mike admitted.

Madeleine took me aside while we were skating.

"What did Isabel say to you? Is she alright?"

"She's in pregnancy-induced euphoria. She knows it's a crappy apartment but she's in a great frame of mind."

"That's a good way to put it. I'll have to tell Mom about Isabel's euphoria. She'll love it!"

Jerseys

The stalls were ready and the great day arrived. Four Jersey cows were delivered at the beginning of April, as promised. The truck backed up into the yard and a ramp was lowered for the cows to walk down. Although Jerseys are considered small, they seemed enormous. I stayed back as they were led to their stalls. They were pretty with their soft eyes and caramel and cream colouring.

"We've been milking them around 5 in the morning and 4:30 in the afternoon. They'll let you know if you're late. You have my number if you have any problems." The farmer got back in the truck and drove away.

"Wow, they're ours now!" Patrick said.

"Wow," I echoed.

They stood in their stalls, reaching down to grab mouthfuls of hay, chewing happily. What placid creatures, as happy here as they had been in their old barn. I loved them immediately.

"Did he say 5 a.m.?" Patrick groaned.

Patrick and I invited his family to come for Easter weekend. We hadn't seen them for a few months and there were lots of changes at Buttercup Acres to show them. As usual, the Andersons planned to stay at the Skylane, while the Lynches would stay with us. It took planning to figure out where everyone would sleep.

Gita and Jiddu's room was now Ellen's. She was delighted to have a room of her own for the first time, and especially pleased with the twin beds, as she had visions of having a sleep over. She made a few changes, immediately removing the clown lamp and putting it in the back of a closet. She went up to the attic and found a lamp with a yellow shade on a curved brass stem. She liked to read in bed and this gave much better light. She also found a desk and chair which she said she would study at, although she usually did her homework in the kitchen, where it was bright and cheery, with one of us always close by to assist.

She loved yellow. Together we made yellow curtains for the windows and found yellow chenille spreads for the beds. I also gave her the primrose quilt to use when it was extra cold.

Patrick and I now had the master bedroom, which looked to the east. We had been using the mahogany bedroom set that Maureen had installed, but the double bed was terribly small. We went to Williamsville and bought a new teak set, with a beautiful queen size bed, and moved the mahogany set into a room on the west side. That would be Maureen and Harry's room. I wasn't sure where the twins could sleep but Maureen said she would take care of it.

It was lucky we had such a large house. There were rooms we had barely looked into. There were two small rooms at the back looking over the barn, with sloped ceilings and dormer windows. We furnished them with cast iron single beds, slipper chairs, and pine bedside tables that we bought at a farm auction. There was also an entire trunk of wool blankets which I purchased, praying they wouldn't be full of moth holes. To my delight they were in beautiful shape, in many colours, some with stripes, some plain. I used these as bright covers on the beds and bought new mattresses, as the old ones had springs poking through. I was enchanted by these back rooms once we got everything in place.

The Andersons and Lynches travelled separately, as Maureen's family was now too large to fit in Mr. Anderson's Cadillac. Maureen travelled with a mountain of supplies for the babies, including their crib. They'd purchased a station wagon to accommodate the family. Not quite as smart as Maureen's Mercedes, but much more practical.

The Andersons arrived first, mid Saturday afternoon. I was somewhat nervous as it was our first time hosting the family since we were married. They came into the front hall in a flurry of presents, cigar smoke and beautiful perfume. The snow was gone, but Mrs. Anderson still wore her mink. I introduced Ellen, who was meeting them for the first time.

Ellen asked me what she should wear and how she should address Patrick's parents. She was very aware of wanting to make a good impression. I was pleased, although I hoped it didn't mean that she was still fearful we wouldn't keep her.

We got settled in the living room and Ellen said, "Could I pour you a sherry, Mrs. Anderson."

Evelyn looked pleased. "Thank you dear, I'd love that."

Mrs. Anderson took to Ellen immediately, and Ellen returned the sentiment.

"I've never been to Toronto, but I've heard they have the most wonderful stores. Someday I'd like to go to Holt Renfrew," Ellen said.

Holt Renfrew? Where had Ellen picked this up?

"It is a great place to shop. You'll have to visit and I'll show you my favourite haunts."

"I'd love that," Ellen said.

Maureen and Harry arrived with the children around 4:30, laden with suitcases and packages. Maureen was looking healthy again. She'd regained the weight she lost in the winter when she had been so depressed. Having challenging work had brought her back to life.

"I'm so excited about seeing the cows," Maureen said. "It's really happening. Soon the cheese production will start. You've probably thought of this already but I have the perfect name for the company – are you ready? Buttercup Cheese."

"I love it," said Patrick.

"Me too," I agreed. "I can't believe we didn't think of it. It's got great connotations of richness, nature and beauty. A winner for sure!"

"We haven't had the barn tour yet," Patrick said. "Shall we go out and see the girls?"

"It's too muddy for me," Evelyn said. "I'm going to stay here and enjoy my sherry."

"I'll stay with you," Ellen offered, "I've seen the cows."

Gita and Jiddu were delighted with the Jerseys. They patted them and declared they were the prettiest cows in the world.

"Clare, will the cows be sent to an island in the summer?" Gita asked.

"What's this?" Mr. Anderson said.

"It's the story I've been telling about cows on an island in the river. These cows won't be doing that. They'll be out in the pasture, eating grass."

Gita held my hand and stayed glued to my side.

"Will you tell us more tonight?" she asked.

"Yes, but I'll have to tell it before you go upstairs to bed. You and Jiddu have new rooms of your own."

"I don't want a new room," Jiddu said.

"I don't either. Why can't we sleep in our room with the clown?"

"It's Ellen's room now," I said.

"That's not fair!" Jiddu was getting upset. Maureen intervened.

"You needed rooms of your own, like you have at home. I'm sure you'll love them and you can get special lamps, ones that you pick out yourself. How's that?"

"Okay, but when can we get the lamps?" Jiddu asked.

Gita whispered to me, "I don't want a new girl to have my room."

"Don't worry darling Gita, you'll always have a place here," I assured her.

When we went inside Ellen and Evelyn sitting side by side on the couch, with cards laid out on a TV tray in front of them.

"I'm learning Solitaire," Evelyn said. "Ellen's a great teacher."

"I didn't know you were interested in that," Maureen said. "I could have taught you."

Now Maureen was jealous. It was going to be an interesting weekend.

We wouldn't be having any wonderful meals at the Skylane with the Anderson's. The babies couldn't be taken to an elegant restaurant yet. The au pair had the weekend off so we were all taking turns watching over Bobby and Patty. They were crawling now, and cried to be picked up and carried almost all the time. It was exhausting. I would have given anything for an au pair that weekend. I was glad to escape to the kitchen to start supper.

After dinner the Anderson's went to the hotel and Patrick and Harry went upstairs to assemble the crib. Ellen helped me with the dishes while Adrian entertained Gita and Jiddu in the living room. He had them singing the songs he'd taught them the summer they'd spent at Buttercup Acres. I could hear the happy sounds of Pete Seeger's songs as we worked in the kitchen. The twins roamed around on the floor, looking for things to pull down and put in their mouths. Maureen followed them around, taking things away.

"I need a playpen," she called out to me.

"There's one in the attic," Ellen said. "Shall I show you?

I watched over the twins while they went to find the playpen. They managed to get it down the narrow staircase to the second floor, where Harry took over and brought it to the living room.

"This may save my sanity," Maureen said.

She plunked them down and gathered up a handful of toys to amuse them. They showed their skills immediately by pulling themselves up and howling at the indignity of capture. There was no easy solution to make these two happy.

Eventually all was quiet. Maureen had the twins asleep upstairs in the crib, and Gita was anxious to hear more about Martha, Morris and Sheila.

We sat on the couch together and I read, for it was now on paper, since I'd gotten my typewriter.

"When we left off, winter was starting. Martha and Sheila were going to hibernate for the winter, and Morris would be out, frolicking in the snow. Now though, winter is over."

> Martha and Sheila had woken up on the first warm morning in spring and realized they'd slept long enough. Sheila stretched and left their shelter, scurrying to her treetop summer home. "See you later, I'm going to find out where I left those nuts," she called as she hurried off.
>
> It was a blue sparkling day on the riverbank. Martha was anxious to start her spring cleaning. It had been a long, snowy winter and there was lots of debris left from storms. Martha sang as she swept, scrubbed and polished, "Oh, how I love a sparkly warkly floor, how I love a sparkly warkly floor." She made up the melody as she went along, and whisked her tail back and forth in rhythm.
>
> She heard a knock at the door and yelled, "Hello, who's there on this beautiful day?"
>
> Morris came in. "I heard sounds and was hoping you were up. It's been absolutely ages since I've seen you. I thought you'd never get up."

"You think that every year. You have to be patient, it always warms up."

"Time to put the old sailboat in the water, eh?"

"As soon as I have everything put to rights we'll head off to see who else is up."

"Poor Bobby Beaver had a shock. You know how hard he worked making his home? Well, just when he'd made a beautiful pond on one side, and a creek on the other, someone came and took it all apart. Can't understand some folks."

"Happens every year. Poor Bobby. Anything else new?

"No leaves to report yet. But there are a few flowers here and there. Mostly snowdrops and croci."

"Croci?"

"Croci. That means several crocuses, to those in the know."

"That's it for tonight," I said. "Time for bed."

"Croci," Jiddu murmured. "I like that word."

We went upstairs and I showed them their new rooms.

"This is charming," Gita said, "like a cottage."

Patrick, Harry and Adrian were out in the cabin, playing poker. Patrick didn't stay late as he had to be up so early for milking. He came upstairs at 10 and dropped into bed.

"I can't keep up with those guys. I've become an old farmer," he said.

"You just have to get used to this schedule. I know some old farmers who party until at least midnight."

On Sunday morning Ellen and I went to early Mass at Sacred Heart, while the Andersons and Lynches went to hear Mike preach at Saint Matthias. When they came home we had breakfast together and the children were given their Easter baskets. They were packed with chocolate eggs and jelly beans from Laura Secord, as well as marbles and skipping ropes. The twins each got a stuffed white rabbit.

The day was perfect for Easter, sunny with a cool breeze. There was almost no snow left, but there were remnants of ice on the pond and the ground was muddy. Maureen and I stuck close to the kitchen, keeping an eye on Bobby and Patty, cooking the ham and scalloped potatoes, and catching up on what had been going on in our lives.

Patrick's father complained again about us still not having a television. "Maureen's not here anymore. There's no reason not to have one now," he said.

"I'm open to the idea. I think we can keep it under control," I said. "Ask Patrick what he thinks."

Gita and Jiddu played with their skipping ropes on the front walkway, then brought toys to the front porch where it was warm in the sun.

"How's Patrick's book going?" Maureen asked. "Does he have any time to write?"

"He's working on it, but as soon as the garden season starts we're going to be busier than we've ever been. I'm not sure how I'll cope."

"I'm excited about the first cheese. I'll order packaging with "Buttercup Dairy" on the label and get it to you soon."

"It won't be ready to sell until July. That is, if our first batch turns out."

"I'm going to work on finding vendors in Toronto, but I better not promise until we have a product. I have a feeling it's going to be great. Let's take some pictures of the Jersey's. It would be good for promotion."

"Let's do it now," I said. I got the Leica and we left the babies in the playpen, with Evelyn in charge.

"Don't be long," Evelyn said. "I won't know what to do if they start howling."

The sun was shining through a small window onto the stalls. We took turns standing beside the prettiest cow and photographing each other. Maureen managed to look absolutely elegant, even in a barn.

When we returned Evelyn and Ellen were sitting together again, talking quietly. Evelyn had tears in her eyes. Ellen had been telling her about how she had been left when she was a baby.

It was funny that she had tears for Ellen but none for me. After all, we both had the same story of loss.

"Poor child," Evelyn said.

On Monday the guests went home and we had a quiet day, although there were no days off for Patrick and me now that we had milk cows. He got up at 5 to do the first milking, and later I strained the milk and got it ready for the cheese making process. Already we had a good quantity of milk ready for our first batch of cheddar. The Augsbergs told us this was a reliable cheese and a good-seller. I was planning to make curd too, and sell it in Lawrenceville, since it needed to be squeaky fresh. I was planning to approach the small grocery store on the main street, as soon as I had my first batch.

Ellen was working on a speech that she needed to research, write, memorize, and deliver to the class. Her topic was the Seaway Canal. I knew a bit about the subject, having lived through the building of it. Patrick said he would go with her to the library one evening that week to see what information they could find.

"How did you pick that subject?" I asked.

"All the other ones were taken," Ellen said. "But they were all just as hard as this one."

I'd forgotten how hard school could be. I used to dread projects because I didn't have a clue how to start. I was better at memorizing and giving it back on tests. Dorothy had never had any interest in what I was doing at school, and my father was too tired to help with schoolwork.

"I only have to talk for about 3 minutes. How many pages do you think that would be?" asked Ellen.

""Let's try it out," Patrick suggested. "Read from your notebook and I'll tell you to stop at 3 minutes."

"How do you come up with such great ideas?" I asked Patrick.

That night I went in to say goodnight to Ellen she was at her desk, sitting in front of the cards.

"Do you tell fortunes?" I asked.

"Only for myself. It puts me into a place where I see things in a new light. Not the future. It's hard to explain but it helps me see more clearly what's going on."

"Dorothy read the cards. I used to tell her it was the work of the devil. It still makes me nervous."

"I don't do it for others, like Shilta and Mercy do. I don't even talk about it because some girls made fun of me about it when I went to school in the country."

"I'm sorry to hear that. Was that a bad place to go to school?"

"Only for us. We weren't like the other kids, our hair wasn't combed, we weren't dressed like the others; it was horrible. I stayed away as much as possible."

"Oh sweetie, I'm sorry to hear that." This brought me to tears. "If anybody's mean to you now, you tell me right away."

"Sacred Heart School is different. Sister Mary Francis watches over me, and she must have spoken to the class, because they're always nice to me. Tell me about our parents, I hardly know anything about them."

I sat down on the edge of the bed.

"Mom, who I called Dorothy, lived with us until I was 10. When they were first married, and when I was little, she was happy. Like you, she wanted to get away from the hard life in the country. Dorothy was glamorous. She spent the morning smoking and drinking coffee in her bathrobe, then she put on her makeup, got dressed up, and her friends came over to talk and have their cards read. She always wore beautiful high heels and tight sweaters. I used to feel she didn't care for my company and I was alone a lot unless Dad was home. I even ate by myself most of the time. Dad worked hard and was only home on the weekends, at least until Dorothy left. I'd been to friend's houses and I knew our family wasn't like others. I was proud in a strange way, and told myself it was a good thing, that I didn't need any mother telling me what to do, watching over me all the time."

"That's sad," she said.

"It makes me sad even now. I wasn't fooling myself. I wanted her to love me."

"What about Dad?"

"He was kind," I said. "You would have loved him. He was quiet, but he paid attention to me. Dorothy shut him out too, so I suppose he was lonely. It's getting late; we can talk about this more. I'll tell you anything you want to know about them. I have a few pictures. I'll get them out tomorrow."

"Good night Clare. I'm sorry you were sad."

"Thanks Ellen, good night."

The Martin

A week after Easter, I was surprised to find a letter from Patrick's mother, inviting us to come for a weekend as soon as we could get away. "Be sure to bring Ellen," she said.

Adrian could handle things for a few days. We drove to Toronto on a Saturday morning in May. The trees weren't yet in leaf, but the grass was starting to grow and the world was turning green. Ellen was excited. It was her first visit to Toronto.

I learned that much of Ellen's fashion sense came from watching Emma Peel on the Avengers. Mrs. Peel seemed like a great role model to me too. Ellen was also aware, from the cruelty of children at her first school, that it was important to know how others dressed and behaved, and to fit in. I was gradually getting a picture of how her life had been, and could understand why she was so anxious to stay with us. She was more self aware than the other children, and this made her life harder. Dorothy had probably been the same. As Dorothy's sisters said, Dorothy was noticeably smarter than the rest of the family.

Ellen was given Maureen's old bedroom at the Anderson's and we had the beautiful suite we'd had at Christmas. Maureen's room was full of her old toys and interests. There was a guitar hanging on the wall.

"Would it be okay if I took this down?" she asked Mrs. Anderson.

"Of course, dear. Do you play?"

"No, but I want to learn."

It was a big guitar but Ellen had obviously picked up guitars in her house as she knew exactly how to handle it. She put the strap around her neck and strummed it.

"If only I knew a few chords. I'll bet this is a great guitar."

"Maureen took lessons for a few months, but she lost interest. I don't think she'd mind if we gave it to you. Do you have anyone who could teach you in Lawrenceville?"

"I could look into it," I said. "There must be teachers."

"There's a big case for it in the closet. You can take it home in that," Mrs. Anderson said.

"Thank you!" Ellen looked ecstatic. "You can't imagine how much I want to play."

I knew Ellen was serious about this. She really didn't ask for a lot.

"As soon as you're settled I want to take Ellen downtown. I promised to show her the shops."

I didn't seem to be invited, but I was fine with that. Patrick and I hadn't had any time to wander freely together in ages.

"Let's go back to that Italian shop where we had espresso, then wander around the Market," I suggested to Patrick.

"Dad and I are going to go out for some guy time. Can you find that area without me?"

"I'll see if Maureen can meet me. I don't know my way around."

Maureen picked me up and we went to the restaurant she'd taken me to at Christmas time. We sat amongst the hanging plants, feeling very private.

"This is still my refuge," Maureen said. "I'm in a much better frame of mind, but I still like to come here to be alone. You used to love your solitude, Clare, your morning cigarette as the sun rose. Do you still find a way to be on your own?"

"It's harder now. I often go to morning Mass just to have time alone, Sometimes I go in early to pick Ellen up from school, and sit at Woolworth's lunch counter, dreaming."

"It's funny how much Moms seems to have taken to Ellen."

"I never expected it. It appears to be mutual. Ellen is drawn to your mother."

"I know it sounds crazy, but it makes me jealous."

"Feelings aren't crazy. They're signposts. Feel them, observe them, but don't act on them. At least, that's what Adrian has been suggesting."

"Adrian gave me a Krishnamurti book at Easter. It's hard stuff. I don't think I can take it in."

"Me too," I said. "Sometimes I think it's just words, no content, but it has helped Adrian. He stopped smoking pot, and got his freedom back. That's worth a lot."

"When I read it, I think, what point would there be in me looking deep within, I'm a wife and mother, and I'm stuck with that. If I go off on a spiritual tangent would good would that be to anyone. I mean, I have my commitments."

"This is leading to a conversation Patrick and I have been having about 'guilt and obligation'. It's one of Dr. Murphy's rules for a healthy life." I explained it to Maureen.

"When I think of my own life right now, it looks on the outside like I'm living by obligation. I know Harry is a rat. It's no secret he's after anything in a skirt."

I started to protest. Maureen held her hand up.

"Don't try to defend him. I see him clearly, and I'm not planning to leave him. That probably looks like obligation, but it's not. It's more a case of making the best I can of my life, as it is now. I question whether anyone truly lives by guilt and obligation. We're always getting something out the situation, whether we let ourselves know, or not."

"Do you mean you think it's a good deal for you, even if he's not perfect?"

"Something like that. I've had lots of time to think it through. I don't see my own love as perfect either."

"I aim for perfection," I said. "I believe in love and honour."

"Clare, darling, you are perfect! Now, let's shop."

When we were reunited at the Anderson's late in the afternoon everyone had an exciting tale to tell about their day.

Patrick was the first to share. "You're going to love this, Clare. Dad bought us a colour TV. It's going to be delivered next week."

"Great, thanks Gordon."

I pictured future holiday gatherings, with Patrick and his father ensconced in the living room watching football. I liked the idea.

"Mrs. Anderson took me to tea at the Royal York," Ellen said. "There were all kinds of sandwiches, little cakes, sausage rolls. And it's so beautiful in there, like heaven."

"It's a pleasure to go there with Ellen. She makes me see it with new eyes," Evelyn said.

"And I saw Holt Renfrew. You wouldn't believe it Clare, everything was so elegant."

"How did you know about Holt Renfrew?" I asked. I had always wondered about this.

"From Vogue magazine. I saw one in the doctor's waiting room."

"Next time, we'll go together," Evelyn said. "We'll find something we really want and we'll all get something new."

"I'm going to start planning for it now," Ellen said. "I want to pick exactly the right thing."

"I can't picture myself in anything remotely Vogue-like," I said.

"You can't go wrong with a cashmere sweater," Ellen said.

Evelyn laughed. "That is so true! A girl after my own heart."

That evening we had supper at the Anderson's. Harry and Maureen came with the children and the au pair. Gordon cooked hamburgers on the barbecue. It was informal and fun. The doors were open to the back yard and the kids ran in and out. It was still fairly cool, but I took my wine and sat by the fountain. Harry came out and sat beside me.

"I hardly get a chance to talk to you," he said.

"Now's your chance. I'm totally available."

"Don't tease me, Clare. You are more beautiful every time I see you."

"You know what, you should save all this for Maureen."

"She doesn't understand me."

"She understands you perfectly."

Patrick came over and said, "Burgers are ready. Moms wants us to come to the table."

239

I jumped up, happy to escape Harry. I didn't think I'd ever understand Maureen's point of view on their relationship. I didn't want to see them divorce. I wanted him to become a man worthy of Maureen.

At dinner Evelyn said, "I gave that old guitar to Ellen."

"The Martin D-28? My guitar?" Maureen sounded upset.

"You haven't touched it in years. Ellen's going to take lessons."

Maureen didn't say any more, but I knew she didn't like it. After supper we were sitting on our own and I said, "If you don't want Ellen to have your guitar we'll leave it here. I don't want you to be hurt."

"Mom's right. I never played it. I'm feeling jealous of Ellen and it's misplaced. It's because I can't let myself feel how angry and jealous Harry's unfaithfulness makes me. What I said earlier really isn't true. I don't feel it's good enough to make the best of it. Something has to give."

"I want the best for you, Maureen. I'll pray for Harry to change."

"It would take a miracle."

Blackmail

Ellen started guitar lessons from Mr. Arthur, a man from Mike's congregation. He lived within a block of Sacred Heart School so Ellen could walk over for her lesson. She didn't need any prompting to practice. She was entirely self-motivated on this. Soon she was playing accompaniment to the Pete Seeger songs that Adrian taught us, and learning to play Gordon Lightfoot, Joni Mitchell and Bob Dylan songs. She had a natural talent for singing too.

I picked Ellen up after her lesson and visited with Mrs. Arthur while I waited. She always offered tea and shortbreads. They were retired but he taught for the pleasure of sharing his love of music and she loved to socialize with the students and their parents. It was a pleasurable routine.

One afternoon when I arrived Mrs. Arthur looked upset and asked me to sit in the kitchen, where we couldn't be heard.

"A terrible thing happened on Ellen's way here. A boy tried to steal her guitar. She was crying and hanging on to it and he was saying he was going to tell on her. I went outside when I heard the commotion and told him I'd call the police if he didn't leave immediately. I know the neighbourhood kids and didn't recognize him."

"Did Ellen know him?"

"That's the funny thing. She wouldn't say a word about it. She dried her tears and went in to her lesson, as if she just wanted to forget about it."

On the way home I asked her about it and she told me it was a rough boy from the public school and she didn't think it would happen again.

Right around that time she asked if she could have a bigger allowance. She said the girls in her class liked to stop for a coke and a bag of chips at lunch time and she wanted to join them. It seemed like a small thing and I gave it to her.

One night I went up and she was in bed reading and I saw that her arm was black and blue.

"What happened to your arm?"

"I slipped and fell against the school gate."

"It looks sore. Should I get you some liniment?"

"It's nothing. It just looks bad."

Ellen started looking pale and sad, and often said she couldn't eat breakfast because it made her feel sick.

"Do you think we should take her to the doctor?" I asked Patrick.

"Something's going on. She's not herself. Maybe we could ask Madeleine if she's noticed anything at school," Patrick suggested.

I called and Madeleine told me she had been planning to call me about it.

"There a dark haired boy who's been hanging around the school yard. I saw him talking to Ellen. The Janitor went out to see who he was and he ran off."

"It must be Timbo. She hasn't said anything about it but she's obviously unhappy and worried about something. I'll have to get to the bottom of it."

When I picked her up from school I said, "Let's have a treat. How about a Coke at the Miss Lawrenceville?"

"I'd rather go home."

"Something is bothering you. I think it's your brother. You need to tell me about it."

She began to cry loudly. "You'll send me away."

"No, don't worry about that. What's going on?"

"He's been taking my allowance but he wants more and more. He says if I stop giving him money he'll tell that I'm a thief and then you won't want me around. Now he wants the guitar. I can't give him that."

"You need to tell me everything."

"When we used to go to town shopping, I'd steal things. Silly things, woolly hair ties, false nails, small things I could hide. I didn't even want them. I don't know why I did it. I never do it now, but my whole life is ruined!"

"You're life isn't ruined. I knew girls who stole when they were around your age. They weren't bad. It might just have seemed like an adventure." I handed her a Kleenex. "You can go to confession, and put it completely behind you. I won't ever speak of it again."

Ellen cried harder then. "I'd hate to go back there. I love this life with you and Patrick."

"I promise we won't send you away. Will you promise to let me know if you have a big problem like this again?"

"Alright."

We went home and Ellen went up to her room. I found Patrick in the barn and told him what had occurred.

"That rat. To think I was so good to him."

"Should I call Shilta and tell her what he's up to? She'd want to know he's skipping school and coming to town."

"Yes, and we should tell the school to call the police if they see him. It's against the law for him to be hitchhiking and skipping school."

"Maybe it will wake them up," I said.

"Don't count on it," Patrick said.

"How did Ellen turn out so well, coming from that environment?"

"That is a mystery!"

When I called Shilta she wasn't very concerned. "I knew the kids stole. It's just kid stuff."

"I'm more upset with how cruel Timbo has been? That is serious," I said.

"Gurly will fix him," she said. As if that was all it would take.

"We haven't seen Ellen since she moved in with you. Doesn't she want to visit?"

"Right now she wants to stay as far from Tim as possible."

"She'll get over it."

Shilta clearly didn't take this incident seriously.

***

Timbo stopped tormenting Ellen, but she continued to be upset. She was having nightmares and bursting into tears over nothing.

242

"Something is still bothering her," I said to Patrick. "What can I do?"

"She's had a lot of change in the past few months. Maybe it's catching up with her," he suggested.

"Let's talk to her together. Let her know that she's safe. These bad dreams make me think that she's had to face a lot on her own."

On Saturday we had our usual breakfast together and then we walked down to the water. We sat on a log and I said, "We need to talk about how upset you are."

"You could never understand."

"We could try."

"I'm afraid I'm like the Hearne's. I can never escape it. I'll say something, or do something, and everyone will see what I am. I've tried to be a new person, but my mind is full of the old life. I always believed that I didn't belong with them, but now that I've gotten away, I'm even more afraid of it pulling me back."

"You can't imagine how different you are from the Hearne family. When you first came to stay, I had no idea who you were. Every day that goes by I see what a miracle you are," I said.

"The things you tell yourself are important," Patrick said. "You need to start with a new story about who you are. Be grateful for where you came from, but aware that you are more than that. Tell yourself you are the luckiest person on earth. My father told me that a long time ago. He lives by it, and it makes him a wonderful person."

"I like your father," Ellen said. "He's warm and safe."

The word safe struck me. I feared Ellen had come from a world where she wasn't safe.

Once home, Patrick went to his study and came back with a notebook.

"I wrote this down when I was feeling troubled," he said. "I thought you might find it helpful, Ellen. 'The Lord is good to those whose hope is in Him, to the one who seeks Him; His compassions never fail. They are new every morning; great is His faithfulness.' As it says, 'You are new every morning'. There is so much hope in that. I try never to forget it."

The beauty of this brought tears to my eyes.

"Thanks Patrick. If I could convince myself that I'm here for good I'd stop being so sad."

"You're my sister. I'll always want you with me," I said.

"Let's talk about something good that's coming up. School is ending soon, we should plan a holiday," Patrick suggested. "Does anyone like to camp?"

"I hate it," said Ellen.

I started to laugh. "Me too."

"So much for Algonquin Park! That's okay, I'll go with Mike. Maybe we could take in some of the Mariposa Folk Festival."

Ellen and I loved that idea.

Partners, Curses and Spells

Our lives were now fully occupied with the farm. The garden was planted, and we had our first batch of cheddar ready to taste. Maureen was going to come for the weekend and make a ceremony of this first tasting. I'd made several batches of curd and it was selling well in Lawrenceville.

Ellen was on summer vacation and enjoyed helping in the garden. I lent her my bicycle which allowed her to visit her friends in Lawrenceville and go to the pool. She'd never learned to swim, so she took lessons that summer and soon could keep up with the other girls.

Kate called and said she'd like to meet with us.

"It's something important I want to discuss with you and Patrick."

We hadn't been visiting as often because the farm was taking so much of our time but I agreed that we would be there the next morning at 10.

Kate launched straight into her proposal.

"I want to make you my business partner, Clare."

"I'm flattered, but I don't know how I'll find the time."

"It won't take much time at present. I'll continue to do most of the work myself. I want to make you my heir, and if I show you properties and how I handle them, it will help you to understand what to do when you inherit."

"I'm shocked. What about your great-niece?"

"I said I was cutting her off, and I meant it. I want you to inherit because no one else will respect what I have. I know you won't go tearing it all down. What I want is for you to spend a few hours with me each week, going over the accounts, seeing what I rent, how much it brings in, learning about upkeep, practical things. Are you willing?"

"I'm willing, but I hope this doesn't mean you're ill."

"No, I'm perfectly fine. I could go on for decades, but I want to have it settled. It will bring me peace."

"I never expected anything like this. You know I love Lawrenceville and believe it's one of the most beautiful and historic towns in Ontario. I'd do anything to keep it that way."

"That's why I want you to take over. You may be shocked when you see what I own. I'm on the Chamber of Commerce and in the past was also on the Town Council. I'd like to bring you to the Chamber meetings if you can possibly manage it. You'll learn so much and bring such a fresh perspective. It's only once a month."

"I'll give it a try. I hope I can stand up to that crowd. I feel too young and inexperienced to take part in running the town."

"You're exactly what Lawrenceville needs. I've asked my lawyer to draw up the will, and the business partner agreement. It will make everything easier for you when it's time to take over. Do you and Patrick want to talk this over?"

Patrick and I looked at each other.

"It's entirely good news and a great opportunity for you Clare. I have no reservations," Patrick said.

"I'm a little scared, but definitely want to go ahead," I said.

"Good, my lawyer's on standby. I'll call and have him come right over with the papers."

On the way home I was in a fog. It was unbelievable that I could become a major property owner, and possibly one of the movers and shakers of the town. Patrick was thinking the same thing.

"Here I married a waitress and next thing I know she's a millionaire. How do you like that?"

"It's earth shattering, impossible to believe, yet true!" Then I had a more sobering thought, how would I find time for all this?

"Are you happy about this, Clare?"

"I'm not sure, but it definitely feels like the hand of Providence. I just hope we have many more years of Kate in charge."

***

Maureen came that weekend with Gita and Jiddu, leaving the twins at home with the au pair. She pulled up in the black Mercedes, looking like a movie star. We came out onto the porch when we heard her car.

"Darling Clare, darling Patrick! We're here!" Maureen called out.

Gita and Jiddu jumped out of the car and ran up the steps. Patrick picked Jiddu up and said, "That's it buddy, you're too heavy now. All of a sudden you're a big boy."

Gita smiled wide. "I lost some teeth and have some new ones."

"I've brought some wine for the cheese tasting, and we'll need the camera to take some publicity shots," Maureen said. "This is going to be great! I can feel it in my bones."

"We invited Mike and Madeleine to join us for the tasting. They're coming at 8."

"We get to be part of it too. Mummy says it's our first wine and cheese party," Gita said.

"You'll be important participants. I'll need you to use all your senses to describe exactly how you experience this cheese," Maureen told them. She turned to us, "Children are sensitive to tastes. They'll notice things we might miss."

"The cheese is rather young," I said. "It may taste ordinary, bland even."

"That's okay. That's where the children come in. They much prefer new cheese to aged," said Maureen.

We set up the tasting on the front porch where we could watch the sun set over the water. It was a warm evening. Gita, Jiddu and Ellen were playing hide and seek, calling out with glee whenever one was found. Maureen and Patrick were playing Rummy, while I sat on the porch swing with my book. A table was set up with wine glasses, bottles of white wine on ice, red wine opened and breathing. There were cheese straws that Patrick and I had made that afternoon, and several varieties of crackers. The Buttercup Cheddar was on a cheese board, in its colourful wrapper.

Mike and Madeleine arrived in the large black sedan. Madeleine wore a sleeveless, yellow cocktail dress for the occasion and Mike had on his summer whites. They were a beautiful couple. Maureen noticed.

"Those two will be fabulous in the promotion photos."

They joined us on the porch, commenting on the heat and the strange lack of mosquitoes.

"It's Citronella," I said. "It seems to be working."

We called the children over and Maureen unwrapped our first cheddar. It had been sitting for a while on the table and was sweating slightly. We were going for the natural look so it was white. Maureen used a cheese slicer to make a pile of cheese.

"Is everyone ready? We need silence. Just taste, allow the experience to be all around you, and permit whatever is evoked to emerge."

Maureen was good, almost like Stargaze, I thought. She handed a slice to everyone.

"Okay, let's taste!"

It was like communion. What a flair for drama Maureen had. She waited a full minute.

"Well?"

"I like it," Jiddu said. "It tastes like cheese."

"Thank you darling."

"It's very fresh," I said, "and nicely salted."

"I taste a hint of clover," Patrick said.

"I'll pour everyone some wine, and we can keep on tasting, and as you have impressions please let me know," Maureen said.

Once the wine was flowing there was lots more talk about cheese and other things. The children went back to their games, which were even more fun as the darkness progressed. Fireflies were coming out and the sun was red over the water.

I was satisfied. Our first cheddar tasted fine, but I knew from my manuals it needed time to develop mature flavour.

Gita and Jiddu were too tired for a story and went straight to sleep. I went in to say good night to Ellen and she said, "I want to ask you a question."

"Okay."

"Do you know anything about curses?"

"Like bad words?"

"No, I mean spells."

"I don't know much. I tend to think it's impossible."

"Mercy puts spells on people. She put one on a neighbour and he got sick and died. I'm worried, what if she put one on me?"

"Why would she do that?"

"She might be jealous."

"Is that worrying you?"

"Yes. I have bad dreams about her."

"We'll ask Father Kelly about it and make sure she can't hurt you. How's that?"

"That would take care of her. I'm sure Father Kelly will know how to undo her curse."

I came back to the party and asked Mike what he thought about curses and spells.

"We don't take it seriously in the Anglican Church. We don't have exorcists any more, but I'm inclined to think such things are possible. Why do you ask?"

I didn't want to tell Ellen's secret. "Just curious," I said.

"We're past all that," Maureen said. "Thank goodness I don't have to add being under a curse to the things I do worry about."

"What do you worry about?" Madeleine asked.

Maureen, normally so confident, was hesitant. "Oh, this and that," she said evasively.

"I worry about the Jerseys," Patrick said. "They're always on my mind. The responsibility is overwhelming. We should never have given them names, now I worry about them as individuals."

"Who are you thinking of right now?" Mike joked, "Vanilla, Caramel, Butterscotch or Cream?

"Butterscotch," Patrick said. "She doesn't seem as perky as usual."

After Madeleine and Mike headed home, and Patrick went to bed, Maureen and I sat on the swing, drinking wine and listening to the crickets in the fields.

"What are you really worrying about Maureen?" I asked.

"Harry. I feel so humiliated and helpless. He's always flirting, right in front of me. How much worse is he when I'm not present? He's making a fool of me. A real low point this week, the au pair's boyfriend threatened to kill him. I overheard. Harry follows her around like a puppy and I can tell she despises him."

"Have you talked to him?"

"He says it's a sickness and he can't help himself, but I know he just doesn't want to change."

"You sound like you're at your wit's end. Is this worse than how you felt two years ago, when you left him?"

"Much worse, but I feel more stuck because of the babies."

"You don't need him for financial support."

"No, I don't. I'm just making excuses. I know how much I missed him the last time. I feel completely confused."

"'Stay still until the stream clears.'"

"What does that mean?"

"It's from the Tao Te Ching. It means don't do anything in the midst of turmoil and confusion. Take care of yourself and the kids, and live with the awareness of this problem until the answer becomes clear. It's hard to be patient, but eventually answers come."

"When we get back I'm going to insist he sleep in another room. I hate myself for allowing any intimacy with him."

"That should help you get clear. Is it hard living with his parents?"

"Their place is so big, I don't even run into them unless I want to. I can't tell if they're aware of our troubles. That would be another humiliation. His parents are sweet; they don't deserve a son like him."

"I'm still praying for a miracle for you."

"Thanks Clare."

On Saturday Maureen and the kids slept in, but I woke up and went down with Patrick for the early morning milking.

He sat on the three legged milking stool, wiped off the udders with some antiseptic, and then starting the rhythmic squeezing that gave us the beautiful pails of creamy milk.

"Patrick, Ellen is worried about something that is completely outside my experience."

"Uh-huh." He kept on milking.

"She's worried that Mercy has put an evil spell on her."

"What!" The milking stopped. "Are you serious?"

"She told me about it last night. She said Mercy put a spell on a neighbour and now she's afraid she could do it to her."

"We'll talk when I come in. The milking helps me to think."

"I'll put the coffee on."

The barn smelled sweet now that we had the cows, a combination of hay and milk, and their natural smell. Who could help but love cows, I thought.

I went in and started the coffee and set out plates for breakfast. I hoped no one else would get up before we had a chance to talk about this strange idea of Ellen's. Between worrying about Maureen's troubles and Ellen's fears, I hadn't gotten much sleep. By the time Patrick came in I was almost asleep in the rocking chair, with Sophie purring on my lap.

"What did you say when she told you this?" Patrick asked.

"I suggested we go to Father Kelly."

"I haven't had any direct experience with witchcraft, or whatever you want to call this sort of thing, but a good friend from my Fundamental

Theology class told me about his experiences. He was convinced evil was real, and could only be fought by holiness. I had a lot of trust in what he said and only hoped I would never experience this in my own life. You're right, we need Father Kelly's help."

"Fear itself is dangerous; it's quite possible to scare someone to death."

"I agree."

I felt a hand on my leg and saw Jiddu beside me.

"I woke up. Is it too early?"

"It's early, but that's okay. Do you want breakfast?"

Before long everyone was up, despite our late night. We all worked together that day, gardening, shovelling the barn stalls, and helping in the kitchen. It was fun, chatting as we did our chores. Gita and Ellen got along well as they weeded and thinned a bed of carrots together. Jiddu stuck by Patrick all day, helping with whatever he perceived as a manly task.

That evening Gita and Jiddu asked me to tell more of the story. As it was another warm evening we sat on the porch swing.

Martha gave Morris a broom.

"You can help," she said, "then we'll be out on the water quicker."

Morris grumbled as he swept.

"Bleep, bleep, bleep, why do I have to sweep? Mean, mean, mean, why does she make me clean?"

This was Morris's cleaning song, and he thumped his tail as he sang. Despite the words, it sounded cheery.

"We're done."

Martha hung up her cleaning cloths and mop, took off her apron, and grabbed her sailing cap.

"Avast. Ahoy. Asail! Off we go!"

There was a fresh breeze. Cat's-paws and williwaws ran across the water. Clouds raced over, changing the colour of the water from blue to green to grey to silver.

"It is a most magnificent day to be awake and alive," shouted Martha into the wind. "Where to?"

"Up the channel, on the leeward side. There's a sweet little mink there I've been keeping my eye on. We'll just pass, as if we had other business in the neighbourhood," Morris said.

"You're sly, I had no idea you were sweet on someone."

Morris blushed.

"Be casual. Now, look to your left, see that hole in the bank. No don't look. No, look. Oh my stars. There she is!"

A petite mink had come to sun herself on the rocks, grooming her mustache as she lolled.

"Ooh la la, c'est magnifique!" Morris was swooning.

"Do you know her name," "Martha asked.

"I'm too shy to ask. Could you find out for me?"

"No time like the present. Hoo there! You, on the rock, what's your name?" Martha called as loudly as she possibly could.

"Me?" She gave a demure look. "I'm Sweetie Pie."

"I'm Martha, and this is Morris."

"Pleased to meet you," Sweetie Pie replied.

"The fire flies are out. It's getting too dark to read," I said.

"Will Morris get married, or does he just want a girlfriend?" Jiddu asked.

"I think he's looking for a wife," Gita said. "How did Morris learn to speak French?"

"From a coureur de bois he met on the river, but that's another story," I said.

The kids ran off to play hide and seek again in the dark. It was another perfect night by the river.

***

After Mass the next morning I asked Father Kelly if he had time to talk to me and Ellen somewhere private.

"If you can wait, I'll be free in about 10 minutes. We can talk on the terrace."

He was soon back. "It's good to have a chance to chat."

Father Kelly knew all about how Ellen had come to stay with me, and about the family background. I didn't think any of this would be a surprise to him.

"Do you want to tell him, honey?" I asked.

"Yes. I'm afraid of my Aunt Mercy. She put spells on people she's angry with. I fear she's put one on me, one that will make Clare and Patrick send me back to my old home."

"It is a terrible thing for you to have lived in a household where someone was practicing these dark arts. I take it seriously. Above all, I

251

know the light will always overcome the darkness. Do you know what that means?" Father Kelly asked.

"That God and goodness are stronger," Ellen said.

"Yes. Now I'm going to give you a blessing and no matter what your aunt has done, she will have no power over you."

We both knelt on the grass. Father Kelly held his arms up, with his palms open as if to gather us into his arms.

"I ask for blessings on Ellen, let no evil be allowed to touch her. Father, I also ask that you bless Patrick, Clare and Ellen and bring light and love into their home. In the name of the Father and the Son and the Holy Spirit,"

"Thank you Father."

"I thought your aunts and uncles were Catholics," Father said.

"They are, but they also practice the old ways," Ellen said.

"As you remember these 'old ways' tell Clare about them, so she can help you to sort these things out."

"I learned to read fortunes," Ellen said. "Clare told me it was wrong, but I thought it was okay if I only did it for myself. Should I give it up?"

"Yes. Don't give the Devil any means of getting to you. I'm going to give you a miraculous medal, blessed by the Pope. Wear this every day. It will protect you."

Ellen attached the medal to her blouse.

"I'm not afraid anymore," she said.

***

Joe graduated in May and found a job at the River Authority Headquarters. He and Isabel moved to a small town 20 miles east of Lawrenceville, where they bought a three-bedroom bungalow with a yard, and a clothesline, and a garage for their first new car. In July their son was born, and Isabel asked me to be the godmother. Patrick and I visited while she was in the hospital. Isabel had on a lacy, baby blue bed jacket and was holding the well-wrapped baby in her arms.

"What are you going to call him?" Patrick said.

"Lawrence, for our home town."

Isabel's euphoria continued. She was completely in love with the baby and with Joe and with the little house in the small, flat town.

"It's the strangest place," she said. "I can look out the window and see everything; the river, fields, the highway that's a mile away. There's nothing in the way, not even trees."

It was a funny little village but if Isabel and Joe were happy, that was all that mattered. It was good to have them settled and not too far away for regular visits.

Isabel got her license and was soon able to bundle up the baby and visit her mother a few mornings a week. Whenever I could get away, I would join them. It was like a dream come true, three married ladies enjoying coffee together, Isabel, me, and Mrs. Bergeron. It made me laugh to think of it. How did we go from schoolgirls to grownups? I was grateful we had managed to find such wonderful lives after the confusion of our late teens.

The Augsbergs came to stay for a week in August. They observed our cheese-making procedures and gave us feedback on how we were doing. They also got us started on a Camembert. After this visit they were headed to Germany for a long awaited holiday. They promised to visit again when they returned and bring some cheese with them from the Old Country.

Another Summer Gone

The Sears catalogue came in August, with styles for fall and winter. I had it on the kitchen counter and then it disappeared. I found it in Ellen's room. She pored over the girls fashions, almost wearing the pages out. I asked her about it.

"I love the catalogue. It puts me into a sort of daydream. I used to just look at the toy section. The Christmas catalogue was my favourite."

"I used to pick out boyfriends from the catalogue."

"Catalogue guys are cute!"

"School starts soon. Is there something you'd like to order?"

"Thanks, but I'd rather to go to Williamsville to shop. Then I can try things on."

"That's sensible."

I thought a lot about Harry. I didn't understand what led him to be such a pain. I remembered once, when Isabel and I were around 15, she asked her mother if she could go to a friend's house for a sleep over. Her mother was surprisingly vehement that Isabel could not go, and should not even visit the house.

"Sally's father is a sex maniac. He can't be trusted around girls," she said.

We puzzled over this for ages. What was a sex maniac? For some reason we didn't ask her to elaborate. I wondered if she would remember and explain it now. If Harry had some kind of mental disorder, maybe there was a doctor who could cure him.

I was also trying to fill Ellen in on my memories of Dad. As I would think of things, I'd tell her about him. "Dad ate two fried eggs and toast with 'Good Morning Marmalade' on it every morning. He was at his most cheerful when he got up in the morning. We had a radio on the kitchen table which he had on all the time. He loved listening to baseball and talk shows."

"I wish I had known him," Ellen said.

"Me too. Dorothy can be infuriating. Keeping you out of Dad's life is one of many things she's done that are impossible to fathom."

"Tell me more about her. Does she look like Shilta and Mercy?"

"Slightly, but she's flashy, always dressed up, with jewellery, makeup, fancy shoes, the works. She knows how to create an impression. Now that you and I are together, I expect she will visit us."

"She never visited us in the country. She used to call, and sometimes write, but I didn't pay much attention because I didn't know she was my mother."

I was spending more time now in my role as Kate's business partner. She was very organized and kept meticulous records of all her business dealings. I was also getting to know her lawyer and realized he was like a business partner to her. He gave her a lot of advice and it seemed he watched over her to protect her interests.

I attended two Chamber of Commerce meetings. We followed a set agenda and two of the members did all the talking. Kate spoke up now and then, but there wasn't much that was controversial. Everyone wanted the same thing, customers and prosperity for Lawrenceville.

Kate pressed me to run for Town Council in the fall election. I was dragging my feet, feeling inadequate to the task, but when the deadline approached I let my name stand. Dolores Black, from Save the River was already on council and was running again. I told her I was considering council and she encouraged me to run.

"You'd be good on council. You clearly love this town, and you see how it's been going downhill."

I was almost hoping that I'd lose, but we were elected by acclamation. There were five positions, and five in the running. This added more meetings to my already busy life. We would need to hire someone to help with the cheese business.

Thanksgiving was approaching again, and the family would soon be descending upon us. I was beginning to feel like an old hand at this sort of thing. I had a 25 pound turkey in the fridge, and had already made the pies. I tried to be organized about it. I had a list of all that needed to be done, and shared the tasks with Patrick, Adrian, and Ellen.

Maureen called to ask if we minded them coming ahead of schedule. She said Harry had a desire to go apple-picking and she hoped to find time for a drive in the countryside to enjoy the fall foliage.

"Of course, I'm happy to have you here. I'll have your rooms ready. Is Inger coming?"

"Yes, she loves Buttercup Acres. Do you have room?"

"We can always fit in one more. I'll figure it out."

After I hung up I said to Patrick, "Harry wants to go apple-picking. That doesn't sound like him."

"I suppose not."

"We're going to have a full house. I'd better get busy."

The Lynches arrived before noon, pulling up in their Oldsmobile Vista Cruiser packed full of people and luggage. They also had packages tied to the roof.

"Yaay, we're here!" Jiddu jumped out first. Maureen was in the front with Patty on her lap. Inger held Bobby in the back. Harry got out and came around to take Patty so Maureen could get free of the seat belt and emerge. Patrick grabbed Bobby, giving him a little toss in the air. The excited, happy squealing began.

"We brought lunch with us," Maureen said. "We stopped in Williamsville and got French bread, Italian ham, pickles, and onions. I didn't get cheese, of course. We thought we'd have lunch and then set out for the apple orchard."

"How about lunch at the picnic table in the back yard?" I suggested. "It's warm and sheltered there in the sun."

We brought their luggage in and up to the rooms.

"Did you bring the crib?" Patrick asked.

"We did," Harry said. "Shall we assemble it now? You and I are getting good at this. I even brought all the nuts and bolts this time."

I gave Inger a choice between the sleeping porch and the daybed in Patrick's office.

"Ooh, I love the sleeping porch," she said.

"It could be chilly," I said.

"I will find it refreshing!"

Maureen and I set out lunch on the picnic table and called everyone to come. Patrick and Harry came arm in arm, talking and laughing, as happy as I had ever seen them together.

"Look at that," I said to Maureen. "Harry is looking so.... I'm not sure what the word is. But it's a good thing."

"We have lots to tell you," she said.

After lunch we took two vehicles and met at an orchard on the Third Concession. It was a perfect day for apple-picking; blue sky, light breeze, and just cool enough. Maureen and I kept track of the twins while the rest of the gang climbed ladders and filled baskets with apples. There were McIntosh's and Spy's, and we came away with a bushel of each. We put the baskets in the back of our truck and Maureen suggested we go to the Park in Williamsville for a walk. She and Harry held hands as we went down the hill to the beach, and Gita and Jiddu ran ahead.

"They look happy together," I said to Patrick, indicating Maureen and Harry.

"Something's up, that's for sure," Patrick replied.

That night Harry said he and Maureen had made a dinner reservation at the Skylane and wanted Patrick and I to join them.

"Inger will stay with the kids," he said. "It's all arranged."

"Adrian can help out," I said.

When we left, Inger was cooking dinner, while Adrian had the children singing, with Ellen accompanying on guitar.

We were given a table by the window, looking out over the hills and the thin red line of the sunset. The sky was still turquoise and pink.

"What a lot has changed since my first visit to this restaurant," I said. "It was an unforgettable occasion, and I had no idea that eventually I would be part of your family."

"It has been a wild couple of years," Maureen agreed.

We ordered and sat with our wine, chatting happily. Maureen was glowing with happiness. I didn't think she would look like that if she was pregnant again. Her good news had to be something else.

As we sat over coffee after dinner, Harry said, "I have a story to tell you."

"We thought something was up," Patrick said.

"I think you know, Maureen and I were having problems. I'd say we were on the verge of divorce. I wasn't living up to my commitment to her, and I hated myself for making her miserable. A lawyer from the firm where I'm articling asked me if I wanted to try acid. He told me he'd done it several times, and it was a real kick. Well, a kick seemed like exactly what I needed. I was smoking lots of pot and I wanted a bigger thrill. We met at his apartment and he gave me what he called a blotter and told me to put it on my tongue. His girlfriend was there, and a few of their friends, they were all joining in the acid experience. Believe me, it was an experience."

"Did you have a bad trip?" I asked. "I'm terrified of that stuff."

"For at least an hour, nothing happened. Ravi Shankar was playing on the stereo and I was starting to get totally bored. There is nothing worse than being stone cold sober while everyone else in the room is tripping. Finally, I told my friend I wasn't feeling it and I was going to head home. I set out and walked miles, eventually reaching the docks, and all of a sudden it hit me.

"Colours started appearing around everything, even though it was dark. As I walked I felt the ground grow soft and spongy under my feet. It seemed funny, and I was laughing and talking to myself, thinking, have I hit the jackpot! This is the best thing ever! The world was dissolving in a sheen of colour and I didn't care. It was all good. Then there was a bright golden light, brighter than anything I've ever seen, and I tried to go towards it, but I was held back, because the ground was dissolving. I started crying and begging for the light. I felt desperate to be part of it. Then I must have lost consciousness.

"When I came to, it was dawn, and I was frozen. Luckily I hadn't been robbed or beaten. I was in a scary area of town. I made my way to a phone booth and called Maureen to pick me up. When I got home I slept for 24 hours. Now I come to the strange part. When I woke, I knew I had a choice to make. I could see clearly what a mess I was making of my life, and that I was making everyone suffer. I decided to kill myself.

"I went in the bathroom and found sleeping pills and a big bottle of cough syrup and downed all of it, then reached for some painkillers with codeine to make sure I did the job. I tried to wash it down with a cup that must have had shampoo or something sweet and soapy in it. Next thing I knew I was throwing up. This went on until I'm pretty sure there was nothing left in my stomach. I sat on the floor in the bathroom, and all of a sudden I saw golden light in the room, and knew I'd been given another chance."

Maureen had tears running down her face as he got to this part of his story.

"That's it, Harry added. "I changed. I'm not the same person who set off to take LSD that night."

"He's a different man now," said Maureen. "I can feel it in my heart."

"Harry, this is amazing! I was so worried you and Maureen wouldn't make it," I said.

"You've been like a brother to me," Patrick said. "I feel I've got that great guy back, the Harry I met in my early teens, and felt so close to."

Harry held up his wineglass. "A toast to rebirth!"

"It is a miracle," Maureen said. "You two are the only ones we can share this with."

We drove home and as we got out of the car Maureen said, "We want you to do one more thing with us. Let's go down to the water."

The night was clear, with many stars and a crescent moon.

"We want to renew our marriage vows, with you as witnesses."

They took off their wedding rings and handed them to Patrick.

Harry took Maureen's hand in his and said, "Maureen, you are the one and only love of my life. I believe in this marriage more than ever. I honour the light within us and I reaffirm my love and commitment to you." Patrick gave him the ring and he placed it on Maureen's finger.

Maureen looked up at Harry, she glowed silver in the moonlight. "Harry, I honour the light within us and I reaffirm my love and commitment to you." She placed the ring on Harry's finger.

"Hallelujah!" Patrick shouted.

We hugged and cried, then walked up the lane and home to bed.

The Anderson's arrived the next day. As soon as they came in, Gordon said, "What will it be, football or baseball? I've been looking forward to getting together with my boys and seeing some great Thanksgiving sports on that new TV!"

It was a grey, wet day, perfect for watching sports on TV, and for indoor games for the kids. Inger kept the twins entertained while Maureen, Evelyn and I worked in the kitchen.

We sat down to Thanksgiving Dinner and Patrick said grace. Then Harry said, "I'd like to make a toast." He stood up. "A toast in thankfulness for my wonderful wife and children, and for all our family who are so special to us."

"Hear, hear!"

Gita stood up. "Can I make a toast?"

"Of course darling," Maureen said.

"I toast in thankfulness to Mummy and Daddy who are in love again."

There was a silence, Then Gordon stood up.

"Well said, Gita! We are all thankful for love." He turned to Evelyn, "To love! Now, I'll slice the turkey.'"

Magic Shadows

That fall we watched Magic Shadows together every evening on television. Every week a classic movie was played in half hour segments, with commentary by film critic, Elwy Yost. It was truly an educational experience and gave us a great appreciation for old movies.

Ellen was in Grade Eight and doing well with school and guitar lessons. She sometimes felt sad because she didn't have a best friend. She said all the best friends were taken by the time she got to Sacred Heart.

"Maybe when you get to high school you'll find a best friend," I suggested.

"I suppose there will be a lot of new kids meeting for the first time. I won't be the only one."

After Thanksgiving Patrick went back into his shell. I had seen it before, but it was still disturbing. He was silent and spent a lot of time in the barn or in his study.

"What's wrong?" Ellen asked. "Patrick looks mad at me."

"I don't know what it is, but I've seen it before. He has moods," I explained.

"It makes me sad. Is there anything we can do to cheer him up?"

"No, we have to wait it out, and try not to take it personally."

"Are you sad, too?" Ellen asked.

"I try to stay cheerful, but if I seem sad you can talk to me about it. I don't want to go around gloomy just because Patrick is. It helps having you here. It's worse if it's only Patrick and I when he's not talking," I said.

"I don't understand it. He's usually so nice."

"There are things in life we can't change. It's been a lesson for me. I often feel responsible to keep everyone happy, and this helps me see it isn't possible; it isn't even desirable."

"Should we leave him alone?" Ellen asked.

"Maybe."

"I miss having him look over my school work."

"I can look it over."

"No, thanks. It's something special that Patrick does. I can wait until he gets happier."

"I won't take that personally either," I said, laughing.

Ellen was going to the afternoon matinee that Saturday with her girlfriends, just as Isabel and I had done for years.

"What's on today?" I asked.

"I never know until we get there. It's always fun, no matter what the movies are."

"I'm going to stay in town until you're ready to come home. I'll browse around," I said.

I brought the Leica with me and took a picture of Ellen with her two girl friends as they waited in line in front of the Princess Theatre. Then I set out for a long walk. I went to the train station and sat on the bench to wait for a train. It wasn't long before a freight train came rattling by. This put me in a state of calm detachment.

I sat for half an hour, through three sets of trains. I took a few photos of the fall scene; the leaves in piles, trees partly bare. I wandered back downtown and ended up in Woolworth's. I was already in a wonderful peaceful state, now I could simply float down the aisles, examining every wonderful ware they sold. Colourful ceramic salad bowls from Japan, Mickey Mouse colouring books, crayons in 48 shades, barrettes for little girls in the shape of Scotty dogs, black slips. Hmmm, black slips, they reminded me of Dorothy.

"Clare. Is that you?"

"Mrs. Dell! How are you?"

"I've heard so much about you lately, on town council, owning a cheese factory, marrying that handsome young man from Toronto. My! My! What a wonderful life you've got."

"It is wonderful," I admitted.

"You were always a good girl."

Mrs. Dell wandered off to do her shopping and I saw it was time to pick Ellen up. I felt completely refreshed by my afternoon in Lawrenceville. There was something healing in walking around a familiar world.

The house was brightly lit as we pulled up the drive. Patrick was in the kitchen, cooking spaghetti and singing. He was back from the underworld. He had the table set and an open bottle of Chianti on the counter.

"Hello darlings." He kissed me and gave Ellen a hug. "Adrian and I have been talking about how many milk cows would be optimum for the cheese factory. Do you think we could handle more?"

We were back to normal. Ellen told us all about the double bill of Gidget movies. After supper we played Euchre until it was time for Ellen to go to bed. I went up to say goodnight.

"He's happy again," Ellen said.

"Yes."

"But what if he didn't come out of it?"

I had no answer for that.

When I came downstairs Adrian had gone to the cottage. Patrick had Pink Floyd playing on the stereo.

"Let's sit for a while," he said. "You probably want to know what goes on with me, why I get depressed every so often. I can't explain it, because it's a mystery to me, too. I would probably be fine if I lived alone. It would come and go, and it wouldn't matter to anyone."

"Mike told me you were like that at University too."

"It started then. It's a cloud of self-doubt and despair. I can't even talk when it comes over me."

"Do you think a doctor could help?"

"Yes, Dr. Murphy, I bet he knew exactly what to do."

"You're joking, but I'm serious."

"I'll be serious too. I don't think it's a medical problem. I see it as a spiritual condition, a call to retreat. The most painful part is being forced to face people while I'm in the midst of it. What I need is to go into a forest hermitage. I feel that if I were to be totally away from everything, I could look more closely at this spiritual emptiness that I feel, confront it. Wrestle with the Devil possibly – or encounter God in the depths of my soul. Ordinary life doesn't make room for this."

"Why couldn't you go into retreat? We could build a cabin at the back of the property. When you felt the need, you could ask Adrian and me to take over here, and you could head to the cabin and be on your own."

"I never allowed myself to think it was possible, it seems too selfish, but a retreat cabin is exactly what I need."

"It would be good for me, too. I don't experience depression exactly, but I have a longing for solitude. Being able to leave everything behind, even for a day or two, would be a God-send."

"I'll get started on the plans with Adrian. Mike would probably like to be involved too. We'll have to work fast before it gets too cold. I wouldn't be surprised if our friends find out and start booking time in it."

"I'm first on the list," I said. "It has to be simple. No electricity. A monk's cell."

"This may be your best idea ever," Patrick said.

The Hearnes

After Mass the next morning Ellen and I drove out to the Fourth Concession. I didn't want her to be cut off completely from the family she'd known. She said she missed Bella and Uncle Django, so she wouldn't mind a short visit. She clearly didn't have a great longing to see them again. I promised we would only stay for coffee and come right home.

As usual there were dogs snarling and jumping on the car as soon as we pulled in the driveway.

"They're just stupid," Ellen said, "they won't bite you."

She jumped down and yelled at them. I cautiously opened the door and we made it to the side door.

"Hello," I called.

"C'mon in. We're watching Billy Graham. He's doing a special crusade."

Ellen gave me a 'what did you expect' look, and we went in the living room.

"Coffee's ready. I'll get up in a tick and bring some for both of you," Mercy said.

Ellen sat on the edge of the couch and Bella squeezed in beside her.

"Are you coming back home," Bella said. "I miss you. I have to sleep alone now, and haven't got anybody to go to school with."

"Don't whine, Bella," Shilta said.

Tim came in and pushed Bella over so he could sit next to Ellen. Ellen moved as far from him as possible.

"What's the matter? Do you think I have cooties?" Tim asked.

Little Django danced around, "Timbo has cooties, Timbo has cooties."

Bella started sniffling, "Timbo pushed me. I want to sit next to Dottie,"

One of the dogs snuck into the house with Timbo and jumped onto the couch beside me. His breath was hot against my ear and I shrank away from him.

"Shut up, all of you," Mercy gave the command. She handed a mug of coffee to me, but brought nothing for Ellen. She yanked the dog off the couch and it scuttled into the kitchen.

It was quiet then, except for Reverend Graham's voice, calling on us to give what we could. Uncle Django walked with us out to the truck, shooing the dogs away so they didn't jump on me.

"Now don't you go worrying about us," he said. "We have our good and bad days. Today's a bad one."

"I'm sorry," I said. "It was bad timing."

"Well, we're family, you have to take what you get," he said. "Goodbye Dottie. It's good to see you so healthy and smart-looking."

As we drove away, Ellen sighed deeply. "Man, am I glad I'm outta there!"

"From now on, I won't insist we visit."

Soon after that visit I had a call from Dorothy, asking me how Ellen was doing.

"She's doing well with us but it's a miracle considering her deprived childhood. How could you have left her with your family?"

The memory of our last visit to the Hearne's was still painful.

"I survived it," Dorothy said. "Besides, I couldn't leave her for you to look after. You were 10 years old. Given all the possibilities, it was the best one at the time."

"Ellen would like to meet you," I said.

"That's what I'm calling about. I'll be in Ottawa for two days and I thought you could bring Ellen and we'd spend a few hours together. I'm speaking at the Friends House, in the Glebe area. Do you know it?"

"I'm sure I can find it."

"We'll meet at Mrs. Tiggy Winkles. Ellen would get a kick out of it."

"I'm not sure she would. She's 13 you know."

"I can hardly believe it. It would still be a good place to meet. Everyone loves looking at toys. I'll see you at 2 on Saturday."

It was a cold, clear day when we set out. I was relieved that it didn't look like we would encounter snow or rain. We stopped for lunch at a Lebanese Restaurant on Bank Street. We both had shawarma and salad. I made a mental note to come back with Patrick some day. We were early so we browsed around Mrs. Tiggy Winkles, looking at all the beautiful books and toys. Dorothy was right; Ellen was charmed by the store, as was I. It was a magical place.

Dorothy peeked through the window and waved at us. She'd been giving a talk and had on her sparkling sari, with a wool cape over it. Her black hair was piled high on her head and held with a copper dagger. She could hardly have been more exotic. She swept us immediately into a large sedan and gave instructions to the driver. He headed north and drove over a bridge and then into the woods.

"Where are we going?" I asked.

"You'll see. I want it to be a surprise."

Dorothy sat behind the driver and placed Ellen beside her. She was at her most dramatic. She took Ellen's hand.

"My child," she said. "I am your mother, but I am also Stargaze. That is my calling. I could not deny it. The world needed me more than my two girls did. I hope someday you can understand."

Ellen was staring into Dorothy's eyes, giving her all her attention. I was feeling annoyed at Dorothy's theatrics, but what did I expect? I tried to prepare Ellen, describing Stargaze and the costumes and the jewellery, but, no matter what I'd told her, this had to be a shock.

The car pulled into a driveway and stopped at a grand country house.

"It's the McKenzie King Estate. I had a vision of us here, wandering through the ruins," Dorothy said.

We followed a path and came to stone ruins. It was enchanting. Ellen and I were both surprised and delighted. There were trails through the woods and beautiful trees everywhere. Dorothy took charge.

"Let's walk in silence," she said. "I want to feel the energy between us."

So we did. It was actually kind of a relief. After all, what could we talk about? It was better than my last encounter with her, having to hear all about the shadow. We walked for at least 30 minutes and had come in a circle, back to the house.

"Now for tea," Dorothy said, and led us to a tea room. She ordered for us and poured when it arrived.

"The frequency is high between us. I believe we have been together for many lifetimes."

"Do you mean reincarnation?" Ellen asked.

"That's just a word," Dorothy said. "I mean so much more."

Dorothy went on to talk about cosmic consciousness, past lives, the spirit world, the coming enlightenment; all the things she talked about when she lectured.

"How did you learn about all this?" Ellen wanted to know.

Dorothy never directly answered questions, but talked and talked, even in the car on the way back to town, barely letting us get a word in. She dropped us off on Bank Street and drove off. By then it was getting dark. Ellen shivered and I asked if she wanted to go straight home, or stop for supper.

"Home, I'll get warm in the truck."

We were both silent as we travelled down the highway. I thought Ellen might have fallen asleep, but as we neared Lawrenceville, she said, "You warned me, but nothing could have prepared me for how awful our mother is."

"I'm sure you hoped for someone much different. Someone motherly, at least."

"I thought there would be a connection, some love that only a mother and child would recognize, but there was nothing. Does she always talk and talk and not listen?"

"She was at her worst today," I said. "She was nervous about seeing you and put up all her defences."

Ellen didn't say anything more until we got home. Patrick greeted us and said, "What did you think of your mother, Ellen?"

"She's a witch!" Ellen answered, and burst into tears. "I hope I never see her again."

"Ellen, I'm so sorry," Patrick said, at a loss.

"I'm going upstairs to write in my diary," she said, and disappeared.

"Wow, I didn't expect that. Did you know she was so upset?" Patrick asked.

"I didn't know she was on the verge of tears. Dorothy was at her worst. She was in her Stargaze sari and jewels and went on and on about crazy stuff. I'm almost immune now, but Ellen was hoping for a mother."

I described the afternoon, the walk in the ruins, tea at the country house.

"What a setting! Your visit sounds like a nightmare, but that place sounds wonderful. I'd like to see it."

"I thought about how you would enjoy it. We should go together, maybe in the summer when the gardens are blooming. We also had a wonderful lunch in a Lebanese restaurant that I'd like to take you to."

"Did you have supper? I could make an omelette and salad." Patrick had been perfecting his omelette technique.

"I'd love that."

I went upstairs and called to Ellen through the door, "Do you want some supper? I could bring it up to you on a tray."

"I can come downstairs. I'm getting over it already. Could we play cards after supper?"

Mike and Madeleine

I no longer went to the Bergeron's for breakfast after Mass. Now we had our own tradition for Sunday breakfasts after church. Ellen and I got home first. Adrian was waiting for us, with a pot of coffee ready.

"Hey kid, sorry to hear about your meeting with Stargaze," he said to Ellen. "I hear it was painful."

"Thanks Adrian. You know what really bugs me? She never asked me one thing about myself, not about how I'm doing in school, not about friends, nothing! It's like I don't even exist to her."

"I've met her a few times."

"Then you know what I mean."

"I do, I'm not surprised at how it went. She's a star amongst the New Age crowd but she doesn't let anyone get close to her."

"Now I've met her and I'm disappointed, but I'm not going to let it get me down."

"Good. Krishnamurti says 'The bitterness of every day makes life meaningless,' but as long as you don't allow bitterness to take over, you'll keep peace of mind and a loving heart. It's also a good practice to avoid judgement," Adrian added. "That's also K's constant message – no judgments."

"I like that advice," I said. "I try to approach Dorothy without judgment, but it doesn't always work. I usually end up angry and resentful."

When Patrick got home from the Anglican service he told us how popular Mike was with women from the congregation.

"I stood outside waiting for Mike," Patrick said, "and there was a crowd of at least twenty women waiting to talk to him. He's like a rock star at St. Matthias."

"It's understandable. He's handsome, charming, witty, and a bachelor."

"Anglicans prefer their priests to be married. It's dangerous - all that adoration could go to his head."

Adrian had bacon sizzling in the big iron frying pan, and pancakes on the griddle. The kitchen was warm and cozy. We sat down and Patrick said grace. He ended with, "and thanks for all the good, loving people in our lives."

"Mike's coming over later. We're going to take a walk around the property and decide where to put the cabin. Do you want him to bring Madeleine?"

"Sure, maybe I can get her to help me with my sock monkeys for the St. Matthias Bazaar."

Madeleine and Mike arrived early afternoon. It was getting colder, a wind had sprung up and there was a feeling of snow in the air.

"Brrrr, I'm glad to be indoors," Madeleine said.

Patrick and Mike set off. I showed Madeleine my pile of grey socks with red heels and the sheet of instructions.

"Do you want to help? They have to be finished in two weeks and I haven't started."

Madeleine put on her reading glasses. "I'm going to make sure I understand the instructions before we start."

I'd already read the instructions and had gathered together the equipment we'd need; needles, thread, thimbles, sewing scissors, cotton batting, buttons and ribbon. We worked together at the kitchen table. With Madeleine's help the work went quickly. She was good as seeing the most efficient way to proceed. We completed three monkeys, and now that I'd done it, I knew I could easily make another three in time for the bazaar.

"They are adorable," I said.

"Now that you know how to do it, you can make one for everyone in your family," Madeleine said.

"Patrick has been telling us what a hit Mike is with the St. Matthias congregation," I said.

"Don't tell me, hordes of women awaiting him on the church steps! I've seen it."

"The remedy is marriage, I hear."

Madeleine looked serious. "It's not turning out to be that simple."

"What do you mean?"

"He needs an Anglican wife. Remember when you thought Patrick was headed for the priesthood and you wondered how a Catholic girl could be the wife of an Anglican priest. Well, it is a problem. Eventually he'd have his own parish and his wife would be a sort of unpaid assistant. It wouldn't make sense if she wasn't Anglican. Also, if I converted, I couldn't teach at Sacred Heart, and my family would be devastated. Especially my father. It would turn my life upside down. I couldn't do it. I'm a Catholic, for better or worse."

"Are you sure about all that? Have you and Mike even discussed it?"

"He's said things like; can you see yourself as a priest's wife? usually when we're at a tea or a youth group gathering, and I see the priest's wife there, leading the way."

"I have a different idea of it. I read a Barbara Pym novel about an Anglican priest's wife in England. She doesn't do any of those church-wifely things. She potters about with her own life and interests, and her husband never says a word about it, maybe because there are tons of women waiting to do all those church-wifely jobs. I'll bet it's not as prescribed as you think."

"But was the wife in the story an Anglican?" Madeleine asked.

"Yes," I replied, "but she seemed more of an agnostic."

"Mike hasn't asked me to be his wife, so we haven't had a conversation about how it could work. It's good to talk about it. I may be making a lot of assumptions. One thing I know, I don't want to leave my work. I love teaching. There, that's the first time I've said that. Maybe I always assumed I'd find 'the one' and walk away from my work, but I don't want that."

"Well, if the question does arise, it will be good for you to be prepared, to know what you want."

"Life is so perfect right now that I can't bear for it to change. Between work, Mike, friends and family, I have it all. I have as great a life as Helen Gurley Brown could imagine."

"I feel the same. Although life is bursting at the seams with commitments, I'm happy and don't want it to change."

"Do you mean change as in having a baby?"

"I guess so. I don't even want to contemplate it."

"My most important goal is finishing my Bachelor's degree. I'll have it by next September. Who knows, maybe I'll continue and get my Masters. I can't bear to think that I would have to leave all that behind. I want Mike, but not at the cost of losing such a big part of my life. Isn't it possible that life can just go on as it is?"

"I remember feeling the same way, but change can't be stopped," I said.

Patrick and Mike returned.

"We've found the perfect site," Patrick said. "We've got time to show it to you before dark if we leave now."

"I love the idea of a retreat cabin," Madeleine said. "Although when I'm in my own apartment, I'm more or less on retreat, as long as I don't pick up a book or a record, or turn on the TV."

"Or answer the phone, or a knock at the door," I said.

"I hadn't thought of it that way. I guess to be alone, in silence, you need to plan for it," Madeleine said.

"It has to be a deliberate space, away from others, away from the daily things that distract us. There won't be any cooking either. Whoever's at home will bring food to the one on retreat," Patrick said. "It's not a place for camping in the woods. It is truly intended to be a place to encounter your soul."

"I wonder how many people have a need for this," Mike mused. "I may do it, just to test my spiritual mettle, but I'm pretty happy in the midst of the hurly burly of life. I get lonely fast." He took Madeleine's hand. "You may have noticed."

"Yes, I've noticed. We can spend the whole day together, and as soon as I'm home, you phone and have more to say. You thrive on connection," Madeleine said.

"Not just any connection, but definitely this one," he said.

I thought about my conversation with Madeleine. Life was probably going to move too fast for her, and she would be forced to make some tough decisions.

It was snowing softly and the light was dim. We hurried back to the house while we could still see. As we came in I heard Adrian and Ellen in the living room. She was playing guitar and Adrian was playing a ukulele he had picked up recently. They were singing along to Gordon Lightfoot's *Song for a Winter's Night*. We stood in the kitchen and listened, not wanting to break the spell. As soon as they stopped I called out, "We're back," and we went into the living room to join them.

"That was wonderful," Mike said. We're having a folk night at the church. Any chance you two would like to perform?"

"I will, if you will," Adrian said.

"I'd like to," Ellen said. "I've never played in public. When is the folk night?"

"Two weeks from now, the night of our Christmas Bazaar. It will be a full day for me. Can I count on you for the Fishing Booth again, Patrick?"

"I'd be disappointed if you took it away from me," Patrick joked.

"Madeleine, if you're taking care of the Jumble Sale I'd be happy to help," I said. "I have on the kilt that I bought last year. I don't think I could ever wear it out, it's such good quality. Gee Adrian, last year we met you there and you were still living in Copper River. Such a lot has changed!"

"I couldn't be happier with the changes," Adrian said. "I feel healthier and more sane since I found Krishnamurti, and since I've come back to live here. Goldilocks' Cottage is a magical haven for me."

"Who's Krishnamurti?" Mike asked.

"He's a spiritual teacher who was found by the Theosophical Society when he was a child. They saw his aura and believed he was the new World Teacher."

"A familiar story," Patrick murmured.

"He was raised by the society to be adored and followed as a guru. Then, when he was in his 30's he brought it all to a halt. He disbanded the society, and told everyone they had to find their own path. He said truth is a pathless land."

"How is it that you know about him if it was all dissolved?" Mike asked.

"He continued to write, give lectures, start schools and communities."

"But always with the message to find your own way?" Mike asked.

"Yes. I can share some of his writings with you, if you're interested," Adrian said.

"It might be good to have a little shakeup. Sure, I'd like to borrow one. I hope his ideas don't get around too much though, my living depends of followers."

We all laughed, although what Mike said was simply the truth.

Over the next few weeks Ellen and Adrian worked on perfecting three songs for the folk night, including *Song for a Winter's Night*, which I could never tire of hearing. That song captured the beauty of this time in our lives perfectly.

I managed to finish the other three sock monkeys and also to knit little scarves and hats for them. The St. Mathias Christmas Bazaar was turning into one of the highlights of the season. Earlier in November I made four fruitcakes with assistance from Ellen, who had never seen fruitcake before. She was shocked at how much effort went into making them. I gave two of them to Mike to sell at the bazaar bake table.

There were great items for sale again that year. I bought books to give as Christmas presents, a Shetland wool cardigan for me, and was unable to resist a crocheted poodle toilet paper cover to match the tissue box cover I'd purchased the year before. The sock monkeys were selling fast, and I had to admit they were irresistible.

I was surprised to see Aunts Mercy and Shilta having tea and shortbreads. I went over to say hello and they asked me to join them.

"I'm sorry your last visit was so rough," Shilta said. "It's hard for us to see Dottie so changed, even a new name. I don't know if you can understand. Anyway, let's have a nice visit and put it behind us."

"I'm glad to see you here," I said. "Patrick and I love this bazaar. We helped out with it last year, too. There's a folk music night after this ends. Ellen's going to play."

"Ellen!" Mercy said. "It's Timbo should be playing!"

I didn't know what to say to this. Madeleine came along and rescued me.

"Your turn to handle the Jumble."

I hurried off.

It was a full day. We hurried home after the bazaar to have a quick supper before we had to be back at the church for the folk night. The tables that had been used for tea were left up, and all the baking that hadn't been sold was set out on little plates at each table. The church women had decorated with candles and greenery. There was a stage, but the musicians were set up on a small riser so it would feel more intimate. Mr. Arthur, Ellen's guitar teacher, played first. He was a well-seasoned player and gave a great start to the night. Ellen and Adrian were wonderful. The evening closed with all of us singing carols.

"That was a perfect day," I said, as we went to bed.

Loss

The phone rang at 6 the next morning. I ran downstairs to catch it before it woke up everyone on our party line.

"Clare, it's Kate. There's been a fire. Can you come right away?"

"Are you okay? Where was the fire?"

"I'm fine. Just shaken up. It was the block on the water where I have stores and apartments. The fire is out, no one's hurt, but I don't know how much damage was done. I need you here."

"Of course I'll come. I'll bring Patrick too."

We found Kate sitting in her kitchen with a pot of coffee perking on the stove.

"I made coffee in case you came out without stopping for some."

"Thanks, we did come straight here. What have you heard so far?" Patrick asked.

The fire chief was here at 5:30, as soon as the fire was out. I was up already, because I'd heard the sirens. I had a feeling the fire was close by. I could smell the smoke when I went out onto the porch. I couldn't see anything from here though. I'd like us to go down there and see for ourselves what it looks like. I couldn't face it by myself."

We drove a few blocks but weren't able to stop near the fire. The street was cordoned off. We got out and saw there was still a fire truck standing by, and firemen doing various tasks.

"What about the tenants?" I asked Kate

"They're all at Sacred Heart parish hall. Father Belfast was one of the first on the scene. He suggested they go there and stay warm until we figure out what next. There are four families, about 20 people in all. About 12 are children, a couple are seniors. Oh, what a terrible thing for them to face on a cold night. Just think of what they have lost!"

"We don't know how bad it was yet," Patrick said. He stopped one of the firemen and said, "We're here with Miss Murphy who owns the building. Can we walk down the street and get a better look at the damage?"

"Sorry, no one can go near for now. Not until the fire chief gives the word. I'll tell you it was a big fire. I don't think anyone will be going back in there again."

Over the next few days, Kate and I helped the families find new homes. In the interim they stayed at the hotel. The local churches held a campaign to collect money, furniture and clothes to replace all that had been lost. One of the families ended up with an apartment in Jessup Manor. The furniture store that took up most of the space on the ground level had too much smoke damage to save anything. There was also a photography studio and record store that lost all of their equipment. Kate's building was slated for demolition. According to the engineer it was too compromised to repair. Of course she had it insured, but we were both horrified at the loss. It was a stone building that had stood for 150 years. It was truly irreplaceable!

This was my first taste of what a heavy responsibility these properties could be, also a first experience of seeing how the business community worked together to try to figure out what to do with this valuable space. The experience was hard on Kate and she started to show her age. She came down with a cold in December. I found her so sick when I came to visit one morning that she could barely get to the door.

"Have you seen the doctor?" I asked. She looked terrible.

"He came over. Said I'd better stay in bed and rest, gave me some pills, too." Kate coughed. "I'm doing what he told me."

"You need someone to look after you. Is there anyone who could come and stay and help you out?"

"The thought of a stranger here makes me feel worse."

"Well, that's it then, you're coming with me."

"What?"

"I'm taking you to Buttercup Acres. I can easily look after you there. Tell me what you want to bring and I'll pack your suitcase."

"I'm too sick to argue."

I helped Kate up the stairs at home and offered her Maureen and Harry's room. It had a good view of the river and a comfortable bed.

"Do you have a room with a single bed? That's what I'm used to."

I showed her Gita's room. "This is cozy. It feels just right," Kate said.

As soon as Kate was settled, I came back to see if she wanted anything, but she was fast asleep. I called her lawyer to let her know where she was. "You can call me about anything that comes up," I told him.

"I'm glad to know you're looking after her."

Kate was too weak to come downstairs for about 10 days. We took soup to her, and Ellen read to her, and finally she started to feel better.

"I thought my time was up," Kate said, "but I'm back in the land of the living. You saved my life, Clare. I believe I feel well enough to come to the table today."

After so many days in bed, Kate needed to be supported to get down the stairs, but once she started moving, she felt better quickly.

There was a good cover of snow by mid December and we had been doing lots of cross country skiing. Kate said she wished she were young enough to join us.

"Did you used to ski?" I asked.

"Down-hill skiing, mostly at Mont Tremblant. Those were great times. I don't remember anyone cross-country skiing back then."

"I'm new to it. Patrick got me skis and lessons last year and now it's one of my favourite things in the world. We're buying Ellen skis for Christmas."

"It's coming up soon, I should be getting home," Kate said.

"Why don't you stay for Christmas?" I suggested.

"No, I'm used to my own routines. It will be good to get back to normal. This has been a wake-up call though. I need to think about moving to a smaller place. I don't know what to do about the family homestead. I can't bear to see someone move in and change it."

"I'll keep this in mind. We have a lot of planning to do, figuring out what to build on the fire site, and how to handle a possible move for you."

"Thank goodness I have my business partner! I don't know what I'd do without you."

***

The retreat cabin was ready. It was simplicity itself; one room with a door, a window and a raised wooden floor. Patrick hauled a small woodstove out to it and declared it ready.

"Where will you sleep?" I asked.

"I'll set up a camp cot and bring a sleeping bag. Now I just have to wait for a black mood."

274

Patrick's family came to our place again for Christmas. Patty and Bobby were still able to sleep in their crib, but they were growing fast and would soon need their own beds. Gita and Jiddu came in and ran straight up to their rooms. They each had a special lamp to place on their bedside tables. Jiddu had a cowboy, and Gita had a ballerina.

"We picked them out ourselves," Gita said.

The twins came in wearing pale blue snowsuits, hats, mitts, and tiny white snow boots.

"They must have been awfully hot in the car," I said.

"Not hotter than Inger and I were, having them on our laps," Maureen said. "They're getting too big for that. Soon we'll need to trade the Vista Cruiser for a bus."

"We could get a Volkswagen van." Harry said.

"Mom and Dad are going to bring the presents. We couldn't fit everything in this time," Maureen said, "not with all the skates and snowshoes and the baby sled."

"May I sleep on the porch again?" Inger asked.

"You may, but this time it will be very cold," I said.

"I will love it!"

"As soon as we're unpacked we want to head out on our snowshoes," Harry said. "This is our first time. It will feel great to get moving after that long drive."

We were a large group tramping over the fields and through the back woods. We went as far as the retreat cabin.

"Wow, a playhouse," Gita said.

"It's a retreat cabin," Patrick said, "a place to come and be silent."

"Not for fun, then?" said Gita.

"No, but a playhouse is a good idea. Maybe that will be our next building project," Patrick said.

"A tree house would be better," Jiddu suggested.

"A playhouse and a tree house," Gita said.

We were happy to get back to the house. Walking in snow shoes was tiring work. I made tea and put out plates of fruitcake and cookies. We sat at the kitchen table and visited. Sophie wound around our legs, saying hello to everyone. The twins were running around and had to be watched carefully as they were longing to grab Sophie. She was elusive but there were two of them and they had figured out how to work as a team.

I told them all about the fire and Kate's sickness.

"She may not be able to keep up with her big house for much longer. We're going to have to start thinking about what to do with it," I said.

"Would she rent?" Maureen asked.

"It's too special. She hates to even sell it to someone who might not appreciate what a treasure it is."

"We have some good news," Harry said. "I've been offered a partnership in a law firm."

"Congratulations, Harry," I said.

"Well done!" Patrick said. "Is it in Toronto?"

"Here's the big surprise." Harry waited a few seconds. "It's in Lawrenceville! We're moving in June. One of your local lawyers is retiring and I'm taking his place."

"I never thought you'd leave Toronto," I said.

"I want a place with clean air, safe streets, and good neighbours. Lawrenceville fits the bill," Harry said.

"I'm thrilled too," Maureen said, "and Gita and Jiddu are always asking to move back here."

"Wow, what spectacular news! I can hardly take it in," I said. "I feel like dancing around the kitchen."

"That's what we'll do! Tonight, the four of us can go dancing at the Regent Hotel," said Patrick.

"We could get a group together," I suggested. "I'll ask Mike, Madeleine, Isabel, Joe."

"What about baby Lawrence?" Patrick said.

"Just Mike and Madeleine, then."

There was a good band that night. We got there early to make sure we had a table together.

"I told Isabel about tonight. She said maybe in 10 years, when Lawrence is older, she'll come with us. Can you imagine?" Madeleine said. "She's perfectly happy at home with Joe and the baby."

We had a wonderful time. Harry was fun to be around, now that he wasn't flirting with every woman around.

"Your brother-in-law seems different, more civilized," Madeleine commented. "Have you noticed the change?"

"He's matured," I answered.

One other thing I noticed; we were older than most of the crowd. We weren't the younger generation anymore.

Ice

The ice on our pond was well frozen by Christmas. I organized a skating party on December 27 in the early afternoon. Patrick and Adrian spent hours clearing a huge space to skate on. Ellen invited several girls from her class, and I invited everyone I knew, whether or not they could skate. We all worked together to make platters of turkey sandwiches, pots of tea, and shortbread cookies.

Mrs. Nelthorpe came with her sister, all the way from Copper River. I borrowed the Vista Cruiser and went into town to pick up Kate and Ellen's friends. The house was full. Patrick's parents brought their skates and showed us what beautiful style they had on the ice. Isabel held Lawrence and watched from the side. The house was full of laughter and happy chatter. We decided to make this an annual event.

At 4:30, as it was starting to get dark, I drove the girls and Kate back to Lawrenceville.

"That was the best party I've been to in years," Kate said. "We used to have skating parties on the river. I don't see that anymore."

"I'll ask at the next Save the River meeting if anyone knows why we don't skate on the river."

Patrick invited Mike, Joe, Harry, and a few young men from St. Mathias to come and play hockey the day after our party. Inger asked if she could join in. She played hockey in Sweden and was quite able to keep up. I hoped she would keep the game from getting too rough. Gordon came but he didn't join in.

"That would be too hard on these old bones," he said. "I'll watch from the sidelines."

Isabel came with Joe and she stayed inside with the baby. Gita and Jiddu were making a Lincoln Log cabin and the rest of us were working on a large puzzle and trying to keep Patty and Bobby entertained. They had a treasure trove of new toys from Christmas, but still preferred to torment the house plants and look for other mischief.

"Were Gita and Jiddu like this when they were toddlers?" I asked Maureen.

"They were easy. The twins are a whole different breed."

"I could take them out and pull them around on the sleigh," Ellen said.

"Would you darling? That would be wonderful," Maureen said.

Getting them into their snowsuits, caps, mitts and boots was a chore. They fought every step of the way, but once they were outside, they were smiling and happy. I ran up to get the Leica to photograph them in the bright sun.

"How is that darling girl doing in school?" Evelyn asked.

I told her about Ellen's progress. "She had some catching up to do, but she has good habits and is staying on top of her schoolwork. She loves the guitar. She played at a folk night at Mike's church."

"Have you thought about next year?"

"You mean high school? There's one in Lawrenceville. She'll even be able to take the bus and I won't have to drive her every day."

"I would be happy to pay for her to go to my old alma mater. It's all girls and has the highest standards. She could live with us. It would be a great opportunity for her."

"Thanks Evelyn, I'm sure it would be a great opportunity, but I'm afraid it would be too big a disruption for her."

"Well, if you change your mind, let me know."

I didn't say it, but I hated the idea of Ellen going to school in Toronto. I didn't want her to become a private school girl, spoiled and privileged. Was I being selfish? I didn't want to hold Ellen back from a great opportunity. I was left in confusion, but afraid to ask Ellen what she wanted, in case she jumped at the chance.

Patrick came in for some water, hot and thirsty from playing.

"I'm going to order a bunch of pizzas. The guys are staying for supper. We also need more beer. Could you go to town for me? I hate to leave the game."

"I'll go with you," Evelyn said. "We can take the Cadillac."

As we drove she talked about the girl's school in Toronto.

"Girls who graduated from there have gone on to be Members of Parliament, university professors, famous writers, not to mention those who married successfully. Those girls continue to be my closest friends."

"Lawrenceville High has a prize-winning marching band," I said. Not a great recommendation I realized but I couldn't think of anything else.

For a second day we had a big crowd of partiers at our house. The hockey players were finished their game and were hungry. They dove into the pizza and beer. I picked up more pizzas than I could ever have imagined needing, but they managed to polish them off.

"How are you holding up?" I asked Isabel.

"This has been a lot of partying for me, but I'm enjoying it. I know how quiet it will be after the season is over and Joe is back at work. I'm thinking I should get to know my neighbours, find out if there are any other young mothers and organize a coffee klatch."

"I expect being alone for hours every day with an infant must be lonely."

"I don't know if it's loneliness, but it can feel like I'm cut off from the world. I see how full your life is, and I feel jealous."

"Is the euphoria wearing off?"

"A bit. I'm truly grateful for my life, especially for Joe and Lawrence, but I need more."

"I'm going to need help with the cheese-making and in the garden. You could bring the baby with you. Would you be interested?"

"Not yet, maybe in the spring. I couldn't commit to that drive every day in the winter. Also, despite what I've said, I'm busy all day with the baby and taking care of the house. I can't think why I'm complaining."

I continued to be disturbed by Mrs. Anderson's proposal to send Ellen to private school. I felt that it would be wrong to let her go, yet fearful that I was cutting Ellen off from an incredible opportunity. I hoped to talk to Patrick about it that night, but by the time I came upstairs he was fast asleep.

The Anderson's went back to Toronto the next morning, so I didn't hear any more about it and hoped Evelyn would drop the subject.

Maureen and her family stayed on with us for a few more days.

"I hope you don't mind. I love it here, and the kids are having a great time," she said.

"I feel like you belong. It's how we started out," I said.

"That day, when we arrived here on the run, I had no idea the direction life would take."

"Buttercup Acres has been a blessing."

"Amen to that!"

Spring Planning

One day towards the end of January, Ellen ran back from the mailbox at the end of our driveway with a bundle of mail.

"Clare, your seed catalogue is here!"

She brought it to me in the cheese room where I was finishing up a batch of mozzarella.

"Wonderful, that means spring can't be too far away. This is the catalogue that I dream over, now that I have my dream man."

Ellen had mail too, a big thick envelope. I looked at it and she said, "It's from Mrs. Anderson. I'll take it in and see what she's sent."

Patrick was in the barn, doing the afternoon milking.

"Your mother sent Ellen some mail today."

"Uh-huh."

"I've been meaning to talk to you about something she asked me at Christmas."

"Does it have something to do with Ellen going to Mom's high school?"

"You knew about it?"

"Ellen asked me what I thought."

"Ellen knew about it?"

"Sure, Mom talked to her at Christmas about it."

"Why didn't Ellen say anything to me? I've been so worried about it. Hoping Evelyn would forget about it, and feeling guilty in case I was keeping Ellen from a great opportunity. What do you think?"

"It's a great school, but Ellen should stay here."

I went inside and saw Ellen at the table with brochures from the high school laid out around her. She was writing a letter.

"Are you writing to Mrs. Anderson?" I asked.

"Yes. She invited me to stay with them and go to the school she went to when she was 14. I'm writing a thank you but no-thank you letter. I thought about it. They have a swimming pool and the girls take riding lessons. It's elegant, but I don't want to leave here. I love my room, the cows and chickens and Sophie. I love finally having some friends. How would you feel if I went to that school?"

"I hate the idea. I love having you here, and I'm afraid it would change you."

"I don't want to leave you and Patrick."

"When Mrs. Anderson has plans, you have to watch out."

"I talked to Adrian too. He said it would make me a babbity little babbit."

I laughed. "It's exactly what I feared would happen if you agreed to go."

"But what does it mean?" Ellen asked.

"It means a soulless conformist to society. It's a line from a play about an orphaned boy who goes to live with his eccentric Auntie Mame. He's taken away from her and sent to a private school where he becomes a prig."

"Adrian also said I'd never find a better place to grow up than here."

"I agree with that."

Patrick came in from the barn and spied my mail.

"The seed catalogue! I'd better get working on the book before all the garden work starts again. I have a few more of his prescriptions to add: always be grateful; be alone with God; allow spirits and fairies to dance in your garden."

"I like the last one," Ellen said.

"Did he really say that?" I asked.

"Not in so many words. How about, don't compare yourself to anyone?" Patrick said.

"That's an excellent one. Comparing can only lead to scorn for yourself or the other," I said. "Does he say, do not judge? I'm working on that."

We went through the seed catalogue and filled out our order that night. The seeds would arrive in March, and then we'd be busy starting them in flats in the greenhouse.

Kate's building was slated to be torn down in March. For now it was boarded up and had lots of police tape and warnings around it.

"We must save all the stone and hardwood and anything else that can be salvaged," Kate said. "Whatever we build next should include some of the heritage that's been lost."

There were discussions on town council and among the chamber members about what should be built. Many of the suggestions seemed like a poor substitute for the grand building that was lost, but the problem was money. It was extremely expensive to build. The chamber suggested a competition so we advertised in the paper for a company to design and build on the space. Since we didn't have a plan this seemed like a good idea.

There were submissions for strip malls and one for an eight-story apartment building. None of these were acceptable to Kate.

One from a development company in Montreal called Edgewood looked promising. They were a firm of architects and engineers who specialized in urban development. Their proposition was a two-story building with a medical clinic and retail space on the ground floor, and apartments above, more or less what had been lost. They presented an attractive model that seemed to fit nicely with the town and promised to use stone from the old building in creative ways.

Edgewood sent their representative to give a presentation at council. She was a good saleswoman. She brought many more drawings of the proposal and sketches of the apartments looking like they could be used in a Hollywood movie. We never met with any of the architects or engineers from Edgewood but spent a lot of time on the phone with them and received lots of mail. We were getting close to a deal.

"That model looks like what we want," Kate said at the joint meeting of the town council and chamber of commerce, "yet I feel we're missing something."

"It's a big decision, we should be sure before we go ahead," Dolores said. "Let's look at the drawings again."

The model and drawings were set up on a long table at the edge of the room and the group slowly walked by, examining them.

"They seem too perfect," Dolores said.

"Maybe it is perfect," the mayor said. "I can't imagine anything better for that spot."

"There's something funny about this," said one of the counsellors. "I could swear I saw one of these drawings in the past week, somewhere.... I'm racking my brains to remember."

"We need to make a decision soon, the mayor said, "Edgewood's lawyers are coming in a week with an agreement to sign."

"I remember where I saw the drawing. Somewhere in Williamsville. Gosh, I hate those memory blanks!"

That wasn't much to go on.

The next day, Patrick, Ellen and I decided to check out a new grocery store on the outskirts of Williamsville, called Shoppers Paradise. It was a warehouse filled with grey steel industrial shelves. I'd never seen anything like it and we were all dismayed at its bleakness.

"Wow, this place is ugly," Patrick said. "The prices are low but it's soul-chilling."

"Well, we've given it one visit, but I don't expect to come here again," I said.

Because it was brand new, there was a drawing of the proposed design for the store. It stopped me in my tracks. The design looked suspiciously like the one Edgewood had proposed to Kate.

"Take a look at this," I said. "Does it remind you of the proposal for Kate's lot?"

"You're right. It does. And do you notice that this building looks nothing like the proposal? See on this plaque, it says Edgewood."

"What? I can't believe we're going down this road again!"

"We need someone to dig into Edgewood and find out who they are. We also need to see some real live examples of their work," Patrick said.

"I thought Kate's lawyer would have taken care of this."

As soon as we got home I called Kate to tell her what I'd seen.

"I'll get Crockett on it right away. Did you know he's retiring and handing his business over to a young fellow? He may be distracted with trying to wrap things up."

"My brother-in-law is taking over a practice in Lawrenceville. It must be Mr. Crockett's."

"What a small world. I hate to lose Crockett. I always thought he'd outlast me. I never thought he would give up his practice at only 75."

"A trip to Edgewood's office in Montreal could tell us a lot," I said.

"Let's go! We'll surprise them. I'll ask Crockett to find their address."

Kate called back a few minutes later.

"The address is only a mailbox. Crockett said he'll do some digging."

***

Maureen came to stay with us for a few days so she could scout out a house in Lawrenceville. I was telling her about the proposal for Kate's new building and she said, "I've got the most amazing idea! What does Toronto have that Lawrenceville doesn't?"

"Traffic, crime....."

"No, what I'm thinking of is a farmer's market building. That's what Lawrenceville needs. It's the perfect spot for it. It will give local producers a place to sell their goods, craftspeople too. I picture a building of glass and stone that will look incredible on the water."

"We never considered that in our discussions. None of the ideas so far was at all exciting. This would be fabulous."

"It could be an attraction for people from all around. We could have a cheese booth. Some of those farmer's who do their own butchering would probably love to have a place to sell their meats, and of course all the market gardeners."

"Can you sketch your vision?" I asked. "You could bring it to the council meeting. I'll talk it over with Kate before you present it but I think she'll love it."

"I'll see what I can do."

"Let's go and see her now," I said. "I'm too excited to wait."

Kate had interesting news when we arrived.

"Edgewood's proposal is not going to fly. Crockett says he's called the office and they're dodgy about where they actually are, and not forthcoming about showing us completed projects. Thank goodness we didn't get as far as signing!"

"Maureen has a totally new proposal."

Maureen showed Kate her hastily made sketch and explained the idea for a farmer's market building.

"This is the first idea that excites me," Kate said.

"My father could probably give us a good lead on an architect for this project. He recently had an expansion of the factory and it was wonderful work."

"We'll follow that up," Kate said. "One thing's for sure, we'll be a lot more careful about checking references. My next project is trying to figure out what to do with this house. It's too big for me now, but I can't bear to see it ruined. I could move and leave it empty I suppose."

"We're looking for a house in town," Maureen said, "but I was thinking of something modern, on the river. So far there's nothing available. Would you consider renting? It's definitely big enough for the six of us."

"Let me show you around," Kate said. "Of course, you've already seen the rooftop apartment."

"We don't have any furniture," Maureen said. "We've been living with Harry's parents, and before that our life was the ashram. They owned everything. We've never had a proper family home."

"I plan to move to a small place with no stairs. I could leave a lot of furniture here."

Before I knew it, Maureen and Kate had an agreement.

***

On Saturday we had a dinner party and invited Mike and Madeleine. Patrick made one of his great roasts and there was plenty of wine. After dinner we stayed at the table, talking about Dr. Murphy and his rules for a healthy life. Patrick read out the rules he had so far.

"They all sound reasonable to me," Mike said.

"Let's all try to come up with our own rules for life?" Maureen said.

"How about, 'work hard and you'll get what you deserve'," Patrick suggested.

"I can think of lots of exceptions to that one," Maureen said.

"To thine own self be true, as per Polonius," Madeleine suggested.

"First find out what the self is," Adrian said.

"This is hard," I said. "Everything I think of sounds trite."

"Do your homework early," Ellen said.

Everyone laughed.

"I mean something much bigger," Ellen said. "Something like, 'look ahead, do your homework, be prepared.'"

"Wise," Patrick said.

"May I be excused?" Ellen requested, "I have studying to do."

She had a brand new Nancy Drew mystery upstairs on her night table. Our conversation couldn't compare with the pleasure of that.

"Goodnight, Ellen," everyone said.

The conversation continued.

"Be open to miracles," Patrick said. "Don't get mired in a materialistic view of life."

"Mine is trust in Providence," I said.

Mike, who I might have expected to express something spiritual, surprised me by saying, "Be a happy animal."

"What does that mean?" Patrick asked.

"Enjoy breathing, seeing, smelling, eating; revel in what has been given in having a body."

"I can see you living that," I said. "You're one of the earthiest and happiest people I know. What about you, Maureen?"

"Don't give up on love," she answered.

"Dr. Murphy has a lot of good advice for couples. Patrick will put it in the book," I said.

"I can hardly wait to read it," Mike said.

"He was completely convinced of his viewpoint," Patrick said. "He treated the citizens of Lawrenceville for 60 years using sugar pills and morally uplifting advice. He trusted that people could be their best selves."

"Sounds patronizing," Madeleine said.

"It was of a world view that made sense at the time. What do we have now? One view fighting another. There would be a lot of peace in knowing you had one source for wisdom," Patrick said.

"But what if that wisdom didn't make sense to you?" Madeleine said.

"There were other options. He wasn't the only doctor," I said, "but he was the most respected one, at least as Kate sees it. Getting back to rules, I would have expected your rule to be more religious Mike."

"But it is. I'm an enthusiast of creation theology, the brain child of a Catholic priest, Father Matthew Fox. He praises creation, the body, nature, all the wisdom of the tribal peoples connected to the earth."

"He doesn't sound Catholic to me?"

"He belongs to a religious order. Surely they would stop him if he was out of line."

"I don't know much about theology, but what you're describing sounds like paganism."

"What's wrong with that?" Mike asked.

I laughed and said, "Are you sure you're a priest?"

Suddenly Mike was serious. "The world is changing, Clare. So is Christianity."

"It won't be Christianity if it changes," I said.

"We're in for a revolution. But don't worry, it will all be good!" Mike enthused.

"Adrian, it sounds like we're back to the New Age," I said.

"Truth is a pathless land," he answered.

It was impossible to talk to Adrian now that he was so fixated on Krishnamurti. He was even becoming a man of few words. I missed the loquacious Adrian.

"You should stick to Oswald Chambers," Patrick said. "Remember how much we used to discuss him?"

"Yes, good old Oswald, always telling us God is in our circumstances, and not letting us get away with anything except total commitment. I'm not sure he and Fox would see eye to eye," Mike said.

"Can you tell us something about Dr. Murphy's advice to couples?" Madeleine asked.

"You may find this hard to believe, but he told couples they would only have children if they wanted them. Your body has a wisdom that controls this," Patrick said.

"Come on, did he really believe that?" Madeleine said.

"Kate says so, and she believes it too," I said.

"There is something mystical about Dr. Murphy's advice," Patrick said. "He believed he was channelling information directly from God. Some of it may have sounded homespun, but it was divine advice. Sometimes the advice from God would be to tell his patient to go the city to a specialist, and he'd pass that on."

"It's such a mystery," Maureen said. "Was he truly inspired by God, or deluded? We'll never know."

"The proof is in the good work he did," I said, "and in the wonderful advice he gave. I truly believe you can live a better life by following his rules."

"I thought of a rule I've always tried to live by," Adrian said. Don't be part of the rat race. Make sure work doesn't take over your soul. I've seen what happens when I don't follow that. Speaking of which, we need more help here. We're turning Buttercup Acres into a rat race, slowly but surely. Look at you, Clare. You're run ragged with meetings. I'm not sure that's a life you would choose. It's been thrust upon you."

I started to protest. "I want to help Kate and the town. How can you say I'm being run ragged?"

"I'm saying what I see. You don't have to acknowledge it. Think Clare, when's the last time you had time to read, or get up on your own and quietly watch the sunrise?"

"It's possible this is something you need to look at, Clare," Madeleine said. "I remember how often you told me you needed solitude and time to wander."

Our conversation moved on, but I was left thinking about what Adrian said. I knew there was too much work for us to handle, but when I thought of hiring people to work in the garden and the dairy, I realized I was being left with work I didn't like, and was hiring people to do the things I loved. How could I hire someone to be on council or to be Kate's business partner? I was stuck!

The next morning Patrick was up at 5:30 as usual, to do the milking. I was exhausted after our late night and slept until 9. When I got up I was dizzy and sick. Did I have too much wine? I stumbled back to bed and waited for someone to discover that I was missing. Ellen peeked in at me.

"Are we going to Mass today?" she asked.

"I'm too sick."

"You look terrible. Can I bring you something?"

"No thanks. Could you ask Patrick to come up?"

"He and Maureen went to St. Matthias to hear Mike preach."

I went back to sleep and woke up when Patrick returned.

"Clare, how are you?" He sat beside me and put his hand on my forehead. "Do you have a hangover?"

"I'm sure it's not that. I don't know what's wrong with me but I feel terrible, worse than the flu."

"Don't worry about anything. I'll take care of things. If you need anything just ring this bell."

He left a small brass bell on my bedside table.

"There's so much to do, and I have no strength. I'm so worried."

"Don't give it a thought. Maureen can stay for a few more days."

"I'm sure I'll be fine tomorrow," I said, before falling back to sleep.

I could not have been more wrong. I developed a fever and was hallucinating for days. I was back at Jessup Manor with my father. I was with him eating TV dinners, watching baseball games, skating together on the schoolyard rink, swimming at a small beach under a willow tree. They were sweet dreams of being taken care of.

There were terrifying dreams too, where I tried to call my father and couldn't remember his number, and I tried and tried with mounting frustration. I dreamed about the night he called from the hospital, and I say to him, I'm coming, I'll take care of you, and I try to leave but my legs won't carry me. I woke up often in tears, calling out for my father. I had nightmares about Dorothy, where I beg her not to leave.

After a few weeks of being extremely sick, I recovered enough to get up for a brief while each day, but I didn't recover enough to return to my usual life. When I finally saw the doctor he sent me for tests and he told me I had mononucleosis. I remembered Madeleine's year off for this illness. How could I possibly spends months resting and recovering? It seemed impossible. My mind was sick too, I could barely read more than a few pages and couldn't focus on anything.

This lassitude went on for months. Once Patrick knew how sick I was, he advertised for help and had lots of applicants. He hired a young woman who had just finished high school and was trying to decide what to do with her life. She wanted to explore untraditional options and the cheese-making sounded ideal. Her name was Joanna. Patrick said he chose her because she had grown up on a farm, but I think it was something more. She had a quiet strength and depth of character unusual in such a young person.

Patrick kept in touch with Kate and kept me informed about happenings in Lawrenceville. Maureen made her presentation to the Chamber of Commerce and the Town Council. Everyone agreed it looked like a great idea, but when it came time to vote on it, the council turned it down. Patrick also found out that Edgewood was building a warehouse grocery store a mile out of town, on farm land.

"Why would the town allow that?" I asked.

"It wasn't their decision. It's outside their jurisdiction, although I did hear that one of the Chamber members owns the land. He's going to make a killing."

Luckily I was in a state where nothing touched me deeply. I heard these things but didn't react.

Ellen spent time with me, often reading to me because my eyes ached. I asked her for some of my old favourites; Gothic suspense stories with young heroines, thrust into danger. I often fell asleep as she read and would wake up thinking about the characters in their simple, clear cut world of strong men, secrets, castles, plots to defeat the innocent but smart heroine, and always a happy ending.

I continued in this state into summer, although I got up for a few hours every day and pottered around, sometimes cooking or tidying, occasionally going out to help in the garden, but I couldn't trust that I could complete any task.

Maureen and Harry moved to Kate's house at the end of June. The kids loved their new house, especially the top floor. Maureen made it a space for them alone, and called it The Saturday Kids' Clubhouse. She somehow managed to get a small piano up there, and all their toys and art supplies, and left them to create their own wonderful world together.

Kate was settled in a new apartment building on the water. She had a ground floor suite that looked out on the river, and very little she'd need to take care of. She came to visit me every few weeks and told me how happy she was with the arrangement.

"Are you disappointed about the farmer's market building?" I asked.

"It's a great idea, but I can't force it through. I have a little power, but there are competing forces."

I should have asked her more, but I was already losing the thread. It must have been painful for my visitors to see me so vague and empty-headed.

Gradually I regained my mind and my energy. When the cool weather came in autumn it was like a tonic. I felt the frosty mornings and drifting leaves bring my strength back. I also felt a change in my sense of what I wanted to accomplish in my life, and realized the task I'd set myself of holding back the tide of change was impossible.

I looked with detachment at what had been going on for the past four or five years. I saw that the river was no cleaner, despite the efforts of our committee, although there a sense that government was beginning to pay attention to pollution. Kate still had her beautiful stone buildings downtown, but she was having a hard time renting them. Her usual tenants told her it was hard to get people to shop in Lawrenceville. They preferred to drive to Williamsville and stock up at the malls and warehouses.

While I was sick, my beloved Woolworth's was bought by a discount store chain called The Fifty Cent Store. The first thing they did was remove the lunch counter. The new store sold many of the same things that Woolworth's sold, but somehow they seemed shabby. When I mentioned it to Isabel she told me it was always like that.

"All that stuff was tawdry, even in the past. You looked at it with the eyes of a child," she said.

Was that true? I couldn't imagine how I could have been so deluded.

I told Kate I wasn't up to the task of preserving her family's legacy.

"I hate letting you down," I said, "but I know I can't do it."

"No one is up to this task, not even me. I've done everything in my power to keep the beauty that my parents and grandparents built, but I'm just one woman. There are people who can't wait to put up malls and fast food restaurants. They'll make lots of money, but where are they going to live when they've destroyed this town?

"The lot where we had the fire is still sitting vacant. I can't come up with any plan that makes sense. I don't know if I'd get anyone to rent space if I do build. We've got a lot of empty stores now on the main street."

As I listened to Kate, I was thinking of how in the past I would have been worried by what she was telling me. Instead I felt sorry that Kate was having difficulties, but didn't feel compelled to try to fix things.

"Man proposes. God disposes," I said.

"Have you become cynical?"

"It's not a cynical statement. I still want the best for Lawrenceville, but I know it's not up to me. It's hard to explain it, but I know I wasn't trusting in Providence, instead I was trying to carry it all myself. I was forcing myself to be a businesswoman and a politician, a person that I don't recognize in myself at all. I don't have endless energy. I hate being on committees. It wears me out at the same time as I feel I accomplish nothing. Do you know what I mean?"

"It's not who you are, dear. You were doing well at it, but it's no good if your heart isn't in it. Your position on council is coming up in a few weeks. Are you going to let your name stand?"

"No. Now that I'm up and around I'll go to the last few meetings, but that's it."

"Maureen plans to run if you don't. She's eager to keep on pushing this market building and she likes to be in the thick of things. She loves adversity."

"It's amazing, even though I've been unable to work for the past six months, nothing has fallen apart. The world went on perfectly well without me."

"Does it upset you?"

"It frees me."

***

"Now that you're feeling better, let's have a night out on our own," Patrick suggested.

"How about the Skylane?"

It was a clear, cold evening. We sat watching the sun set over the hills, turning the sky and the hills bright orange. Patrick reached across the table and held my hand.

"I'm so happy to have you back. It feels like you were gone forever."

"I have few memories of the past months. What did I miss?"

"One of the first things was a big argument with Adrian. He told me I was abusing his friendship, that he'd never intended to work like a dog, and I was a slave driver. He really let me have it. Finally I got him calmed down enough to discuss it. He said he wanted to live like the monks, on a schedule of four hours of labour, and four hours of prayer. Fine with me I told him. I apologized for how far we had strayed from our original agreement."

"That's always been Adrian's desire, to make sure work doesn't encroach on his soul."

"You also missed the Lynch family's move to Lawrenceville. Despite the fact that they didn't have furniture, they still had a lot of stuff. They suit that house, somehow. Harry is happy in his job. He's taken over all the things you were helping Kate with, and Maureen has taken over in becoming an advocate for the preservation of Lawrenceville. She's still helping promote Buttercup Cheese, but she's putting lots of energy into town politics. It's great for her."

"It's worked out so well. What about Joanna? How is she doing?"

"Joanne's a God-send. She's strong, she knows how to milk, she can change the oil on a truck, she loves the cheese making, and so far she has no plans to leave us. She's enthusiastic about everything, happy to join in if we're fixing a fence or picking baskets of produce to take to the farmer's market. She and Adrian have become great friends. He has her reading all sorts of books."

"Where does she live?"

"She has an apartment over one of the shops in Lawrenceville. She travels by motorcycle. Shows up every day in her black leather jacket and high black boots."

"Wow! Did you ever use the retreat cabin?"

"Ellen has taken it over. She spends hours in it, playing her guitar and writing songs. She asked if she could decorate, and I said yes, and now it seems more like her clubhouse. We'll walk out there tomorrow. She had a friend over in the summer and they decided to sleep out there, but around 11 they came in because they got scared."

"You did a good job of looking after her without me. I know I still saw her every day, but I wasn't tuned in to her. Were there any big crises?"

"The first week of high school was a big change. Some of the kids on the bus were crude and picked on her. I told her I'd drive her to school and pick her up if it was making her life hell. Maybe knowing she wasn't stuck allowed her to fight her way past it. Now she has someone who saves her a seat, and they just roll their eyes at the bullies, and talk to each other. Having one friend makes all the difference."

"High school has changed so much since I went there. We wore skirts every day, no matter how cold it was. I see she's a lot more casual."

"The school councillor tried to say she should be in the four year commercial program, but I pushed and made sure she got in the five year program. I'm sure she can do it."

"No one did that for me," I said. "Ellen is so lucky to have you going to bat for her."

"Ellen spent a few weeks with Mom at the end of August. She learned to play tennis and came back with lots of new clothes. She travelled by train on her own."

"I knew about that. My memory was starting to clear by then. What about you, did you have any black moods?"

"They're less likely in the sunnier months, and I was so occupied that I barely had time to think of myself. Working hard is good for me." Patrick paused, then said, "You were very upset when you first got sick. You spoke endlessly about your father. You cried a lot. Do you remember any of that?"

"I know I was back in my childhood. The dreams of happiness and of being with my father were painful. I would feel loved and protected and then it would all be gone, in an instant. I lived that loss over and over. I dreamt constantly of Dorothy too, sad lonely dreams."

"Mrs. Bergeron was worried about you. She called every day at first, and sent Isabel over with a Sacred Heart prayer card and a bottle of holy water."

"Dear Mrs. Bergeron! I'll go see her this week. I'm so happy to be back to our life together, but I'm not going to be the same Clare I was when I got sick. I need what Adrian has, time for work and time for my soul. I'm not sure exactly what the ratio is for me, but I have to pay attention and not go back to being a slave to work."

"I hope you didn't think I was running you ragged," Patrick said.

"It wasn't you, or anyone who was to blame; it was me taking responsibility that wasn't truly mine. It was my ego too, enjoying being so important."

"The doctor says you should ease back into life, and watch that you don't get too tired. All I want is for you to be healthy and happy with me. I love our life together."

"You know what I love? Waking up and seeing the river; sitting in the kitchen with a cup of coffee while Sophie stares at me from the rocking chair; going out to the barn and having the chickens come rushing over to see me; playing cards after supper; talking to you about Dr. Murphy's ideas. I love everything about our life together. I want to have time to savour it. Does that make sense?"

"'Yes, it does."

"You know, I feel giddy, rather like Ebenezer Scrooge after he's seen the error of his ways."

"Uh-huh."

"I am the luckiest person in the world," I said.

"Here's to us," Patrick said, "the two luckiest people in the world!"

The End